It had to have been that last sip of tequila.

The one where she clearly remembered saying to herself, "Well, I shouldn't waste it."

Unfortunately, that was the last thing she really remembered.

No, she wouldn't be getting up anytime soon if she could help it. And to prove it, she buried her face deeper into the pillow. It felt good to do that, so she did it again. In some bizarre way, the action helped her headache—she'd never call it a hangover out loud—so she did it again. Then she rubbed her head against the pillow.

It was that scent. She wanted that scent on her. A very shifter thing to do and one she'd never really be able to explain to a full-human without getting that telltale "ewww" response.

As her brain began to slowly process whose smell this could possibly be, she felt the bed dip and a heavy weight rest against her side.

"Baby?" a deliciously low voice said. "You awake? I need you, baby."

Sissy's eyes snapped open, but she immediately closed them again when bright sunlight brutally seared her brain right inside her skull.

"Mitchell?"

"Yeah," he purred, nuzzling her chin, her ear. "You up for more of me, baby? 'Cause we are so not done."

Not caring how much the light hurt, Sissy slammed her hands against Mitch's chest and pushed him off while scrambling back until her shoulders hit the headboard. Using both hands, she held the sheet under her chin.

"What the hell is going on?"

THE MANE ATTRACTION

SHELLY LAURENSTON

BRAVA

KENSINGTON PUBLISHING CORP.
http://www.kensingtonbooks.com

BRAVA BOOKS are published by

Kensington Publishing Corp.
119 West 40th Street
New York, NY 10018

All Kensington Titles, Imprints, and Distributed Lines are available at special quantity discounts for bulk purchases for sales promotions, premiums, fund-raising, and educational, or institutional use. Special book excerpts or customized printings can also be created to fit specific needs. For details, write or phone the office of the Kensington special sales manager: Kensington Publishing Corp., 119 West 40th Street, New York, NY 10018, attn: Special Sales Department, Phone: 1-800-221-2647.

Brava Books and the B logo Reg. U.S. Pat. & TM Off.

ISBN-13: 978-0-7582-3487-2
ISBN-10: 0-7582-3487-2

First trade paperback printing: November 2008
First mass market printing: March 2012

10 9 8 7 6 5 4 3 2 1

Printed in the United States of America

To Ma.

I didn't realize how much like Sissy Mae you really are.
A charming Southern lady who loves fast cars,
lazy summer days, and Alpha Males. I miss you more than
you'll ever know, but it occurred to me while writing this
book that you're still with me every day.

Chapter 1

It was hard to think about death at a wedding.

Yet he was managing it pretty well.

And it wasn't because he was bored or the bride didn't look beautiful or the venue wasn't amazing. It was because of that damn call.

One call and his mind was filled with images of death. *His* death. But it wasn't every day a man got a call that informed him there was a two-million-dollar bounty on his head. All that money for his big lion head.

He should be wallowing in depression. He should be having one of his panic attacks when he couldn't breathe or see straight. He should be doing what any normal human being—normal being relative since he could shift from human to feline in about thirty seconds or so—would be doing when finding out someone wanted him or her dead so badly.

But he couldn't be depressed, he couldn't panic. Not now. Not with *that* staring him in the face.

Okay. So it wasn't right in his face, but if he dropped to his knees and crawled over to it . . . his face could be right there. Now that was something worthy of wallowing in.

Happily wallowing.

"You're staring at my ass again, aren't you?"

Normally when coldbusted this way by a woman, Mitchell Patrick Ryan O'Neill Shaw would begin some serious lying. He knew females well enough to know there were times when a man had to lie or risk losing important parts of himself. But every once in a while, if a man was lucky enough, someone would come along who went past the whole male-female flirting dynamic. And that someone was Sissy Mae Smith.

They didn't start off as friends. Not surprising since she stole his damn jacket. He'd lent it to her underdressed friend—at least she'd been underdressed at that moment—and Sissy had done what scavenger wolves did . . . she took it for herself. But Mitch was feline—king of the jungle and all that—so he took the damn thing back. That led to Sissy wrapping herself around Mitch like a monkey and demanding he, "Enjoy your taste of nirvana, bitch!"

To be honest, he really hadn't known what to make of her at that point, but Sissy had a way of making people feel like they'd known her for twenty years. She'd walk into the security office where they both worked for her brother—a job that kept him busy and out of trouble until he had to go back to Philly to testify—and drop into Mitch's lap like she belonged there. Then she'd say something along the lines of, "I know my beauty is enthralling, but do you think men realize I have substance, too?" or "Would you take me more seriously if I weren't so pretty?" But it was when she would find him wandering his brother's hotel in the middle of the night that he realized how much he liked her. She'd never ask him questions like, "Why are you sweating and jumping at everything that remotely sounds like a gunshot?" and instead, she would drag him off to some late night diner for what she referred to as "breakfast and mocking."

And it was over one of those breakfasts that Mitch realized Sissy had become one of his best friends.

"Yes, I'm staring at your ass," he told her as plainly as she'd asked, "but I can't help it. It keeps talking to me."

He wasn't kidding either. It was the way that stupid bridesmaid dress hung off her that was making him crazy. It was a millimeter too tight around her ass, and he couldn't do anything but stare.

Like most shifter females from the Smith Pack, Sissy was a lot of woman. Strong, powerful, built. She could take down perps better than most linebackers could take down a quarterback. He'd seen her take a punch to the face and then kick the living shit out of the guy who'd done it. He'd also seen her whine over her stubbed toe. Sissy would never be a supermodel but that's what Mitch liked about her. You took Sissy to bed, you never had to worry about breaking her.

She was pretty, too. She looked a lot like her big brother, but her features were softer, her fighting scars a little less dramatic. She kept her dark hair in a shaggy layered cut that teasingly covered and illuminated sharp, light brown eyes and well-defined cheekbones. The hairstyle appeared casual and easily maintained, but Mitch had grown up in a house with women, and his mother, a former registered nurse, now owned her own salon chain. He knew a three-hundred-dollar cut when he saw one. But the designer shoes on her feet were her first and only pair. Same thing with the designer gown. Sissy liked to be comfortable and look comfortable, and she wasn't afraid to put in a little work to get that across.

Yeah, Mitch liked that she was a walking, talking contradiction. A backwoods hillbilly who'd traveled the world and understood more cultures than some PhDs. A woman who'd barely finished high school but still managed to earn and keep the respect of people with multiple degrees. A shit-starter who lived to torture anyone stupid enough to get caught in her web but who would die to protect her family and friends.

Sissy had turned out to be everything he expected and nothing like he'd thought.

So it seemed inevitable they'd end up in bed together, at least for one night, but then Sissy had suddenly looked at him one day and said in her straightforward way, "You know, I like you too much to ever fuck you." Sissy wasn't much for vague euphemisms. In her world, if you were "sleeping together," you weren't doing something right. "Sex" was for prostitutes. And "making love" was for people who never got out of the missionary position.

And in some bizarre way, Sissy's blunt pronouncement made complete sense to Mitch, and he'd shockingly agreed. They'd been best friends ever since.

Of course, that was before she put on that damn dress. Now he was all distracted and horny, and Sissy had no one to blame but herself and her good-size ass.

"Did you say my ass was talking to you?"

"Yup."

It had talked to him all through the ceremony and now while they were being forced to take pictures under the burning Long Island, New York, midday sun. A simple thing like taking pictures had turned into a good hour for Mitch to stare at her ass some more.

The whole event was out of control really. Such a huge wedding for two people who couldn't care less about marriage. There were fifteen people on the groom's side and fifteen on the bride's, an interesting mix of males and females—and breeds. Cats and canines comingling. Maybe not happily but politely. Sissy stood up with her brother, and Mitch had ended up on the bride's side.

It had taken him by surprise when the bride had asked him. Why would she want him in her wedding? And that's exactly what he'd asked her. She'd smiled up at him, those big, brown wild dog eyes of hers making him feel all protective of her, and then she'd told him, "Because, dude, you're our karaoke king, and we worship at your altar."

The bride was an odd girl. But adorable as only a canine could be.

But really, how many shifter weddings would he ever be invited to? Unlike many full-humans, his kind kept their commitments once they made them so wasting money on a big wedding or bothering with all the paperwork usually amounted to a complete waste of time. Of course, getting shifters—male and female—to make the commitment was often like pulling teeth, but once trapped, they were in for the long haul.

Of course, Bobby Ray Smith, Alpha Male of the New York Smith Pack and local hillbilly, wasn't marrying just anybody. He was marrying Jessica Ann Ward, Alpha of the Kuznetsov Wild Dog Pack and worshipped geek hottie. And a wedding like this didn't happen every day . . . or millennium, for that matter. So to be part of it was kind of an honor for Mitch. Add in that Jess's Pack was as rich as Bill Gates, and you had a wedding on par with a Kennedy event.

In fact, the wedding was taking place at an actual *castle*. And Mitch didn't even have to pay for anything. His tux, shoes, the attempted haircut—already grown back out to his full mane in less than twenty-four hours—all paid for. Rooms in seriously expensive hotels down the road had also been booked. He knew the food would be stupendous, and there was apparently a room called the Chocolate Room. Chocolate was the theme for the entire wedding, but there would be desserts of all kinds in that one room. There was also the Gambling Room, the Gaming Room, and the Sing Your Heart Out Room for the karaoke fans.

Yeah. He liked how these wild dogs lived. They knew how to enjoy life and felt no shame when caught chasing their tails.

But now he had to get through all these pictures. One after the other with a goofy smile on his face.

While the bride and groom took pictures with the groom's parents, Sissy Mae turned to face him. "Did you just say my ass was talking to you?"

"Again. It's talking to me *again*."

"Again. I see."

Standing next to him, Sissy leaned her shoulder against his. With those heels on—that she'd been complaining about for days—she was nearly as tall as Mitch. "And what does my ass say to you exactly?"

"I don't know. It's speaking in tongues."

Sissy's laugh rang out across the Long Island acreage surrounding the castle. But it quickly faded when a voice snapped beside her, "Sissy Mae, try not to embarrass your brother today. If you can manage that for once."

Yup, there went that twitch. It was a small one, right in the corner of her left eye, and most people probably never noticed it. But Mitch had been hanging out a long time with Sissy, and he'd learned her facial expressions because a certain expression would probably be the only warning he got before she started some shit. But that twitch was new and only seemed to happen when her mother was around.

"Think you can do something useful," her mother went on, "and help Jessica Ann change her gown now that we're done with the photos?"

"Why? Has she lost the use of her arms?"

The thing that was kind of scary about Sissy's mother was that she didn't get hysterical and mad like most mothers who fought with their daughters. Instead, she got this frightening little smirk on her face and stepped close so that she was only inches from her child.

Softly, she said, "Get up them steps and help your sister-in-law before I make you wish I'd left you at the pound."

Sissy sighed. "If only *not* being your daughter was remotely true, there would be a reason to live."

"Well, Lord knows I wouldn't want to give you that spark of hope."

"I'll take her," Mitch volunteered, grabbing Sissy's hand and pulling her toward the door the rest of the females had gone through.

Most of the time, Mitch loved watching family strife from a distance. But he knew when two deadly predators were squaring off, and if someone told him to put money on who'd win between Sissy and her mother . . . well, Mitch wouldn't know.

Sissy had youth, and she was wicked fast when she wanted to be. He'd worked with her long enough to know the damage she could do. Especially if you pissed her off.

But there was something in her mother's eyes. Something hard and dangerous that Sissy didn't have. At least not yet. And since Mitch had actually been invited to the bachelorette party, he felt a certain loyalty to making sure Jess's day stayed perfect. He didn't want her having to worry about blood on the walls of her lovely wedding venue.

"Explain to me again how matricide is illegal in some states," Sissy growled from behind him as he pulled her toward the enormous staircase.

"In *all* states. Plus, I think there are some moral restrictions around it, too."

"That's not fair. Clearly, these lawmakers haven't met my mother."

"I wouldn't know. Besides, this is all so foreign to me," he explained once they hit the top step. "My mother loves me and would do anything for me, so I've never had a desire to kill her."

Light brown eyes abruptly narrowed. "Throw that in my face again, and your sweet momma will be nursing your mauled body back to health."

"Sweet talker."

They neared the set of rooms that had been set aside for the bride and her bridesmaids. Mitch heard all the giggling and felt right at home. He'd been raised by women. His mother's Pride had taken good care of him throughout his childhood. They had taught him a lot over the years, and what they couldn't teach, there'd always been a male or two around the house to help out. Then the day after he'd turned eighteen, one of his aunts walked into the kitchen where he stood leaning against the counter, downing a bowl of cereal. She stared at him like she'd never seen him before and demanded, "Are you still here?" He knew then it was time to move on. He'd always be welcome in his mother's house, but it would never be his Pride.

And Mitch had never done the Pride thing. He'd been the only male offspring in a house run by hard-core Philadelphia girls who spoke pretty freely. So he'd known at a young age how Pride females really felt about the males who ate their food and got them knocked up, and Mitch didn't want that.

But being a nomad had its benefits, and he liked that the only enemies he had were the ones he made himself. Joining up with a group was a little too "gang mentality" for him. How these Packs of canines did it, Mitch had no idea. The wolves seemed to tolerate it as their lot in lives. The wild dogs seemed to love it.

Mitch stopped short when Sissy refused to go any farther.

"You can't make me go in there," she said as the giggling and laughing became louder and more hysterical.

He turned to face her. "Not still holding that punch over her head, are you, Sissy?"

"No. And stop reminding me about that." Sissy and the bride had a colorful history from years past, and Mitch took delight in torturing Sissy with it.

She stepped closer and whispered, "They're all so . . . so . . ."

"Girly?"

"Golden Retrievery."

Mitch laughed and continued to drag Sissy toward the door. "You guys are family now. That means you help out."

They stopped in front of the open double doors and stared in fascination at the suite full of wild dogs chanting, "Jess! Jess! Jess!"

And Jess, in wild dog form, chased her tail in circles over and over and over again.

Mitch glanced at Sissy, and she didn't even bother to hide her embarrassment.

"Well," he pushed. "Get on in there."

She pulled her hand away. "There has got to be a bar around here somewhere." She walked off, and Mitch turned back to Jess. She'd stop spinning, but now she stumbled all over the room because she was dizzy.

As she sat down hard, her legs going out from under her, the other wild dogs caught sight of Mitch.

"Mitch!" they all cheered, and grinning, Mitch walked inside.

Sissy walked up to her best friend, throwing her arm around Ronnie Lee Reed's neck. "Did you scout the area?"

"Yup. Two full bars in the front of the ballroom, two in the back, and three others scattered near the gaming and karaoke rooms."

"Karaoke?" Sissy shuddered. "Make it stop."

"Yeah. But there's Texas Hold 'Em and blackjack in the gaming room."

"Thank the Lord for small favors." She glanced around. "Seen the old heifer?"

"I haven't seen *either* old heifer in a while. But you know how they like to stalk their prey, waiting until we're at our most vulnerable before pouncing."

"I'm in hell, Ronnie Lee. Absolute hell."

Her momma had been in town for three weeks . . . three of the longest weeks in Sissy's entire life. She didn't know what was up her momma's ass, but the woman had been riding Sissy from the day she'd arrived in New York, and Sissy's patience was running thin.

"At least your momma clearly states what her problems are with you. Mine just keeps sighing at me and shaking her head."

"I don't know. After the last three weeks of constant Janie Mae chatter, disappointed sighs sound pretty good. And when's dinner? I'm gettin' hungry."

"Another half hour at least. Maybe you could go back up and gently coax the bride to dress faster."

"I am not going back up there. You're asking too much. Besides, Mitch is up there. He'll get her to move along."

Mitch held one end of the rope, and the wild dogs held the other. With one leg crossed over the other, he rested his left elbow on his knee and studied his nails.

"Pull!" They did, and Mitch didn't budge.

"Ladies, aren't you getting a little embarrassed by this?"

"No!" they all yelled. He wasn't exactly surprised. African wild dogs had high embarrassment thresholds.

Jess, who hadn't participated—this time—in the game of tug, sat down next to Mitch. She wore a satin robe and not much else.

"How you doing, beautiful?"

"Fine. Glad that part is over."

He glanced at her flat belly and asked his daily question since finding out she was pregnant with Smitty's love child, "And how's Mitch Junior?"

Jess shook her head. "You have got to stop calling her that. Smitty will have your head."

"But I love watching how red his face gets." He looked at

the clock on the wall. "You better get dressed. There's still more to your day."

She rolled her eyes. From what Mitch could tell, Jess hadn't had much to do with arranging this wedding other than to insist on the Karaoke Room and no real flowers at the ceremony or the reception since she was violently allergic. From the flowers on the tables to the bride's bouquet, all were fake flowers but so artfully done, he wouldn't have known if someone hadn't said something about it.

"I haven't seen the other dress. Put it on, and I'll see if I can give it the Mitch seal of approval."

"Okay." She glanced longingly at the rope and the She-dogs still attached to it.

"No, Jess. You can't play tug."

She gave a cute little growl before storming off. "My day my ass!"

"I knew you'd be back here. Hidin'."

Sissy smiled up at her daddy. She wasn't surprised he'd found her in the back of the kitchen, hiding in the room the staff used to take breaks. He knew his daughter better than most people realized. But they'd always been close. "You're one of the few who don't piss me off, Shug," he used to tell her when she was only five. Bubba Ray Smith was a unique good ol' boy, but Sissy loved her father and would destroy anyone who messed with him.

"I'm not hiding. I'm taking a much needed break." She stood and hugged her father. "Hey, Daddy."

"Hey, Shug." He always called her that when they were alone. It was his pet name for her. He started off calling her Sugar, but when she'd turned four or so, he'd gotten lazy and shortened it to Shug. "How are you holding up?"

"I'm trying, Daddy. I really am. But she's pushing me."
Like always.

"You gotta stop letting her get to you." Her father pulled out the chair for her, and Sissy sat down, her father taking the chair next to hers. "She pushes you because she wants you to be the best."

"The best at what? Matricide?"

"That ain't funny, and you know it."

It was kind of funny.

"You're grown now, Shug. You can't let her get to you anymore. You've got your own Pack, and you don't even live at home anymore. Although I'd never stop you from moving back if ya want." And she heard the hope in his voice. It broke her heart and made her feel very loved.

"You know I can't come back, Daddy. Not to live." She smiled. "But at least I'm in the States now."

"Yeah. That's true. And here I know my little girl's safe."

Yeah, her father still saw her that way. His baby girl. Sweet, delicate, his princess. Of course, everyone else knew better. And most women would be annoyed, wondering why their fathers didn't see them as adults who could manage their own lives. That wasn't her father, though. Sissy never felt like he thought less of her. He'd trusted her to handle most things when everyone else still treated her like a kid. So no matter where she went or how far away she was, she was Bubba Smith's baby girl, and she always would be. It didn't bother her because she didn't doubt herself as a woman or a She-wolf. You couldn't when you were Alpha. You couldn't afford to.

"I was real worried you'd stay over there in Asia, and then I didn't know what I'd do without my baby girl."

Because God forbid the man would actually leave the country.

"What's outside of America that's all that interesting?" he'd grumble. The fact he was taking an actual vacation starting tomorrow still amazed her. Her mother must have had to work some major Lewis Mojo to make that happen.

"Do your old man a favor, Shug," he said, taking her hand.

"Anything, Daddy."

"Don't get into it with your momma today. Promise me."

"But—"

"Promise me, Sissy Mae." Okay. He'd pulled out the full name. Not Shug or darlin' girl or any of his other nicknames. So he was serious.

To Sissy's surprise—and especially to her brother's surprise—this wedding meant a lot to Daddy, and she wouldn't ruin it for him. She'd simply avoid the heifer. Hell, she'd been doing it since grade school, what was one more day?

"I promise, Daddy."

He leaned in close and kissed her forehead. "That's my Shug."

"Your tits will fall out."

Jess blinked big, brown dog eyes at him. "What are you talking about?" She looked down at the sleeveless ivory dress she had on. Her ceremony dress had cost a small fortune. This one, specifically for the reception, cost a lot less. Like a mini fortune.

"I've seen you dance, Jess. Your tits are going to fall out."

Jess took a step back and stretched her arms out. "Nipple check."

The She-dogs surged forward and stared intently at the dress.

"I see nothing," Sabina stated as if her word was the only one that counted. Sabina was Russian, Jess's second in command and the one whom the pack had been named after, and she had the sexiest accent Mitch had heard in a while. "You are wrong," she told Mitch.

"I'm not wrong." He moved behind Jess, placing his hands on her sides. He lifted her up and shook her around for a few seconds. As he knew she would, Jess giggled like a six-year-old.

When he put her back down on the ground, the wild dogs took another look.

"Nipples, my friends," May announced. Maylin was Mitch's other favorite wild dog. Originally from somewhere in Alabama, she was cute, Asian, and thought he was "just a darlin' sweetie!" Unfortunately both females were thoroughly mated. And they had a ton of kids each to prove it. What did one do with so many children? It's not like you could put them to work in a factory to earn their pay—some considered that wrong.

"We have nipples," May finished.

Mitch rested his chin on Jess's shoulder and looked down. "How bad is it? I should examine the area closely. It's all right, sweetie. I'm a cop."

Jess reached back and slapped at his face. "You're disgusting," she laughed.

The dressmaker, who they had at the wedding for just such situations—*who can afford that?*—was summoned to the bride's suite.

Mitch sat in a chair and watched them add matching satin straps to her dress so that it would stay up. Still sleeveless but much safer.

"Better?" Jess asked while she stood in front of him.

He leaned up and put his face right against her breasts. "Give me a moment to investigate."

"Or," a really angry voice snarled next to him, "I could tear your throat out now, and we can have a wedding *and* a funeral."

Without actually moving away, Mitch turned his head and looked into the angry wolf eyes of Bobby Ray Smith, Smitty to his friends.

"Don't get mad at me because I'm only trying to be helpful."

That got Mitch a flash of wolf fangs before Jess pushed Smitty away.

"If either of you get blood on my dress, there will be hell to pay," she told them.

"Sissy Mae!"

Sissy turned from the bar and faced her most favorite aunts in the world. Her mother's sisters, but she didn't hold that against them.

Squealing, she threw herself into their arms, and her aunts hugged her and showed her she wasn't a complete failure, no matter what her mother said.

"Look at you, darlin' girl. Ain't you as pretty as a picture!" her Aunt Francine, the oldest of the Lewis sisters, exclaimed.

"Thank you." Her momma had told her to lose a few pounds. "I have to admit, I was afraid of what the wild dogs would come up with for the gowns. Especially when I saw Jessie Ann's wedding gown." It wasn't that the bride's gown wasn't beautiful. But it probably fit in a bit better in the year 1066.

Leave it to Jessie Ann to go for the weird.

Sissy pulled back from her aunts.

"I like that color on you, though," Francine told her. "Although brown at a wedding . . ."

"It's not brown," Sissy explained because she'd heard it ten thousand times in the past six months. "It's chocolate. Dark chocolate. Seventy-two percent—"

"Stop." Francine held her hand up. "I can't listen to any of that."

Sissy laughed. "Leave it to Bobby Ray to catch himself a Jessie Ann."

"Has she forgiven you?" Roberta, the next oldest, asked.

"She says she has, but I don't believe her. I come in the room, she finds a way to leave it."

"No one to blame but yourself on that, Sissy Mae." Francine never let Sissy forget anything. "You tortured that little thing something fierce."

"Torture is a harsh word. Accurate," she added, "but harsh."

Sissy smiled warmly at her Aunt Darla, the youngest of the sisters. "How's my Uncle Eggie? I wish he'd come."

"Aw, darlin', you know better than that. My man is not good in crowds." And Darla wasn't much better.

"He's probably in a Dumpster somewhere in Smithtown."

"He better not be," Darla playfully growled. "I warned him I better not find him in one again."

"And Dee-Ann?" Sissy asked about her favorite cousin, Darla and Eggie's only child.

Darla opened her mouth, then shrugged. "Honest, darlin'. Your guess is as good as mine."

"I wouldn't worry, Aunt Darla. I'm sure Dee-Ann's just fine." At least Sissy hoped so. She loved her cousin, but Dee worked for the government and whatever she did kept her away from her family and out of touch for way too long in Sissy's estimation.

"So . . ." Aunt Janette asked, her eyes bright, "when are you coming home, Sissy Mae?"

"Aww. Do you miss me?"

"Sure . . . and some cat heifers need another smack-down."

Typical. "No. Absolutely not."

"Oh, come on, Sissy—"

"No, Aunt Janette." Sissy shook her head for emphasis. "I told you before never again, and I meant it."

"Ungrateful."

"Am not, and stop trying to use guilt."

"Now," Francine cut in, "when are we gonna get our Sissy Mae settled?"

"Uh . . ."

But before panic could set in fully at that ugly question, Mitch suddenly grabbed her from behind.

"Excuse me, ladies. I need to use Sissy as my human shield."

He lifted her up, and not surprisingly, she was abruptly face to face with her brother.

Sissy sighed when she saw her brother's scowl. "What did he do now?"

"The boy needs to keep his hands to himself."

"Actually, my hands weren't involved at all."

Bobby Ray reached around her, trying to grab Mitch's throat.

"Now ya'll stop it, right now! Bobby Ray, go on. Dinner will be soon, and you need to drag that bride of yours away from the other Pound Puppies."

"Stop calling them that. And remember what I told you, boy."

After her brother stalked away, Sissy slapped at Mitch's hands. "Let me down right now, Mitchell Patrick Ryan O'Neill Shaw."

"Uh-oh," he said to her aunts while placing her on the ground. "She used my full name. That means I'm in trouble."

"I thought the rules were set?" Sissy faced him, and she barely stopped her frown. Not for what Mitch had done. Hell, that was downright tame. No, it was because Mitch had been looking . . . she couldn't explain it. There were dark circles under his eyes, and he was losing weight. He was smaller than his half-brother, Brendon, but she had the feeling that wasn't quite right. Mitch was one of the swamp cats. They were bred big and powerful. But she'd noticed that

Mitch didn't eat much, and that was only getting worse. She tried to get him to eat more, but he'd been picking his food lately. Something was going on with him. Something more than usual, and she had to find out what. There were not a lot of guys she respected enough to call friend. Females were her friends; males she actually respected were usually family or damn near. But most men were simply potential fucks in her mind and nothing more. Mitch had been the first who'd moved past that in Sissy's world, and Sissy took care of her friends.

"Look, Mitchell, if I can't start shit, *you* can't start shit."

"I was helping out the bride." He looked at her aunts. "I was merely checking to ensure her bodice was fitting her properly."

Francine asked, "And I guess you had to get right up in there with that pretty face of yours to check that out, huh?"

"If my friend needs me to do that, then—excuse my crude language—dammit, yes. That's what I'll do."

Sissy chuckled and started to scratch her head, then remembered she still had that damn fake flower wreath in her hair. According to the bride, these things were big at Renaissance Faires . . . Sissy still had trouble dealing with the fact she now knew people who openly admitted going to those things. "You're simply not happy if your life isn't in danger, are you?"

Mitch grinned. "Don't be jealous of me and Jess. You know I'd check your bodice anytime you wanted me to."

"Stop talking." She grabbed his arm and tugged him closer to her aunts. "Mitchell, these are my momma's sisters. Miss Francine, Miss Darla, Miss Roberta, and Miss Janette. Ladies, this is Mitchell Shaw, Brendon Shaw's baby brother."

Busy shaking each aunt's hand, Mitch still managed to glare at her over his shoulder. "Is that the best way you can describe me? Simply as Brendon Shaw's baby brother?" He sighed sadly, sad gold eyes looking at her aunts. "She's afraid to tell you lovely ladies the truth you know. What she wants to say is Mitchell Shaw, the man I love and adore with all my sassy Southern heart."

"Pathetic, isn't he?"

Mitch suddenly cringed. "Gotta go. Reed boys at ten o'clock."

"What did you do to them this time?"

"It'll take too long to explain, but it involves a call to a lovely Long Island matchmaker named Madge who believes the Reed boys are looking for love. Shit." Mitch took off running, and Ronnie Lee's brothers were right behind him.

Sissy shook her head. "I don't know what to do with that boy sometimes." She scowled when she realized all her aunts were smirking at her. "What?"

The dinner turned out better than Sissy thought it would. First off, important, older shifters were put up on the long dais at the front of the room. Usually, that space was reserved for the bride and groom, but Jessie Ann had come up with some crap about the importance of elders and family and Sissy's daddy got all puffed up because Jessie insisted he and Janie had to sit right in the center. In other words, they were the most important.

Then again, maybe they were the most important to Jessie Ann. She'd lost her parents when she was only fourteen, and Sissy's parents had warmed to Jessie Ann right off.

Even more important, the seating worked to Sissy's advantage. Instead of being trapped with her momma for an hour of feeding, Sissy thankfully sat at the table with the bride and groom, who kept the wedded-bliss cooing to a minimum. Mitch sat on her right, and Ronnie Lee sat on her left with her mate and Mitch's half brother, Brendon. Desiree

MacDermot-Llewellyn sat across from her with her mate and Smitty's best friend, Mace. The rest of the table held Jessie Ann's friends, Sabina, Phil, May, and Danny.

The massive room not only boasted enough tables for all the attendees, but it even had a dance floor right in the middle. Although Sissy doubted she'd do any dancing to some lame band or even worse, a lame DJ. But her steak was bloody and delicious and the company tolerable.

Although Sissy had known this was going to be a big wedding, she hadn't realized the kind of people who would be attending. On one side of the floor were some of the biggest names in the oh-so-boring universe of software and computer . . . stuff. Sissy only knew that because Brendon mentioned them, and he seemed pretty awed. Being a lion, he wasn't easy to awe. Surrounding that unwitting group of full-humans were more Packs and Prides and unattached cats than Sissy had ever seen in a room together. Some of them she recognized from her work in New York City. Others she'd never seen before, but she'd heard about them. They came from all over the States, as far away as the West Coast.

Then there were the wild dog Packs. Asian wild dogs, dingoes from Australia, and more African wild dogs than you could shake your fist at. And since they never shut up— Lord, those dogs could talk and talk—Sissy would love to shake her fist at them, all right.

The rest were Smiths. Either blood relations or related by mating. They'd come from all over, including North and South Carolina, Alabama, Mississippi, Louisiana, Virginia, West Virginia, and Texas. The only area feebly represented was her own damn home, Smithtown.

Now Sissy had known right off Sammy couldn't make it to the wedding. He had ten pups and a diner that he and his wife ran in the heart of Smithtown. Vacations for them were pretty much nonexistent. But Sammy had contacted both

Sissy and Bobby Ray to let them know and offer his apologies. Because that was the way it was supposed to be done.

That, however, did not explain the absence of Travis, Donnie, or Jackie. How her own kin could treat their brother like this was beyond Sissy. You simply didn't do that, no matter what you felt about a person. Blood was blood, in Sissy's mind, and there was nothing she wouldn't do for her kin no matter how much she hated them and wanted to smash their faces in when given the first opportunity.

She'd deal with that on another day, though. But she'd damn well let Travis know how she felt about this. She wouldn't even bother with Jackie and Donnie. They only did what Travis told them to, anyway.

Mitch leaned back in his seat, one long leg stretched out, his arm resting on the back of her chair.

The man did look good in a tux. Of course, she preferred men in jeans and a T-shirt to a stuffy suit or tux. Well, actually, she preferred them naked, but society frowned on that sort of thing.

His gold eyes scanned the room, and she knew he was thinking what she'd been thinking.

"So much shit to start," she murmured next to his ear, "so little time?"

He grinned. "It's too easy. Like lambs to the slaughter."

Sissy leaned in closer, enjoying the big cat's scent. "This is almost over now, right?"

"Not even close, sweet cheeks."

He was right, of course. But Sissy still figured the worst of it was over.

Until the music started . . .

Mitch *loved* it. The wild dogs were the absolute best. They'd heard less than six bars from George Clinton's "Atomic Dog" before they all "whooped!" as one and rushed the dance floor.

Even the bride left her new husband and got on that dance floor bow-wowing with the rest of them.

The rich geeks joined in, completely oblivious. The rest of the breeds, though, appeared thoroughly horrified. The cats were astonished since they were used to the wolves, who were more predator than goofy canine. The wolves were embarrassed by the goofy canine behavior. The bears were typically bored.

"Why are you smiling?"

Mitch laughed at Sissy's question. "Come on! How cool was that? It was like that Dog Whisperer guy came in and rallied them all to the floor!"

The lions and Dez laughed. The wolves . . . not so much.

"Don't walk away mad," he said as they did. "You're completely missing the humor in this."

Sissy gripped her brother's hand and pulled him into the kitchen, smiling and waving when everyone called her name.

"How do you know these people?"

"You were never a people person, Bobby Ray."

"These people" were the kind of people who helped Sissy when she needed it most. These were the people she always made sure she took care of when they performed a service or gave her a little non-job-related assistance.

Sissy led Bobby Ray to the room she'd been sitting in with her father and closed the door behind them. "I wanted to give you something."

Her brother crossed his arms over his big chest. "Another lecture about the perils of hybrid children?"

"Why bother? You'll just have to learn it for yourself, I guess." She picked up the wrapped package she'd left on the table and handed it to him. She had known the staff would leave the gift there. The chef adored her.

"This is for you."

Bobby Ray stared at the package in his hand. "For what?"

"For your wedding."

"You said having a wedding was stupid and that marriage was stupider."

"That hasn't changed. But since you went through with it, I wanted to get you something. Open it!" She bounced up on her toes while her brother pulled off the wrapping. He opened the box and blinked. Then he closed his eyes, and his smile was slow and warm.

"Where did you find this?" he finally asked.

"Going through your room looking for cigarettes. You'd only been gone to the Navy a month or so."

"I'm surprised you didn't throw it out."

"I never hated her, Bobby Ray. I wasn't nice to her, but I never hated her. And based on that," she pointed at the gift she'd given him, "I knew you loved her. Even then. I never mentioned it before because I thought I lost it. But I found it last time I was home, buried with my stash of old *Playgirls*."

Bobby Ray lifted the ID bracelet from the velvet-lined box. Inscribed on the front was Bobby Ray's name, but it was the inscription on the back that at the time, told sixteen-year-old Sissy what she'd already suspected and had her feeling like a bully for the first time: "*To my Jessie Ann*."

"I figured you could give it to her now since you pussed out when you were eighteen."

"I didn't puss out; I just didn't think it was the right time. Judgmental heifer."

"Gelding."

Sissy wrapped her arms around her brother and hugged him tight. "You have a happy life, Bobby Ray."

"Yeah. I'm fixin' to."

And Sissy laughed.

* * *

Mitch threw his arm around his older half-sister's shoulders and smiled when she went tense and her hands clenched into fists.

Marissa Shaw was Brendon's twin and Mitch's older half-sister. Thankfully, she was not his *only* sister. There was still Gwenie. Five years younger, sweet, innocent Gwen would never be so mean to Mitch. She worshipped him!

Rissa, however, seemed convinced that Mitch was nothing more than a scumbag who wanted to steal their vast fortune from them. And he was so nice to her, too . . .

"Those shoes were an interesting choice. Were they out of the official clown shoes, and you had to go with the cheap imitations?"

Marissa scowled at him. "Aren't you needed somewhere? I'm sure Sissy wouldn't mind you staring at her big ass some more."

"Don't be jealous, sweetie. I'm sure someone wouldn't mind staring at your big ass."

She abruptly pulled away from him. "Feel free to stay away from me today."

"I try and stay away from you every day."

"You don't try hard enough."

Mitch watched her walk away. "Love you, Rissa."

"Shut up."

Laughing, Mitch pulled his vibrating phone out of his pocket. But the laughter died when he recognized the number.

Sissy saw her mother going up on her tiptoes, looking over the crowd for something. Probably her. Panicking, Sissy took several steps back, but those damn shoes went out from under her. Who the hell paid seven hundred and fifty dollars for shoes anyway? In what world was that okay?

Give her a pair of boots and a leather jacket, and Sissy was a happy gal for a lot less money.

Figuring she'd hit the floor, Sissy shut her eyes and gritted her teeth. And although she hit something hard, it wasn't the floor.

Slowly, she opened her eyes and bit back her smile. "Oh. Hello, Brendon."

"Uh . . . hi." He looked so fabulously horrified sitting in that chair with his mate's best friend on his lap that Sissy couldn't stop herself. All the rules drummed into her by Bobby Ray over the last few weeks disappeared as she stared at Mitch's big brother.

"I guess this is a bit awkward, huh?"

"Well . . ."

"But I couldn't hide it anymore." She put her arms around his neck, and his whole body tightened as his eyes looked around the room, practically begging someone to rescue him. "You and me . . . perfect together, Brendon."

"What?" His gold eyes grew wide. "Uh . . . Sissy . . . wait a second—"

"Seriously. I've seen your kids. We'd have beautiful babies."

"What's going on?"

Poor Brendon. He didn't know whether to be relieved or scared to death when Ronnie Lee walked up to them.

"I finally told Bren that he was mine and we would be together forever."

Ronnie's eyes turned toward the ceiling, and she brushed her hair away from her face. "I thought we were going to discuss this first."

Sissy felt Bren's big lion body jerk, and she had to fight hard not to laugh.

"I'm Alpha Female, darlin'. I don't have to discuss a damn thing with you or anyone."

Ronnie nodded and cleared her throat. "She's right. I'm sorry, Bren." She sniffed back a nonexistent tear—Ronnie never could fake actual ones. "I hope you'll remember me fondly." Then she ran off into the crowd.

Now Sissy frowned. How had Ronnie learned to run in those damn shoes?

"Ronnie, wait!" Brendon stood and practically tossed Sissy off his lap. "I'm sorry but . . . forget it." He ran after Ronnie, and Sissy started to laugh until she caught her mother's scent.

She spun and ran out a set of big glass doors leading to the gardens. She debated not stopping, just running all the way back to the city, but Mitch's scent caught her attention. She followed it and found him by one of the marble benches they had all over the property. Like most of the males in the wedding party, he'd lost the jacket, removed his tie, and undone the collar of his shirt. Mitch had also rolled up his sleeves to his elbows, and Sissy could see the tattoo on his forearm. He was on the phone and pacing back and forth.

He looked . . . tense. And she didn't know why. She should find out.

"Are you sure?"

"Of course I'm sure," Jen Chow snapped. "Do you think I'd call you about this if I weren't sure?"

"I don't know why *you're* getting so tense. It's me with the bounty on my head."

"I really wish you'd take this seriously, Detective."

"I take everything seriously." Especially what life he had. "But trust me. No one's getting into this wedding who shouldn't be here. I'm probably safer here than anywhere."

"Yes. You're probably right. I want you back here by Monday, though. I'll send—"

"I'll get there."

"Detective—"

"I said I'll get there."

"Fine," she snapped again. ADA Chow had the shortest fuse on record. And after working together for so long, it amazed him that she still called him Detective.

"Talk to you later, Jen."

"Monday, Detective. I'll speak to you on Monday."

"Yep." Mitch disconnected his phone and stretched his neck. It was a full moon out tonight, illuminating everything around him. Of course, he didn't need any of that to see. Not with his eyesight.

Now he knew what those lions in Africa felt like when they were being tracked down by great white hunters.

Two million dollars would bring out the top-drawer hitters. Would he even last another week? Around his own kind, he felt safe, but once he went into the system, he had serious doubts. But hanging around wasn't an option either. He wouldn't be responsible for getting one of his family or friends hurt or killed. Everyone meant too much to him.

Nope. He'd leave tomorrow. But tonight . . .

Mitch slipped his cell phone back into his pants pocket and turned around, ready to head back to the party. What he didn't expect was to find Sissy Mae Smith stretched out on the marble bench watching him. Christ, she looked good with her legs crossed at the ankles and her body propped up by her arms, the palms flat against the bench.

The dress she wore was made of the softest, lightest material Mitch had ever seen. The color a dark brown that contrasted brilliantly with her light brown eyes. He could say he'd never seen her look sexier, but that would be a lie. He'd seen this woman in shorts—absolutely *nothing* was sexier than that.

"Hey."

Sissy gave him that little knowing smile. "Hey."

Mitch waited for her to ask him what was going on, but she didn't.

"I've been bad, Mitch," she said instead.

"Oh?" Mitch crouched beside her, his elbows resting on his knees. "Do tell."

"I was torturing Brendon again."

"Isn't that a little too easy, sweet cheeks?"

She smiled, blinking in surprise. "I hate that nickname."

"I know. And yet, somehow I don't care."

"Keep it up, and it's my windmill arms and legs of fury with wild hitting and kicking."

"An effective fighting skill."

"I think so."

"And you torturing my brother . . ."

"I know. Too easy. And he falls for it every time. I need something else to fulfill my needs."

"A greater challenge?"

"Exactly."

He stood and held his hand out for her to take. She did, her fingers warm against his, and he tugged her to her feet. "Let's go."

"Where?"

"We've got a castle filled with shifters, alcohol, and a barely contained predatory instinct."

"We promised Bobby Ray."

Leaning down, he rested his forehead against hers. "Come Monday, feel free to blame it all on me."

A small frown creased her brow, and she petted his cheek with her right hand. "Don't think I won't."

"But tonight, we're gonna have a great time. Aren't we, Sissy?"

Both hands cupped his cheeks, and Sissy pulled back a bit, staring into his eyes. For the most amazing split second ever, he thought she was going to kiss him. It would have been perfect, too. In the beautiful garden, under the moonlight, just the two of them . . .

"*Sissy. Mae. Smith!*"

They both jerked, and Sissy quickly stepped back, but she didn't have anywhere to go except back on the bench. She sat down hard. But it couldn't match the hardness in her eyes when she stared up at Mitch.

"Yes?"

Miss Janie stepped closer. "They're giving toasts. Aren't you supposed to be giving one?"

"Yep." Sissy stood and brushed off the back of her dress.

"Think you can manage keeping it clean and respectful?"

He didn't know what Sissy was about to say, but Mitch had a feeling that silence at this moment was her best friend. Determined to keep the bloodshed nonexistent, he grabbed Sissy's hand and yanked her back toward the ballroom. Her mother watched them go, and when Mitch looked at her over his shoulder, the smile she wore reminded him of Sissy.

Although telling Sissy that would only get his skin torn off. And he'd really like to avoid that for as long as possible.

Besides, kissing Sissy now or hell, doing *anything* with Sissy now was a mistake for both of them. And they both knew it.

Chapter 2

R onnie patted Sissy on the back. "Great toast."

"Thanks."

"Only one barely veiled insult toward Jessie Ann. I think she was impressed."

Sissy winced. "I actually wasn't trying to insult her. Figured I should keep this one clean for Bobby Ray since it's his wedding and all."

"You did the best you could manage."

"Gee. Thanks."

Ronnie put her arm around Sissy's shoulders and pulled her friend in close. "What's this I hear about you and Mitch out in the garden?"

Sissy rubbed her forehead. "You're telling me my own mother is spreading rumors about me?"

"No. I heard it from Mitch. He said y'all got busted by her."

Sissy gave up. *That idiot.* "Nothing happened."

"Because y'all got busted. He thinks you're in love with him. Want his babies . . . and life insurance."

"It's like he *wants* me to slap him around."

The friends were silent for a moment and then said together, "Although he might."

Sissy grabbed a glass of champagne off a passing tray, and that's when she saw him staring at her. He was really cute, although a little short for her. Asian, dapper as hell . . . and really cute. Had she mentioned that already?

"I know you two," he said. She could tell English wasn't his first language, but his accent was flawless, and she detected a bit of British there. He snapped his fingers. "You took my Lotus!"

Sissy choked on her champagne, and Ronnie started looking for the exits or law enforcement with arrest warrants.

Lord, what is the statute of limitations again?

Giving her a teasing smile, he said, "Some would say you won it fair and square, but I still doubt it."

Realizing she wasn't being accused of thievery—that was a load off—she took a closer look at the man in front of her. He was Asian wild dog and really cute. Wait. She'd already thought that. "Now I remember. In the Philippines. Right?"

"Right. Did you enjoy my car?"

"Oh . . . sure." Until they'd sold it. That little baby financed their next six months in Asia.

"I'm Kenshin Inu, in case you don't remember."

"Sissy Mae Smith. Ronnie Lee Reed."

"You're related to Smitty, yes?"

"Yep."

"Interesting. You know I'm working with him and Mace to start a Japanese division of their business."

"You are?" Bobby Ray hadn't told her, probably because he knew she'd beg him to let her go to Japan for the initial setup.

They were so discussing this when he got back from his honeymoon. The thought of getting back on the road again made her almost giddy. It wasn't like before. She didn't need to escape for years, only to be forced back for holidays and guilt visits to Tennessee. Now living in the city she adored and as Alpha Female of the New York Smiths she had a reason to come back, but she'd always need to travel and Bobby Ray had to know that. Besides, Ronnie Lee could handle the She-wolves when Sissy wasn't there.

Already her mind was turning with the possibilities of this.

"I see the bride signaling for me. If you ladies will excuse me." He smiled and walked off.

"You gonna wait until after the honeymoon or before to torture Bobby Ray about this?"

"After, of course! But Mace will hear from me on Monday."

Ronnie laughed, shook her head. Sissy didn't know what she'd do without her regular traveling partner. Together, she and Ronnie had done some major damage around the world and weren't allowed in quite a few countries because of it.

Wait, is Tokyo still on the list?

But Ronnie was with Brendon Shaw now and madly in love. Although she loved to travel, she didn't have the same drive that Sissy did to keep it up.

"Oh." Ronnie motioned over a pretty, slim woman in a sexy as hell dress. "I don't think you guys have met yet. Gwen O'Neill, this is Sissy Mae Smith. Sissy, this is Mitch's baby sister, Gwen."

Lord in heaven! *This* was Mitch's baby sister? His "innocent" baby sister? His "sweet, adorable" baby sister? Maybe it was Sissy's imagination, but the woman was too hot in her sleeveless black dress with the low-cut front and even lower-cut back, five-inch heels, and a short mass of black, curly hair that teasingly swept across bright gold, almond-shaped eyes to be anyone's innocent anything.

According to Mitch, she was only half lion. Her father

was a South China tiger, which made her one of the rare Tigons. And she'd picked up the best of both her parents. Beautiful, classy, and—

"I'd give my left tit to get laid sometime this weekend, but I don't think that's gonna happen."

Now it was Ronnie's turn to choke up the champagne she'd only just sipped, and Sissy stared at Mitch's "innocent" baby sister, fascinated.

"I thought I'd find somebody here, but"—hands on hips, she looked around—"nothing is real promising." The voice was low, husky. Over the phone, she could easily be mistaken for a man.

"Ya know," she went on, "Mitch talks about you all the time." She eyed Sissy before turning back to scan the crowd. "And I'm always like, 'Dude, if you like her so much, fuckin' marry her.' And he's all like, 'Shut up.'"

Sissy didn't dare look at Ronnie. Nope. If she looked at her, forget it.

"This is a nice wedding, though, huh? Although we weren't invited. But Ma made up her mind. She was coming, and I figured I better go to keep her out of trouble, ya know? A couple of margaritas in my mom, and all hell breaks loose. But Brendon got us in with no problem, and everybody has been pretty friendly. Except that bitch." She snorted and glared across the bar to Brendon Shaw's twin sister. "Marissa 'I'm God's gift to the universe' Shaw. She's this close"—Gwen held up her thumb and forefinger a small bit apart—"to getting acid tossed in her face. I don't think she realizes no one talks shit about my brother. I don't give a fuck who you are. Or in her case, who you *think* you are."

Sissy physically turned away so she was in no danger of even *glimpsing* Ronnie's face or body language. She wouldn't be able to take it.

"What I love is she acts like her shit don't stink. Like I don't know who she is and where she came from. But I know 'cause I came from the same place she came from. You know what I'm sayin'?"

Waiting a moment, Sissy realized that yes, Gwen did want an answer.

"Absolutely."

"I know a lot of these bitches, they forget the men once they're old enough to go out on their own. But not me and not my Ma. This is Mitch I'm talking about. No one fucks with him." Again, those dark gold eyes sized Sissy up. "You know, you're cuter than I thought you'd be. I'm surprised he hasn't fucked you yet. But he says you guys are friends, although why anyone would have a male as a *friend* is completely beyond me. But maybe it's a wolf thing, huh? 'Cause other than for fuckin' or tunin' up my car, I don't see their purpose. But hey, that's me."

Mitch walked up to them and handed his sister a glass of champagne. "Everything going okay over here?" And he gave Sissy a warning glance to not mess with his sister.

Not that he had anything to worry about. Personally, Sissy would like to avoid having acid thrown in her face. She was wacky that way.

"Everything is fine," Gwen assured him. "Stop worrying about me." She slipped her arm around Mitch's waist and rested her head against his chest. Considering her stock, Sissy thought Gwen would be considerably bigger. At least taller. But she wasn't even five-nine. Most Smiths would consider her "tiny." No wonder she wore those shoes, although how she managed to walk in them, Sissy didn't know.

"I'm your big brother. I'll always worry about you." Suddenly, Mitch's gaze locked on something at the bar, and he snarled.

"What?"

"He's checking you out."

Gwen rolled her eyes, and Sissy didn't even bother looking to see who he was talking about.

"I'll handle him." Mitch pulled away from his sister and walked to the bar.

"Well," Ronnie, who loved to state the obvious, sighed out, "now you know why you won't be gettin' laid this weekend."

Mitch walked back to his sister, feeling pretty cocky about scaring off that puma.

"Are you done?"

"Yup. Just protecting my little sis."

"Gee. Thanks."

Mitch glanced around. "Where did Sissy go?"

"All she said was, 'Momma's at six o'clock.' Then she and Ronnie took off running. It was . . . interesting."

"You and Ma get along. You don't know how people who don't get along with their mothers suffer."

"I like Ma. And she's worried about you."

"Nice how you slipped that in."

"Just warning you she's going to be bugging you tonight."

A waiter arrived with two bottles of Guinness.

"You saint," Mitch sighed happily, grabbing his bottle. After a healthy drink, he said to his sister, "You know what's funny about you and Ma being here?"

"What?"

"Neither of you were actually invited."

Gwen rolled her shoulders. "You know Ma. Not a chance in hell she was going to miss out on seeing her only son in a tux. Besides, this is considered the party of the century. She wasn't about to miss it."

"Yeah, but you had a table and everything."

"Brendon took care of that for us." Gwen grinned. "He

always said if we need anything to go ahead and call him, so Ma did."

"He meant that. You ever need anything, go to Bren. He'll always watch out for you guys."

"Uh . . . okay."

"Why are you staring at me?"

"You look tired. And thin. Too thin."

"I'm fine. Just a lot going on."

"Any of that going on with Sissy?"

"You're gonna start this now?"

"I hadn't met her before. Now that I have . . . not sure what you're waiting for. She's hot. And sturdy. Uncle Joey always says O'Neill males need sturdy women."

"You start quoting Uncle Joey, I'm walking away."

"I just don't know what the problem is."

"There is no problem. And I'd like to keep it that way."

"Fine, ya big pussy."

"You have to know that's *not* an insult to me, right?"

Sissy tapped her foot and watched her friend. "Dez, you have to make a choice here."

Dez was probably the only full-human Sissy could say in all honesty that she trusted. A tough cop, an amazing mother, and a great friend, Dez was not to be trifled with. She was a deadly predator like the rest of them. When she'd asked Sissy to be her son's godmother, she'd specifically stated, " 'Cause I know you'll kill anybody who tries to hurt him." Truer words had never been spoken, but the fact that Dez realized it and acted accordingly was what set her apart from her weaker full-human counterparts.

But when it came to chocolate, Dez could be as big a pain in the ass as Jessie Ann.

"I can't. You do understand that, right?" She started at

one end of the U-shaped table. "Here we have the candy. Chocolate with nuts. With caramel. With fruits."

"Dez—"

"Then we have the fresh fruit and the dark chocolate waterfall. Of course it's all dark chocolate. At least seventy-two percent cacoa. There's chocolate fondue and twelve—yes, twelve—different kinds of chocolate cakes. Then there are the brownies and pies—"

"Desiree!" Sissy cleared her throat. "Just. Pick. Something."

Covering her mouth with her hands, Dez's eyes went from one end of the table to the other. "I . . . I can't! I'm in chocolate overload!"

Good Lord.

"Darlin', you know I love you, but there is a table of unsuspecting males playing Texas Hold 'Em, and it's calling my name."

"You can't," Dez said offhandly, reaching for a plate. "Maybe I'll take a little of everything . . . except the fruit. I can do without the fruit. Why screw up chocolate with fruit?"

"Why can't I?"

"Last time I was in there, so was your mother."

"That woman is *everywhere.*"

"Should I mention she was in the Karaoke Room belting out—"

"*No!*"

"All right then."

Dez walked over, her plate piled with bits of this and that from the available chocolate selections.

"Desiree."

"What? I wanted to be covered."

"Your thing for chocolate is unhealthy."

"And there's still the wedding cake. That thing is dark chocolate. Wish my wedding cake was like that."

"Your cake was chocolate."

"Not dark chocolate. Not like that."

"I can't have this conversation with you anymore." Sissy turned to walk away.

"I'm sure you could have this conversation if I were Mitchell. And we were outside in the garden . . . under the romantic moonlight," she taunted.

Sissy squinted. "You're armed, aren't you?" Dez kept her service weapon on her at all times. She even had a small pistol on her at her own wedding. Yup. A full-human predator all right.

"Every day," Dez confirmed.

"Damn." There went that potential beating Sissy had been all ready to give.

Mitch sat alone at a big table and picked at his slice of wedding cake. It wasn't that the cake wasn't delicious. It was. In fact, the cake wasn't just chocolate; it was dark chocolate with seventy-two percent cacao. He knew this because the bride had announced it before cutting the cake and a collective "ohhhh" had come from the wild dogs—and Dez. To Mitch, chocolate was chocolate.

Nah. It wasn't the cake. It was him. His family was right. He was getting thin. He simply wasn't hungry these days. Must be the overall fear of death that had screwed with his appetite.

It had been, what? Five years ago when he'd used his old high school connections to dig his way into the O'Farrell crew. His department had made him look like a dirty cop, and his old history of being the high school football star had greased the wheels.

But after all that work and risk, it mostly wasn't for shit. Almost all the charges against the O'Farrell crew had been dropped after more legal wrangling than seemed possible. In fact, this whole situation should be over now. Except for the one charge that wouldn't go away. The one that had blown Mitch's cover, that he couldn't bring himself to tell his family about, and that still gave him nightmares.

First-degree murder against Petey O'Farrell, head of the O'Farrell crew. Mitch was the only witness to what that sick old fuck had done—and Mitch was now the only thing between freedom and life for O'Farrell.

If Mitch didn't testify, the case would crumble. If Mitch was dead, O'Farrell would be out of jail faster than he could spit.

Bottom line . . . he needed Mitch dead.

Not a very comforting thought. No wonder Mitch no longer had an appetite.

Sissy dropped into the empty seat beside him, undoing her shoes and kicking them off her feet. Funny, her mere presence soothed him. He'd never noticed that before.

Turning the chair around, Sissy pushed her feet into his lap, ignoring the fact he was still eating . . . or in this case, picking.

"Rub my feet."

Mitch placed his fork on the table and looked down at her feet. "Don't I need a veterinarian's license to handle hooves of this size?"

She lifted her foot a bit and brought it back down onto his groin, causing him to grunt.

"Rub them," she ordered.

Liking his balls in working order, he did what she told him to do. "How are you holding up?"

"So far, so good. I've avoided her. She's on one side of the floor, I make sure I'm on the other. If she starts looking above the crowd like she's trying to find me, I run like I'm going for the gold in the Summer Olympics."

"That's your plan for the rest of the evening? Dodging your mother?"

"Yes. That's my plan. And since you're insistent that killing your parents is so wrong, I really have no other choice."

"Good point. It's almost over, though. A few more hours of New Wave music and bad wild dog dancing, and this all will be a distant memory."

Sissy stared out over the dance floor. "Lord, that is some bad dancin'."

"But it's exuberant."

She shook her head and looked away.

"I have to say, Sissy, I thought you had a few more brothers." Sissy followed his gaze to Smitty, who stood talking to one of the cousins who'd bothered to attend, and he'd come from Smithville or Smithburg . . . one of the other Smith places the States were apparently littered with. It seemed that many of the family from Smitty's hometown were woefully absent.

"I tragically do have more brothers, but they don't know how to act right." She sighed. "That ain't fair. Sammy has ten pups and a diner he and his mate run. But Travis Ray and Donnie Ray could have shut the garage down for a few days. And last I heard, tax accountants weren't dramatically needed in the middle of June, so I think Jackie Ray could have closed up his little piece of shit office for a weekend."

"So why didn't they?"

"Because they're bastards. Because they think this is stupid. Because when Daddy's not there, Travis wants to think he's in charge. And, most importantly, it's football season."

Mitch frowned. He loved most sports, but football was his true passion. "It's not football season."

"Yeah, well . . ."

"Yeah, well what? I know for a fact it's not football season."

Sissy shook her head. "I don't want to discuss it."

"Yeah, but—"

"I," she cut in roughly, "don't want to discuss it."

"Okay. Okay. No need to get your thong in a bind."

"And stop telling people Momma busted us in the garden."

"She did."

"And that I'm in love with you?"

"You are," he teased, loving how he got her to smile with the silliest stuff that most females didn't find remotely funny. "You simply haven't faced it yet. You saucy siren, you."

"You know, you look like the high school football star—"

"I was."

"—but you talk like a dweeb."

"It's called being complex and dynamic."

"It's called being a geek." Her body suddenly tensed. "Is that her?"

Mitch looked around. "Don't see her. I think you're safe for the time being."

"Thought I scented her."

"Isn't your mother leaving tomorrow?"

Sissy's whole body dropped, her limbs sort of relaxing so that she looked like she'd passed out. "Yes! Her, my daddy, and Ronnie's momma and daddy are going on that cruise. And not soon enough. I've got one nerve left, Mitchell. One. And she's playing 'Dueling Banjos' on it."

Mitch laughed as Sissy motioned one of the waiters over. "Darlin'," she said to the waiter with her most luxurious drawl, "could you please get me a shot of tequila?"

Staring at her, his mouth kind of open, the waiter nodded and started to walk away. Mitch caught hold of his jacket and asked, "You gonna ask me?"

"Oh. Yes. Yes. Of course. What would you like, sir?"

"Beer."

"We have over seventy—"

"Bud."

The waiter looked disgusted at Mitch's love of good ol' American brew. "Of course, sir."

Really big feet waved in front of his face after the waiter walked off.

"Hello? You ain't done. And get the instep this time."

Mitch gripped her feet and raised an eyebrow. "Oh, I'll get the instep."

"Don't you tick—"

He started tickling her feet, and laughing hysterically, Sissy desperately tried to pull her feet back.

"Stop, Mitch! Stop! *Ow!*"

The woman had this ability to come out of nowhere. One second, she wasn't there, and then suddenly, Miss Janie was not only there but also yanking her daughter by the hair.

"Sissy Mae Smith," she ordered. "Act like ya got some damn sense."

Mitch kept his grip on Sissy's feet, afraid she'd get up and get into a full-on dogfight with her mother.

As quickly as she showed anger, Janie Mae just as quickly calmed down. She kissed Mitch on the forehead. "Hello, pretty kitty."

Strange how Sissy's mother had seen Mitch several times during the day, but this was the first time she'd greeted him . . . and definitely the first time she'd kissed him. He got the distinct feeling he was being used here. Not that he minded. He actually liked the crazy She-wolf. Of course, not quite the same way he liked her daughter.

"Hi, Miss Janie." Everyone called her Miss Janie, and Mitch was afraid to call her anything else.

She patted his cheek in that motherly way she had. "I met your momma. I just love her."

Mitch blinked. "You do?" Even he had to admit his mother was not an easy woman to get along with. She was loud and raunchy and rude. But that didn't mean anything to Mitch because the woman amazed him. Her dream had always been to own a high-end salon, but the Pride wouldn't pay for that. They would, however, pay for her to go to nursing school. She ended up being a nurse for years, putting money away and taking stylist classes in her free time. It took her years, but eventually, she opened her own place and now had three of them in the Philadelphia area. With her own grit and determination, she'd moved the O'Neill Pride up in the ranks and had offered Mitch more than once to "help you get your ass in your own Pride."

"She's lovely. I'm planning a big end of summer party in August, and I invited her and that gorgeous baby sister of yours. I want you to come too. Okay?"

"You want us in Smithtown?"

"Oh, no." Miss Janie shook her head. "We'll be having it here somewhere. Lord, son, I'd never bring you down to Smithtown." She gripped his face with one hand, long fingers on both sides of his face, and squeezed until his lips pursed out. His mother often did the same thing. Was it a maternal instinct like breast feeding? "This face is simply too gorgeous to have it ruined like that."

Mitch laughed, and she patted his cheek and walked away.

When he looked at Sissy, she was glaring at him like he'd betrayed her somehow. "What?"

How did she do that? Sissy was thirty-one, and her momma still had a way of making her feel like a twelve-year-old. All the wedding planning had been kind of fun until her mother had practically moved to New York for the final preparations. For a month, she'd had to tolerate that woman on a daily basis. And every day, Bobby Ray had to talk her out of taking the first plane to Japan or Australia or anywhere her momma wasn't—and that they legally allowed Sissy to enter.

It wasn't that she didn't love her momma. She did. But did she have to make Sissy look and feel so small? And did she have to do it in front of Mitch? True, doing it in front of any man was mean, but in front of Mitch, it was particularly bitchy as far as Sissy was concerned.

"All right, Shaw." Trying to get her mind off Mitch, Sissy motioned to the three-hundred-plus crowd at her brother's wedding. "I'm on the hunt for my next conquest. See anyone with potential?"

"Sure." Mitch glanced around and pointed at a cheetah across the room. A female. "What about her?"

"What is wrong with you?"

"Don't give me that tone. Have you even tried it?"

"Mitchell—"

"How do you know if you'll like it or not if you haven't tried it . . . with me watching . . . and filming?"

"Forget I asked."

Sissy ran her finger over his tattoo. A four-inch green shamrock. "Could you be more Irish?" she laughed.

"Not really." He grabbed her hand. "Come on. We're dancing."

"To the Go-Go's?" Sissy had successfully managed only two dances, and both had been to slow songs. It wasn't that she couldn't dance but come on! The Go-Go's? Did these wild dogs not have any music from the twenty-first century? Or even the nineties?

"We're gonna rock out." He dragged her toward the dance floor, stopping briefly so she could knock back the shot of tequila the waiter brought.

Once on the dance floor, she watched in horror as Mitch did something some people—no one she knew, of course— would call dancing.

"Mitchell," she whined, "this is just embarrassing."

Mitch stopped, looking around at all the wild dogs dancing. Even the bride was doing the pogo like she was at a 1985 prom.

"As compared to what?"

He tragically had a point.

Mitch walked up behind his brother and slapped him on the back. The thing about Brendon was that Mitch didn't have to hold back. His brother didn't go flying across a room or snap like a twig from one little hit. Instead, Bren didn't move a step, glancing at Mitch over his shoulder and asking, "What?"

"Are we having a good time?"

From the balcony overlooking the dance floor, Bren gazed down with that intense stare of his. He always looked like he was sorting out the world's problems. Finally, he answered, "Yes. I am." Twenty minutes to answer a simple question . . .

Mitch leaned back against the railing. "You and Gwen getting along?" he asked.

"Of course. You know I love Gwenie."

"And Marissa—"

"Takes a little longer to warm up to people," Brendon explained about his twin.

"Gwen's thinking about coming out here to visit in a couple of months. Maybe she could—"

"She'll stay at the hotel."

Mitch opened his mouth to say something, and Bren cut in, practically snarling, "And if you mention paying for that room, I will toss your ass off the balcony."

Mitch looked over the rail and gauged the distance. It wouldn't kill him, but it would hurt, so best not to push it.

"I just don't want some people—I won't mention any

names—but some people who look like you, share similar DNA, and came out of the same womb ten minutes before you did accusing me of taking advantage."

Now Bren laughed. "I wish you'd stop taking what *some* people say to you at face value. Besides, the hotels are as much yours as ours, and if you want to put up guests in one of the top floor suites that go for ten grand a night, that's up to you." Bren sipped his beer. Unlike Mitch, he went for one of those obscure label beers. "Besides, Mitch, Gwen is family."

"You're not related."

"Your sister is my sister, shithead. If she ever needs anything, all she has to do is ask."

Mitch nodded and felt relief wash through him. He'd been worrying about who would watch out for Gwen if—when—anything happened to him. Knowing Brendon would do it for him made Mitch feel more relieved than he could say.

"Thanks, bruh."

"Shut up, Mitch," Brendon growled.

And Mitch smiled.

Sissy held up her shot glass of tequila, and Ronnie did the same. "To good friends, good times, and the hope that we never have to do this again."

Ronnie laughed as they touched glasses, then they took their shots in one gulp. Sissy kind of shuddered. Damn, that was good tequila. But no more. Not tonight. As much as she might want to get loaded so she could drown out the never-ending criticism coming from her momma, Sissy had promised herself—

"Why do you drink that?" her momma snapped from behind her. "You know you can't handle it."

"My hope is that'll blind me to you still being here."

Sissy motioned to the bartender for another shot, and she didn't even have to look to know Ronnie had made a desperate escape. Not that she blamed her. Ronnie had her own mother to deal with. "You are still leaving tomorrow, right, Momma?"

A glass of champagne in her hand, Janie Mae Lewis rested against the bar. Her momma never had to *try* to look scary. She simply was. While at the same time, pleasant looking. No one had ever accused Sissy of being pleasant . . . ever. Lookswise, she took after her daddy's side. Dark hair, light brown eyes—as opposed to her momma's amber ones—and a square jaw.

The other Lewis sisters weren't nearly as hard looking, nor did they work Sissy's last nerve the way her mother did.

Mostly because her mother had the tendency to say things like, "You know if you tried not glaring so much, you could look real pretty."

Sissy let out a breath at her momma's words, remembering her promise to her daddy. She wouldn't fight her momma no matter how much she wanted to. "I'm sure somewhere in there, you've hidden a compliment. So thank you for that."

"I just want you to be happy, Sissy Mae." And Sissy felt so proud she kept that snort all to herself. "And you won't be happy if you keep scaring off every male that comes your way. I mean look how happy your brother is. And Jessie Ann's already pregnant. So they'll be happy with a passel of kids, and you'll be their pups' favorite aunt. You can visit them during the holidays, and maybe their dog will sleep on your feet at night."

Sissy turned, ready to tell her mother to shut the fuck up when someone slammed into her from behind.

"Oh, sweetie, I'm so sorry." The lioness had gotten a bit of champagne on Sissy's dress and was desperately wiping at it. "I'm so so sorry. Let me help you get that clean." She smiled at Janie Mae. "I swear, I'm such a clumsy ass, Janie.

Let me get her cleaned up. We'll be right back." Then she was dragging Sissy out of the ballroom and off into the darkness until she stopped at a marble bench.

"Sit, baby-girl. Sit."

Sissy did, and that's when she felt the wave of pure rage wash over her. If this lioness hadn't pulled her away, Sissy would have broken her promise to her father—and possibly ended up going to jail for the night—and she'd never have forgiven herself.

"Easy. Just breathe. Here," a firm hand against her back pushed her down until her head was below her knees, "breathe, baby-girl. Just breathe. Deep ones in and out until the ringing stops."

How did she know there was a ringing in her ears? Because there definitely was ringing.

After a good ten minutes or so, Sissy finally felt strong enough to sit up. The lioness sat next to her, smoking a Marlboro Light, and Sissy got a good look at her.

"Miss O'Neill?" Mitch's mother. Sissy had only had a chance to say a quick hello when she'd passed her in the Gaming Room. The lioness had been cleaning out some wolves, and Sissy had left her to her work.

"Oh, darlin', call me Roxanne. Or Roxy. It's not my real name, mind you. A nice Irish girl gets a nice Irish name. But do you know how many friggin' Patricia Maries there are at Mass every Sunday? So when I was nine, I decided I wanted to be called Roxanne." She grinned, and in that moment, she looked just like her son. "One of my aunts was a big reader, and when I told everybody at Sunday dinner that I was now Roxanne, she asked me if that was because of that book, *Cyrano* something. And I told her—and the priest who was having dinner at our house—that I got the name from the hooker who worked the corner near the ice cream parlor me and my sisters hung out at after school."

Sissy burst out laughing while Roxy shook her head. "Let

me tell you, baby-girl, that night, I did not sleep on my back. My ma tore my ass up." She shrugged. "But everybody still calls me Roxy."

She reached into her small Gucci purse and pulled out a half-used pack of cigarettes. "Here."

Sissy shook her head. "I quit." About twelve years ago, in fact.

"Do you want to get through the rest of the night without killing your own mother?"

Realizing she was right, Sissy took a cigarette from the pack and let Roxy light it up for her with her gold lighter.

As Sissy sat back and smoked her cigarette, she looked closely at Mitch's mother. Like all lionesses, she was sort of gold all over. But her hair had lighter blond streaks and was combed out so it looked like a sexy wild mane. She wore a tight gold dress that may have been a few years too young for her and gold designer shoes that probably cost a fortune. Although Sissy wouldn't know much about that since she was a boot girl. Work boots, cowboy boots, biker boots, whatever. If they were boots, Sissy wore them.

Mitch's momma was beautiful, but there was a wildness to her that made Sissy take to her instantly. None of that stuck-up lioness shit she'd seen from the Llewellyns and the other East Coast Prides attending the wedding. This woman was classless and tasteless, and Sissy knew in that instant that she adored her.

"I gotta say, baby-girl, my boy talks about you all the time. But the conversation is definitely weird." She turned a bit and looked at Sissy. "Did he really give you a wedgie the other day?"

Sissy laughed, remembering their tussle during the rehearsal dinner. She thought her momma was going to have a stroke she was so embarrassed. "Uh . . . yeah. But I kind of deserved it."

"So you and my boy . . . uh . . ." She wiggled perfectly waxed eyebrows, and Sissy laughed harder.

"God, no."

Now the lioness looked insulted. "Why the hell not? Is my boy not good enough for you?"

"Miss O'Neill—"

"Roxy."

"Roxy, trust me when I say that there are few Smiths who can accuse anyone of not being good enough for them. But we're buddies. Friends."

"Let me tell you something, baby-girl. My Mitchy—"

Mitchy?

"—I love him more than any woman can love her son. But me and his daddy, well . . . let's just say that was more about obligation to the Pride than any great love affair. But my pretty little Gwen . . . me and her daddy . . ." Then she purred. Seriously. Purred.

"Let's just say I've never gotten it like that before and not since. Gwenie is my love child. And that's what you want. Someone who makes you feel that way."

"What happened with Gwen's father?" Sissy knew something must have happened because Roxy spoke of him in the past tense. And she had no idea how Mitch made her "feel," and Sissy was okay with that. No use analyzing everything. That had never been her style.

Roxy shrugged shoulders that looked strong and powerful. Typical swamp cat and probably why Roxy didn't look scared of anybody. Why would you be when you're built like a tank?

"I screwed that up. He had obligations to his family in Hong Kong and I was too scared to leave my Pride or Philly." Gold eyes locked on her. "You weren't afraid to leave your Pack, though, huh? Mitch says you've been damn near everywhere."

"Smithtown has too many Alphas and not enough territory."

"Plus, you didn't want to have to take down your own mother so you could be in charge."

"Like I could."

"Oh, you could. And she knows it." Roxy moved a little closer. "Take it from someone who does it to her own sisters, baby-girl. She does what she does to keep you off balance."

"But I'm not in Smithtown anymore."

"But until you settle down, until you have a mate and your mate is some place *other* than Smithtown, she'll always worry you might move back. For good. When you meet someone as strong as you, you've gotta find other ways to keep control."

She took another drag from her cigarette before carelessly tossing it. Sissy's had already burned down, nearly singeing her fingers. "So when you gonna tell her you don't want kids?"

Sissy froze. "Who says I don't want kids?"

"Look, when someone mentions having kids to someone who wants to have kids, you see all sorts of longing and shit in their eyes. You know what I saw in your eyes when your mother mentioned kids? Impatience."

Sissy laughed so hard she started coughing, and Roxy nodded her head. "I thought so."

She patted Sissy's knee and leaned in close, whispering, "Just FYI, baby-girl, but Mitchy doesn't want kids either."

"Stop." Sissy pushed Roxy's granite shoulder with a chuckle. "Please stop. And shouldn't you be trying to hook him up with a nice Pride female or a full-human? I thought most cats would rather see their cubs with a full-human than a canine."

"I want my Mitchy to be happy, and he won't be happy in anyone's Pride. And he's much too good natured to be around other cats." She took out another cigarette, her face getting serious. "I worry about him, though. He's not sleeping. Or eating enough. I can tell."

"It's this upcoming trial and everything. And now there's the bounty on his head."

Legs crossed, eyes focused on the sky, Roxy pursed her lips. "He's had a bounty on his head. That's why he came to New York, right? A few grand?"

"I think they raised it. Based on what I heard, it's mighty."

"How do you know this?"

"I was nosey and listened in to his conversation."

Roxy nodded approval. "Good girl. What else did you hear?"

"He's heading back to Philly on Monday."

"And you're going to miss him."

Sissy answered honestly. "He's my best friend, Roxy. Next to Ronnie Lee. So of course I'm gonna miss him."

"I tried to talk him out of this, you know? Tried to convince him to keep his mouth shut and pretend he didn't see anything. I'm from the neighborhood. I know what happens to snitches."

"He's not a snitch," Sissy snapped, automatically defending him. "He's a cop doing his job. And he's doing a good job. Putting his life at risk to take down scumbags like Petey O'Farrell takes guts most of us don't have." Sissy took a breath to calm herself down. "You're his mother, and I respect that," she finished, "but watch what you say. I don't want Mitch hurt because someone's being careless."

That gold gaze watched Sissy for a long time, and when Roxy moved, Sissy braced herself, expecting to get punched. Instead, Roxy kissed her forehead. Almost on the same spot her father had. What was going on with everyone today? Was it the wedding? Did it affect people the way funerals did?

"You are a darling, wonderful girl, and I'm so glad you're Mitch's"—she paused for a moment, but it said volumes—"friend."

Roxy stood, tugging her dress back into place. All those voluptuous curves, the woman knew how to work a wardrobe. "Come on, baby girl. Let's get you a real drink. I know I could use one."

"I better not. I've already had two . . . or three."

"What's one more? Don't worry." She grinned, and Sissy would swear she saw fangs peeking out of her gums. "I'll watch out for ya."

Mitch was being thoroughly entertained by Ronnie Reed's uncles and brothers getting sauced on the homemade 'shine they'd brought from Tennessee when he saw Dez MacDermot strut out of the ballroom. He liked Dez. She was a good cop. Little crazy, but you had to be to do the job.

"All right, gentlemen. Let's go."

"Go where?" Rory Reed, Ronnie's oldest brother, asked way too loudly. Wolves . . . they simply could *not* hold their liquor.

"Out front. The bride and groom are leaving, and there's a whole tossing of flowers and garters thing that's involved. So let's go."

"The flowers are fake," Mitch reminded her.

"You're gonna start with me now, cat? 'Cause I'm tired and cranky, and the chocolate is wearing off."

"I see why Mace loves you."

"Yeah, yeah, yeah. Fuck youse, too."

Mitch and the Reed boys laughed as they followed Dez back into the castle. You really could take the girl out of the Bronx but not necessarily the Bronx out of the girl. Dez proved that.

As they headed toward the front and the throng of people blocking the entrance, Dez motioned to Mitch. "Could you take care of Sissy before her mother sees her?"

"Where is she?"

"Over at the back bar." That didn't worry him. It was her next sentence that caused the intense panic. "With your mother."

Mitch stopped cold and grabbed Dez's arm. If he didn't know better, he'd swear she was moments from going for the piece she had hidden on her somewhere.

"Say again?"

"Sissy's with your mom. Roxy, right?"

"What she's doing with her?" Mitch knew he sounded desperate, but didn't Dez see the recipe for disaster this was?

"Drinking, last I—where are you going?"

Mitch ran, cutting past people and trying to pretend nothing was wrong. Especially when he saw Miss Janie. Her eyes narrowed, and her gaze immediately scanned the crowd, looking for Sissy no doubt. Moving past Ronnie, Mitch tugged her hair and motioned to Sissy's mother. It took her a second, but then she was up and moving, stepping in front of the woman before she could go looking for her daughter.

As Dez had said, Mitch found Sissy and his mother in the back bar.

When she saw him, Roxy stood and smiled. "There's my baby-boy!"

"What did you do to her?" he demanded.

Sissy's head rested on the bar, her body moments from sliding off the stool.

"Just getting to know baby-girl here." Roxy grabbed his arm. "I like her, Mitchell. She's smart and funny and sturdy. You know what your Uncle Joey says."

"No! We're not discussing Uncle Joey now."

Mitch grabbed Sissy's shoulders and pulled her back. "Sissy? Can you hear me?"

Her eyes opened. "Mitchy!" she crowed, and he covered her mouth with his hand.

"I don't know why you're upset." His mother shrugged. "If you can't handle her, I'm sure her mother will take her."

"Don't even think it."

"Fine." Roxy shrugged. "Hey, at the very least, I've loosened her up for ya."

"Ma!"

Roxy held her hands up. "Just kidding. Gawd! Where did your sense of humor go?"

"That wasn't funny."

They both heard it at the same time. Ronnie's voice over the well-wisher's din outside.

"I'm sure she's in the bathroom, Miss Janie. *Really!*"

"Why the hell are you yelling, Ronnie Lee Reed?"

"Move, baby-boy." Roxy motioned him away, and Mitch immediately picked Sissy up and placed her over his shoulder. He could only hope she didn't start throwing up.

"And don't take her to her room at the hotel. That's the first place her mother will look."

Mitch nodded and slipped out through a back door . . . barely missing Miss Janie as she stomped in.

"I know she's been in here, Ronnie Lee Reed. I can smell her . . . and the tequila!"

Mitch moved fast, cutting through the castle and out the back. He had to get Sissy's drunk ass back to the hotel. Of course what he'd do with her after that, he had no idea. Especially when she suddenly blurted out, "You have the best ass, Mitchell Shaw!"

Christ, it was going to be a long night.

Chapter 3

Sissy Mae turned over and buried her head back in the pillows, trying her best to block out the sunlight. Since she'd never been a morning person, Sissy always kept the blinds in her room at the Kingston Arms Hotel closed. Why she didn't do that last night, she had no idea.

Well, it didn't matter. She was too exhausted to care at this point. Exhausted and in pain. Her throat was sore and raw, and her head throbbed. It felt like her brain was rattling around inside her skull.

It had to have been that last sip of tequila. The one where she clearly remembered saying to herself, "Well, I shouldn't waste it."

Unfortunately, that was the last thing she really remembered.

No, she wouldn't be getting up anytime soon if she could help it. And to prove it, she buried her face deeper into the pillow. It felt good to do that, so she did it again. In some bizarre way, the action helped her headache—she'd never call it a hangover out loud—so she did it again. Then she rubbed her head against the pillow.

It was that scent. She wanted that scent on her. A very

shifter thing to do and one she'd never really be able to explain to a full-human without getting that telltale "ewww" response.

As her brain began to slowly process whose smell this could possibly be, she felt the bed dip and a heavy weight rest against her side.

"Baby?" a deliciously low voice said. "You awake? I need you, baby."

Sissy's eyes snapped open, but she immediately closed them again when bright sunlight brutally seared her brain right inside her skull.

"Mitchell?"

"Yeah," he purred, nuzzling her chin, her ear. "You up for more of me, baby? 'Cause we are so not done."

Not caring how much the light hurt, Sissy slammed her hands against Mitch's chest and pushed him off while scrambling back until her shoulders hit the headboard. Using both hands, she held the sheet under her chin.

"What the hell is going on?"

"What's wrong, baby?"

She stared at him in horror. "Mitchell Shaw, tell me you didn't!"

"Didn't what?" He crawled across the bed toward her. "Didn't turn you inside out and work you like you've never been worked before? Well, if you're asking me to be honest, I guess I'd have to say—"

"Don't." One hand released the sheet she had such a grip on to halt his words. "Not another word."

"Don't be that way, baby."

"And stop calling me that!"

He took hold of the sheet and began to pull it away from her. "Don't be shy, baby. We have no secrets now."

This wasn't happening! This wasn't happening! She was fully dressed!

Wait. She was fully dressed.

Sissy stared down at the clean white T-shirt and white sweatpants. She clearly smelled Ronnie's scent. These were Ronnie's clothes. Had to be. Sissy never wore white. She had a tendency to get food on clothes within seconds. And something told her it was Ronnie who'd put the damn things on Sissy in the first place.

"You are so hot, baby."

Slowly, she looked up at Mitch, and forcing herself to look past her hangover, she could see he was fighting hard not to laugh out loud.

"You. Big. Haired. *Bastard!*"

Sissy launched herself onto Mitch, knocking him off the bed and onto the floor. She punched and slapped at his face, and he held off her blows with those sides of ham he called arms. And it didn't help that he was hysterically laughing the whole time.

"I hate you, Mitchell Shaw! I hate you!"

"You *love* me, sweet cheeks! Admit it!"

"One day," she told him between blows, "you're gonna meet me in hell! And I'm gonna kick your big, white ass!"

"Last night you told me it was the best ass!"

"Shut up!"

He grabbed her wrists and turned, putting her on her back with him between her legs. "Are you going to keep fighting me, or you going to admit I'm your lord and savior?"

"Blasphemer!"

"That's what the priests all said."

"I should tell my daddy to kick your ass."

"He's on vacation. With your mother. Remember?"

And like that . . . all the fight went out of her. "She's gone? Really and truly?"

"Really and truly." He leaned in and kissed her nose. "Now are you going to keep fighting me, or are we going to get some breakfast?"

"Breakfast, you evil bastard. But this will not be forgotten."

Grinning, Mitch released her wrists and easily got to his feet. He reached down and grabbed Sissy's hand, pulling her up.

"You sure you feel okay?" He still held her hand. "I was just messing with your head."

"It was mean." And she shrugged. "Of course, when I think about it, I have to appreciate the evil of it."

He moved closer. "So you're not mad at me?"

"I should be—" Sissy looked up into Mitch's handsome face, and her words died in her throat when she saw something there she didn't see very often—maybe because she'd never really looked before. She saw desire. Pure, clear. It was there on his face and the way he stared at her lips.

She swallowed and was about to lick her suddenly dry lips, but quickly realized that would probably be a bad idea.

He let out a sigh. "We have to go, don't we?"

"Yeah. We do." She did, right? Somewhere in the universe, it would be considered the right thing to do. Only she couldn't remember why it would be the right thing to do.

"You're right. I know you're right." He shook his head the tiniest bit. "It's a real damn shame, though, huh?"

"Maybe. For all I know you're a dud in bed."

"Now see, that was just cruel . . . and challenging."

Laughing, Sissy playfully swiped at Mitch's head. He ducked it, his body moving to the side a bit to avoid her swinging arm and then . . . then everything went weird. She heard small pop sounds, and Mitch pitched forward, slamming into her and dropping them both to the floor.

"Lord, Mitchell! What are you—"

Then she smelled it. The predator in her could smell it—and hungered for it.

Blood.

Mitch's blood.

"Mitchell?"

She gripped his shoulders, and immediately, she felt blood drenching her right hand. Pushing him onto his back, she straddled his waist and looked down into his face.

"Mitchell?"

He opened his eyes, looking up at her. "Get out, Sissy," he managed. "Get out now."

"You don't get rid of me that easy, darlin'." She examined the length of his body and immediately spotted his cell phone. He used it for personal calls, but it was set up for their business, too.

She used the walkie-talkie part of it.

"This is Sissy. Answer back."

Her brother was a brilliantly distrustful man, and he'd arranged for security from the time guests began to arrive on Long Island until everyone had left. She'd never been so grateful.

"This is Té, Sissy. What up, girl?"

"Té, I need you to get Mace and Brendon to Mitch's room now. He's down, bleeding from his neck and shoulder."

Her voice no longer relaxed, the six-foot, six-inch She-bear answered back, "Hold."

Sissy pulled the sheet off the bed and shredded it with her claw. She took several strips and pressed them against his neck and shoulder. She was more worried about the neck.

"Mitch darlin', I need you to stay with me." She made her voice commanding, although she felt like a panicked mess. "You just keep those freakish cat eyes on me."

He did, but she knew it was a challenge for him. He wanted to sleep.

Té came back on the line. "Sissy, you there?"

"I'm here. Go."

"We're moving." That's all she said, and that's all Sissy needed to hear.

"No hospital," Mitch told her, his gold eyes staring at her. And she knew he was right. She couldn't take him to a hospital. Not a regular hospital anyway where their ability to protect him would be seriously limited.

Into the phone, she said, "No ambulance, Té. No cops."

"Got it."

"I need to go home, Sissy. I'll be safe at home." She somehow doubted that, but she wouldn't argue the point with him.

"I'll take care of everything, Mitch. Don't you worry about a thing, darlin'."

"You need to go."

"You know She-wolves only do what we want. We're difficult that way. So you just think about holding on for me, darlin', and let me worry about the rest."

She didn't know how long it took, maybe two minutes, but it felt like thirty hours until that hotel door was kicked open and Mace walked in. Dez was behind him wearing only a long T-shirt that had "I love my Rotties" emblazoned across the front. Sissy almost laughed, which seemed really inappropriate at the moment. Typically, Dez was well armed with a .45, and she slowly moved to the window, keeping close to the wall and out of the direct line of fire.

Mace crouched down by her and Mitch.

"No ambulance," Mitch said again.

"Don't worry, kid," Mace told him. "We've got it under control."

But the strips of sheet she'd balled up and pressed against his wounds were already saturated in blood, and blood covered Sissy's hands, up her forearms, damn near to her elbows.

Dez walked back over. She glanced down at Mitch before heading to the door. "I'm checking outside."

"Dez—" But Mace didn't get to finish since she was already gone.

Suddenly, Brendon and Marissa were there, but without Ronnie, which struck Sissy as really odd. Mace moved so Brendon could get close. Marissa didn't say anything, simply braced her back against the wall, wrapped her arms around her stomach, and stared. Sissy could see the terror in her eyes, in her pale face. She was terrified for her baby brother. And she'd probably never admit it.

The brothers locked eyes, and Sissy felt the connection that went through them. She had it with Bobby Ray. That connection that went beyond simple blood ties and to something so much deeper.

Brendon took Mitch's hand in his own and held on tight. "We need to get him out of here."

"No ambulance," Mitch repeated. "No police."

"We can't leave him here," Brendon said calmly. "Do we know a local doc?"

"I don't," Mace said. "But I'm sure—"

Ronnie ran in, and behind her were Mitch's mother and Gwen.

Roxy motioned Brendon away and crouched next to Mitch. She pulled the pieces of sheet away and examined his wounds. "I need water. Gwen, go to the car and get the kit."

Gwen moved without question, and Ronnie swept up the ice bucket before heading into the bathroom to get the water.

Roxy grabbed clean strips of the ripped up sheet and pressed it against Mitch's wounds. She called Sissy over with a tilt of her head. "Hold these against his wounds until I tell you to stop."

Sissy nodded and did as she was ordered.

No more than two more minutes passed before Gwen came back into the room with a metal box, "First Aid" written in red on the top. She popped the clasps and pulled out a huge roll of gauze. Ripping off strips, she handed them to her mother.

By then, Roxy had her water. She pushed Sissy's hands

away and carefully wiped off the blood. More seemed to pour out, but her expression never changed. She looked intensely interested but nothing more. She didn't show any signs of panic or fear or rage. She simply cleaned her son's wounds and examined the area.

"I see three entrance wounds. The one on his neck is mostly a graze. The other two . . ." She reached under Mitch's shoulder, managing to ignore the way he winced, and felt around. "Yeah. They went through. Which is good. Won't have to dig around."

She gripped Mitch's shoulder, and he snarled at her. "Yeah. The bullet hit some bone on the way through. That's gonna hurt like a bitch when it heals."

She grabbed more gauze and again put pressure on the wound. "Sissy." Immediately, Sissy replaced Roxy's hands with her own and applied pressure.

"Gwen, what have we got in the kit?"

"For closing his wounds?" Gwen looked inside without waiting for her mother's response. "We've got your staple gun."

And Mitch snarled again.

Roxy patted his head. "The last thing we need is for him to heal over those. They're a bitch to get out after. What else?"

"Butterfly bandages."

"Perfect. We'll work with those."

"Why not stitches?" Brendon asked, pacing restlessly while he watched.

"I don't know when they'll get taken out. And again, I don't want his wound healing over them. Gwen, take Sissy's place. You'll help me."

Sissy stood up and moved out of Gwen's way. She stared down at her blood-drenched hands, quickly realizing the white sweats she wore were also covered in blood.

Mace took her elbow and steered her toward the bedroom

door. The last thing Sissy saw was the tears streaming down Marissa Shaw's face before Mace pulled her into the small living room of the suite.

"Talk to me."

She shrugged. The blood was drying on her hands and arms. Right now, it was sticky. Soon it would be dry and—

"Sissy. Tell me what happened."

"We were standing at the window, talking. And then I heard pop sounds, and he went down." She closed her eyes as the recent memory washed over her. "He moved, Mace. At the last second he moved, and if he hadn't—" The words stopped as an image of Mitch's brains covering Ronnie's nice white sweats nearly choked Sissy to death. Lord, she was barely holding it together.

"He's one of us, Sissy." Mace stroked her back. "And God knows he's tougher than most."

"I know."

"Now what about Smitty?"

Sissy blinked and looked up at Mace. "What about him?"

"We need to let him know."

"He's already on a plane. They left before the sun rose. Besides, what's he gonna do except worry and drive you insane?"

"You've got a point," Mace grumbled.

"No. We leave him out of it for now."

Ronnie tugged on her shirt. "I got you clean clothes."

"Thanks." Sissy looked back down at herself. "I'll need to clean up first."

But before she could escape to a bathroom, Té appeared in the doorway. The She-bear almost had to duck to walk in. "We lost him."

Sissy could see Mace getting that look on his face. This was why the staff liked dealing with Bobby Ray instead of Mace. Mace had a very low threshold for failure. Even failure that couldn't be avoided.

"Any sign of where they were?" Sissy knew that this third-floor room had been chosen specifically for Mitch because of its location and his need for additional safety. No trees for anyone to hide in right outside the window and no buildings remotely close. And he was surrounded by shifters, so no one would be sneaking in.

"No. But we're still looking." Té leaned to the side, trying to see into the bedroom. "How is he?"

"Alive."

Té's brown eyes closely examined the bloodstains on Sissy's clothes. "Okay."

"So what now?" Mace asked. "What's the best thing we can do for him?"

Brendon walked into the room—Sissy got the feeling Roxy had thrown him out—and said, "I can take him to Philly on the family plane."

"And we can give you protection for as long as you need it."

Sissy shook her head. "You can't take him to Philly."

"Why not?"

"Everyone who wants him dead is there."

"But we're not there now. We're in fuckin' Long Island. And he wasn't safe here."

"She's right." Roxy walked in, wiping blood off her hands with a hotel towel. "He shouldn't go back to Philly. Not yet. Not until he at least has his full strength back."

"So then where?"

Mace rested his butt against the back of the couch. "Will Witness Protection take him?"

"Maybe."

"Forget it. I won't have my son trapped with some useless full-humans when he's still too weak to protect himself. Even if they are armed. He'll stay with his Pride if he has to go back."

Brendon's barely held patience snapped, and he stepped into Roxy, shocking Mace and Sissy—but not Roxy.

"Look, I won't leave him vulnerable in the middle of Philly with a bunch of uncaring females."

"We can't do any worse job than you and that father of yours."

Sissy let out a breath. She wasn't in the mood for this. And her usual patience was currently nonexistent.

"Stop it. Both of you." She didn't raise her voice or even rush her words. At the moment, she sounded more like Bobby Ray or her daddy. Still, they both pulled back and looked at her. "How long for him to be ready to travel?" she asked Roxy.

"We've stopped the bleeding, and I've dealt with his wounds. Gwen's cleaning him up now."

"Get him ready, get his stuff together. He's coming with me."

Brendon frowned. "Coming with you where?"

"Home." She looked at Ronnie, and her friend's eyes grew wide when she realized which home Sissy meant. "I'm taking him to Smithtown."

The last thing Mitch really remembered was . . . being on top of Sissy. He'd had a split second of thinking, "Wow. This feels really good." Then everything else went kind of hazy.

Opening his eyes, he looked around, and that's when he saw Sissy sitting on the floor opposite where he was lying. She had her head bowed while her legs were raised and her elbows rested on her knees.

"Sissy?"

She lifted her head and smiled, but he could see how tired she was simply by looking at her face. Exhausted even.

"Hi," she said, and she looked relieved.

"Hi." Mitch blinked and looked around again. They were in a plane. His brother's plane based on the level of luxury. A hell of a lot better than coach on one of the airlines.

"We're going home, right?" he asked Sissy, worried about her. She shouldn't have come with him. And where was everyone else? Something wasn't right, but he couldn't focus enough to figure out what.

"Yeah, darlin'. We're going home. Now go back to sleep."

"Are you okay?"

Her smile grew, but he didn't know why. "Yeah, Mitch. *I'm* fine."

"Oh. Good." He started to drift off, but he jerked awake again. "But—"

"Sssh." And good thing she cut him off because he really didn't remember what he'd been about to say. "Sleep. Everything's okay." Something soft brushed against his forehead, and if he didn't know better, he'd swear Sissy had just kissed him.

He grinned as he started to drift off again. "Dirty She-wolf. Trying to take advantage of me in my weakened state."

She gave a soft laugh and whispered, "Bonehead."

"Sassy pants," he shot back.

He heard Sissy chuckle again before he fell completely asleep. The sound soothed him and made him feel safer than he had in a very long time.

Chapter 4

Mitch jerked awake when he heard a door slam and raised voices. He looked around the room he was in. In the bright light of morning coming through the window, he knew he didn't recognize his surroundings. He didn't recognize anything. The smells, the sounds—nothing.

He wasn't dead, and if O'Farrell's guys had caught up with him, he'd be dead. Guys like that didn't waste time with hostages unless they had a use for them. Besides, he didn't think any of the guys who worked for O'Farrell were big Marlon Brando fans from his *A Streetcar Named Desire* days. Maybe when he was in *The Godfather* . . .

Slowly, Mitch looked away from the Marlon poster hanging over the bed and glanced around the room. NASCAR posters and muscle car pictures torn out of magazines practically covered all the wall space. NASCAR toy cars were lined up on a desk that looked seriously unused. There were few books except for those on car repair and car building. A stack of car magazines was piled in one corner, and another corner had a little shrine to NASCAR racer Dale Earnhardt, Sr.

Mitch smiled even while he was annoyed. This had to be

Sissy Mae's room. Although he'd never known she was that big a car fan.

Still, she hadn't sent him back to Philly like he'd told her to. One simple thing, and she went another way—just like always.

Trying to turn his head, Mitch immediately regretted it. Because it hurt like all hell.

Not surprising. He could actually feel things repairing themselves inside his body. Bones knitting back together without any help except his accelerated metabolism and the gift given to him by his pagan Irish ancestors.

As long as he didn't do anything stupid or get shot again, he should live. But still . . . his wounds would hurt like hell for a few more days. He wasn't looking forward to that. So really, he should just relax back and let his body heal before he worried about . . .

Mitch jerked again, then again wished he hadn't when he heard another bang and voices shouting.

Worried about Sissy, Mitch slowly and carefully pushed himself into a sitting position, using only his left arm for leverage. Then with another grunt, Mitch slid his legs off the bed, took another breath, and pushed himself to his feet. He made a mad grab for the headboard and forced his body to remain steady. When the wave of pain and nausea passed, Mitch looked around, and he smiled when he saw his .45 next to the pillow his head had been on.

Picking up the weapon, Mitch slowly walked to the bedroom door, opened it, and went down the hallway. He silently groaned when he saw a long set of steps leading downstairs, but the yelling and slamming sounds were getting nastier.

Determined, Mitch moved down the stairs. He rested his left shoulder against the wall and used it to rest his weight against. He also had his weapon in his left hand since his right was currently useless.

He wasn't the best shot with his left, but he could do enough damage for Sissy to get out if she needed to.

Relieved to finally see the bottom of the stairs, Mitch carefully managed those last few steps, stopping on the last one. The stairs led to a hallway. If he turned left from there, he'd be in what looked like the family room. If he turned right, he'd be in the living room. He assumed it was the living room because it was absolutely spotless and unused, the other room . . . not so much. And if he went straight, he'd go right into the kitchen.

And that's where Sissy was. Mitch had never seen her that angry. She had a finger-pointing thing going on with another male who Mitch didn't recognize. The only thing that prevented them from slamming those fingers into each other was the second male who stood between them, trying to calm everybody down.

Shaking his head and unbelievably exhausted, Mitch sat down hard on the steps. "Family," he said to no one in particular. He knew from experience that only family could make someone *that* insane.

"Don't think for a second, Jackie Ray Smith, that you can bring that fat ass of yours in here and tell me what I can or cannot do!" The wolf did have wide hips for a man.

"If I remember correctly, Sissy, this ain't your Pack anymore. You're here only as a guest."

"That isn't true," the other male said, pushing his brother back. This one looked so much like Smitty, it was kind of weird. "Sissy is family and will always belong here."

"Sissy is a whore, bringing some—" He didn't get to finish that statement as the Smitty look-alike slammed his fist into the other one's mouth. Good thing, too, otherwise Mitch would have had to do it himself because that had just been a damn rude thing to say.

"Get out," the wolf told Jackie with deadly calm. "Get out

right now." Mitch knew who'd win a fight between these two. And apparently, so did Jackie.

"This ain't over," Jackie warned, inching toward the door.

"It amazes me you have a college degree." Sissy waved him off. "Go on. Go run over and tell Travis like the big, fat baby you are."

He slinked out. If he'd had a tail, it would definitely be tucked between his legs.

Once the door closed, the wolf turned back to his sister. "You all right, darlin'?"

"Yeah." She shrugged. "Yeah, I'm fine."

The big wolf wrapped his arms around Sissy, burying her head against his chest. "If it helps any, *I'm* glad you're home."

She laughed. "That's better than nothing, I suppose."

"You're going to have to talk to Travis at some point. With Daddy out of town—"

"Yeah, I know." Sissy's head suddenly lifted from the wolf's chest, and she sniffed the air. She looked at Mitch and blinked in surprise. "Mitch? What the hell are you doing out of bed?"

He didn't have it in him to yell that answer across the room, so he waited until Sissy stood in front of him, the big wolf behind her. "I heard a fight," he explained. "Thought you were in trouble."

"And you were gonna help?" She crossed her arms over her chest. "You can't even stand."

"I brought a gun."

"You shoot with your right." She took the gun from his hand and tucked it into the back of her denim shorts. They were tiny little shorts, too, and looked so amazingly good on her.

"You should have called for me," she chastised.

"Why? Since you seem to have such a problem doing what I tell you to?"

Sissy's head tilted to the side, and she stared at him. "What does that mean?"

"I told you to do one thing. One. Take me to Philly."

"No, you didn't."

"Sissy—"

"You said to take you home. So I did."

Mitch glanced around again, staring through the stairway banister into the family room. It was a small house but cozy. Worn furniture that had taken a lot of abuse over the years but had held up well because it had been quality when purchased or made. There were dozens of pictures, some with humans and canines and some with canines only. A giant TV took up a good portion of the far wall. The kitchen wasn't that big, either. It had a Formica table with eight matching chairs around it. But the unused living room was nice, yet still homey. Then he thought about Sissy's room—that was not the room of an adult Sissy.

Taking a deep breath, Mitch picked up two important scents . . . canine and fresh air, and it all fell into place.

His eyes locking with Sissy's, he barked, "*I'm in Tennessee?*"

"Well, where did you expect me to take you?"

"I expected you to take me to Brendon's plane, and I expected the captain to take me to Philadelphia. *I'm not sure why that was so hard for you to understand!*"

Sissy's jaw worked. "Stop roaring at me, Mitchell Shaw. I did what I thought was best."

"If that's your best, I'd really hate to see your worst."

Hands fisted at her side, Sissy stepped back. "You wanna go to Philly, hoss? There's the damn door." She pointed toward the door in the living room, but each room had a door leading outside. "Have at it."

"Fine. I will."

"Fine!" She turned and headed back toward the kitchen.

Mitch pushed himself to his feet, stood there for a second, and then his whole body sort of quit on him.

Sammy Ray Smith stared down at the two hundred and . . . *what?*—fifty, sixty pounds of naked cat passed out in his arms. Simply put, this was one of those great things he'd get to tell his mate when they met for dinner later because it would make her laugh so hard.

Glancing over his shoulder at his baby sister, "Uh . . . Sissy?"

She barely spared either male a glance. "Oh, leave him there. Let him rot on those stairs for all I give a damn."

Oh, Lord. Nothing he hated more than a pouty, unreasonable Sissy. That Sissy didn't make an appearance often, but when she did, she could be the biggest pain in the ass.

As soon as he'd heard Sissy had come back to town, Sammy had come straight over here, missing the morning rush at his diner. But he'd known with both his parents out of town, Travis, Jackie, and Donnie would start on Sissy. Their baby sister annoyed them because she didn't back down. If you wanted a fight, she'd give it to you. If you were rude, she'd tell you so and act accordingly. She never averted her gaze; she never let anyone pin her down.

Unlike Sammy, who knew and accepted what he was, Sissy would never bend to anyone's will but her own. She was an Alpha through and through. And that made her a problem for Travis, who wanted his mate to be the next Alpha Female when he took over for their daddy. Shame Patty Rose was nowhere near as strong as Sissy. And in the end, that's what it came down to. Not mere physical strength either, although that helped, but strength of will. Sissy didn't back off until she got what she wanted, no matter the consequences.

"Why don't I take this big buck upstairs, and you make him something to eat? I'm sure he's starving."

"Let him starve."

Sammy shook his head and let out a sigh. "Sissy, just make the man some soup. Please."

She stood in the middle of the kitchen, her arms crossed over her chest, one bare foot tapping against the linoleum floor. Yup. She was pissed.

"Do you have any idea how bad cats smell after they die? The whole house will be funky, and then you'll have to answer to Daddy."

She rolled her eyes even as her mouth twitched.

"He'll come in complaining about a 'cat funk.' And I won't take the blame for it."

"All right, all right." She waved him off. "Take the big idiot upstairs, and I'll make him soup or something."

"Thank you, darlin'." He lifted the man over his shoulder and carried him back to the second floor. Sammy started into Sissy's room, but he really didn't like the idea of some guy being in there. This was his baby sister, after all. So he went down a few doors to Bobby Ray's old room. He dumped the cat on the bed and stared down at him.

After a few moments, he slapped him on the forehead. "You awake?" When he didn't get an answer, he slapped him again. Harder.

"Huh? What?" Gold eyes opened. "Smitty?"

"Don't insult me, son." He crossed his arms over his chest and stared down at the cat. "Name's Sammy Ray Smith. I'm Sissy's older brother. Now, she's gonna take care of you while you get better. And I know how you cats get when you're sick. You snarl and snap and are basically unpleasant. But if you don't want me coming over and peeling off big portions of your skin while you scream and cry for help, you'll be nice to her. You'll treat her with respect, and you'll keep your dirty cat paws off her. Understand me, hoss?"

Those gold eyes narrowed. "You sure you're not Smitty?"

That made Sammy laugh. "Nope. Not Smitty. But I'm not surprised he'd tell you the same thing. And probably has. Now Sissy will be up here in a bit with some soup for you."

"Soup? What am I? An eight-year-old with the flu?"

"Now see, that's what I mean. That's not nice and respectful. That's rude and unpleasant. Nice and respectful will keep you covered in the skin God gave ya as opposed to donor flesh. Understand me, hoss?"

He knew the cat wanted to snap and snarl again, but he probably also knew he wasn't strong enough to take on Sammy Ray's youngest daughter, much less Sammy himself. "Yeah," he finally grumbled out.

"Good." Sammy pulled a blanket from the end of the bed and covered Mitch from the chest down. The last thing he needed to think about was a naked cat running around in front of his innocent baby sister. "Enjoy your soup."

Sammy walked out and headed back to the kitchen. Sissy stood at the stove stirring a saucepan filled with canned soup and water. Dumb cat. If he'd been nice, she'd probably make the big oaf soup from scratch. That's something his bonehead brothers, besides Bobby Ray, had never understood. Sissy had the biggest heart Sammy had ever known. And she protected her own. But you had to treat her right, and Travis, Donnie, and Jackie never did. They let those jealous girls say all those horrible things about Sissy and sometimes joined in. It was the one thing Sammy wouldn't tolerate. Not from anyone, but especially his own kin. Alpha or not.

"Chicken noodle," he said, walking into the small kitchen—small for a family of seven anyway. "My favorite."

"You want some?"

"Nope." He kissed her forehead. "I need to get back to the diner."

"Okay. Thanks for coming by."

He walked to the door and had it open when Sissy's voice stopped him.

"How bad can this get, Sammy? With the Pack. And don't sugarcoat it."

"They tolerate you, darlin', because you're family. But you didn't come alone, and Travis is going to try and use that to his advantage."

"Fine." She slammed the soup spoon down. "I'll go over there right now and—"

"No. You won't." He moved next to her again and placed a hand on her shoulder. "Let him make the first move."

"Why would I do that?"

"Because when it all blows up, you can tell Daddy and the Elders that Travis started it. When the time comes, that'll work in your favor." He placed the spoon back in her hand. "Now feed that boy before he starts whining."

Sissy stood in the doorway of her room, wondering where the hell Mitch was. Then she remembered that Sammy had put him to bed. No way would he have put a male in her bed.

Smiling, she headed down the hall, checking rooms as she went.

She found Mitch asleep in Bobby Ray's room. Well, asleep or out cold. She really couldn't tell at the moment. He'd been in and out of consciousness since his mother had patched him up. Roxy had warned Sissy then that Mitch might or might not get the fever that most shifters got when seriously ill or wounded. It wasn't an easy thing to go through, but those who survived the fever usually felt stronger and healthier than they had before they'd been hurt.

More importantly, it was over in twenty-four hours. No fever for Mitch, which meant longer to heal until his return to full strength.

"Hey. Shithead. You awake?"

Frowning, Mitch opened his eyes and looked at her. If she hadn't known him and been a predator herself, Sissy probably wouldn't hang around with that frown.

"Keep looking at me like that, and I'll put a pillow over your head and end this right quick." She held up the tray holding his soup and toast. "You wanna eat, or you just gonna keep glaring at me?"

"I'm sorry," he said, taking her by surprise. "I'm not trying to be an asshole."

She successfully resisted the urge to say, "And yet you're succeeding quite nicely." Instead, she said, "You're just in pain. When you're feeling better, you'll be your much more jovial asshole self."

She put the tray on the dresser and helped Mitch to sit up. Once settled, she put the tray down so it rested over his thighs.

"Can you eat with your left?" she asked when Mitch only stared at the food.

"Yeah. Sure." But he still didn't go for the spoon. He looked so tired.

Glad no one could see her, Sissy sat on the side of the bed, grabbed the spoon, and scooped up some soup. "Here. I'll help."

Mitch stared at the spoon, then said, "Aren't you going to make choo-choo sounds?"

She snorted a laugh. Even at the worst of times, the man never failed to keep that sense of humor.

"Open your mouth before I give you a reason to cry."

He did, and Sissy fed him a spoonful of soup.

"Good?"

Mitch nodded even as he looked ready to go back to sleep. Sissy had rarely seen Mitch without his clothes on, and now she knew what his sister and mother saw. He was too thin. Too thin for their kind anyway. Compared to a full-human, Mitch was still huge, but Sissy knew better. She'd seen Brendon walking around his hotel apartment in a pair of jeans only, and the boy had been built. But Mitch had always been more the athlete of the pair. He should at least match his brother in size, if not be a little bigger.

She'd have to work on that while he was here. Get him to eat more. A few deer, some wild boar, and he should be right as rain. Of course, that was later. Right now, she had to make sure he got stronger. She'd never seen him so weak before. So . . . fragile. That simply wouldn't do. Not for her feline.

"Come on, another spoonful."

He took it, swallowed, and asked, "Where is everybody?"

"That can wait."

Sissy tried to feed him again, but he turned his head. "Answer me, Sissy."

"Everybody is back home. And let me tell ya, convincing them to not come with us was one of the hardest things I had to do. I had to be my most persuasive, which says a lot."

"I'm surprised you managed."

She chuckled, offering him another spoonful. "Yeah. Me too. I told Brendon he had to stay in New York. Whoever did this, I want them to think you're still there, recuperating. If he leaves, they'll know for sure you're not there. But your momma was a little easier to manage."

Mitch shook his head. "Only because she's plotting something."

"Yeah. That's what I figured. I told her not to do anything. I told her how it would piss you off."

"Think it'll work?"

"No. But you can't say I didn't try. Anyway, she went back to Philadelphia with Gwen. They're fine. And so is Brendon."

"What if the ones who did this know I'm here?"

"We didn't file a flight plan for the jet, and I left our cell phones with Ronnie."

"No cell phones?"

"Don't worry. We have phones here in the sticks, too. So you can get that look off your face. Some of them even have push buttons."

"I didn't say anything."

"You didn't have to. Your Yankee face said it all. But no calls for you or me. I don't want anything traced. No e-mails either."

"What if you need something from Bren or Ronnie?"

"Don't worry. There are other ways to handle this sort of thing."

"Yeah?"

"Yeah. I mean, once my granddaddy learned that the government could tap phones, we had to come up with another way of getting information to each other without them bastards knowing or understanding what was being said. We've got code words and a process. It's real intricate. So Brendon will know you're fine."

Sissy held up the spoon for him again, but Mitch didn't open his mouth. He only stared at her.

"What?"

"Why does it matter that the Feds can tap phone lines?"

"You ask a lot of questions for someone who can barely keep his eyes open. Come on. One more spoonful, and then you can get some sleep."

He let her feed him the soup even while he watched her.

"What about your Pack?" he asked after swallowing.

"They're in New York. They'll watch out for Bren and Marissa, so don't worry about that."

Mitch smiled. "Will Marissa know?"

"Of course not."

"I guess she's probably handling this well."

"You'd be wrong. It really . . ." She couldn't get the memory of Marissa's tear-stained face out of her mind. "It tore her up, Mitch."

"See, Sissy, when you lie to me, you strain the love and trust we've built."

"Don't believe me. But I know what I saw, and I know Ronnie looked freaked out because she had to calm Marissa down. She was crying. But don't believe me."

"I won't. Although I appreciate you trying."

She put the empty bowl on the tray and helped Mitch to settle back down on the bed.

"Sissy . . ."

She finished tucking in the sheet and looked at Mitch. "What, darlin'?"

"I know this can't be easy for you . . . bringing me here. How much trouble will this get you into?"

Sissy gave her cheeriest smile. The one she used when she didn't want her father to know she'd just shoved some boy out her bedroom window moments before Daddy had walked in. Her momma never bought it, but Daddy usually did. She'd never used it on Mitch before.

"Not a bit of trouble, darlin'. Don't you worry." She picked up the tray and headed toward the door before her smile could slip.

As she used one hand to hold the tray up and the other to close the bedroom door, she heard Mitch mutter, "That has to be the fakest smile on the planet, Sissy Mae."

Chapter 5

Desiree MacDermot-Llewellyn watched her new partner sniff a tree. *If she lifts her leg, I'm leaving.* Wait. She was feline. That meant lifting her tail and . . .

Dez shuddered.

She still wasn't quite sure how this all happened. She'd gone into work like she did every Monday morning only to find everything had changed. Absolutely *everything*.

She now had a new partner and was part of a new . . . unit? Actually, the unit had been around when most cops were still Irish and really did *walk* a beat because there were no cars. But the unit was new to her.

She knew there were things Mace hadn't bothered to tell her. Not because he was hiding anything, but he didn't think about it. Some things simply never occurred to her husband.

Telling her that the NYPD had its own shifter unit had apparently never occurred to the man. They were based out of Brooklyn—and true, she wouldn't mind the convenience of not battling into Manhattan every day—and had their own foot patrol, detectives, and SWAT Unit. All of them had been cops in other precincts, and about ninety-five percent were shifters. All kinds of breeds. But five percent were like her.

Full-humans who had a link to the shifters, which made them . . . safe.

For Dez, what made her safe was her son.

He was too precious to her, too important for her to ever risk him.

Especially when she already had so much to worry about when it came to her boy. Just the other day, they had to change out his crib because he'd punched through the wood slats. Once he had done that, he had grabbed hold of the broken pieces of wood and yanked until he'd made himself a nice hole. If the dogs hadn't barked like the house was on fire, he would have tumbled out headfirst.

But because they knew how important her son was to her, the shifters felt they could trust her to protect them all. When she'd called Mace, he'd sounded part impressed and part worried. The cases this unit took on could be more dangerous in some instances and safer in others. But to get in, even for a shifter, was a big deal. It was an important unit, and silence was mandatory.

And her first case . . . Mitch's attempted murder. The attempted murder no one else in the NYPD knew about.

"No one was here."

Dez turned to face her new partner. Her name was Ellie Souza, out of the Bronx. She was strikingly beautiful and freaky tall. But it was those light gold eyes that Dez found most disarming. Mace's always seemed like melted gold; this chick's were a stark light gold that did nothing but make Dez feel she never wanted to meet this woman in a dark alley. Apparently, she was jaguar, the product of a full-human West Indian mother and a shifter Brazilian father. She didn't say much, which Dez appreciated, but she did have a tendency to stare.

And that stare wigged Dez out.

Dez again gauged the distance from this tree to Mitch's room. "It had to be here. Look at the distance."

Souza said nothing, simply turned and walked away. Dez followed, annoyed she felt compelled. But this woman had a way about her. Dez wondered how Souza's other full-human partners had dealt with her before she'd gotten moved to this unit. This unit with no name and no official record? Hell, at least Dez knew what Souza was. Had a handle on what to expect based on breed. She did wish, though, that they'd hooked her up with a wolf instead. She was a total dog person.

Suddenly, Souza's head swung, and she sniffed the air. Her head moved as she searched for the scent. It reminded Dez of when she hid treats around the house and sent her dogs off to find them.

After several hundred feet, Souza stopped. "Here. She was here." She leaned against the tree and sniffed. "Yeah. Right here."

"She?"

"Definitely." She climbed the tree, slipping effortlessly up and briefly getting lost in the branches and leaves. "Definitely a she. On her period."

Dez threw her hands up. "Hey! There are some things I don't need to—"

"Lion."

Shocked into silence, Dez watched Souza flip back out of the tree. She landed with ease and shook her head. "Yeah. You heard me right."

"That can't be right."

"I've got the best nose in the NYPD. She was lion. She was female." She stared at the tiny stamp that was the hotel Mitch had stayed in. Dez didn't realize how far away they were until this moment. "And she was a really good shot. Even for a shifter."

Souza looked at Dez and gave a small smirk—she didn't seem to be real big on smiling—and said, "Exactly who did your friend piss off, MacDermot?"

* * *

Sissy stared down at Mitch. She was getting worried. He slept so much. At least, she pretended he was sleeping. It was more like he was passed out. It was Tuesday morning, and except for helping him to the bathroom and spoon-feeding him some more soup, he hadn't moved a muscle.

She was used to fevers. Her daddy had gotten them more than once, and he usually recovered in about twenty-four hours. During the fever, her father shifted from man to beast many times over. He had delusions, and he had a thing about grabbing Janie Mae and tussling with her.

But Mitch had been down since Sunday with no fever and very little movement.

It began to worry her so much she even called in the town doc. He didn't seem real happy to deal with a cat, but he'd always liked Sissy and wanted to help. But even he didn't know what to do with a non-fever-having shifter.

"Keep an eye on him," he'd told her. "And hope he don't die in his sleep."

What kind of bedside manner was that anyway?

Letting out a breath, Sissy tried again not to panic. She felt so alone. How did full-humans live like this? No Pack. No one who watched her back or was just there when she needed someone. She'd give anything to have Ronnie here. Someone who could tell her, "Don't worry. Mitch will be fine. He's too crazy to die."

But they were still on "radio silence," as Bobby Ray always put it.

She sighed when she thought of her brother. She really missed him. He was the rational brains in their partnership, and she was the crazy one who made everyone afraid to push them. It worked brilliantly for them. She wished he was here, but she wouldn't be the one to ruin his honeymoon. She had a feeling Jessie Ann would think Sissy had used this just to ruin her time with Bobby Ray. They had lots of years to get on each other's nerves; Sissy would rather not start right away.

So instead of being surrounded by her Pack and even those annoying dogs, she was trapped in hostile territory with a sick cat and her eldest brother Travis less than a hundred miles away from her.

She and Travis had never gotten along. He wanted everyone to submit to him, but she never had. Neither did Bobby Ray. And he hated both of them for it.

It surprised her he hadn't come by yet, but she knew he would. He'd try to push her out—of that, she had no doubt. Whether she could stop him was a whole other thing. With both her parents and Ronnie Lee's out of town, she had no backup and no Pack of her own to protect her.

And it wasn't only her brothers she had to worry about. Without her mother's protection, she had to worry about those who lived on the hill. No one spoke of them. No one uttered their names unless absolutely necessary. They'd been howling for her every night since she'd arrived. It was becoming more insistent, too, the more she ignored them.

For the first time, Sissy knew what it was like to be completely alone, and she hated it.

Okay. That was wrong. She wasn't completely alone. Her aunts had stopped by quite a bit to keep an eye on her. "You need us, you just call," each of them would tell her on her way out the door.

She hadn't told any of them about the calls from the hill. To be honest, she was afraid of what her aunts would do. Those on the hill didn't get along too well with the Lewis sisters, and Sissy didn't want to be responsible for anything happening to her aunts. She loved them too much. And she really didn't want to hear the shit she'd get from her momma.

Sissy frowned when she realized the corkboard over Mitch's head was moments from falling on him. It had been part of her room since she was twelve and held her all-important travel list. All the places she'd been planning to go since she was seven or eight. She left the board up there to remind herself she'd been to most of those places. It helped her deal with her mother. And more than once, after one of her mother's "lectures," she'd look at the list, call up Ronnie Lee, and ask something like, "Ever wanted to go to Sydney?" If she didn't know better, she'd swear the woman did it on purpose.

No. She better move that board, or Mitch would wake up with more wounds than he went to sleep with.

Mitch opened his eyes, closed them, and then opened them wide.

"There are big breasts in my face," he announced to anyone who would listen.

"Wha—oh, stop it."

He didn't know why Sissy was hanging over him, but waking up to her breasts was definitely enjoyable.

Reaching up with his left hand, he palmed one and got a slap across the offending limb.

"Stop that right now, Mitchell Shaw."

He grinned. "Your nipples are hard."

Sissy sat back, placing a small corkboard on the floor, and that's when Mitch realized she was straddling his waist, wearing nothing more than a tiny pair of shorts and a cutoff AC/DC band shirt. Exactly what *was* she doing?

"What is wrong with you?" she demanded.

"I've had a near-death experience, Sissy . . . and I'm really horny. Uh . . . think we can—"

"No. We can't. And you couldn't even feed yourself not too long ago."

"It was all that chicken soup. It cured me."

"Yeah. Right. And stop touching!" She slapped his hand away again.

"Oh, come on, Sissy. I almost *died*. Can't you help me out?"

"You did not. And I'm not having sex with you 'cause you almost died."

"Fine. Hand job?" he asked hopefully.

"No."

"Blow job?" Christ, he *was* horny. Horny, hungry, and . . . safe. It had been so long since he felt that way, he almost didn't recognize it. But that's what being here with Sissy made him feel. Safe.

"Mitchell!"

"At least let me bury my face between your breasts. Just for like five seconds."

"Don't make me hurt you."

"If I do, will I get to call you mistress?"

She slid off his lap and ended up staring at the tent she'd left behind. "What *is* wrong with you?"

He grinned, happy to see that all of his important parts were still working. "Apparently nothing."

Smirking, Sissy suddenly grabbed the sheet and lifted it, taking a look.

"Hey!"

"My, my, my. Look what you've been hiding, Mr. Shaw."

He snatched the sheet back. It was one thing to be the predatory male in this scenario, but Sissy had turned it on him like she did with everyone else. "Hands to yourself, Smith. I won't let you turn me into your sexual plaything."

Sissy laughed. "Not yet you won't."

She might have a point.

"I'm hungry," he announced.

"I've got some more soup—"

"Any more soup, and I'll start roaring. You know you hate that."

"Are you implying you want some meat?"

"No. I'm telling you I want some meat. Feed me."

"I'll bring something up."

"Actually . . ." Mitch sat up a bit. "I'd rather get up."

"You sure?"

He nodded.

"Okay." Sissy walked across the room and grabbed the duffel bag he'd brought with him to the hotel. She must have brought it with them when they left. "Your sweatpants okay?"

"Perfect."

She walked to the bed and pulled out sweatpants and a T-shirt. "Here."

"Thanks."

He waited for her to leave, but she just stood there.

"Yes?"

"Don't you need help getting dressed?"

"No." He made shooing motions with his left hand. He knew it was ridiculous, but he didn't want Sissy to see him as weak and needy.

"Can you move your right arm yet?"

"I'll make do. Go away."

"Fine. Suffer." She moved toward the door. "Let me know when you're ready to come downstairs. I'll help you."

"I can manage."

"Fine," she said again. "But if you fall, I'm leaving you there until you learn a lesson."

"Very nice."

"I'll get food started. It'll take a bit, so don't rush."

He didn't think he could even if he wanted to.

By the time Mitch made it downstairs, Sissy was pulling the mac and cheese she'd mixed the night before out of the oven. She'd made quite a few meals over the last three days in between checking on Mitch. She couldn't sleep well anyway, and she was afraid to sleep for long periods of time, should something happen. So Sissy did what she always did when she was stressing out—she cooked. She found it soothing, and she was pretty good at it. In the time it took Mitch to really wake up, she'd completely filled both freezers with potential dinners. Whatever remained when she and Mitch left would feed her parents for a couple of months.

His long time getting ready gave her time to bake up the food and get her uncontrollable nipples in order. What exactly were they thinking anyway? Getting all hard and needy just because Mitch Shaw, of all people, had his face between her tits? She blamed them. Not herself. Damn nipples.

"That smells good."

Sissy jumped a bit before turning around and helping Mitch into one of the table chairs. She felt his forehead as she'd been doing over and over again for three damn days.

"Am I okay, Mom?"

"Don't be a smart-ass."

"Yup. You even sound like my mother." Mitch let out a sigh. "I'm worried about her. My mother."

"She's fine. And she knows you're fine."

"She does?"

"Yeah. I called my Aunt Janette, and she called my other aunt, one of Daddy's sisters—he has six—in Alabama; she called my uncle—one of my momma's brothers—in North Carolina who called—"

"Stop it. Please. I'm begging you."

"I was only trying to—"

"I know. And I appreciate it. I *adore* you for it. But . . . stop talking."

"Fine. Be that way." Sissy walked to the stove. "What do you want to drink? Milk, juice, or sweet tea?"

"Tea."

Sissy nodded while she put some of the mac and cheese on a plate and put it in front of Mitch. From the refrigerator, she pulled out the salad she'd made and a pitcher of sweet tea. When she turned around, Mitch was still staring at the plate of food she'd put in front of him. He didn't seem worried about his mother anymore as much as simply disgusted.

"Is there a problem?"

"There's ham in it."

"Yeah. So?"

"I hate ham in my mac and cheese."

"You haven't even tried it."

"I don't need to try it to know I don't like it."

Sissy rolled her eyes. "Do you like ham?"

"Yeah."

"Do you like mac and cheese?"

"Yeah."

"Then what's the problem?"

"I don't like them mixed together." He stared down at his plate like a five-year-old looking at a vat of broccoli.

Sissy walked to the table and slammed the bowl and pitcher down on it.

"Take a bite."

"I don't want to."

"Mitchell Shaw, you take a bite right now. If you don't like it, then fine. But you'll goddamn try it first."

Clearly disgruntled, Mitch picked up his fork and poked at his food for a bit.

"Mitchell. Shaw."

"Okay. Okay." His mouth twisted in disgust, Mitch put a forkful of her mac and cheese into his mouth. He started to chew, and she watched him. She waited for it. And like with most things, she wasn't disappointed.

"Wow," he said after he swallowed. "That's . . . that's . . ."

"Really good?"

"Amazing."

She grinned. "I know. That's the best mac and cheese— with or without ham—that you'll ever have. So enjoy it since I don't cook very often. Now eat."

He did, too.

While Sissy watched, Mitch went through the mac and cheese—even what she'd left on the stove—the salad, and the pitcher of sweet tea like he hadn't eaten in years.

Glancing around at the empty bowls and dishes in front of him, Mitch frowned. "Got anything else?"

Sissy blinked. "Anything else?"

"I'm still a little hungry."

"Is this normal for you?"

"No, no." Mitch peeled melted cheddar cheese off the near-empty baking dish and tossed it in his mouth. "I usually eat a lot more until the stress started getting to me. But you'll see. When I get my hunger back."

Sissy calculated the money everyone had handed her before she'd left and the few dollars she had in her wallet.

Depending on how long they stayed, she may have to start getting their food the old-fashioned way . . . running it down and ripping it open herself.

Travis slammed the hood down on the twenty-year-old Ford truck his cousin had dropped off the night before and looked at the typically freaked-out Jackie. If he wasn't blood, Travis would slap him around on principle. But he was family, and Travis couldn't afford for his weakness to make the rest of them look weak. So he kept Jackie close and used him to do things he and Donnie didn't want to. Like sending him to find out what Sissy was up to. He'd known even before he sent Jackie there what would happen.

Sometimes he was such a bastard.

"So Sissy slapped the shit out of you—again. What do you want me to do about it?"

"She did not."

That was true. It had been little brother Sammy. Next to Bobby Ray and their daddy, Sammy was the only one who could get a leash on Sissy. Still, Sammy had a thing about calling a spade a spade. Or in Sissy's case, a whore a whore. It was the one thing that brought out his rarely used temper with Donnie and Jackie. Although he'd never try that shit with Travis. Not if he liked having two working legs.

"I thought you would have gone over there by now," Jackie whined. "Told her to get out."

"Is that right?" Travis picked up the team's playbook from the counter and flipped through the pages. They had practice this afternoon, and he wanted to be prepared. The upcoming game was one of their most important.

"She's got the cat," Jackie insisted.

"A sick cat. Throw her out now, and I just look like a son of a bitch. Wait until he's at least walkin'."

"If he were real bad, Sissy would have taken him to the hospital over in Waynesburg," Donnie explained, easily moving out from under the car raised above his head. Travis and Donnie coowned Smithtown's main repair shop. It was a good living, and Donnie didn't piss Travis off too much, which he did appreciate.

"Gotta play this smart, boys." Travis looked between his brothers. "She's alone. She ain't got Smitty or Daddy or those She-bitches of hers. And Sammy ain't no real threat. It's just little ol' Sissy and a sickly cat."

Travis stepped away from his kin and looked out the garage door at the clean, quiet streets of his town. "It'll be pure pleasure bringing that little bitch down."

Mitch opened his eyes, quickly realizing he was sitting on the couch in what he had found out from Sissy was definitely the family room.

As Sissy told him, "Momma doesn't let anyone but special company use the living room. But my daddy doesn't like many people, so special company doesn't ever come. So that room never gets used."

The strange thing was, he could have sworn that only moments ago, he'd been sitting in the kitchen.

He looked at Sissy, and she gave a small shrug.

"You fell asleep at the kitchen table," she explained.

"Oh. Uh . . . sorry."

"No need to apologize. I'm glad it was actual sleep this time, and not total unconsciousness. Although it is hard to tell the two apart. With both, you just sort of drop where ya are." To illustrate, her entire body went lax against the couch, her eyes closed.

"Then you wake up." She opened her eyes, sat up a bit. "Then you suddenly drop again." Again she went lax, making Mitch smile. "But this time," she whispered without opening her eyes, "there was snoring . . . and a little drool."

Mitch laughed and shoved his bare foot against hers. "I do not drool."

"There's no shame in the drool," she said, sitting up.

"I don't drool."

"Then you won't fit in here. Smiths are known for drooling and knuckle dragging."

"I thought I saw scrapes on your knuckles earlier."

Sissy stuck her tongue out and crossed her eyes, making Mitch laugh harder.

Smiling, Sissy turned up the sound on the TV. She had on a sports channel so she could catch the latest stock car race results. "You know," he said after a few moments, "I wanted to thank you for all this, Sissy."

"That mac and cheese was good, huh?"

"I'm not talking about that." Although he may have seen God after his first bite of that delicious meal. "I'm talking about this. You bringing me here. Taking care of me. Thank you. For everything. And sorry I was such a prick before."

"I understand, but thanks for apologizing."

They fell silent, and it had to be their first awkward silence ever. He hated it.

"Want to watch a DVD or something?" Sissy finally asked, sounding desperate. "My parents have a good selection."

"Sissy, it's okay."

Sissy frowned. "What's okay?"

"You . . . being madly in love with me. It's okay. I know how enticing it must have been to have me lounging around your house . . . naked. And deliciously vulnerable." Mitch raised his eyebrows. "*Needy* even, while in your bed."

"Mitchell . . ."

"No, no. There's no need to deny your feelings. Not when we both know the truth."

"Are you done?"

"For the moment." He grinned. "Saucy."

Finally, Sissy laughed, the uncomfortable moment gone. "What is wrong with you?"

"My mother constantly indulged me."

"Clearly. DVD or not?"

"Whatcha got?"

"Everything probably." She stood and walked to the bookshelf filled with DVDs and old VHS tapes. There weren't a lot of books. Mitch sensed the Smiths were not big readers. Sissy went on her toes to see the higher shelves, and Mitch had to bite back a growl.

Christ, the woman had the *best* legs. The kind of legs Mitch could easily imagine wrapped around his neck.

"*Deliverance?*"

"That's not funny."

Sissy giggled. "You Yankees. Mention *Deliverance,* and y'all get so freaked out."

"And with good reason."

"How about *Die Hard*?"

"Perfect. Lots of shit blowing up and guns."

"And hot German men for me." She pulled the DVD box down and went to the good-sized TV across from the couch. It wasn't as big as Bren's or even a flat screen, but Mitch felt more comfortable in the modest digs of the Smiths than in the wealth of his father's.

The movie started, and Sissy sat at the far end of the couch.

Mitch cleared his throat and stared at her.

"What?"

"Get over here."

"I'm comfortable."

Mitch sighed. "Do I really have to pat the couch and say, 'Here, doggie'? Are you really going to make me sink that low?"

"But I'm comfort—"

"I'm sick!" he howled, forcing Sissy to quickly slide over until she sat next to him. He didn't stop until she did, either.

"Happy?"

He settled down, resting against her side. "Very."

The movie had barely started when a knock at the door had Sissy up. What bothered him was that she had one hand on the butt of the .45 she'd taken off him earlier, which was still tucked into the back of her shorts. She even released the safety.

She sniffed at the door and frowned, glancing at him. She opened the door slightly.

"Yes?"

"Hey, Sissy Mae." When she only stared, "It's me. Frankie. Big Joe's boy."

"Frankie?" Sissy pulled the door open to reveal some . . . wolf. "I can't believe it."

To Mitch's surprise, Sissy threw herself into that wolf's

arms, and the wolf looked real happy about it, too. Of course, it didn't hurt much that she was wearing nothing more than that damn T-shirt and those unreasonably tiny shorts.

"How are you?" Sissy asked, finally pulling back.

"Doing good." The wolf actually whistled. *A wolf whistle?* "And look at you. You are looking mighty fine."

"Thank you."

He rested against the door frame, staring down at Sissy. "So . . . uh . . . got plans tonight?"

Sissy looked unusually befuddled. "Um . . ."

"Thought maybe we could catch a movie, get some dinner."

That was rude. He was sitting right here, and that *dog* was acting like Mitch was invisible.

"That's real sweet, darlin'. But I've got a guest, and we already have plans."

"Who?"

Sissy pointed at Mitch, although they all knew the bastard had seen him.

"You're gonna stay home for . . . him?" He snorted, clearly feeling pretty cocky since he probably knew Mitch was still too weak to put up much of a fight. Too bad for him that lions had very long memories. "Hasn't he healed up yet?"

"He's doing much better—and you can tell Travis that."

The wolf frowned. "What does your brother have to do with this? I came here to see you. I didn't know you'd be all wrapped up with *him*."

"That's real sweet to hear, but I am all wrapped up with him so—"

"I knew Ronnie swung that way, Sissy, but you too?"

Sissy raised her hands and dropped them in a helpless gesture. "What can I say, Frankie?" She placed her hand on the wolf's chest and gently pushed him back so he no longer blocked the door. "But what's a girl without her pussy?"

And if it wouldn't have hurt beyond anything, Mitch would have rolled right off the couch he was laughing so hard.

"Sissy."

He'd murmured that against her ear, his hand rubbing up and down her spine.

"Sissy. Wake up."

She did somehow. Not even sure when she'd fallen asleep. Or how long she'd been draped over Mitch Shaw while she slept.

Her cheek rested against his chest, and she could feel his heartbeat. Her hands rested against his shoulders, and she'd splayed the rest of her body between his thighs.

When she realized, she jerked in surprise, but his arms wrapped around her, holding her close. "It's okay. It's me." He kept his voice low, almost a whisper. And she knew it was him. That was the problem.

"What . . . what time is it?"

"Late." He held her tighter, and she realized all the lights were out and it was pitch black outside. Lord, how long had she been asleep? "Do you hear it?"

"Hear what?"

But she did hear it now. Sissy heard that persistent, demanding howl through the darkness.

"Sissy . . ."

"It's okay, Mitch."

Resting her hands against his chest, she pushed until she sat up. The central air conditioning had kicked on, and the loss of Mitch's body heat made her feel like she was freezing.

"What is it?"

"Family stuff."

"Your brothers?"

She wished. They were easy. Easy and stupid and she had no problem handling them, even when they made her angry.

"No. Not my brothers. I've gotta go." She stood, but Mitch grabbed her hand. "I can go with you."

How could she not have realized it before? He was so sweet. Really. Just . . . sweet. She'd never known anyone sweet before. Although in her family, sweet translated to wuss.

"I'll be fine." And if he came along, he wouldn't be. There were some parts of this town that cats could never go to. Not if they liked breathing.

"I won't be long."

"Okay." He smiled. "I'll be here when you get back . . . hungry."

Her arms dropped. "Again?" She'd fed him earlier . . . food that should have lasted days was quickly disappearing in a night.

"Yes. Again. So don't be long, okay?"

The concern he showed made her feel kind of warm inside—or she was getting a rash. She got those when she came home to visit.

"Okay. I'll even try and bring home something bloody." She handed him the .45 she'd taken from him earlier.

"If it's still moving and bloody, that would be great."

Sissy left the house and headed into the woods surrounding her parents' territory. She shifted as she walked, shaking off her clothes before breaking into a run.

She never thought she'd think this, but she missed her parents. She didn't realize how much family crap they protected her from merely by their presence.

Sissy ran on. She felt safe in her parents' territory, even though if she went too far west, she'd cross from Smithtown into Barronville. Cat territory run by the vicious backwoods Barron Pride that even Sissy avoided unless she had her She-wolves with her. If she went too far south, she'd cross into bear territory. They were much more welcoming than the cats, but Sissy had a reputation there that didn't exactly make her a welcome canine in their town.

But go too far north, and she crossed into territory that few ever ventured into. Not the Pride, not the bears, not the wolves. And a good deal of the Smiths didn't go there either. No one. And with very good reason.

Sissy knew the moment she crossed into that territory, too. She *felt* it in her bones. In her soul. The power of it infused the ground beneath her feet. A place of power. A power that was neither good nor evil. Instead, it was how that power was wielded that was the problem.

They waited for her about a mile in. Sissy stopped ten feet from them. She didn't shift until the first one did.

"Gertie," she said after she'd shifted.

"Sissy Mae."

The three other females shifted, but none of them came near her.

"So, what do you want?"

Gertie shrugged. "Just wanted to see you. Thought you'd like to come up for some sweet tea." She gestured behind her. "She'd love to see you."

"Forget it. I ain't goin' up there."

"Sissy, you know she wouldn't harm you." Harming her wasn't what had Sissy worried.

Everyone called her Grandma Smith, but the most she was to Sissy was a great-great aunt. No one knew for sure, but they said she was a teen during the Civil War. She didn't choose sides since she considered all of that "full-human business," but Lord forbid some soldier from either side strayed on Smith territory.

Even Sissy's daddy feared her, and the man didn't fear many. As old as the hills and as mean as a snake, Grandma Smith was a powerful witch and shifter who led by fear. She didn't like males much, and she took Smith females with power from their mommas and raised them herself. And to hear Sissy's aunts tell it, Grandma Smith had wanted Sissy and had come down from her precious hill to get her. It was Janie Mae who backed her off. And in that one move, ensured her place as Alpha Female and the eternal enemy of one cranky old bitch who lived up on the hill.

"Look, I'm just here for a few days. Then I'm gone again."

"We know what your momma's told you about us, but she doesn't know anything. You're a Smith female of the bloodline. One of us. We'll always have a place for you here . . . among us."

Sissy forced her body not to move. Not to run. Even as they moved closer, she didn't back down. She kept her voice calm. "I'll never belong here. You know it. *She* knows it."

"That's your momma talkin', Sissy Mae. You know better. You know where you belong."

"I know I'm done with this conversation."

"That whore has turned you—"

Sissy didn't even know she'd do it until her claw slashed across Gertie's cheek. Blood sprayed across a tree trunk, and the others snarled, fangs extended.

"Call my momma that again, Gertie, and that'll be the last thing you ever do."

Then Gertie was there, her forehead resting against Sissy's, her fangs bared. "Remember who you are, little girl. Remember who you come from."

Keeping her fangs in and sheathing her claws, Sissy said flatly, "Get off me."

She could see Gertie deciding what she wanted to do, but a low howl from higher up on the hill had the four females looking nervously over their shoulders.

Gertie stepped back. She stared at Sissy. "We'll talk again."

They walked away from her, but they never turned their backs on her. At least not until they were out of her sight.

Mitch had worked his way through most of the cereal Miss Janie had in her cupboards before he realized that Sissy had made it home.

He found her sitting on the porch swing, her legs tucked up under her, her eyes focused out into the dark.

Sitting down next to her, he got the swing to rocking gently. He'd never been on a porch swing before. He liked it.

"You all right?"

"Yeah."

"Sissy . . ." Mitch blew out a breath. "I'm much stronger now, and I'm going to leave tomorrow."

"It's not about you, Mitch." She looked at him. "Me sitting here, thinking. This isn't about you. But you do need to promise me one thing."

"Anything."

"Don't go up that hill." She pointed to the freaky hill with the scary woods surrounding it that she had run into earlier. "Don't ever go up there. And if anything calls to you, like a dead uncle, or if you think you see a pet dog you once loved when you were ten, ya know . . . ignore it."

"I'll keep that in mind." Sissy had nothing to worry about. Some places a man instinctively knew not to go. That hill was one of those places.

Mitch scratched his chin. "So can we get back to me now?"

Sissy smiled, looking relieved he hadn't asked more questions. "Yes, we can get back to you now."

"Me being here is not helping you with your family, is it?"

"Other than your frightening appetite . . . you're the least of my problems when I come home."

"Then what is it?"

When she only shrugged, Mitch patted her thigh. "I'm a very good listener." When Sissy only stared at him, he added, "I have very soulful eyes. Women love that shit."

"It's nothing really," she finally told him. "It's just disappointing when you realize that nothing has or will ever change. Just like my grandpa used to say . . . same shit, different day."

"You can't let your family get to you."

"Easy to say. Your family adores you." And she rolled her eyes at that.

Mitch scratched his head. "Who are you talking about?"

"You. Your mother adores you. Brendon brags about you all the time. And your sisters haven't tried to kill you once."

"Hold it." Mitch held both forefingers up and rolled them back. "Let's rewind. *Who* brags about me all the time?"

"Brendon." Sissy turned on the swing to face him. "You do know he brags about you all the time, don't you?"

All Mitch could do was shake his head. His brother? Bragging? About him?

"How could you not know?"

"What does he say?"

Now fully annoyed at Mitch, she began checking things off on her fingers. "That you were a football star at your high school. That you graduated high school and college with honors. That you've been awarded citations or whatever in your little police department." Only Sissy would dismiss the entire Philadelphia Police Department as that "little police department." Christ, he liked her.

"How proud he is of you. And how you're his brother. Blah-blah-blah. His chest puffs out when he's talking about you, and he's already a large man."

"Wow."

"You really didn't know?"

"Nope." Resting his chin against his fist, his elbow on the back of the swing, he asked, "And Marissa?"

"Let's not ask for the unobtainable, hoss."

"Good point."

"So while your siblings are running around bragging about you and sobbing over your lifeless body, I'm stuck with my crew."

"Is it that bad?"

"One time I told Travis I was thinking of applying for a receptionist position at a law office, and he said, 'Don't they usually hire pretty girls for that?'"

Mitch gritted his teeth. He hadn't even met Travis yet, but he already hated the man.

"Luckily, I already know how amazing I am, otherwise I would have been devastated."

"And he's just jealous."

"Jealous? Of what?"

"He's jealous of you."

"Is that right?"

"Of course! Because no matter what he does, when he puts on your shorts and one of your bras, he never looks as cute in them as you do."

And keeping her laughing for the next hour made *Mitch* feel amazing.

Chapter 6

Sissy woke up about one in the afternoon . . . alone.

They'd gone from the porch to the family room and spent a good portion of the night watching late-night television and laughing. The last thing Sissy remembered was resting her head on Mitch's shoulder while they discussed the benefits of doing an infomercial for Mace and Bobby Ray's security business and how disgusted both former Navy SEALs would be if they even tried to suggest it—which meant they would.

And now she woke up on the same couch but with no Mitch. Maybe he'd gone back to bed. She hoped so. The man needed sleep. Real sleep, not simply unconsciousness from blood loss.

Sitting up, she rubbed her face and stretched until she heard all sorts of pops and snap noises that did nothing but make her worry about her general bone health. Then her stomach grumbled, and everything else took a backseat. Throwing off the blanket she had on her legs, she stumbled into the kitchen. She pulled open the refrigerator, determined to get to the food before Mitch had a chance to clean her out, and froze. There was nothing left but a carton of rancid Chinese food her parents had left behind. She went to the overhead cabinets and checked there, but all the cereal and Pop-Tarts that her parents kept for their grandkids were gone as well.

Selfish feline!

Annoyed beyond reason, Sissy stomped upstairs, hoping to wake his big cat ass up with the noise. She took a quick shower and went to her room to get clothes. Once she'd pulled on a pair of denim shorts, bra, and T-shirt, she stomped down to Bobby Ray's room and threw the door open. But the bed was empty.

Sissy turned back toward the hallway. "Mitch?"

No answer, so she ran down the hallway and stairs, calling out for him.

As she slid into the kitchen, she noticed for the first time the folded notebook paper on the table.

> *Starving. Went into town for food. We need supplies, woman! You're not caring for me properly.*

Then an annoying smiley face.

Her eye twitched.

Went into town? By himself? What is wrong with that man?

Sissy charged outside, running full speed toward town, her rental car completely forgotten since she walked most places when she visited anyway.

It had never occurred to her that he might wander off on his own, but she should have remembered that he'd never go hunting if he could help it. Male lions were scavengers at heart. Used to being taken care of by the females in their life. Since Mitch didn't have his own Pride to feed him, he spent most of his time in restaurants or getting his food delivered.

Sissy cut through the woods far opposite from the part of the woods she'd traipsed into last night.

She cut through several of her relatives' backyards, waving to the ones who yelled out greetings while she ignored the small deer that leaped into her path. Her stomach growled, but she kept going until she hit the main road that led into town. Of course, that's when she slammed right into the side door of a bright red '78 Camaro, the impact tossing her back into the woods.

Times like this, she was grateful to be a shifter.

She heard tires squeal when the person driving hit the brakes. A few seconds later, a door opened, and a gruff female voice called out, "Hello?" Then Sissy heard sniffing as the She-wolf tried to track her.

"I'm over here," Sissy responded while pushing herself up until she was on her hands and knees.

Footsteps moved closer, and then she heard, "Hey. Sorry. Are you . . . wait. Sissy Mae?"

Sissy lifted her head, and her gaze traveled up a long, powerful body wearing worn jeans, a worn T-shirt, and not much else. But when Sissy saw that face, she grinned. "Holy shit. Dee-Ann?"

"Figures," Dee-Ann sighed. "I've killed my own damn cousin. Momma's gonna have a fit."

Laughing, Sissy grasped Dee's hand and let her first cousin drag her to her feet. Dee-Ann was her cousin twice over. Her mother, Darla, was Janie Mae's sister, and her father, the infamous Uncle Eggie, was the older brother of Bubba Smith. She was three years older than Sissy, but they'd had some very good times back in the day.

"Well, don't get any ideas. You are not in my will."

"Damn. I had it all planned out, too."

The pair hugged, and Sissy let out a relieved breath. "Dee, I didn't know you were home."

"Only been back a couple of days. I'm out for good now, Sissy," she finished on a murmur.

Sissy tamped down her desire to grill her cousin on how

she felt and instead said, "Well, darlin', you missed the wedding of the century."

"So I heard. I am real sorry I missed it."

"Don't worry. Bobby Ray understands."

Together they walked back to the main road, and Sissy glared at the still running Camaro. "And you have the nerve to be tooling around town in *my* car."

"Oh, no, no, no." Dee shook her head. "Don't even try it. I won this car fair and square. Besides, I look much better in it than you ever did."

"I still say that race wasn't fair."

"Ignoring you," Dee stated flatly. Of course, she stated most things flatly.

Sissy laughed, giving her cousin another hug. "Take me into town, bitch," she said as she walked around to the passenger side.

"All right. But you owe me from where your big, fat head dented my driver's side door."

"Maybe if you weren't speeding."

Hands slapping against the roof of the car, Dee stared at her. "You didn't say that. Those words didn't come out of *your* mouth."

Sissy gave her most innocent expression. "Why, cousin, I don't know what you mean."

The waitress placed another hamburger with fries in front of him and stepped back.

"Anything else?"

His mouth filled with food, Mitch held up his empty glass.

"More milk," she said. "Got it." Grabbing several empty plates, the waitress let out a little sigh and gave a small shake of her head before she walked away.

Why everyone was staring at him, Mitch didn't know. He was hungry, dammit; that didn't make him a freak.

As he dove into his seventh Smithtown Diner's Mighty Burger, the rumbling sound of a modified muffler caught his attention, and the sweetest cherry-red Camaro tore past the big front window of the restaurant. Tires squealed, and the car returned, practically diving into the empty space right in front.

He really shouldn't have been surprised when Sissy laughingly stumbled out of the passenger side, nor when the waitress placed his milk-filled glass down and said, "Oh, Lord. Here comes trouble."

"There you are!" Sissy said as she walked into the diner, another woman right behind her.

Mitch had to admit he liked how Sissy walked into a room. Every male became instantly aware of her. But Sissy either never noticed or she went out of her way to never notice. Mitch didn't know, but he enjoyed how oblivious she seemed, annoying every male in a thirty-foot radius.

She pulled out a chair and dropped into it. "Next time when you leave the house, why don't you just wear a big bull's eye on your chest?"

"What does that mean?" he asked around his burger.

"I'm trying to protect your dumb ass, and you go wandering off."

"You weren't fulfilling my needs," he said simply. "And I have big, demanding needs."

"You're a glutton," she snapped and took a fry off his plate. He snarled at her, but she only snorted. "And stingy."

"I don't share."

"Get over it." Taking more fries—and risking her hand in the process—Sissy motioned to the woman who had come in with her and who now sat in the chair across from Mitch. "This is my cousin, Dee-Ann. Dee-Ann, this is Mitch Shaw. He's a cat and my personal pain in the ass."

"Hey," Dee-Ann mumbled while she looked around the diner. Mitch immediately noticed that look. He used to have it himself until he learned to be more subtle about it. This was a wary, untrusting woman. With one look, she probably could tell him every exit in the room, who she thought would be the most trouble, and what her escape plan would be if someone who made her nervous came through the front door.

Dee-Ann's hair was darker than Sissy's and much shorter. Her eyes were a bright yellow, and her body made Sissy's look almost petite. She was blatantly strong and sported scars that didn't come from claws or fangs.

"She just got back from overseas," Sissy told him, and her eyes made everything clear.

Sissy twisted in her chair and looked over at the counter. "Sammy . . . *Sammy Ray!*"

Mitch's eyes crossed at her screams, and he glanced at her cousin only to see that Dee-Ann didn't even seem to notice.

"What?" Sammy Ray yelled back. It was like the Smith family had only one volume level.

"I want the burgers deluxe." She looked at her cousin. "What you want?"

"Same."

Sissy nodded and looked back at the counter. *"Make it two!"* she screamed. She turned back around and shrugged at Mitch. "What?"

Ronnie hadn't slept well during the night and had over-slept the morning straight into the afternoon, so she wasn't surprised to wake up and find her mate gone. Nor was she shocked to find him pacing his office.

Shaw thought he could hide his feelings from her. But they were mates. She felt what he felt. Not on some wacky metaphysical level either. Simply the way one who loves another does. And all heaven knew she loved Brendon Shaw.

"You're gonna wear a hole through that carpet, darlin'."

He stopped and immediately glared at her. Then he closed his eyes and pulled the simmering rage back. She'd rarely seen Shaw this angry. He had a wonderful nature and made being with him easier than she could have imagined. But his love for his brother was deep and abiding and tinged with guilt over the way Shaw's father had seemed to forget Mitch's existence for fourteen years.

Shaw had tried so hard to protect Mitch, but after what Dez had told her yesterday, they needed to take different precautions to protect Mitch. But Ronnie still had a hard time wrapping her mind around what Dez had told her. Even when she knew it was true.

"I'm sorry," he said.

"And stop apologizing. You haven't done anything wrong." She walked over to him, put her arms around his waist. "None of this is your fault."

"Then why do I feel like it is?"

"Because it's in your nature. Protecting everyone around you is what you do."

"We need to make sure Sissy knows what she's dealing with now. How everything has changed."

"She will."

"And then we need to make sure—"

Ronnie put her hand over his mouth. "Stop." She moved her arms until they were around Shaw's neck and pulled him in until his face pressed against the side of her neck and his arms tightened around her back.

He held her so tight that a lesser woman would have had broken ribs.

"Do you trust me, Brendon?"

He nodded, and she knew he couldn't speak at the moment. That was okay. She didn't need him to.

"Then leave this to me, baby."

Finally, Mitch seemed to have finished feeding that fat face of his and leaned back in his chair with a sigh. "Now that was good."

"And hopefully, you left enough food for the rest of the town," she sniped.

"Someone's testy," Mitch replied, following that with a mocking hissing sound and a flash of slashing claws. "Saucer of milk for dessert, dear?"

Rude son of a—

"Thank you," Mitch told the waitress as he took the check from her. He glanced at it and handed it to Sissy.

She pointedly looked at the piece of paper in his hand and then back at him, one eyebrow raised. "And you're giving me this why?"

"Ain't got no money, sweet cheeks."

Her eye twitched. She hated when he called her that. "Well, *Mitchy*"—and she truly enjoyed that glare she got in return—"who the hell told you to inhale half my brother's food supply?"

"Your brother owns this place?"

"Yeah."

Mitch snorted, balled up the bill, and chucked it at Sissy, hitting her in the head. "We both know you don't have to pay to eat at your brother's if you ask him nice. Now go ask him nice."

Snarling and glaring, Sissy reached for the knife on the table, but Dee moved it first.

"Lord." Dee grabbed the balled up bill and stood, taking it to the counter.

"You're gonna make your cousin pay?"

No. She was going to make Mitch pay.

"Done," Dee told them as she walked back. "See? Not brain surgery. You need a lift, Sissy?" Sissy smiled, and Dee took a sudden step back. "What?"

"Well . . . he has—literally—eaten me out of house and home. Think you can take me to the Mega Store?"

"You have a car."

"I have a *rental* car. Not a pretty little Camaro that you won unfairly." The Camaro hadn't been Sissy's first, but she'd loved it like all the others. "Dee, don't make me whine."

Dee held up her hand. "Please don't. You know how that sound annoys me."

Sissy held her hand out. "Keys."

"You're not driving."

"Hell I'm not. Gimme."

Dee blew out a breath and handed the keys to Sissy.

With a grin, Sissy stood. "Come on."

"Shotgun," Mitch called, and Dee shook her head.

"I'm not sure that's such a—"

"He called it," Sissy cut in. "Shotgun for the cat it is."

Mitch walked out onto the sidewalk and glanced around. Smithtown was a nice little place. Real homey and clean. The kind of place where people left their front door unlocked during the day. Even with all the local canines glaring at him, he still felt pretty comfortable. Although he had checked each burger to make sure no one had spit in his food.

Opening the passenger door to the '78 Camaro, Mitch waited until Dee-Ann got into the backseat, then he slid himself in. The car had been expertly maintained and practically had Mitch purring as he sank into the seat.

"Buckle up," Sissy told him.

He almost snorted again. What? Did she think she could scare him by going eighty or something? One of the reasons he'd become a cop was because he'd become so friendly with the ones who'd pulled him over on a regular basis. Finally, one told him he wouldn't take him in for speeding—again— if he'd stop by during the high school's job fair that week. It seemed like a real easy way out of a ticket or jail time, so he went. And shortly after Mitch turned twenty, he was a cop.

To humor her, Mitch buckled himself into the seat, chuckling when he realized they had the kind of safety harness the NASCAR racers used in their cars.

"Locked in?"

"Yup." He grinned at her. "Go for it."

Sissy smiled back at him. "If you say so."

Mitch wasn't sure, but he thought he heard Dee-Ann grunt something—the woman was not a big talker—before Sissy Mae turned over the motor and Mitch's desire to purr got even worse. Nothing sounded sweeter than a souped-up engine.

Slowly, Sissy pulled away from the curb. She glanced down both sides of the street and made a U-turn.

Sitting in the middle of the street, the motor rumbling, Sissy stared at him, and Mitch stared right back. Eventually, when the staring went on past what even shifters would consider normal, he grinned. The one he used when he really wanted to annoy her. He'd gotten more things thrown at his head using that smile. This time, however, Sissy only smiled back. Even Mitch had to admit she had a killer grin. Kind of like her brother's, but Sissy's did stuff to him Smitty's damn sure never could.

"Hold on," she murmured, and he briefly wondered if she ever used that particular tone of voice in bed.

Mitch snorted, trying to stop where his thoughts were headed—again. "Yeah, yeah. Show me what ya got, sweet— *Mother of God Almighty!*"

*   *   *

Sissy never knew Mitch had such a colorful vocabulary until she shifted her old Camaro into gear and hit the gas.

When she took those tight turns on Deer Road doing about ninety, he called her all sorts of names her daddy would slap him upside the head for. When she played chicken with a couple of her cousins—at least, she was pretty sure they were her cousins—in that pickup truck, he slammed his hands down against the dashboard and gritted his teeth. When she was doing about a hundred and thirty on Duckbill Drive, she might have actually heard some rather violent roaring and a whimper or two. But when she hit one hundred and sixty-four and took that turn on Watermans Way, she knew she'd have to replace the dashboard for Dee. Those claw marks would do nothing but devalue the vehicle.

With gravel and dirt flying, she spun into the store parking spot. A grocery store that catered to their kind safely ensconced between canine, cat, and hyena territory. The simply named Mega Store was one of the few local "safe zones" where different breeds could mingle comfortably.

Sissy cut off the engine and tossed the keys to her cousin sitting quietly in the backseat. "Man, that felt good. You just can't do that sort of thing in New York." She patted Mitch's knee, delighting in the way his entire body jerked away from her. "Come on, Mitchy. Let's get some supplies to handle that lion-sized hunger."

Biting her lip and enjoying her life way more than she really should, Sissy got out of the car and headed toward the big glass doors of the store.

When she realized Mitch Shaw wouldn't be moving anytime soon, Dee-Ann Smith moved to the other side of the backseat and got out of the driver's side of the car. Leaning down, she looked in and frowned a bit when she saw how pale the big cat had gotten since she'd first met him.

Pale and a little green.

"There's a quiet little spot behind the garden outlet over there. If you need a few minutes."

Without looking at her, Mitch nodded his head. "Thank you."

"Sure." She stood and closed the car door, careful not to slam it shut since she really didn't want the man unloading his cookies inside her vehicle.

Dee-Ann caught up with Sissy right inside the store. She had tears in her eyes, and Dee knew she'd been laughing at poor Mitch.

"You are mean."

"He asked for it!"

"Right now, that poor boy is yakking up his cookies behind the garden center and you—"

"Ooh! Give me your phone. I wanna take a picture." She tried to grab for it, but Dee caught her arm and yanked her back.

"I'm not in the mood to tussle."

"You don't know how to have any fun."

Dee didn't even bother arguing. She knew her cousin to be amazingly oblivious and clueless about many things. She could be selfish, slightly obsessive, and a shitstarter of the highest order. But overall, Sissy was a good person, and Dee had been real sorry to see that her cousin wasn't Alpha Female of Smithtown. Of course, Dee hadn't known Sissy had moved to New York for good until she'd gotten home. Her life the last five years hadn't offered much opportunity to get regular updates on her kin.

And Sissy had been right. Dee didn't know how to have any fun. Not anymore. Her life the past few years had not been fun, and she had the beginnings of an ulcer to prove it.

But she knew that Sissy had been somewhat deceptive when she told Mitch Dee had been "overseas." To Mitch, that probably meant Dee had been fighting in Iraq like the rest of the Marines she'd trained with. But that would be wrong. She'd been sent off to do other things and had never even been to any Arab country, much less fought in one. When she'd been honorably discharged from duty, she figured coming back to Tennessee would be the best thing for her. But except for her joy at seeing her parents and the territory she loved to run and hunt on, she was already getting fed up.

But Sissy had a way of bringing out the "fun" side of anybody if she'd a mind to. To quote Janie Mae, "Sissy came out of my womb with her middle finger raised."

Mitch walked up to the women, his glare for Sissy and Sissy only. He'd gotten some of his color back, and he was already popping a piece of chewing gum in his mouth—yeah, he'd lost his cookies behind the garden outlet, she realized with a smile.

Sissy grinned up at him. "How ya doin' there, Mitchy?"

Gold eyes narrowed, and Sissy, to Dee's shock, tried to make a run for it. But Mitch caught her, spun her around, and suddenly, his hands were in the waistband of Sissy's shorts.

"Mitchell Shaw, don't you—*ack!*"

But it was too late. He'd already reached inside the back of her shorts and yanked up, giving her the wedgie to end all wedgies.

Sissy's squeal hit notes Dee never knew her cousin capable of, irritating every shifter in the building, before Mitch stepped back, briskly brushed his hands against each other, and grabbed a shopping cart. "All right, ladies. Let's go get me some supplies."

Trying for a modicum of dignity, Sissy tossed her hair back and kept her spine straight as she headed toward the bathroom so she could dig her underwear out of her ass.

And that's when Dee realized that she'd never met a man brave enough to give Sissy Mae Smith a wedgie. Beyond the entertainment factor alone, Dee found the whole thing kind of interesting.

Mitch slowly pushed his cart down the meat aisle. He loved shifter-friendly stores. Not only could he find the largest cuts of meat anywhere, but he could also find the most interesting.

Yumm. Impala. It had been ages since he'd had impala.

Grabbing a frozen rack of rib meat, he dropped it into his carriage and moved on.

He was eyeing the leg of zebra when he realized he was being eyed the same way, and he turned to find three extremely hot lionesses standing behind him.

"Hey," they said in unison.

Mitch grinned. "Hi."

"I'm Paula Jo Barron. These are my sisters, Lucy and Karen Jane."

"Hi. Mitch Shaw."

"You're new to town, huh?"

"Yup."

"Any chance you're planning on staying?"

"Well . . ." Mitch watched their expressions change as they looked to his left side. He followed their gazes and stared into the big, dumb dog eyes of a wolf. Another male. Who were all these males? How many did they have in this area anyway?

"What?"

"Sissy with you?"

Mitch felt the desire to bare his fangs. "Why do you ask?"

"Just wanted to say hey."

Then he stood there, saying nothing. Smitty did that

sometimes. And the Reed boys. They'd just stare for absolutely no reason whatsoever. It was irritating.

"Well, she's not here at the moment."

"Is she staying at her parents' house like usual?"

"You're gonna walk away now, and I won't hurt you because you walked away."

The wolf nodded. "Fair enough. Tell her Lou said hey."

The wolf ambled off, and Mitch shook his head. What weird Southern shit was that?

Mitch heard a throat clear, and he looked up into three sets of gold eyes watching him. "Yes?"

All those gold eyes blinked in surprise, but before Mitch could figure out why, another cart slammed into his.

"If you think," Sissy Mae snarled, pulling back and slamming her shopping cart into his again, "for a damn second I'm paying for zebra meat, you've lost your goddamn cat mind!"

"That's impala. I haven't even grabbed the zebra yet. And you are too paying for it. And who the hell is Lou?"

"Who? And what makes you think I'm paying for shit?"

"Because I want it."

"I want world peace and not to have you around. And yet we don't all get what we want."

He rolled his eyes. "I'll pay you back, you whiny canine."

"We can hunt deer down right in the backyard," she told him, exasperated.

"Hunt? Me?" He placed his hands on his hips. "Your job is to *bring* me food. Why haven't you grasped that concept?"

"I can bring you a fist sandwich." Then she put her fist under his nose. "It's my specialty."

Just to disgust her—and because he kind of felt like it—Mitch dragged his tongue across her knuckles.

"Eww!" she quickly wiped her hand on his T-shirt. "You're disgusting!"

"You have one job, canine. Tend to all my needs and wants."

He glanced at the lionesses still avidly watching. "Tell her what her role is. And how she should adore every minute of catering to my needs and wants."

Sissy eyed the lions. "Paula Jo."

"Sissy Mae. Having fun?"

"No!" She turned back to Mitch, putting her hands on her hips, imitating his stance. "I'm not having a good time. How do you put up with them?"

The lioness shrugged and admitted, "It's their sperm. We put up with a lot to get that."

"Or I could simply have a specialist remove his sperm and toss him out of my house just like y'all would."

Mitch sniffed, wiped a nonexistent tear. "That was cruel. You've hurt me deeply."

"No. I hate you deeply. There's a difference."

Moving fast, Mitch grabbed her around the waist and dumped her butt right into her cart, then he shoved it, sending it speeding down the aisle.

"And that's for your little driving bit!" he laughingly yelled over her squealing his name.

He grinned and turned back to the lionesses, who only stared at him. "We're friends," he explained.

Sissy grabbed a box of cereal. It was the biggest box they had. *This should work.* She dropped the box into her carriage.

"Might as well grab four more if you want it to last past today."

Sissy briefly closed her eyes. "Tell me you're just being cruel 'cause we hate each other."

Paula Jo shook her head. "Wish I could, you know, 'cause I do hate you. But it's true. Of course," she gave a slow smile, "you could send him my way. Me and my sisters know how to take care of lion males, and we'll get him off your hands. And you can go back to whatever it is you do. Lick your ass. Chase your tail."

Sissy barely heard the old insults. They didn't even register. She was too busy realizing that Paula Jo was serious. She wanted Mitch. For herself and her Pride.

And Sissy would be damned before she let that happen.

"Sorry. I promised I'd keep him with me."

"Yes, but he's eating you out of house and home. And he'll keep doing it, too. We both know times are tough right now, so why don't you let me have him?"

Sissy pressed her hand to her chest. What was this strange feeling she had? It was something . . . weird. And she'd never experienced it over a man before. But she'd felt this way once before with Paula Jo. When the lioness had taken the first deer Sissy had ever brought down on her own. It was just a little thing and sickly, but it was Sissy's. Then Paula and her sister Karen Jane came out of the woods and chased Sissy and Ronnie Lee off. As Sissy watched them eat her prize, she'd been so angry she couldn't see straight.

Lord in heaven . . . she was jealous!

"Sorry, Paula Jo. Unlike y'all, when wolves make a commitment—even to a cat—we keep it."

In typical fashion, it was at that moment that Mitch suddenly glided by at the end of the aisle. Really. He glided. Because he had his feet on the cart and had pushed himself past.

"Was he—" Paula Jo frowned. "Ballet dancing?"

Based on the positions of his arms . . . "I think he was, yes."

Sissy rubbed her eyes with her fists and wondered how much shame she'd bring to the Smith name if she actually ran away from Paula Jo.

The lioness slowly inched away. "Interesting."

* * *

Mitch stuck his arm all the way to the back of the potato chips shelf, made it a little U, then dragged it forward. The big bags of chips fell off the shelf and right into his cart. He did the same thing with some pretzels.

His nose sniffed the air, and he glanced over his shoulder. "Hi, Dee."

"Hey."

"Stocking up."

"Uh-huh."

She walked around him and looked into his cart. When her gaze met his, she didn't say a word.

"What?"

"Nothin'."

Mitch pushed the cart forward, Dee falling into step next to him.

"Dee, can I ask you a question?"

She shrugged. "Don't see why not."

That seemed an odd response, but . . . whatever.

"Who is Lou?"

"Lou? I know lots of Lous. You'll have to be more specific."

"He's wolf and was asking for Sissy about ten minutes ago."

"Oh. That Lou. Yeah. I know him. He's from Smithtown."

"What does he want with Sissy?"

"What every male in Smithtown wants from Sissy." Dee stopped by the candy and grabbed a Hershey bar. Nothing fancy. No almonds or caramel. Just simple milk chocolate. He had a feeling that explained Dee really well.

"And what's that?"

"To fuck her."

Mitch suddenly looked around. He never expected such a . . . blunt response. Not even from Sissy. And he didn't like that particular blunt response one damn bit.

"That's it?"

She bit into her chocolate and chewed. He hoped she still planned to pay for that. He *was* still a cop for the time being. "And to mark her."

"Just like that?"

"She's Sissy Mae. A born Alpha. And direct Smith bloodline. Plus, I've always heard she's a wicked fuck in bed."

"Okay. Stop." Mitch held his hands up. "Just . . . stop."

"You asked."

"Yes. Because I'm an idiot. Thanks for the reminder."

For the first time, Dee grinned. It didn't make her any prettier, but it took away that perpetual glare. "You're welcome."

"*How much?*" Sissy demanded when the cashier gave her the final price.

Mitch nudged her shoulder. "Pay her. I'm getting hungry."

Feeling sick, Sissy looked at him. "Again? You just ate an hour ago." At this rate, the man would use up all of Smithtown's food supply. And eat her right into the poorhouse.

"Almost two. And you're not driving this time. Give the keys back to Dee-Ann."

"Don't tell me what to—"

"Now. Or it's atomic wedgie time." She knew he wasn't kidding either.

Growling, she handed her mother's credit card to the cashier—she'd owe that woman a fortune when she got back into town, but Sissy couldn't risk using her own card—and Dee-Ann the car keys.

"I hate you."

"How could you hate this face?"

"Easily."

"But I'm adorable."

"More like psychotic."

Feeling ill at how much this single food bill came to, Sissy signed the receipt while Dee stared at all the food the two grocery clerks bagged. "We're not going to get all this in the Camaro."

Sissy wasn't exactly surprised. They'd filled up three large carts with all the food they'd purchased. She wasn't exactly sure where she was going to fit it all in her momma's house either. They only had two freezers.

"Sissy could walk home while you drive me and the groceries back."

"Or," Sissy countered, "I could gut you here and let your rotting corpse attract the hyenas while we go home and enjoy a nice, quiet meal at my parents' house."

Mitch thought about that a moment but finally shook his head. "That doesn't really work for me."

"Then shut up."

It took some work, but eventually, they managed to get all the food and all three of them in the car, although Sissy ended up driving because Mitch couldn't fit in the backseat with all the groceries and she refused to get in the backseat since she refused to look weak. It really was never easy to be an Alpha wolf. Mitch suggested he could drive, but Sissy and Dee only laughed at him.

But if Sissy even went above sixty, Mitch started roaring, which got real old real fast . . . and did nothing for her sensitive ears.

Once they got back to her parents' house, she and Dee spent another hour trying to figure out where to put all the food. Of course, Mitch wasn't much help there either. "I'm too hungry to think," he'd claimed and ended up sitting on her parents' couch, eating a big bowl of Frosted Flakes and milk.

"Okay. On my count . . . one, two . . . *three!*" The cousins slammed the door on the chest freezer, and somehow, it sealed shut.

Sissy let out a breath. "Good. We got it to fit."

"You know, in two more days, you'll be buying more food for him."

"I don't want to talk about it."

They walked back into the kitchen. "You want to stay for a while?"

"Can't. Promised Momma I'd be home for dinner."

"Stop by tomorrow if ya want."

"Okay." Dee started out the door. "And remember to watch your back."

"Don't I always?"

"Watch it more," Dee told her before slamming the door closed.

Sissy shook her head. "As always with that girl . . . clear as mud."

Mitch cleared his .45 and checked the clip. "Did you bring any other ammo with us?"

Sissy walked in from the kitchen, wiping her hands on a dish towel. He didn't know what the hell she was cooking in there, but Christ Almighty, it smelled so freakin' good.

"Wha?"

He held his clip up. "More ammo? Or is this it?"

"That's all I brought from New York."

He winced. "This isn't much."

"I know."

They stared at each other for several seconds. Finally, Mitch said, "Thanks for your high level of concern."

"It doesn't quite live up to your high level of whining."

"I'm not whining, I'm concerned about our safety."

Sissy tucked part of the dish towel into the waistband of her shorts and walked across the room. She pushed aside a wood shelf holding all sorts of little curios and things. Stuff that Mitch would only accidentally break so he never had any of it in his own home.

Sissy didn't remove the shelf attached to the wall; she simply pulled it open. That's when Mitch saw the false wall behind it. She moved that aside, revealing a serious safe. He knew the make. It was one of the high-end kind. Sissy punched a code in and pulled down the handle. She opened the door, and Mitch let out a choked breath.

"Holy shit."

"This is Momma's stuff," Sissy said as she stepped back so he could get an even better look at the arsenal behind the wall. "You can use anything in here but her blades. Don't mess with her blades. I nicked one once when I was twelve, and she tore my ass up. And since she seems to like you, I'll be the one to suffer."

When Mitch simply sat there and stared, she motioned him forward. "Come here. I'll show you what she's got. Then I'll show you Daddy's upstairs."

Slowly, Mitch stood. "Can you guys legally have this stuff?"

"Hunting is a way of life around here."

Mitch reached into the eight-shelf safe and pulled out the Tech Nine semiauto. "And what, exactly, do you hunt with this, Miss Smith?"

"Anything," she said simply, "that ain't supposed to be on our territory."

And Mitch knew she wasn't talking about any damn deer.

Chapter 7

Sissy didn't know feeding Mitch would be so enjoyable—except for the expense, of course. He'd pretty much groaned and purred during the whole meal. Everything she put in front of him made him smile, and then he'd feed like he hadn't eaten in days.

It had done her ego a world of good and took the sting out of all the money she'd spent earlier. She so rarely cooked these days, she forgot what it was like to have someone appreciate her efforts.

Of course, she did make him clean up the dishes while she took a shower. He'd tried to fight it, but when she promised him zebra stew for the next day, he'd shut his mouth and gotten to work. When she'd walked through that kitchen an hour later, it sparkled like angels had touched it.

Now, with beer in hand, she got to sit out on the front porch swing wearing her favorite old baseball jersey and enjoying the late summer night. This was what she missed about living in Smithtown. Nights like this. In New York, it was never quiet, and while she adored the energy, there was something to be said about being able to hear crickets and the night-loving birds.

As she combed her wet hair, the howling started. At the farthest part of Smithtown, one wolf would start it, and it would spread until all of Smithtown was alive with the sound. Grinning, Sissy leaned her head back and howled right along with them. She simply adored that sound. Adored the meaning behind it. The power. The—

"Shut the hell up! I'm trying to sleep!"

Sissy's eyes crossed as the howls abruptly stopped. Lord, she'd hear about this until she was in her grave.

With a sigh, she headed up to her room and closed the door. While she finished combing her hair out, she flipped through an old car magazine she'd found shoved in one of her desk drawers. It made her smile, seeing all the notes she and Ronnie Lee had made. Picking out their dream cars and marking all the necessary parts they planned to get one day. Back then, they'd liked their cars the way they'd liked their men. Big, powerful, and mean.

Of course, Mitch wasn't mean. Never on purpose, anyway.

Wait. Where did that thought come from? Why was she thinking about Mitch and what she liked in men at the same damn time? What was wrong with her? And when did she start asking herself so many questions? And why couldn't she stop?

An abrupt knock yanked Sissy back to the moment, and she ended up glaring at her poor defenseless door.

"What, Mitchell?"

Mitch pushed the door open and stood there looking too good to be remotely fair. He had on a fresh pair of sweatpants and . . . nothing else. They rode low on his hips, teasing cruelly. She wasn't a saint, dammit!

"Sexy, sexy," she growled at him before she could stop herself.

"You treat me like a whore."

"You are a whore."

He grinned. "This is true."

She stared up at him. "You can't sleep, can you?"

"I tried."

"The howling?"

"No. That was just really annoying."

"Around here, it's nightly, so get used to it."

"Great."

Sissy pulled her legs up, wrapping her arms around them. "Do you have bad dreams?"

"Not like I used to. Mostly because I simply don't sleep. Guess I'm definitely feeling better since I seem to be back to my old habits."

"Your appetite is A-OK, though."

"It is, isn't it?"

He walked into her room, looking at all her pictures and toy cars.

"Did you sleep last night?"

"Uh . . . yeah. I did." He glanced at her through ridiculously long dark gold lashes she'd never really noticed before. *Lord, help me.* "I think it was because of you, though."

"Me?" *Don't read too much into that. Don't read too much into that.*

"Yeah. I think it was your snoring. It was quite soothing, and all that drool reminded me of a waterfall."

See? Sissy grabbed one of her pillows and pitched it as his head. "Bastard."

Mitch laughed. She appreciated the fact that although the man had been through hell and was forced to stay in a strange town where everyone hated him on principle, he still loved to laugh.

"So do you have a diary I can read?" he teasingly asked. "It would be a saucy tale about a young, firm Sissy Mae discovering her passionate sexuality."

"Have a diary? Around my momma? I thought you had more sense. My daddy doesn't call her the Great Detective for nothin'. If the woman put her mind to it, she could probably find D.B. Cooper and Hoffa. So having a diary with all my deepest and darkest secrets would be one of those dumb things I try not to do."

She reached under her bed and pulled out a photo album. "But I do have pictures of me and Ronnie Lee in bikinis." She moved back on her bed and patted the mattress.

Mitch removed his Glock first, then dived on the bed like a ten-year-old. Once he got himself comfortable with his back braced against the headboard and his too-long-for-the-bed legs stretched out, Sissy placed the album in his lap.

She opened the cover and flipped past a few pages, but Mitch stopped her. He stared at her when she was eight and Bobby Ray ten.

"Wow. Jess was right, Sissy. His head was *huge*."

Sissy crinkled up her nose. "I know. It took him a while to grow into that thing. The Navy really helped there. His head never got any smaller, but thankfully, his body got much bigger."

Mitch began flipping pages himself. He smiled at a picture of her when she was about eleven. She wore a bikini top with denim shorts and had her middle finger raised to the camera.

"Dee took that one. She was in the photography club at school."

"Has your mother seen this picture?"

She laughed. "Oh, yeah. She's torn it up six, seven times— but Dee has the negative and a darkroom."

After a few more pages, Mitch stopped on a picture of her, Ronnie Lee, and her cousin Katie out of North Carolina. All three were in bikinis, and you could see three tigers in the background watching them.

"How old were you here?"

"Sixteen."

"Man, even then."

"Even then what?"

He didn't answer and instead asked, "Who are the alley cats?"

"Some boys we met when I was on vacation in Smithville. You ever been there?"

"No. I've heard about it, though. It's supposed to be fun."

"If you like fighting bears and tigers and hyenas for your zebra dinner, it's a blast. I love going there, but I haven't been in a while."

"Is it true they have seals there?"

Sissy shrugged. "Yeah." She lowered her voice. "Only during the winter, though. They're for the polar bears. They just sit by this saltwater lake and wait for those seals to come close enough."

"You have moral issues with that, don't you?"

"At least my dinners can run fast."

Mitch turned a few more pages. "Uh . . . Sissy?"

"Hhhmm?"

"Why are most of the pictures in this section missing half?"

"Oh, yeah. That."

Mitch chuckled. "Ex-boyfriend?"

"Yup. My first boyfriend. Actually . . . my *only* boyfriend. The males I've been with since I would never call boyfriends."

"Bad breakup?"

"Something like that." She rubbed her forehead and yawned. "What about you? Did you have a girlfriend back when you were sixteen?"

"Yup. A She-wolf. See . . . I'm the United Nations of the shifter world. Willing to take all comers."

"A She-wolf, huh? Do I remind you of her?"

"No." Mitch flipped through a few more pages. "She was really nice." Sissy slammed her fist into his left shoulder. "Ow! What was that for?"

"Are you saying I'm not nice?"

Mitch chuckled. "That's not what I meant. No, you don't remind me of her, *and* she was really nice. Not that you don't remind me of her *because* she was really nice."

"That better be what you meant." Sissy rested her chin on her raised knees. "What happened to her?"

"She dumped me for a tiger with a Mustang."

"I can say that I've never dumped a man over a car. I have, however, gotten shot at over a car."

"That somehow does not surprise me." He looked around her room. "You do have a thing about muscle cars, Sissy."

"Yeah, I do. Me and Ronnie Lee used to rebuild them. We haven't in ages."

"Were you good?"

"Yeah." She studied him for a moment, briefly debating with herself. *Eh. What the hell?* "I can take you to see one tomorrow. It's over at my brother's house. Sammy's house." She wouldn't trust any of the others to hold on to something so important to her.

"I'd love to. I never get tired of cars."

"Good. We'll do that after we go hunting in the morning."

"You mean after *you* go hunting in the morning."

"You're coming with me. We'll hunt down a hog for breakfast. It'll be fun."

"It doesn't sound like fun. It sounds like I'm working for my meal. How is that fair?" He touched his wounded shoulder and gave her big cat eyes. He looked like one of those velvet paintings. "Painful."

"It'll be more painful if you don't start pulling your weight around here, hoss. Besides, you need the exercise to get your strength back."

"You're not taking very good care of me."

"Have I put a pillow over your head while you've slept?"

"Uh . . . no."

"Have I thrown anything heavy and deadly at you?"

"No."

"Then I've taken care of you."

"Nice." He flipped through a few more pages, but she could see he was fighting to stay awake. Good. The more he slept, the better he'd get. "Can I ask you a strange question?"

"No, I won't have sex with you in my childhood bed."

Mitch chuckled. "That's not a problem. I'm more a take-you-up-against-the-wall kind of guy anyway." And she almost swallowed her tongue. "But that's not my question."

"So ask."

"Why does this house have so many doors? You've got one in the family room, the kitchen, the living room, and the one behind the stairs."

"Revenuers," she said simply.

Mitch frowned. "Revenuers?"

"Yeah. That's what my granddaddy called them. He built this house, and he wanted to be able to run when he had to run. Bobby Ray never told you?"

"Told me what?"

"Darlin', the Smith empire—"

"Empire?"

"—is built on moonshine money. Many doors mean many exits. And Granddaddy did like his exits. If he didn't like somebody—and I mean, you could be the queen of England—the man would just get up and walk out."

Mitch examined the walls again. "That explains the car fetish."

"Yup. In this family, you're born knowing two things. How to rebuild a carburetor and how to outrun the revenuers."

"Built into your DNA strain, is it?"

"Yup. The 'Shiner strain, they call it."

Sissy took the photo album from his hands. "We'll look at the rest tomorrow."

"Any nude pictures? Maybe you and Ronnie and some oil?"

"Dream on."

"A man can hope, Sissy Mae. When that's all he has left."

Sissy laughed at Mitch's dramatics and wondered if he'd even realized he'd settled down in her bed, curled on his side, hands under his cheek?

She looked down at her full-sized bed. It was perfect for her when she stayed in here alone, but to share it with a lion-sized male did not sound remotely comfortable.

Resigned to sleeping in the guest room or Smitty's room, she started to move off the bed. But Mitch grabbed her hand.

"Don't go," he mumbled, already falling asleep.

"Mitch, Mitch, Mitch. If I stay, you'll only fall madly in love with me like so many men before you."

"It's you we have to worry about," he sighed out. "You've already been trapped in my erotic web of lust. Might as well give it up to the daddy of all cats."

Grinning, Sissy stretched out next to Mitch, her arm thrown over his waist. "You keep on dreamin' that dream, kitty."

"I will. I own ponies in that dream, too."

Sissy laughed, and Mitch started snoring. Not a scary, annoying snore, just a snore that told her he was out cold.

In his sleep, he grabbed her arm and held it against him. Even if she'd wanted to go somewhere else, didn't look like it would happen.

She didn't mind, though. Sissy knew for a fact there were worse ways to spend a night.

Chapter 8

Mitch woke up feeling better than he had in a very long time. His strength was building back up quickly, and the usual panic he woke up with simply wasn't there this morning.

Of course, that could have a lot to do with the fact his face was buried between two large and perfect breasts.

Opening one eye, Mitch quickly realized he was completely entangled with Sissy Mae Smith. He'd had dreams about this sort of thing before, but usually, they were both naked and covered in scratch marks.

This, however, would do for what he would consider an excellent morning wake-up.

Mitch couldn't believe how well he'd slept. In fact, he'd come to terms with his possible death simply by realizing that for once, he'd actually get to sleep again. A real sleep. Deep and unconcerned and without worrying about everything and anything.

But he didn't have to die to get that kind of sleep. Instead, he simply had to trust himself to Sissy. Not nearly as hard as it sounded because he knew she had his back. If she knew there was danger, she'd get him up and be ready to fight within seconds, and he'd do the same for her.

That kind of partnership meant more to him than some piece of ass because that kind of partnership kept him breathing.

Sissy suddenly moaned in her sleep, and her arms tightened around him, her hands digging into his hair.

Uh-oh. This wasn't good. No, that was wrong. This *was* good. It felt good. It felt amazing, having Sissy wrapped around him like this. But it wouldn't be right to take advantage of her when she was out cold.

Right . . . *right?*

"Oh, God," she groaned, the leg she had around his waist tightening up. Immediately, Mitch's body began to respond, his morning wood taking on gargantuan proportions. "Yes," she whispered. "Oh, yes."

"I'm not a saint," he muttered. "You're asking too much of me here."

He had to push her off. He had to set her aside, and he had to get in the shower and take care of things himself. And he had to do that now.

"Clyde."

Mitch froze. Clyde? Who the fuck was Clyde? And why the fuck was Sissy moaning about him in her sleep? Was that the ex-boyfriend she'd mentioned last night? Was she still hung up on that guy?

And even more importantly, why the fuck did Mitch suddenly care?

She giggled. "Clyde."

That was it.

"Hey." He shook her. "Hey!"

Sissy's eyes fluttered open, and Mitch forced himself to ignore how pretty those light brown eyes were this early in the morning.

"Huh?"

"Who the hell is Clyde?"

"Clyde?" Sissy frowned. "What?"

"Clyde. You moaned Clyde in your sleep. Who the fuck is Clyde?"

"Oh. Yeah." She looked away. "Clyde."

Wait. What did that mean? What was that expression on her face? What wasn't she telling him?

"Yeah. Clyde. So who is he?"

Sissy shook her head and still wouldn't meet his eyes. "Nobody."

"Sissy—"

"Come on. You promised me we'd go hunting." She wiggled out of his arms and scrambled out of bed. "I'm going to brush my teeth first, then we're going."

"Answer my question, woman!" But she'd already skipped out of the room.

Really. She'd *skipped*.

After ordering his cock to get some control, Mitch tossed off the covers and marched into the bathroom. Sissy stood at the sink brushing her teeth. She grinned around the toothbrush, showing a mouthful of toothpaste, before she handed him his toothbrush.

"And this Clyde conversation isn't over," he told her before he started brushing his teeth. She only snorted, spit out the toothpaste, and rinsed her mouth. Then she skipped out of the bathroom.

He was getting tired of the skipping.

Five seconds later, she walked back on all fours, her tail wagging. When he kept brushing, she barked at him.

"Two minutes!" he snapped around his mouthful of toothpaste and went back to brushing. Didn't she know that dentists recommended at least two minutes of brushing twice a day?

Sissy sat and scratched her ear with her back leg. She

looked like all the Smith wolves when she shifted. Dark brown, almost black fur with very small patches of white and gold built in. Unlike his eyes or even Bobby Ray's, Sissy's eyes went from light brown to yellow only when wolf.

And thankfully, she'd finished molting. Although it had been entertaining when he'd walk into her hotel room and find her rubbing herself up against a potted plant or furniture, trying to get the tufts of fur off.

Mitch finished brushing, spit, and Sissy slammed into his side with her paws. *Impatient female.* Then she started barking at him—and wouldn't stop.

Annoyed—and amused—Mitch shifted and roared at her. Sissy stumbled back, wagged her tail, and took off running.

Mitch was right behind her.

It took a while, and to be quite blunt, Mitch wasn't the best hunter she'd ever worked with—in fact, his older sister, Marissa, was ten times better—but they'd finally tracked the wild boar down and had him cornered. The boar was a mean ol' buck, and big. When he realized he'd been cornered, he lowered his head and charged.

Shit.

Sissy dashed to the side as the boar came at her, and when he charged past, she grabbed hold of his leg, dragging him back.

Mitch grabbed the boar on his side, trying to get him into position so he could snap his spine.

But the boar kicked out, his hoof hitting Sissy in the jaw. Not wanting a broken jaw anytime soon, she let go, and the boar tore away from Mitch. He took off down the small hill and toward the lake.

The pair went after him, and Mitch had caught hold of the boar again by the time Sissy got to them.

Mitch dragged the boar back so Sissy could get hold of it. But before she could get a grip, water from the lake suddenly exploded on and around her, and she stumbled back.

Ralph. She'd completely forgotten about Ralph!

How the hell could she forget about Ralph? Who forgets about a ten-foot crocodile living in her parents' lake? Maybe because he'd been part of this lake for so long.

It had been her extremely stupid cousin who'd originally gotten it as a cute *little* croc, but when it finally outgrew the shoe box under the bed, the idiot had dumped the poor thing in this lake.

When Ralph hit a healthy five feet, the family had discussed getting *rid* of Ralph, but he was such a little trooper none of them had the heart, and Daddy figured it would keep anyone who annoyed him away from his lake. It was a real sweet sentiment, too—until Ralph hit ten feet. Then this lake and a good portion of the surrounding property became Ralphie's territory.

Of course, this meant they all stayed away from Ralph. If Ralph got their prey, they found other prey.

That's what logical, *sane* predators did.

Apparently Mitchell Shaw did not fall into that category.

When Sissy had gotten the water out of her eyes, she watched as Mitch played tug with a goddamn crocodile. She barked at him, but he seemed determined not to give up the damn boar.

Sissy barked more and slammed her paws against Mitch's side. But he only dug his enormous paws into the soft earth surrounding the lake and settled into a tug that Ralph seemed more than happy to engage in.

Was the man insane? Had being undercover pushed him over the edge? And why was she having another conversation with herself?

"Sissy Mae."

Sissy looked over and saw Dee-Ann standing about ten feet away, clothes clutched in her hand.

"You need to get . . ." Dee's gaze traveled over to Mitch and Ralph. "Holy shit."

Walking over to her cousin, Sissy barked the whole way. When she shifted and started putting the clothes on her cousin had with her, her barking moved to ranting.

"Can you believe him? I think the boy has lost his god-damn mind. Who the fuck plays tug with a crocodile? No one sane. That's who!" She tugged on the denim shorts before pulling on the T-shirt. "I risk everything to save his dumb ass, and now I'll have to go back to his big brother and tell him the hitter didn't get him—it was a crocodile. *How am I supposed to explain that?* And why the hell are you here anyway?"

Dee didn't answer, her gaze locked on Mitch and Ralph.

"*Dee-Ann!*"

"Don't yell." Her cousin turned to her. "I was sent here to get you." She sighed. "They want to see you in town."

Sissy let out an angry breath. Now? Her brother wanted her now? Then she stopped a moment to think about it. Bastard. It was perfect. Kick her out while Mitch was unable to walk, and the town might turn on him for being a major prick. Wait until the cat could tussle with crocodiles, and the town would have a parade leading them out.

Bastard!

"And you've got some visitors at the house."

Sissy pulled her annoyed gaze away from Mitch and back to her cousin. "I do?"

Mitch had a good grip on the boar—who'd died quite a while ago from blood loss and internal damage, no doubt— but that damn crocodile wouldn't give it up.

And were crocodiles indigenous to these parts? He'd watched documentaries on crocs, and he'd never heard about a huge population in the wilds of Tennessee.

But investigating that further would have to wait because the damn thing wouldn't let go!

His jaw getting tired, Mitch readjusted, but the croc took advantage and scurried back. Mitch tried to grab hold, but the damn croc disappeared into the lake. Mitch roared . . . and roared again.

Now he was hungry, tired, and covered in boar's blood. He hated hunting his own food!

Snarling, he turned and walked back to Sissy's house. He had no idea where she had gone, but she better have some food waiting for him or he'd be a little more than cranky.

But Mitch felt his anger moving to a new level when he neared the house and saw them. There were about eight, and they all held flowers or boxes of chocolate.

What the fuck?

He didn't bother to shift; instead, he kept on walking until he reached the line—a friggin' line!—that led from the house down the porch steps.

And was Sissy shooing these horny wolves away? No! She was looking way too cute and wet from the lake in those tiny shorts and way-too-small T-shirt—did she not have any other kinds of clothes?—while she took their flowers or chocolates and smiled.

Didn't she understand that until he left, her attention should only be on him? True, they only had a friendship, and it would probably stay that way, but until he headed back to Philly, he expected her to focus solely on him.

And he knew he wasn't being unreasonable . . . dammit.

Standing behind Sissy—and getting a delightful look at that great ass—he stared at the wolves who'd come to call. They stared back, none of them making any effort to leave.

So . . . he roared. A few jumped, the others continued to stare.

Sissy looked at him. "Oh?" she asked. "Have we finished tussling with Ralph?"

Now the wolves looked a little concerned. But Mitch had no idea who Ralph was. To make that clear, he tilted his head to the side, and Sissy shook her head in obvious disgust.

"Ralph. The crocodile you refused to give up that damn boar to."

He snorted at her, and Dee shook her head. "That was a sight all right," she grumbled. Mitch was quickly learning not to expect more from Dee than the occasional sentence thrown at him to keep him off balance.

"Well, as you can see, I'm busy. So"—Sissy shooed him—"scoot."

She was shooing *him* away? Not these dogs? How was this okay behavior?

Not about to be put off for some German shepherds carrying flowers, Mitch grabbed hold of the back of Sissy's shorts and tugged her toward the steps.

"Hey! Have you lost your mind?"

He ignored her and kept pulling.

"Can I just say that this is rude? You're being rude!"

Mitch didn't care.

Sissy let him drag her into the house because she knew if she tried to pull away, her shorts would get torn off and she wasn't in the mood for that.

Besides, this was kind of fun.

Although what had gotten into the man, she had no idea.

Dee came in after them and closed the door while Sissy slapped at Mitch's muzzle until he released her.

Motioning to the men outside, Dee said, "Nice move mentioning Ralph."

That had been a tactical maneuver. She didn't want to have to worry about anyone starting shit with Mitch when she was out of the house. At least not until he was back to full strength.

"But you really need to get into town, Sissy."

"Yeah. Yeah. But I got boar's blood all over me, so I better shower." She had her foot on the first step, but one big hand slapped against the wall and the big arm attached blocked her from going up the stairs. She looked at a now human, bloody, and seriously naked Mitch. *Yowza.* "Yes?"

"What about my breakfast?"

"So you lost your breakfast to Ralph, huh?"

"You named him Ralph?"

"What did you want us to name him? Crocky McCrockenson?"

"I'm hungry," he said again.

"Dee, darlin', could you fix the king of the jungle here something for breakfast since he seems to be incapable?"

"Yup."

Mitch leaned in close, his mouth against her ear. "Does she cook as good as you?"

"No," Sissy whispered back, "but at least I don't have to worry about you replacing me with another. Now . . . mind moving that horse dick out of my way?"

He moved his arm, and Sissy headed up the stairs.

"Wait," he said behind her, "was that an insult?"

Sissy was right—Dee wasn't as good a cook as her. She wasn't bad, but Sissy really had a way with the skillet.

Freshly showered and wearing jeans, T-shirt, and sneakers, Sissy trotted down the stairs. She took bacon directly off his plate, and he almost took her arm off.

Dee handed Sissy a paper towel. "You want me to go with you?"

"Nah. I'll be fine."

"You sure? I know how it gets between you and Travis."

"What's going on?" Mitch asked even as he kept eating.

"Nothing to worry your giant cat head about."

"Sissy—"

"Bye. I won't be long." She walked out the back door without another word.

"I hate when she does that."

Dee chuckled or snorted—Mitch couldn't tell—and put the dirty pans in the sink.

Before she could turn on the water, he quickly asked, "Got any more eggs?"

Dee looked at him over her shoulder. "I just made you a carton of scrambled eggs."

"Is that a yes or a no to my question?"

Chapter 9

Sissy walked into her old high school, and memories inundated her, some of them great. Like her and Ronnie Lee teasing every boy in a ten-foot radius. Or the way Sissy and her She-pups ruled these halls from ninth grade to twelfth.

Of course, it was also in these hallways that Sissy's English teacher told her she might want to consider a job that didn't require her to think too much. Or the time the principal called Sissy's momma down to the school because Sissy had chased Jessie Ann Ward into the air conditioning vents where she'd gotten that scrawny little body stuck. Boy, was Momma pissed that day.

No, those were definitely not memories she needed to relive anytime soon.

The local high school was also where the town Elders met. In some of the towns, the board was made up of many breeds. Canines, cats, bears, even hyenas. But not in Smithtown. Because within the Smithtown borders, there were only canines and a few antisocial bears who lived in houses near the caves. The bears who lived in Smithtown were simply too big and mean to fuck with, especially the polars, so the wolves let them be. Town politics, however, came down to the wolves, and that's who she'd be facing today. Her kin.

Her only problem now was that her daddy and momma weren't around, which left this issue to the strongest.

Sissy walked into the band room—she'd only ever come to this room to make out—where the Elders waited. But not only the Elders. Her brothers were there, too, and their mates, quite a few of her cousins, and some She-wolves who'd decided not to follow her to New York.

Everyone, it seemed, except Sammy and his mate—interesting. She wondered if Sammy even knew about this meeting.

"It's nice to see you home, Sissy Mae," her Uncle Sirras said.

"It's nice to be home." *Except for moments like these.*

"Shame you didn't come home alone," Travis Ray said softly. Like always, he spoke softly and carried a big fat paw—and head.

Unlike Bobby Ray, however, Travis had never really grown into his head.

Travis's mate, Patty Rose, stepped forward and hugged Sissy. "How are you, darlin'?" she asked in her most "I'm so sincere" voice. "Are you doing okay?"

"I'm just fine, Patty Rose," Sissy answered back in her best "you're such a friggin' liar but I'm going to pretend you're not" voice. "Thank you so much for asking."

"So what are you going to do, Sissy Mae?"

She focused back on Travis. "About?"

"He needs to go." Travis rarely bothered beating around the bush. He was a direct man who expected direct answers.

"I can't do that. I promised his family he'd be safe here."

"Doesn't he have his own kin?" Jackie Ray demanded, sounding typically panicked. "His own Pride? What about that rich brother of his? Couldn't he protect him?"

Ignoring Jackie like she always did, Sissy stepped closer

to Travis. "They could have killed me, too, Travis. I was right there."

"Then maybe you should pick better friends to be spending your time with, baby sister."

"Now, Travis Ray," Patty gently chastised—as if she thought Sissy would believe any of it for two seconds. The She-wolf hated her. Always had, always would. "Let's all stay friendly about this."

"So you want us to go?" Sissy snapped, ignoring Patty. "Is that what you're saying?"

"You don't have to go anywhere. This is your home. And always will be."

"Okay."

"But this ain't that cat's home. So he goes."

Sissy's hands curled into fists at her side. "If he leaves, I go with him." And her brother knew that about her. Knew she'd never send Mitch off on his own.

"Fine," Travis said simply. "Then go."

"You bastard. You'd throw me out of my own home?"

"Oh, no." Travis took a step closer—but not too close. "You're leaving on your own. I only threw out that cat. And that's exactly what I'll tell Daddy when he gets home from his big vacation."

Angry, exasperated, and ready to kill, Sissy threw her hands up and turned to walk away. "Fine, you big-headed bastard! We'll leave."

"Bye. Don't let the door hit your fat ass on the way out."

Sissy abruptly stopped walking, and she could sense how everyone but Travis took a cautious step back. That was probably smart. Normally, a crack like that would start a brawl, but not now. Not when Sissy had to watch out for the overeating beast recuperating in her daddy's home.

But what stopped Sissy in her tracks was that calendar tacked to the band room wall, specifically that date marked off on it. Suddenly, that date meant more to her than it ever had before.

"Unless . . ." Sissy began.

"Unless what?" The pause was long and dramatic until Travis asked again, "Unless what, Sissy Mae?"

"Unless we can come to a deal."

"Money don't mean shit to me, Sissy, and you know it."

"Oh, I know." She turned around and looked at him. "But there is something that means the world to you. And Mitch can help with that. When he's healed up a bit more, of course."

Immediately, Travis knew what she was getting at. "You have to be kidding."

"He's good."

"Bullshit. We went down this road with his brother, and you saw how well that worked out."

"Mitch is better."

"Yeah. Right."

"I swear. Check online if you don't believe me."

"Okay. So say it's true . . . then what?"

"Then you have a shot at what you want. What you've been wanting for years."

Jackie shook his head. "She's lying, Travis. She's—"

She grabbed that tambourine lying on a desk and chucked it so fast Jackie didn't have a chance to move before it hit him right in the forehead. He screeched like a wounded hyena, and like always, everyone ignored him. To be honest, he might not have even been in the room the way everyone didn't even bother looking at him.

"Well . . . ?" Sissy pushed.

"If it's true—"

"It's true."

"*If* it's true, then that's a deal I'd be much inclined to take. But it better be true, Sissy. And he better be up for it."

She grinned. "Mitch is usually up for anything."

The females chuckled, but Travis only stared at her. "But if you're lying, Sissy Mae, best get that cat out of town before we show him what Saturday nights used to be like back in Grandma Smith's day."

Sissy's eyes narrowed at the mention of that old witch's name, and everyone but Travis took another step back. "That's not funny, Travis."

"Wasn't trying to be funny since I'm not really known for my sense of humor. Now if you don't mind, I need to meet with the Pack—which last I heard, you weren't part of anymore."

Sissy grinned. "Oh, that's very true. 'Cause if I were, I'd have killed you long ago and worn that giant head of yours as a hat as a warning to any challenger."

She turned and again headed toward the door. Before she even made it back to her rental car, her mind was desperately turning over how she would ever convince Mitch to do this.

Mitch was halfway through the unbelievably delicious zebra stew Sissy had made him for lunch when he realized that she kept staring at him. Anyone else, he'd assume they had a little crush on him. But Sissy was the kind of gal who didn't get crushes, and when she wanted someone, she really went for it. No doubts, no obsessing. In a way, she was kind of like a guy. So then why the hell did she keep staring at him?

"What?" he asked when he'd finished his food. Now that he had his appetite back, it would take a hell of a lot more than curiosity to distract him from his meal.

"You done?"

"Yeah, I'm done. Now why do you keep staring at me?"

"Let's talk in the other room."

Mitch watched her get up. She was being really nice, which automatically made him wary. He followed her into the family room and sat down on the couch. She paced in front of him for several minutes before he couldn't stand it anymore.

"They want me to go, right?"

"Well . . ."

"Don't sweat it. I should go back to Philly anyway, and I don't want you to get into trouble because of me."

"Wait. Let me finish." She twisted her hands in front of her as she continued to pace back and forth. "I found a way for you to stay—for a price." She stopped twisting her hands together so she could rub her temples. The pacing continued. "Lord, this is so embarrassing."

Mitch winced. "You don't have to marry your cousin or something, do you?"

Sissy abruptly stopped pacing and turned to him with a lethal scowl. "Think we can put aside the cultural stereotypes until we're done with this conversation?"

"Sorry."

Hands on her hips, Sissy let out a deep breath. "You can stay, but . . . you'll have to . . . do something."

"*I'll* have to marry your cousin?"

"Mitch!"

He chuckled. "Sorry. I couldn't help myself. Now could you spit it out already?"

"You see . . . it's the bears. Of Collinstown."

Since he had no idea where Collinstown was located, all of that was meaningless. "Okay."

"Well, we've had this rivalry with them for years and . . . well, you see . . ." Sissy started to pace again and again abruptly stopped. "The bottom line is they want you to play."

"Play?" Mitch had no idea what she was talking about. "Play what?"

Sissy suddenly found the cracks in the floor fascinating, and Mitch had to admit he was entertained. He'd never seen her so obviously uncomfortable before.

"Uh . . . football."

"Football? The game?"

"Of course the game."

"Hey, excuse me if I find it surprising my life or death situation hinges on my ability to be Joe Namath."

"Look," she sat on the couch beside him, "I know this is a strange request. But I had to think of something. Without my parents here, I am at the will of that asshole Travis, and if I go ahead and kill him like I tried when I was eight, Daddy will have my ass."

"But why football? I mean, let's face it, we could always ask Bren for money or—"

"I can say with all honesty, Travis doesn't care about money. He cares about two things . . . being Alpha Male—"

"And football."

"And football," she confirmed.

"So he needs me to play a little game of pickup against some bears?"

"It's not really that simple." She turned to face him, pulling her legs up on the couch and resting back on her heels. "As you know, each town of shifters is different from every other. And each region is different. But the one thing the Southern and Midwestern shifters have is our love of football. We have official teams that travel, and some of the richer towns have actual stadiums that're for these games specifically."

"You're kidding?"

"Not even a little. Since I was a kid, I've had football shoved down my throat. My daddy and his brothers played when they were young, and their fathers played when they were still using those leather helmets and very little padding. They simply love the game."

"Of course they do. It's like an elaborate game of fetch—ow!"

Mitch rubbed his head where she'd yanked out actual hair.

"If you think this is easy for me, it's not! And you making canine jokes just pisses me off. And for your information, every breed in the Southern states plays."

"But the bears are unbeatable."

"Basically. I mean, their guys can reach eight feet tall and almost four hundred pounds when human. Lord knows they could never legally play in the NFL. It would be lethal."

"And you think I can help?"

"Remember what I told you the other night? Brendon brags about you constantly, especially about how amazing you were in football."

He was, too, but he'd had to "tragically" end his career his senior year of college before he could be recruited by a pro team. Between those blood tests that seemed to get more extensive every year and his not being able to pull back as much if he wanted to win in the pros, it simply had been too big a risk for him and his kind. Broke his heart, too.

Mitch still caught a few pickup games with friends from his old neighborhood every once in a while, but again, he always had to hold back because they were full-humans. The thought of being able to really play the way he'd always wanted to nearly had him wiggling.

Sissy touched his leg. "I know I'm asking a lot of you, and of course we'll wait until you're fully recovered, but hopefully, that will be before next Saturday since that's the day of the big game, but really, I'd understand if you say no, and I'll fight for you to stay anyway. Travis is *such* an asshole, but for you, Mitch, I'll fight him. I swear."

She sounded so sincere, so upset, so traumatized that Mitch could do nothing *but* torture her.

"What do you think you're doing?" He pushed her hand off his leg, and Sissy reared back in surprise.

"Huh?"

"You heard me. Don't you think I know what you're doing?"

"What I'm doing?"

"Trying to use me. To entice me to play on your team."

"Mitch, of course I'm not—"

"*I'm not a whore!*"

Sissy rolled her eyes. "Mitchell . . ."

"I see how this works."

"How what works?"

He moved further away, giving her his best ingénue stare. "First, you sit next to me—a little *too* close—wearing those sexy tight shorts and that begging-to-be-torn-off tank top. Then a few innocent touches in all my favorite naughty areas, of which I have many."

Sissy slapped her hands against her thighs. "Mitchell Shaw!"

"And before I know it, I'm on my back, and you're having your dirty, disgusting way with me. Just so I'll play for your team."

She looked up at the ceiling as if asking it for guidance. "Why do our conversations get so strange?"

"And because I'm weak . . . and your breasts are so large and full—"

"Good Lord."

"—I'll succumb to your She-wolf wiles and agree to play your damn game."

"Or you could just cut the bullshit and agree to play."

"I could. But I figured this was a better way of getting you to agree to let me look down your shirt."

"Mitchell!"

Laughing, he held his hands up. "Okay. Okay. I'll play."

"Only if you want to. Only if—"

"On one condition."

"I'm not letting you see down my top."

"We both know you will eventually, sweet cheeks."

"Stop calling me that."

"But before I put on a pad or pick up a ball . . ."

"Yeah . . . ?"

"I wanna know who the hell Clyde is."

Sissy fell back on the couch, her knees raised, her bare feet digging into the cushions. She always looked so sexy like that. "You can't be serious."

"Tell me, or I go play for the bears."

She shrugged. Sighed. "I'm not sure you're ready for this. Clyde . . . means a lot to me. He knows how to touch all my favorite—what did you call them?—naughty places."

"Bears," he growled.

"Fine," she replied stoically. "If you insist."

"I insist."

"Come on then. We have some time before today's practice, which I'm sure Travis wants you at. But I really hope you're ready for this."

He did not like the sound of that.

Chapter 10

Mitch stepped out of the rental car and glanced around. Sissy had parked them beside a small but nice home that sat right in the middle of a ton of property. Growing up in Philly, Mitch was used to the small covered backyard his mom's Pride had. All this property stunned him. Lots of trees with small rivers and big lakes.

Now Mitch understood why Bren had no problem coming out here to visit Ronnie Lee's family. All Mitch had to do was sit outside on Sissy's porch drinking coffee, and he'd see deer and elk dashing by. Of course, it kept him in a state of constant hunger.

"This is Clyde's house?"

"Nope. This is my brother's house."

Mitch smirked. "Which one? You'll have to be more specific than that."

"Ha-ha."

"*Aunt Sissy!*" a young voice screeched, then Sissy was besieged by five kids who looked barely a year apart. What his mom would call Catholic Twins.

Sissy picked up the smallest one and swung her around while the others surrounded her.

"How are my favorite little terrors?" she asked.

"Fine," they said in unison before inundating their aunt with . . . well, who knew. Mitch couldn't understand them as each yelled to be heard over the other.

The kids were a dirty mess, but that was to be expected since Mitch doubted they'd spent more then ten minutes in the house all day. And shifter kids played rough instinctively. The way they played today would be the way they hunted down dinner tomorrow.

"Where's your momma?" Sissy finally asked after amazing Mitch with the way she'd been able to follow what each child said and comment on it so no one felt left out.

"In the house," they all said . . . or yelled, depending on your perspective.

"Y'all tell her to meet us at the barn. Okay?"

She placed the smallest child on her feet, and the children ran for the house. "Sammy has five more kids somewhere around here."

"Wow."

Sissy gave him a small smile. "I sure do love kids," she said before heading off to the back of the house and the barn. But he heard the last thing she said quite clearly, "As long as they ain't mine."

They walked toward the barn, and Mitch asked, "Is Clyde a cow?"

"No. You know we can't have cows around here. They stampede so easy."

Sissy grabbed the handles on the barn door and pushed them in opposite directions.

"This is Clyde," she said with real pride. But Mitch barely heard her. He was too busy wondering if a man could come without actually ejaculating. Because nothing, absolutely nothing had ever been so beautiful before. So sexy. So . . . so . . .

So goddamn hot!

"Hey, Sissy Mae." A pretty She-wolf with bright blue eyes walked up to them. "Haven't seen you in an age."

"Hey, Violet. This is Mitch Shaw."

She gave him a friendly nod. "Hey." Mitch managed a sort of half-ass wave.

"Where's my brother?"

"Where else? At the diner. Gotta make sure we can feed this pack of rabid dogs."

Sissy held her hand out. "Gimme."

Violet shook her head and laughed. "You ain't never gonna change, Sissy Mae Smith."

"Not unless it's court ordered."

Violet slapped a set of keys into Sissy's hand and walked off, leaving them alone.

"Where did you get this?" Mitch finally asked, moving slowly around the beauty before him.

"We built it," she said simply, but Mitch couldn't help but stare at her in shock.

"This is it? This is the car you talked about rebuilding?"

"Yeah." She walked up to the 1971 Chevrolet Chevelle Malibu and ran her hand lovingly down the hood. "When me and Ronnie Lee were about fifteen, our fathers gave us enough money to buy our own cars. And let me tell you, it was not a lot of money. But they'd gotten real tired of us stealing their cars, and the sheriff at the time said if he caught us hot-wiring another car, he'd definitely throw us in jail. Anyway, they figured we'd get some piece of shit car that would tool us around town. You know, something your grandmother would drive. Instead, we went to the junkyard and found the battered husks for this Malibu and another for a '71 Plymouth Barracuda. Ronnie wanted that one cause she always did love that song by Heart. What money we had left, we started buying parts. When we ran out of money, we started working around town. And we are talking some shitty jobs until we got something steady at Travis's gas station. He taught us a lot about cars and engines. And we put some others together, like the Camaro Dee-Ann's got."

Using the tips of her fingers, she ran her hands along the roof. "It took us over two years to build this one and Ronnie's, but damn if it wasn't worth it."

"Why is it here?"

"When we left the country, we left the cars in the safest places we could think of. I left mine with Sammy Ray 'cause next to Smitty, I knew I could trust him not to sell it or do anything to it. Ronnie left hers at her momma's 'cause she knew that woman wouldn't let anyone near that car. She'd never admit it, but she was real proud of Ronnie Lee doing such a good job."

"They should be proud of both of you. This is amazing."

Sissy grinned. "This is Clyde. I haven't taken him out in ages, but I dream about it a lot."

Mitch laughed. "Hence the groaning his name?"

"Pretty much. But can you blame me?"

"Not a bit." He was moaning now.

"Come on, Mitchell. Let's go for a drive."

Mitch shook his head. "Forget it, Smith. I'm not ready to have any gray hairs in my tawny mane, thank you very much."

"To quote my daddy, don't be such a pussy."

"But I am a pussy."

She folded her hands together as if praying. "How about I make you a promise to stay in the speed limit? I'll take you around town for a bit." She leaned forward, those pretty eyes wicked. "Come on, pretty kitty. You know you want to."

Christ, did he want to.

"Fine. But you promised."

Sissy squealed and pulled open the door. The fact that the car was unlocked, even in this barn, was a testament to the safety of this little town. It was run by predators, however. So steal at your own risk.

The engine turned over, and like a well-fed puma, it purred to life. Mitch squirmed a bit in the seat.

"Whatever you're doing over there . . . stop it."

"Can't help it." Mitch reached over to the radio Sissy had put in. It had a cassette player, and Mitch smiled, remembering his own. "Let's see what tunes our lovely Sissy used to listen to back in the day." He turned it on and after a few bars, looked at her. "Sissy . . . honestly."

"What? This is my 'get out of town' tunes."

"Led Zeppelin's 'Ramble On'?"

"And Lynyrd Skynyrd's 'Free Bird' and Golden Earring's 'Radar Love.' If it was about driving away or leaving, it was on this cassette. So sit back and enjoy the Sissy experience."

"There's so much to mock there, I'll just leave it alone."

Slowly, she pulled out of the barn, and Sammy Ray's kids stood on the porch with their mother, chanting, "Clyde, Clyde, Clyde," over and over again.

"Remember what you promised me, Sissy Mae Smith."

She sighed. "I remember, you big wussy."

The way she drove? Damn right he was a wuss.

Francine Lewis looked up from her accounting paperwork, scowling as her younger sister came rushing through her office door. She didn't have a lot of time in the day to manage the money side of their business, and any interruptions annoyed her. When they closed their pie shop at the end of the day, Francine didn't want to worry about anything. Instead, she liked to go home to her mate and relax, maybe hunt something down.

"What is it, Janette?"

"The old woman has been at Sissy again."

Francine's hand paused over the adding machine. "When?"

"Two nights ago."

"And?"

"You know Sissy. She put 'em off, but I don't like it." Janette dropped in the chair across from her sister's desk. "If Janie comes back and finds out—"

"Okay. Stop. This is Sissy we're talking about. She's not stupid, and let's face it, she's got that big cat to care for."

"She offers all them Smiths power. And Sissy likes power."

"She's just like her momma when it comes to that. But Sissy likes power she has full control over." Francine pushed her hair out of her face, annoyed it was in her eyes. "No, I don't think we have anything to worry about. She knows to stay away from them."

"I hope you're right."

So did Francine. They couldn't afford to lose Sissy to that bitch on the hill. They'd never get her back if that ever happened. And no one really knew the extent that woman would go to obtain and keep her power. And she'd go further than most.

"I trust Sissy. She's crazy, but she won't do anything that will make her stay here forever."

Janette snorted a laugh. "You got a point there."

Chapter 11

Sissy tooled Mitch around town for a good two hours, showing him her high school, where she and her crew of junior She-wolves used to hang out when they weren't picking on the weaker Omegas. Even where she'd been arrested the first time.

"And see that tree over there?" she asked him, pointing at the giant oak off the main road.

"Yeah."

"I fucked under that tree." She nodded at the memory. "It was nice."

"And thank you for that visual."

What Mitch didn't know was she couldn't remember having this much fun before with a man when sex wasn't involved. Most guys bored her right quick, and on more than one occasion, she'd looked at Ronnie and said, "I think those lion females have the right idea. Fuckin' and protection only. Not sure what else good they're for." Then she'd go back to hanging out with her She-wolves who, even when they annoyed the living hell out of her, she found vastly entertaining.

But she simply liked having Mitch around. He made her laugh . . . and not just *at* him either.

"I don't know why I'm bothering asking but . . . you hungry?"

"I thought you'd never ask. I'm starving."

"Shocking." She thought a moment. "There's a steak house near the edge of town. It gets a mixed clientele, but the food is really good."

"Good enough."

"And since your kind comes in now and again," she said, pulling up to a light, "they should have enough to feed your bottomless pit of a stomach."

Sitting at the light, the sound of an engine revving beside them had Sissy leaning over Mitch to look through the window. Immediately, she grinned.

"Roll down the window."

Mitch did, his mouth open in shock.

"What are y'all doin' here? I thought we were gonna wait—"

"Trust me. We had to come. But we can catch up later." Ronnie Lee grinned from the comfort of her '71 yellow Barracuda, glancing up at the light and back at Sissy.

Now Sissy grinned as the pair stared at each other.

"Don't even think it," Brendon Shaw warned his mate. "I mean it, Ronnie Lee."

Mitch's head snapped around, and he glared at Sissy. "You promised me!"

Sissy turned back to face forward as the light dropped to green. "I lied," she said simply before gunning the engine.

Mitch gripped the dashboard. If his love of cars didn't border on the religious, he'd have started ripping that dashboard apart. But he simply couldn't. He simply couldn't do that to this beauty. So instead, he held on for dear life and prayed to any available higher powers for help.

But when he wasn't trying not to pee his pants in fear, Mitch had to secretly admire the way these two females handled cars. Ronnie hit a tight turn, and Sissy was right with her. She didn't flinch; she didn't even look stressed. At one point, she even said, "Did you see that?"

"See what?" And he couldn't keep his voice from breaking as tires squealed.

"Boot sale at Marlands. We are so going back there later."

How she even saw that he'd never know. He couldn't do anything but stare blindly at the upcoming road, praying that something wouldn't suddenly appear. They quickly took the race out of downtown and to the backwoods. Now Mitch understood why the roads were so wide. So two cars could race side by side. From what Mitch could tell, the entire town—not just the Smiths—was filled with the descendants of bootleggers who, when they weren't running from the local law, were racing each other for kicks.

Ronnie passed Sissy, and Sissy let out a curse, but not in English.

"Was that German?"

"Cursing in German sounds much cooler, don't ya think?"

He didn't have time to answer as Sissy shot past Ronnie, her evil cackle doing nothing but making his already queasy stomach a little queasier.

Mitch gripped the dashboard tighter as Ronnie pulled up beside them, the two of them hitting speeds that couldn't be remotely legal in any country on the planet.

"Are you praying?" she asked.

"I was raised a good Irish Catholic. When you know you're gonna die, you pray."

"Oh, calm the—*fuck!*"

Mitch's head snapped up in time to see a Smithtown sheriff's car parked sideways, completely blocking the road. The sheriff leaning against the door, his arms crossed over his chest—he'd been waiting for them.

"Sissy . . ."

She didn't answer, too busy hitting the brakes and spinning the car to the left, while Ronnie spun hers to the right so they wouldn't collide with each other in their effort to not hit the sheriff.

When they came to a screeching, squealing, grinding stop, Mitch realized his side of the car was about five inches away from a rather enormous tree. Visions of him and the car wrapped around that tree trunk did nothing for his current lack of equilibrium.

Gripping the steering wheel, Sissy had her eyes shut and kept muttering, "Shit, shit, shit," over and over again. Although Mitch didn't think her current chant had anything to do with their near miss of the tree. He was positive of that fact when the bullhorn went off.

"*Sissy. Mae. Smith. Get. Your. Ass. Out. Of. The. Car— Now!*"

Sissy cringed even as she reached for the door handle. She'd barely gotten it open when a big hand reached in, grabbed her by the ear, and dragged her out.

"Owww!"

"Barely back two days, and already I find you breaking every law ever put on the damn books."

"We weren't doin' nothin'," she argued, sounding remarkably like a ten-year-old.

"Keep that mouth shut, Sissy Mae. *Ronnie Lee Reed, get your ass over here!*"

Mitch needed to get out of the car, but the passenger side was simply too close to that tree. So he had to do some fancy finagling to drag his big body out of the car and through the driver's side. His brother grabbed him under the shoulders and helped him out the last few inches. Once he stood, the two brothers stared at each other and then threw themselves into each other's arms, sobbing.

They were just so glad to be alive.

When Ronnie Lee jabbed her lightly in the ribs, Sissy never expected to look over and see Mitch and his brother hugging like they'd just been helped off the *Titanic*. When Sissy's gaze moved back to Ronnie's, they both rolled their eyes at the unlimited drama two cats could create.

"*Are you listening to me?*"

Sissy's body jerked at the booming words, and she turned back around. "Yes, sir."

"When's your daddy coming home?"

With a shrug, Sissy said, "Got me."

"*You don't know?*"

Cringing away from the yelling, Sissy shook her head.

"And I guess your parents are with them, Ronnie Lee."

"Yes, sir."

"And you two think you can just come here and start up where you left off twelve years ago?"

"We didn't do anything," Sissy said again.

"Quiet!" The sheriff walked over to Ronnie Lee and stood in front of her. "What have I always told you? She's a bad seed, and you should stay away from her."

"Uncle Jeb, that's not fair."

"And how come you always blame me?" Suddenly, a finger was in Sissy's face. Sissy always called that the "cop finger." Cops were the only breed she knew who could point that one forefinger at you and make you shut up immediately. Hell, Dez did it all the time.

"I clocked y'all goin' a hundred and seventy-five."

"*Jesus Christ! What do you have under that hood?*" When

they all stared at him, Mitch simply shrugged. "I'm curious."

"Now both y'all listen up and listen up good. You get in one more bit of trouble, and I'll come down on you like the Archangel Gabriel himself. Understand me?"

"Yes, sir," Ronnie answered.

But Sissy didn't say anything, and Ronnie's uncle stood in front of her waiting for that answer. They locked gazes, and Sissy didn't back down. She never did. She really didn't know how.

"Sissy promises too," Ronnie said, pushing her uncle back toward the car.

With a snarl, the sheriff walked off, but not before tossing over his shoulder, "She's just like her momma."

She knew he'd said it on purpose. A low blow, but she still nearly had her hands around his throat when a strong arm grabbed her around the waist and yanked her back. She swung wildly ordering the sheriff to, "take that back, you bastard!"

But he only laughed at her and drove off.

Mitch wrapped his arms around her rage-shaking body and kissed her scalp. "Calm down."

"He blames me for everything. I never did a damn thing to him, and he hates me."

"He doesn't hate you," Ronnie corrected her. "He just doesn't like you."

"Thanks."

"Come on." Ronnie smiled. "Let's get out of here. I think we both need a beer."

"I'm hungry," both Shaw brothers stated simultaneously.

"Guess we better go to Sammy Ray's diner then," Sissy sighed. "I definitely don't have enough food for the both of ya, and the steakhouse needs reservations made twenty-four hours in advance when you're coming in with more than one male lion."

* * *

"One of our kind tried to kill Mitch?"

"Yeah." Ronnie put a paper napkin on her lap before looking back at Sissy. "Can you believe it? Where's the loyalty?"

"I don't know. Sounds like Mitchy here just pissed off some Pride, and they want revenge."

"Stop calling me that. Only my mother can call me that because she was in labor for eighteen hours. And no Pride would fuck with me because no one wants to fuck with my mother."

"That's true," Brendon confirmed while taking food off Ronnie's plate—clearly to her annoyance. "The O'Neill Pride may not be in the Llewellyn ranks, but they are definitely feared and breed a lot of females. Personally, I agree with Dez. Some cat is being paid a lot of money to kill Mitch."

"I'm surprised O'Farrell would even hire a woman. He doesn't trust them to do anything but cook and—" He stopped talking when he looked up to see Sissy and Ronnie staring at him. "Forget it."

"He may not have hired her. You do have a bounty on that big head."

"You could stay lion all the time." Now everyone stared at Ronnie.

"Why?" Sissy had to ask.

"I'm sure O'Farrell wants proof of Mitch's death before he'll pay up. And this lioness would know if she kills him as cat, he stays cat. Not like she'll be able to prove dick then."

"Wow." Mitch nodded in approval. "That's not remotely as stupid as it sounds."

"Thanks."

"But I can't." Mitch took a roll off Sissy's plate, and she debated chopping his hands off.

"Why not?"

"Can't play if I'm cat all the time."

"Play?" Brendon glanced between them. "Play what?"

Sissy glanced at the clock on the wall of her brother's diner. "Lord, Mitchell, we better move if we're gonna make this practice on time."

"Practice?" Brendon's eyes narrowed. "Practice for what?"

Mitch gave a dramatic sigh. "You're not gonna believe this, bruh, but in order to stay here, I have to play football."

Sissy saw Ronnie wince seconds before Brendon's hand slammed against the table. "*How come he gets to play?*"

"Now, darlin'," Ronnie rubbed his forearm, "there's no use gettin' upset."

"It's not fair. I'm as good as him."

"Is that why they call you Mr. Fumble Paws?"

Sissy barely ducked in time as that roll came flying at her head courtesy of Ronnie Lee.

"What? It was just a question."

Chapter 12

Sammy Ray stormed into his brother's shop while the big bastard was getting ready to get out to the field for practice.

"You're making him play football?"

Travis barely glanced at him. "Don't see what it is to you, Sammy Ray."

"She's your sister."

"She doesn't have to play."

"You know what I mean."

"Look, I didn't tell her she had to leave. But it's not safe to have him here."

"But you'll let him stay if he plays ball?" That only made sense in Travis's universe.

"I'm willing to take the risk if he's as good as she promises."

Donnie walked out of the office and stopped. He stared at Sammy, and Sammy stared right back until Donnie looked away.

"Meet you outside." Then Donnie was gone.

Lord, Bobby Ray and Sissy had the right idea. Leave this

town and their crazy ways. Because really, Sammy didn't know how much more of his big brother he could take.

"I'll say it again, Travis. She's your sister. And if she needs help, that's all that should matter. I don't care who she brings home with her."

"Let's face it, little brother, Sissy Mae is a—"

Sammy held up his hand, cutting Travis off. He loved his baby sister and wouldn't let anyone call her that. At least not to her face. Or his. "Let's understand each other, Travis. You call her what you're about to call her, and it'll be a dark day for both of us. Understand me?"

Travis shook his head. "Always protecting her."

"Only from you. She or that cat shouldn't have to do a damn thing to stay here, and you know it."

"But he will." Travis picked up all his stuff to bring to the field and walked over to his brother. "And if you have a problem with that, little brother, you're more than welcome to do something about it."

When Sammy didn't say or do anything, Travis snorted and walked out.

"I can't believe I'm back here again." Sissy looked around the huge football field. The town boasted several. One for midget football, one for the junior high and high school kids, and this one, which was reserved for town-against-town battles. Every Saturday during her summers growing up in Smithtown had been spent here. When she and Ronnie Lee had left, she swore never to come back to this damn field. But here she was.

And the Smithtown Field wasn't just a plain old field with some markers up to show boundaries. It was a low-level outdoor stadium where any semipro team would be proud to play.

Even though the home game against the bears wasn't until the Saturday after next, they still sold the usual hot dogs and burgers during all practices for those who came to watch. But Sissy and Ronnie bypassed that for a couple of hot coffees from the Starbucks across the street.

As they walked toward the cushioned bleachers, Sissy looked over and watched Mitch catch a perfect pass. She knew he still hurt a bit, but he didn't show it. Instead, he caught the ball and looked downright bored by the throw.

She smiled.

"So what's going on with you and Mitch?"

Startled, Sissy glanced at her friend. "Nothing. Why?"

And that's when her best friend of more than twenty-five years slapped her in the back of the head.

"Ow!" Sissy stopped walking and glared at Ronnie. "*What was that for?*"

"Because you're an idiot, Sissy Mae Smith."

Sissy didn't understand Ronnie sometimes. "What are you talking about?"

"I'm talking about . . . shit."

Immediately, Sissy checked her bare feet. "Where? I don't smell anything." But when Sissy looked back up, Ronnie wasn't looking at the ground but behind Sissy.

She turned and looked up into eyes she would have done anything for . . . when she was sixteen.

"Gil." Her ex.

He smiled. "Hey, sweetheart."

Mitch easily caught the ball, and he could tell by the wolf's face that he really thought he'd motored that ball right at him. *Canines. Ya just had to love 'em.*

They'd started off taking it easy on him because they knew he was still healing. But that didn't last long when nothing they did seemed to faze him.

"You up to trying a few passes?" Travis asked.

After finally meeting Sissy's brother, Mitch knew for sure he didn't like the guy. Where Smitty had a heart, Travis had nothing but an empty hole.

Mitch moved his shoulder around. It hurt, but if he soaked it tonight, the pain would be tolerable in the morning. "Yeah. Sure."

Travis motioned one of the guys out, and Mitch threw the ball. The wolf caught it, but was slammed back several feet. Startled, he looked at Travis.

"Not bad."

"I know."

"I'm sure my sister told you the requirements for staying."

Mitch smiled. "Let's face it, Smith. You need me more than I need you. Especially if you want to win against the bears. Right?"

"Yeah. And?"

"I'll play."

"But what do ya want? 'Cause I know you want something."

"My brother on the team."

Travis's mouth dropped open, and for a brief moment, he lost that annoyingly cool expression he seemed to wear at all times. "Fumble Paws? Forget it."

"Make him offensive line. He'll never have to touch a ball. But either he's in . . . or I'm out."

Travis glanced over his shoulder at Bren sitting on the bench . . . well, it was more like pouting on the bench.

"And make it sound like ya mean it."

Letting out a sigh Mitch often heard from Sissy, Travis called out, "Hey, Shaw, you want in?"

Bren sat up straight. "Me? Yeah!"

He charged out on the field like he'd been called to pick up his Olympic gold medal.

"This better work," Travis snarled at Mitch.

"Leave him with me." Mitch looked around for Ronnie so he could let her know. But he caught sight of some guy talking to Sissy.

Grabbing Travis's arm before he could walk away, he asked, "Who's that?"

Travis looked in Sissy's direction. "Oh. Him. That's Gil Warren."

"He's part of the Pack?"

"Today. He comes and goes."

"Why's he talking to Sissy?"

Travis slowly turned to look at Mitch. "How do I put this?" He stroked his chin. "You could say Gil was Sissy's . . . first. And a girl never forgets her first now, does she?"

One of the wolves tossed the ball back at Mitch. "Let's do a few more passes."

Mitch nodded. "Sure."

He examined the ball in his hand for a moment, pulled back his arm, and let the pigskin fly . . .

Sissy couldn't believe this. Gil? Gil friggin' Warren? Back in Smithtown after all these years and acting like he hadn't dumped her ass. Or maybe he thought she was one of those females who let things go. Forgive and forget. Finding peace by forgiving.

Well, that sure as hell wasn't Sissy. She didn't forgive or forget a damn thing.

"It's really good to see you again, Sissy."

"Yeah. Thanks."

"How long you here for?"

"Don't know."

"I see your sister's here, too, Gil." Ronnie glared at the female who'd told Gil he could do better than "Bobby Ray's bitch sister." Ronnie had always hated Tina, but not as much as she hated Gil.

That's why Ronnie was Sissy's best friend. She hated all the right people.

"We're back for good."

"Great." Sissy looked for a way out of this conversation, short of kicking the man in the nuts. Which was something she'd wanted to do for years.

"How about we get together for dinner tonight?"

Sissy blinked and looked at Ronnie. "You must be joking," she said to him.

He smiled. She used to love that smile. Now, it just looked smarmy. "Not even a little, sweetheart. We'll have a nice dinner, catch up. It'll be great."

"No."

"Come on, Sissy Mae. It's time to let the past go."

"No, it's not. But nice try."

Ronnie laughed, but it turned into a squeak when a football whacked into the back of Gil's head, slamming the wolf forward. Sissy and Ronnie stepped aside and watched Gil hit the ground.

"Sorry," Mitch called from the field. "My fault."

Sissy stood there, stunned for several moments, until Ronnie grabbed her arm and took her to the stands, stepping around Gil's twitching body.

"If I asked you why Mitch might have done that, will you hit me in the back of the head again?" Sissy asked once they'd gotten comfortable in their seats.

Ronnie nodded. "Yup. I sure would."

"Okay. Just checking."

Chapter 13

Mace Llewellyn walked into his Brooklyn home late in the evening. It had been a tough day with Smitty, Sissy Mae, and Mitch out. He still debated contacting Smitty, but everything seemed to be handled. Was it worth ruining the man's honeymoon for a situation he really couldn't fix anyway? And Mace knew Smitty well enough to know his buddy would want to *fix it*.

"I'm home," he called out.

"In the kitchen."

Mace closed the door and turned to face Dez's dogs. He snarled, and the two males took off running. The puppy, however, didn't move. She didn't seem to be bothered by Mace's snarls or roars. When he was home, she followed him around faithfully. To be honest, Mace had no idea what to do with her. She'd already grown to three times her original size, and she clearly wasn't done if the size of her feet was any indication. Plus, she stared up at him with those big, adoring eyes.

He simply didn't have the heart to be mean to her the way he was to the other two. Glancing around first to make sure no one was around, Mace crouched beside her and petted her head and under her chin the way she liked. Her eyes closed, and her whole body kind of swayed as he scratched a little harder on her neck.

"Mace?"

Hearing Dez's voice, Mace scrambled to his feet and quickly wiped his hands on his jeans. "Coming."

Mace tossed his jacket on the couch and walked through the house and into the huge kitchen. Dez sat at the kitchen table working on her new laptop. One of the perks of her new job. She'd been real unhappy when she'd found out they'd moved her to a new division and a new partner. She still didn't understand how this job was a huge step-up and how it could change her career for the better.

Taking a few steps in, Mace stopped and stared down at the floor. "What is that mongrel doing to my baby?"

Dez glanced down at Marcus and shrugged. "They're playing."

Mace didn't consider a one hundred and fifty-pound dog using his muzzle to push his son in circles playing.

"That can't be safe."

"Marcus is happy."

True, his son was giggling, but he was a toddler. Toddlers laughed at all sorts of shit until blood began to flow.

Grumbling, Mace reached down and grabbed his son. Like the momma's boy he was turning into, Marcus slashed at his father's face with nonexistent claws and screeched until Mace put him back on the floor with the dog. And the dog happily proceeded to spin the brat around in circles.

"Told you," Dez mumbled, her gaze focused on the computer screen.

"Should he even be up this late?"

"He's nocturnal, since you keep forgetting."

Mace growled to himself and decided not to get in a fight with Dez. To be honest, he was horny as hell, and she looked so good in that T-shirt. "Food?"

"Fridge."

Mace opened the refrigerator door and pulled out the three giant sandwiches the nanny had made before she left for the day. "How was work?"

"Fine."

"You and your partner getting along?"

"I guess. I haven't tried to shoot her yet."

"That's good, baby." He sat down at the table.

"Okay. I've got questions."

Dammit. He hadn't even eaten yet. "No, Desiree. There's no conspiracy."

"Oh, yes, there is. But that's not what I'm talking about. You and Smitty were in the SEALs but a special unit, right? Just shifters?"

"Yeah."

"Any females?"

"Nope."

"Any other units like yours but with females?"

Mace nodded, half of his first sandwich already devoured. "Yeah," he said after he swallowed. "I think the Army has something. Don't know shit about the Air Force. And the Marines definitely."

Dez scowled, and Mace shook his head. "Not. A. Conspiracy."

"Fine. But all the years I was in, and I never heard about any special units filled with shifters."

"And that was for a reason, baby."

"Yeah. So you keep saying."

"We keep this secret for the good of our kind."

"Yeah, but you told me."

"I trusted you." He smiled. "And I knew if you told, no one in their right mind would believe you. You have to be smart and know when to break the rules. We're not only protecting ourselves; we're also protecting the next generation."

Dez ran her hands through her hair, revealing her frustration.

"So you think whoever shot at Mitch was military?"

"Yeah. I mean the distance she was at, Mace . . . forget about being full-human. I don't see you or Smitty making this shot."

Mace remembered what Sissy had said when she was still covered in Mitch's blood—"If he hadn't moved . . ."

"Now we just have to figure out who she is."

"Start with the Marines. God knows, you guys love your sharpshooters."

Finally, Dez gave a little laugh and sat back in her chair, cracking her knuckles. "You might as well pick her up, Mace. She'll only start whining."

Mace had tried to ignore the paw that kept tapping on his leg, hoping Dez wouldn't notice. The woman may not be a shifter, but her cop senses were on point.

Grumbling, he reached down and picked the puppy up, placing her in his lap. "And you can just wipe that smile off your face."

"I didn't say a thing." She pushed her chair back and reached down to scoop up their son. "Let's get you upstairs and to bed, baby-boy, so Dad can have his quality time with his girlfriend."

Dez kissed Mace's forehead. "Don't be long. I'm horny." And with that pronouncement, she left the kitchen, her two beasts trailing behind.

Mace gave the puppy a piece of salami from his sandwich. "You are so not helping me keep our relationship a secret."

Sissy didn't know when her favorite Smithtown bar had gotten a karaoke machine, but she never thought she'd see the day when a pair of male lions would stand on that stage singing Bon Jovi songs.

It had been Dee's idea to meet at the bar, and Sissy had jumped at it. Since Mitch had bopped Gil Warren on the back of the head, Sissy had been feeling really . . . strange. Mitch was still goofy . . . right? Still her buddy. Still her friend. And friend only.

Right?

Then why did she keep staring at him?

No, no. She was overthinking this. She probably only felt this way because Mitch had almost been killed right in front of her. That had to be it.

Because how could she be feeling anything else for a man singing his heart out on "Livin' on a Prayer"?

"I've never heard Brendon sing," Ronnie commented while sipping her beer. "And I think I'll be okay never hearing him again."

"Then don't hang out with the wild dogs. Apparently, Mitch is their star attraction at their monthly karaoke nights."

"Dogs singing." Dee curled her lip a bit in disgust.

Ronnie wiped condensation from her bottle. "So . . . Gil Warren."

Sissy picked up her beer. "I don't want to hear it."

"Can't believe he had the guts to come back here," Dee muttered.

"And brought that sister of his." Ronnie sneered. "I hate her. And I heard she hopes to make Gil Alpha."

Sissy snorted. "On what planet would that happen?"

"Having a strong female at his side would definitely help with that."

What insulted Sissy most was the way they were staring at her, like they expected her to have a breakdown or something.

"Do you really think I'm that pathetic?"

When they didn't answer, she slammed her beer bottle down. "I'm going to the bathroom."

"Sissy, wait. We didn't say—"

But she walked away before Ronnie could finish whatever the hell she had to say. She stopped by the bathroom and did what she had to do, but didn't feel like going back to the table yet since she still wanted to punch someone in the face. She went out the back door and into the alley instead. As the door closed, Sissy heard noises coming from the Dumpster. She walked around it and stopped to stare at the wolf half in and half out.

"Uncle Eggie!"

Her uncle stumbled back from the Dumpster, his amber-colored eyes wide.

"You know you're not supposed to be Dumpster divin'." If it wasn't for her aunt and Dee-Ann, her uncle would be living on the streets somewhere. "Now scoot on home"—she motioned him away with her hands—"before someone comes out here and sees you."

His gaze briefly swung back to the Dumpster—who knew what he may have seen in there that he wanted—before he ran off into the woods. Her aunt should be grateful. Sissy had just saved her from having one more thing brought into her house that Eggie promised he'd do something with and never did.

Sissy didn't know how the females of her family put up with the males. Seemed like a lot of work for very little pay-off.

She walked over to the Dumpster and looked inside. The radio. It had to be the radio. Her uncle probably thought he could fix it and sell it on eBay or something.

"Thinking about throwing yourself in?"

Sissy yelped at Mitch's voice. "Don't sneak up on me."

"I came out here to make sure you were okay. You were the one staring longingly into a trash bin."

"I was not, I was just—oh! Forget it." She turned and faced him. "What do you want anyway?"

"You wanna dance?"

Sissy frowned. "In the alley?"

He flicked her forehead with his finger.

"Ow."

"Not out here, buckethead."

"Buckethead?"

"Inside."

"Are they playing real music or more of that karaoke crap?"

"Why don't you admit I've been robbed of my musical career because society can't handle my innate sexuality?"

"Or I could admit that you're a nut job. But that would be redundant." She headed toward the door, Mitch behind her.

"Look at you, using big words like redundant."

While she opened the door with one hand, she swung at Mitch with the other. He caught it and laughed. "No sense of humor."

"Some would say."

She was nearly in the hallway when Mitch asked, "Who was that guy anyway?"

Sissy stopped and turned back around. She immediately knew who he meant. "That was Gil Warren."

"The old boyfriend?"

Sissy stepped back out into the alley, letting the door close behind her. "Yeah. The old boyfriend."

"You didn't tell me he still lived here."

"I didn't know. According to him, he's moved back and planning to stay." Sissy stuck her left hand in her shorts pocket since Mitch still held her right. "Why did you hit him with the ball?"

Mitch studied her hand, his thumb rubbing across her knuckles. "You looked annoyed that he was bothering you." He shrugged, his focus never leaving her hand. "And I didn't like him talking to you. I didn't want him looking at you. Basically, I hated him on sight."

Sissy swallowed. "I . . . uh . . . see."

He finally moved his gaze to her face. "You mad?"

"Not even a little." Then Sissy did what she'd been wanting to do for a long, long time. She went up on her toes and kissed Mitchell Shaw.

Nothing dramatic or movie worthy. She didn't shove her tongue down his throat or jump into his arms. She simply pressed her lips to his. Probably the sweetest, most chaste kiss she'd given to any man not a blood relative.

But if she didn't know better, she'd have thought she'd grabbed the man's dick from the response she got.

Suddenly, Mitch's hands were digging into her hair, his mouth hot against hers as he pushed her up against the door. His tongue slid into her mouth, swirled around hers. Tasting, exploring. And Sissy felt her body melt like it never had before.

Well that had been smooth. Yeah. Very nice, mauling Sissy in the back alley of a bar. But he'd never expected her to kiss him. He definitely had never expected to feel the explosion that came from what was nothing more than sweet, soft kiss. Probably no more than a "thank you" for handling that ex of hers. And here he was blowing it way out of proportion.

But she tasted so damn good and smelled even better. It wasn't really fair. He was only sorta human!

Pull back. You need to pull back.

In a minute. He'd definitely pull back in a minute. He promised himself.

Then Sissy wrapped her arms around his neck, pulling him closer. Her right leg wrapped around his, her bare foot sliding up and down his calf. Her tongue tangled with his, her fingers burrowing deep in his hair and holding him as she turned the tables and took his mouth with more passion than he'd experienced with anyone.

When she abruptly dragged her mouth away, Mitch didn't know what to do. Beg. He wasn't above begging. Especially when his cock was pretty much ordering him to beg.

Beg, damn you! Beg!

Then Sissy pulled her body away, but she grabbed hold of his shirt. "Come on." She stepped back, snatched the door open, and walked back into the club, dragging Mitch behind her. She stopped by the table where Ronnie sat on Bren's lap and Dee was nowhere to be seen.

Sissy swiped up the car keys and walked out, still dragging Mitch behind her.

To the day he died, Mitch would never forget the expression on his brother's face. Bren looked stunned and a little bit panicked to see Sissy dragging Mitch anywhere. It was kind of classic.

Ronnie yawned.

Once outside, Sissy shoved him toward the car. "Get in."

He knew by letting her drive, he was truly risking life and limb, but no one could get them back to the house faster, and he needed to be inside Sissy. He needed to feel what it was like to sink inside her and fuck her until they both couldn't see straight. He needed that more than anything.

Pete O'Farrell, Jr. walked out of the overpriced French restaurant and to his car, which they'd parked in the back alley. They always did this in case there was a reason to make a fast exit.

One of his guys, a slow-witted behemoth called Meat, should have been waiting for him. As soon as he realized Meat was nowhere to be seen, Pete headed back to the restaurant. But she stood in front of the door.

He'd heard about her. You couldn't grow up in his neighborhood and not. Roxy O'Neill. She was strange, they'd say. Strange and sexy and dangerous. But no one knew why. They just knew to avoid her and her sisters.

But he knew why she was here. To fight for the life of her son. Contrary to popular belief, Pete hadn't put the contract on that cop's head. Hell, that kid had done what no one else had been able to do . . . get rid of his old man. True, for a while it looked like the cop would be able to take some of the most important guys in the crew down, but a good lawyer—like him—could find all sorts of reasons to get charges dropped. One thing after another had made those charges go away over the last couple of years. You almost felt bad for the kid.

But the problem with Petey's charges was that the cop had witnessed it firsthand. Mitch Shaw had just happened to be at the wrong place at the right time and caught Petey O'Farrell cutting the throat of some little whore who'd made the mistake of threatening to go to Petey's third wife about their affair. It was a typical stupid Petey O'Farrell move, and the cop happened to see it. Maybe if it hadn't been a woman, the cop would have kept rolling undercover until he had more. But he'd lost it and nearly killed the old man. The guys had told Pete it was weird how Shaw had become . . . different. He was always so good natured and laid back whenever Pete had spoken to him, so no one saw it coming. But somehow, the cop had managed to calm down and had busted the old man right there, blowing his cover for good.

And for Pete, Jr. . . . life had turned beautiful.

"Hello, Peter."

"Miss O'Neill."

"I was hoping you'd have a few minutes to talk to me."

He smiled. Shrugged. "I don't know what to tell you. I've already had the cops at my firm, and I told them what I'm about to tell you . . . I didn't put a hit out on your son."

"And I believe that. And I know your father did."

"I couldn't tell you."

"Shhh." She waved her hand. "I'm not talking about that. I'm talking about what you think."

He shook his head. "I don't follow."

"If the hit went away, what would you do?"

"Are you asking me if I want your son dead?"

"I'm asking you what you'd risk to see him dead."

His smile returned. "Miss O'Neill—"

The loud bang cut off his words, and he turned. They'd dropped Meat onto the roof of his car, and then . . . *it* landed on him. It was big and gold and . . . bloody.

"I need you to answer my question, baby-boy. You see . . ."

And when Pete turned, there was another standing beside Roxy O'Neill, pushed up against her side, and then Pete heard this weird . . . grumble, and he saw two more at the far end of the alley. And two males at the mouth of the alley. He knew they were male because they had those big manes.

He could scream for help, but something told him they'd never give him the chance. He had a gun, but he knew he'd never reach it before they tore him apart.

It was late . . . no one was out.

And who would believe this?

". . . I need to know if your father is my only problem . . . or if you are too?"

Shaking his head as the males neared him, Pete stammered out, "No, ma'am. It's not me."

"That's good, baby-boy. That's good." Then her hand was around his throat, and those big, red gaudy nails she had suddenly felt different—thicker, harder, sharper—and dug into his skin. With no effort on her part, she hauled him back until he hit the car. Meat's head was right by Pete's. If the guy was breathing now, he wouldn't be for long.

The one standing on Meat leaned over, and blood and drool leaked onto Pete's forehead.

"You know me," Roxy said. "If nothing else, I know you've heard of me. And my boy means more to me than I could ever say. I'll deal with your father—and you get to take over without any problems—and you make sure when the time is right that they all back off my baby-boy. Understand?"

Pete swallowed and nodded his head.

"Good. Because no matter what you try to do to me . . . to my boy . . . there will be more of us from all over. And it will be you they come looking for. You understand that, right?"

He nodded.

"I want to hear the words."

"Yes. I understand."

"Good." She stepped away from him, and the rest of them all moved at once, slipping away into the darkness like they'd never been there. "I appreciate that we understand each other." Her hand moved away from his throat, and he blinked because he could have sworn he saw claws or . . . or . . . something before those big, red gaudy nails came back.

Then she was strutting down the alley, a simple gold purse hanging from her hand. "Good luck on taking over the business, Pete. I think you'll be great. You're definitely smarter than your old man ever was."

Then she was gone. And all that heavy French food came flying right back up.

Sissy pushed her car to its limits as she tore through Smithtown trying to get home and get Mitch into bed . . . or on the floor . . . or anywhere she could get him.

Once she made up her mind, Sissy didn't waffle. She didn't agonize over her decision. Or question if she was doing the right thing. Who had time for that? Plus, her body was making demands she needed to fulfill or die trying.

She slammed to a stop in front of her parents' house. Mitch unleashed his grip on the dashboard and relaxed back in the seat.

Sissy didn't know how long they were sitting there, but she finally turned in the seat to face him. "Is there a reason we're still sitting here?"

"Uh . . . I didn't want to rush you."

Sissy shoved his shoulder with both hands. "Out! Now!"

Laughing, Mitch got out on his side, and Sissy snatched the key from the ignition and quickly pushed the driver's side door open. Together, they headed up the porch steps. But when Sissy hit that top step, pain slammed through her foot, and she howled, immediately hopping on one leg while she grabbed her wounded foot.

"What's wrong?"

"*Splinters!*"

Mitch put his hands on his hips. "You're fucking with me right now, aren't you?"

Sissy leaned back against the porch rail and held her foot up to his face. "Splinters!" she yelled again.

"Damn. Those are splinters." Mitch gazed into her face. "Of course, if you insist on walking around barefoot—"

"No one in Smithtown wears shoes in the summertime."

"Is that a law?"

Sissy growled and started to hop into the house, but Mitch grabbed her under the knees and lifted her up. He only held her by her legs, though, and her head dangled dangerously close to the floor. She squealed, and Mitch gave her a shake.

"Stop the whining. You need to toughen up."

Without unleashing her fangs, Sissy bit the back of his leg.

"Do that again," he playfully warned, "and I'm dropping you on your head. Now simmer down."

Mitch took her into the family room and dropped her on

the couch in front of the TV. Sissy started to sit up, but Mitch pushed her back down by her forehead. She started swiping at him, and he batted at her hands while they kept their faces turned away from each other.

When he got bored with that, he said, "Lie down and be quiet. Mr. Kitty is going to make you feel all better."

Sissy stopped struggling. "That sounds creepy—and wrong."

Mitch grabbed a blanket from another chair and began to pull it over her body.

"It's ninety degrees outside. I don't need—"

The blanket covered her face, and Sissy growled. Then he tucked the blanket tightly into the couch cushions so Sissy was temporarily trapped. She had to kick and fight to get the damn blanket off her, and by then, Mitch was back with the first aid kit from the first floor bathroom.

She reached for her foot. "I can do this—"

"No." He slapped her hands away and lifted up her legs so he could sit on the couch. Then he dropped her legs back onto his lap.

"Okay. Let's see what we've got." He lifted up her foot and said, "Well, what we've got here is a freakin' boat."

"Really?" She slammed her heel against the side of his face, snapping his head to one side. "How big are they now, Mitch?"

Rubbing the abused side of his face, "Dainty little elf feet?"

"Exactly."

Sissy bit the inside of her mouth to stop from smiling. She didn't know what it was about him, but the boy did have a way. She'd never really thought of felines as goofy, but Mitch was definitely goofy.

"Is amputation out here? 'Cause we don't want it to get infected."

"Mitchell . . ."

"Okay. Okay. No need to get testy. It was just one of the many options." He pulled tweezers out of the kit and lifted her foot again, studying it closely. "It's in kind of deep, so this will probably not be real pleasant."

"Have you *met* my mother?" Sissy asked. "I put my arm through a window once, and that woman just yanked—*owwww!*"

"Done." Mitch held up the trio of splinters.

Glaring, Sissy reached for her foot again, and again he slapped her hands away. "Those hands are unclean."

"I washed them at the club. And is the iodine really necessary?" she demanded as he poured some on a cotton ball. "Isn't there something in there with pain reliever already included?"

"I'm sure there is." He slapped the iodine-doused cotton ball against her foot. "But I prefer this," he said over her yelp.

Once cleaned and wrapped in a small bandage, Mitch dropped her foot back on his lap. "There. All done. Now that wasn't so bad, was it?"

"Not if you're Dr. Mengele," she muttered.

"I hear that whining again."

Sissy let out a little growl before the pair fell silent, everything suddenly very awkward.

Mitch gave a small shrug. "Guess after all that, the mood's kinda broken, huh?"

"Are you saying that because you lost your hard-on or because you again don't want to rush me?"

They both glanced down at his crotch.

"So you're worrying about rushing me."

"I just want you to be sure."

Frustrated, Sissy sat up and quickly straddled his waist. She grabbed fistfuls of his T-shirt and yanked him up until their faces were mere inches apart.

"You know what I want, Mitchell?" And before he could answer, "To get laid. Preferably by you. If I weren't sure, we wouldn't be here. I wouldn't be on your lap with a wet, unfulfilled pussy, and you wouldn't have a healthy length of lead pipe in your pants. So stop being a tease, get your pants off, and give it up before I get testy."

Mitch gazed at her face. "I am *so* turned on right now."

Sissy leered at the cat, her ass rubbing against his denim-covered cock. "Well, all right then."

He thought after that speech, Sissy would jump him. She didn't. Instead, she stroked his cheeks, his neck, the whole time watching his face. Mitch truly liked Sissy. Liked the way she didn't shy away from anything or anyone. She knew what she wanted, and she went after it. Christ knew, he liked that in a woman.

Sitting on his lap, Sissy gazed down at him. She pushed his hair out of his face and said, "Lord, all this hair."

"Hey," he corrected, "this is not merely hair. This is my mighty tawny mane. It's a sign of my overwhelming manliness."

"More like your overwhelming bullshit."

He grinned. "That, too."

Sissy motioned him forward. "Sit up a bit."

He did, and Sissy grabbed the bottom of his T-shirt, lifting it over his head. She flung the blue T-shirt behind her and ran her hands down his chest.

"Lord, Mitch. You've filled in real nice since you've been eating all my—and the town's—food."

Mitch stroked his hand across Sissy's cheek. "Your fault. No one told you to cook so well."

"I'm just glad something has come out of feeding you." Her hands caressed his shoulders, his neck until they slid into his hair. She gripped handfuls, pulling his head back and leaning up so she could look him in the eye. "I can't wait to have you inside me."

Damn. Really, just . . . damn.

Mitch kissed Sissy, his tongue sliding inside her mouth, reveling in the delicious taste of her. His hands slid down her back until he could grip her ass cheeks, holding her tight until his need to see her naked took complete control. Grasping her T-shirt, Mitch tugged it over her head, tossing it on the floor behind her.

She wore a black bikini bathing top under her T-shirt, the strings hanging down past her shoulders. He wrapped one of the dangling ends around each forefinger and tugged until they pulled loose and separated at the back of her neck. He lowered his hands, the strings still on his fingers, and watched as the top followed.

Sissy, not remotely shy or insecure, kept her hands at her sides while he looked his fill. Her breasts were full but not huge, her light brown nipples already hard and eager. She had several faint scars across her chest and a more recent one near her collarbone. Mitch ran his finger across the scars, immediately noting Sissy's confused expression when he didn't go right for her breasts.

"What?"

Sissy grabbed his hands and slammed them against her breasts. "Get to work, hoss. I ain't got all day."

Mitch pulled his hands back. "Don't rush me. Until I'm done, these are my breasts to entertain myself with. You just sit there and enjoy basking in the sunshine of me."

Sissy was seconds from telling Mitch what he could do with his "basking" when he leaned forward and wrapped his mouth around her left breast. She gasped, shocked at the amount of pleasure that shot through her system. His mouth was hot and his tongue . . . talented.

Wrapping her hands around his head, her eyes tightly shut, she held him close against her. He sucked, hard, and Sissy's pussy clenched in time to the tugs.

She let out a low groan. "I can't wait any longer," she whispered.

He pulled back and pushed her off his lap. "Get the rest of your clothes off," he ordered before he jumped up and ran out of the room and up the stairs.

Assuming he'd return, Sissy kicked her shorts across the room and untied the back of her bikini top so she could finish taking it off.

By the time she dropped it to the floor, Mitch came charging down the stairs, tripping and sliding past the family room entryway, sliding back and into the family room. He slid to a stop in front of her, tossing a handful of condoms over his shoulder onto the couch.

"Where did those come from?"

"Your parents' stash—"

Sissy held her hand up. "I don't want another word."

"You're still not naked," he told her.

"You're never consistent. Either I'm going too slow or too fast."

"Whatever." Mitch pushed her back a bit and dropped to his knees in front of her. He took hold of her bikini bottoms and jerked them down her legs. "Step." She stepped out of them, and he flung them over his shoulder.

"Back in a minute," he said before burying his face against her pussy.

She laughed and gasped again as his tongue swiped against her already wet slit, his hands pushing her thighs apart so he could get in closer.

The legendary lion tongue. Used the way the Lord intended, it could remove flesh from bone. Used another way, it had Sissy squirming and not sure she could stay on her feet much longer.

She dug her fingers into Mitch's hair, hauling him closer, spreading her legs wider. Mitch's big hands slid up the back of her legs until they gripped her ass, kneading and squeezing her while his tongue continued to work her pussy.

Eyes sliding shut, Sissy felt the sensations wash over her. It had been a long time since she'd felt anything this good, anything that had the ability to make her feel like she could simply relax and let him do whatever he wanted . . .

Sissy's eyes snapped open, and she wrenched away from Mitch. What was she doing? She knew her rules . . . boundaries. There always had to be boundaries. But when he looked up at her with nothing but concern and her juices on that handsome face, she felt a little more panic dig in, and her boundaries began to slip away.

Unwilling to let it go, Sissy did what she always did so well. She took control.

"Up," she ordered, grabbing Mitch by the hair and lifting. He went with her and let her shove him back on the couch. Dropping to her knees in front of him, she reached for the button fly of his jeans. Once it opened, she gripped the worn denim and the soft cotton boxers underneath and pulled, grunting at him to raise his hips. He did, and she dragged the jeans down and off.

With him completely naked, Sissy gave herself a moment to stare at the perfection in front of her. All that power wrapped up in one golden package with a cock that could choke a rhino.

Placing her hands on his legs, Sissy started at the knees and slid her palms across the hard, muscular flesh. Raising herself up a bit, she leaned in, her lips grazing his inner thigh, followed by her tongue. She reached his cock, which had grown deliciously harder and thicker in the last few seconds.

Gently, she stroked her tongue against each vein and ridge, circling the head before tracing her steps back down. He growled low, and she knew she was pushing the cat. She didn't care. At this very moment, she had complete control of him and his cock—nothing could be sweeter.

Sissy wrapped her lips around the head of his cock, her tongue licking off the pre-cum while she sucked. Mitch hissed between his teeth, and Sissy took hold of his balls, squeezing at the same time she swallowed him whole.

Holyshitholyshitholyshitholyshitholyshitholyshit.

Other than that, Mitch was pretty much beyond basic thought. Sissy had wiped his mind clean. His ability to reason or plan or fuck with people's lives had been momentarily dissolved with the use of her wicked mouth.

Since it had been a while since he'd trusted a woman enough to have her in his bed, it wouldn't take much more to have him blow. But this wasn't any woman. This was "wicked smile" Sissy. He didn't realize until this moment how long he'd been fighting his attraction to her. How much he'd wanted her. And now he had her—and she was sucking his brain cells right out of his head.

Groaning, Mitch dug his hands into Sissy's hair and pulled her in close. He held her tight against him and let the power of a long overdue orgasm tear through him and straight into her mouth.

Sissy gripped his thighs, her mouth wrapped tight around his cock, swallowing and sucking the come from his body. He jerked three times before he finished coming and let out that sigh of utter relief and delight.

Panting, he dropped back against the couch. He let go of Sissy's hair, and she let go of his cock.

She relaxed back, her ass resting on her heels, her thumb wiping the corners of her mouth.

If she was pissed he'd come in her mouth without warning, she didn't show it. In fact, Sissy Mae looked pretty damn cocky at the moment. Not that she didn't have a right to be, but there was something else there. Something Mitch couldn't quite put his finger on.

She began to speak, and Mitch held up a finger. "Give me a minute," he said, cutting her off.

She shrugged and sat Indian style on the floor.

Mitch pushed his hands through his hair, the sweat keeping it off his face, and he continued to watch Sissy through half-closed lids.

It took him a good minute, but it suddenly occurred to him what that expression on her face was—control. She thought she had it.

He'd seen the same look on the faces of pimps they had absolutely no evidence against or murder suspects who believed they'd successfully hidden the body somewhere.

True, the level of blow job he'd just received probably did make most men her slave until she'd gotten bored with them.

He knew her logic, too. If she kept control of him, she could keep control of herself. She'd be wild enough in bed to keep it interesting and him coming back for more, but her heart would never truly be in it. *She'd* never truly be in it. And why the hell would he want that? He could get meaningless fucks from anybody. He could definitely get them from females who were a hell of a lot less dangerous to his mental health than Sissy Mae Smith.

No, no. That wouldn't work for him. Even if this thing lasted only until the sun came up, he wanted all of her in those few hours. And he'd have all of her, too.

Mitch sat up, his elbows resting against his knees, and then he simply stared at her. Stared at her until her smug smile faded and she began to look a little nervous. Ahh. The wonderful benefits of being a cop.

"What?" she finally asked, her legs rising up until her

knees rested together and her arms wrapped around her calves. In one move, she'd completely blocked herself off from him.

"You wet?"

Sissy snorted. "Most of the time."

Christ, what a match. They had to be two of the horniest people on the planet. When motivated, Mitch could literally go all night. But whatever bullshit women might say to their friends, they were not always down with that.

Yet he had a distinct feeling Sissy was the one female who could actually keep up with him. But he didn't want her spending the whole time trying to figure out how to control him. She could control those dogs who sniffed around her, but he wasn't some dog.

Mitch stood and motioned to her with his hand. "Get up."

Smiling, she slowly rose to her feet. She felt confident again, in control because he was hard again and she knew without a doubt he wanted her. He could see it on her face, in the way she moved.

"What?" she asked softly, now at her full six feet.

Using only the tips of his fingers, he stroked her face, her cheeks. Sissy's eyes started to close, but she shook her head and went to step back. To move away from him.

Mitch slid one hand behind her neck, holding her in place with a loose grip while he moved in closer, until he could feel her skin against his. Like the predators they were, Mitch and Sissy stared at each other, trying to figure out who was stronger, more powerful.

Then they both smiled because at the moment, none of that mattered.

He kissed her hard, his one hand remaining on the back of her neck, the other sliding around her waist and down until he could grip her ass. *He really does have a thing about my ass.* He pulled her in tight, and Sissy could feel his hard cock digging into her belly, and she couldn't wait anymore.

Sissy wrapped her arms around Mitch's neck and brought her legs up and around his waist. Deliciously big hands gripped her ass, squeezing and releasing, while his mouth plundered hers.

Mitch, who always seemed so removed from everything—a true nomad lion without a Pride—made her feel like he was right there with her. She couldn't believe what an aphrodisiac it was.

For both of them, apparently.

Sitting on the couch, Sissy still in his arms, Mitch kept a tight hold on her with one hand while blindly searching the couch for a condom. Sissy stroked his shoulders, his back. Their kiss a neverending thing until Mitch turned, pushed her to the couch, and crouched in front of her. He gripped her hips, lifting them up and pulling her to the edge of the couch. Sissy braced her hands, palms flat, against the couch cushion behind her. She watched Mitch don a condom before he placed his cock against her wet slit.

But then he didn't move. Drenched, horny, and anxious, Sissy had run out of patience hours ago. Determined, she grabbed Mitch by the hair and yanked hard.

The smile he gave her was deadly while he pulled her down and shoved forward, his cock pounding into her with one awesome thrust.

Head falling back, Sissy let out a gasp of pure pleasure. Even better was the way Mitch held still for a good minute, his cock throbbing inside her. He was large, filling her completely and then a little more. There was pain . . . and she loved it.

"Look at me."

Sissy raised her head at the order. His fangs were out, his eyes like a big cat's. Then she realized her fangs were out, too, her eyes probably shifted to wolf. Even more, she'd unleashed her claws, and she was currently ripping into her momma's favorite couch.

She didn't care. She'd buy the bitch a new couch. Later. Much later.

One side of Mitch's mouth lifted, and Sissy marveled at the enormous size of Mitch's fangs. True, she'd seen his fangs before but never when they were both naked and fucking. She should be freaked out. She wasn't. She was so turned on she could barely think straight.

"Fuck me," she ordered, unable to stand another second of this. "Fuck. Me."

Her voice had dropped several octaves. Mitch answered by placing his knees on the couch and sitting up straight. He drew his hips back, dragging his cock from her, and with his eyes on her face, slammed back home.

Sissy snarled again, the complete unleashing of the She-wolf in her an absolute joy while Mitch fucked her hard. He didn't hold back; she didn't want him to. Their eyes stayed locked as Sissy destroyed her mother's couch and Mitch held on to her like his very life depended on it.

When her entire body began to shake, Sissy began to worry. Her orgasms had always been straightforward and simple. It hit, she'd gasp a few times, squirm, let out a sigh, and smile. She was happy, the guy was happy, and all was right with the world.

But this . . . this was turning into something out of control and dangerous. Her body was on fire, sweat poured from her, her moans had turned into short staccato screams, and she couldn't stop the goddamn shaking. And the whole time, Mitch just kept watching her.

That's what did it, too. The look on his face, the hunger in his eyes. He slammed into her one too many times, and Sissy flew over that edge, her entire body locking up as she . . . as she . . .

The scream he tore from her wasn't remotely human, and she was thankful no one lived too close to the house because the sheriff would have been called, and wouldn't that have been embarrassing.

Mitch answered her scream with a roar of his own. He roared, he shook and came. When he was done, he muttered curses before he fell on top of her, shoving her down onto the couch.

Their sweat-drenched bodies stayed locked until their heavy breathing relaxed and their heart rates returned to normal.

Eventually, Mitch levered himself off her and slid down to the floor, his back against the couch. Uncomfortable on the now torn-up cushion, Sissy sat down next to him.

For several long minutes, they said nothing. Instead, Sissy stared across the room, and Mitch took off his condom and wiped off using the tissues in the box on the side table, disposing of it all in the trash next to the couch.

Sissy knew she'd definitely have to take out the trash before they left and her parents returned, or she'd be hearing about it until the end of time.

Finally, after what felt like hours but was really only ten or so minutes, Mitch spoke.

"This is your fault," he said.

Chapter 14

Sissy leaned forward, her arms resting on her raised knees, and glared at him. "*My* fault? How is this my fault?"

Mitch pushed his wet hair off his face, not sure he'd ever recover from that orgasm. "It just is, and we both know it."

Letting out a deep breath, Sissy nodded. "I see." She stroked one finger across the black Celtic tattoo taking up his left bicep. "I like this."

"Thanks," he muttered absently, wondering what he was going to do next.

"It makes doing this so precise." Then that misleadingly small fist slammed into the spot covered by the tattoo.

"*Ow! What the hell was that for?*"

"Do you think I'm happy about this?" she demanded, getting to her feet. "And this is *your* fault. *Yours!*"

Mitch stood. "How is this my fault? I'm not the one with the pussy that drains the life from a man!"

"And I'm not the one hung like an overendowed donkey!"

Holding his hand up, Mitch asked, "Wait—what are we arguing about?"

She was quiet for a moment and then snapped her fingers. "Feeling trapped."

"We are? I don't know. Your damn breasts are mesmerizing me," he finished on a mumble.

"I can't believe you're hard again," she sighed in what sounded like awe.

"It's a lion thing. To be really blunt, I can go for hours."

Panting, Sissy's hand rested on her stomach, and she abruptly moved toward him. Automatically, instinctively, he moved toward her. They were nearly in each other's arms, when they both stopped and turned away.

"We need rules," she said, echoing what was in his mind.

"Rules. Yeah, I like rules."

"Well, you are a cop."

"You're gonna bring that up now?"

"Don't get snippy with me." She paced away from him. "Clear lines. Boundaries. I'm all about the boundaries." And to show how much she liked boundaries, she drew a little square in the air with her forefingers.

"Right. Boundaries."

"There'll be no love talk."

"You mean, like dirty? Like when I tell you where to put your mouth or how I want to stick my fingers—"

"*No.*" She eyed him. "But I'm sensing I won't have to worry about the love talk."

Mitch shrugged, still not clear on what she meant. "What else?"

Rubbing her hands together, Sissy continued to pace, but every time she walked away, all Mitch could do was stare at her ass. The damn thing was talking to him again!

"Outside of fucking, no signs of affection like unnecessary, non-fucking related touching. And we won't go on dates. You won't bring me flowers."

"Or chocolates?"

"Let's not be unreasonable." She walked to the door and

walked back. "We will keep this simple and uncomplicated. No matter how amazing the sex is, it never will be more than that." Standing in front of him now, she placed her hands on her hips. "And do you know why, Mitchell?"

"Why what?"

With a sigh and a dramatic roll of her eyes, she snapped, "Why this needs to remain simple and uncomplicated?"

"I'm sure I do, but at the moment, I am so horny I can barely manage this sentence."

Sissy gripped his face between her hands. "Because you, Mitchell, need a simple uncomplicated woman. Preferably full-human. And I need a male I can control so he won't get in my way. So no matter what happens, we can't let this get out of hand. Understand?"

And she was right. Sissy was the kind of woman who could get him all tangled up, and he'd never get out. She was sexy and demanding and unpredictable and severely unstable. If she wasn't starting shit, she was in the middle of it. She was beautiful and dangerous. A predator's predator.

But even worse, even more devastating, he was leaving. Not simply leaving Smithtown but leaving everyone he knew and cared about, including Sissy. Once he testified, his whole life would change, and Sissy would be nothing more than a sweetly weird memory. So he needed to follow her rules and stay in her boundaries.

Yet Mitch was smart enough to know that none of that logic would matter. Because if he wasn't really careful, he'd lose his heart to this woman and probably regret it for the rest of his life.

"No letting it get out of hand," he repeated back to her.

"You agree?"

"Yeah."

"Good." She walked away again. After a few moments, "You're staring at my ass, aren't you?"

Mitch threw his hands up. "Tongues!"

She turned and faced him, her hands again on her hips. "This isn't going to work if you can't get control, Mitchell Shaw."

"Don't tell me." He pointed at his cock. "Tell him."

Sissy shook her head. "I start talking to it . . . it's going in my mouth."

"See? *You're not helping!*"

She held her hands up. "Sorry. Sorry."

Clearing her throat, Sissy walked up to him. She kept her hands down at her sides and her eyes focused on his Adam's apple. "Would you like to partake of sexual intercourse again?"

Mitch frowned. "What the hell are you doing?"

She stomped her foot. "I'm trying to keep this unemotional, dumb ass. Now work with me."

"Okay. Okay." Now he cleared his throat. "Yes. I'd be quite pleased to partake of sexual intercourse with you . . . again."

Sissy nodded and took a step closer. Her breasts grazed against his chest, and Mitch fought back a shudder of pure pleasure. Leaning down, he kissed her on the mouth. She kissed him back, her mouth closed, her eyes open. That seemed safe enough. So Mitch stroked his hand down her back and rested it on her ass. He didn't squeeze or anything, no matter how desperately he wanted to.

Her ass was made for squeezing.

But then suddenly, Sissy snarled, "Bastard," and dug her hands into his hair, and her mouth was on his. She lifted up her legs until they wrapped around his waist.

Mitch swiped another condom off the couch. He'd planned to head up the stairs, but he really couldn't be bothered, so he slammed Sissy against the wall.

Concentrating on her neck, his mouth sucking against the soft skin while he slid on the condom, Sissy gasped and writhed against him. "Fuck me, Mitch. God, fuck me."

He slammed into her so hard, Sissy's head banged into the wall.

"Sorry," he muttered.

"Yeah, yeah," she growled, her forehead against his shoulder. "Whatever. Just fuck me."

Mitch pulled out and slammed back in, the sound of Sissy's gasps and yelps against his ear. He picked up the pace, Sissy egging him on by digging her heels into his spine, her fingers into his shoulders.

"Harder," she begged. Actually, it was more of an order. And Mitch didn't care. There were times in a man's life when he just needed to do what he was told. Especially when the woman telling him was milking him dry and taking him on the ride of his life.

But when Sissy came and her claws unleashed, tearing into his back, and Mitch roared out her name, he knew they were in the biggest trouble of their lives.

Chapter 15

They never even made it out of the living room. They'd tried. Several times. But they always ended up doing it on the furniture or the stairs or the floor.

Man, she'd have a lot of cleaning up to do before her parents got home. Her father probably wouldn't notice, but her mother . . . shit.

Sissy struggled to roll over since Mitch's arm was across her back and it was damn heavy. By the time she rolled to her back, she looked up to see Ronnie and Dee on the other side of the picture window by the door. Ronnie was busy writing "whore" on the glass with her finger before the pair doubled over laughing.

Idiots.

Sissy tried to fling Mitch's arm off, but it wasn't moving. "Hey." Nothing. "*Hey!*"

Mitch's head snapped up. "Huh? What?"

"Move."

He blinked those gold eyes at her, and she felt an answering tug in her pussy. See? This would never do!

"I'm not getting any morning nookie?" he asked.

"No. Move."

"You're cranky," he complained as he moved his arm, slipping his hand under his cheek and closing his eyes.

He was right, which annoyed her more. She wasn't normally cranky in the mornings unless she'd done some serious drinking the night before. So she mumbled, "Sorry." And got to her feet.

Grabbing the blanket off the floor and wrapping it around her body, she went to the front door and stepped out onto the porch. "What's up?"

"Wanna go down to Parson's Lake?" Parson's Lake wasn't attached to the lake Ralph lived in, so it had become the summer hot spot around Smithtown.

"Yeah. Sure. Give me ten minutes."

Ronnie glanced inside and raised her eyebrows. "Maybe twenty would be better?"

"Don't start."

Dee's gaze on Mitch was unflinching when she finally said, "Lord, he's hung like a stallion."

Laughing, Ronnie walked toward the car, Dee behind her, and Sissy slammed the door.

Mitch grinned. "Like a stallion, eh?"

"Don't start," she repeated and headed up the stairs.

Once in the bathroom, she turned on the shower and dropped the blanket. She looked at herself and winced a bit. She had bruises on her back, hips, ass, and shoulders. Shoulders? Then she remembered Mitch holding her by her ankles and . . . forget it. If she started thinking about any of that, she'd never get out of here.

"Are you pissed at me or something?"

Mitch stood in the doorway, rubbing his left eye with his fist and watching her with his right.

"No," she answered honestly. "I'm not pissed at you. Just hope we didn't do something stupid."

"What do you mean? Like when I had you by your ankles, and I—"

"No," she desperately cut him off. "Not that specifically. All of it."

"We have boundaries, don't we?" And he drew the little square with his fingers. "Remember? You made me swear."

Yeah, she had. But now she didn't know if she could keep her own promise. Or even if she wanted to. And that only made her feel ridiculously weak.

"Right. I remember."

Mitch walked up behind her and put his arms around her waist, his nose nuzzling the side of her neck. "Let's not worry about any of that for now, okay? Let's just enjoy what we've got going at the moment."

"Yeah. Okay."

His lips grazed her neck, and Sissy's eyes crossed.

"Mitch, I've gotta go."

"They went to get food and drinks. Ronnie says I've got at least half an hour before they get back. And we both need to shower."

Without another word, Mitch picked her up and carried her to the shower, seeming to enjoy—and ignore—Sissy's squeal of protest.

Mitch slammed the pillow over his sleeping brother's face and then pressed it down using the weight of his body. Bren's arms flailed wildly, and Mitch laughed like a mental patient until his brother pushed his hands against Mitch's chest and shoved.

Landing in a chair halfway across the room, Mitch only had a second to take a breath before his older brother was out of bed and coming after him.

"Shit." Mitch took off, making it downstairs and through the hall. But he never did make it through the front door before his brother grabbed him by the hair, yanked him back, and then slammed him forward into the wall.

When his ears finally stopped ringing, Brendon had him pinned to the ground, his big, fat face hovering over Mitch's.

Mitch heard his brother make that distinctive sound. "Don't you dare spit on—*you motherfucker!*"

Ronnie Lee sat up, lowering her sunglasses to the tip of her nose. "Please tell me you didn't give him the boundaries speech."

"Of course I did."

"Make that stupid square with your hands, too?" Dee grumbled, searching through the cooler for God knew what.

"The visual helps. You know men are more visual than women."

Ronnie pushed her sunglasses back up her nose and stretched back out on the lounge chair. "Why do I bother with you?"

"Because I'm one of the few people who tolerates your bullshit."

"Good point." Ronnie readjusted her bikini bottoms. She never knew how to just settle and relax. She constantly fidgeted. It drove Sissy nuts sometimes. "I guess he agreed."

"Of course he did."

Dee, who burned pretty easily in the sun, slathered on more sunscreen. "What do you mean, 'of course'?"

"Because he knows a little of me is better than none at all."

"Not really an insecure gal, are you, Sissy Mae?"

Sissy thought a moment before shaking her head. "Nah."

"Is it my imagination," Ronnie cut in, "or is Mitch getting bigger?" When Sissy raised an eyebrow and Dee stared, Ronnie quickly shook her head. "I don't mean that! I mean in general."

"The way he's been eating, he *should* be getting bigger."

Dee tugged down her baseball hat to shield her face. "He'll keep Gil away."

Sissy's eye twitched. "Are we back here again?"

"Who can forget their first?"

Sissy sighed at Ronnie's wistful tone. Since she'd fallen for Brendon Shaw, Ronnie Lee had shown a girly side to her personality Sissy was none too fond of.

"You did," she countered.

"I didn't forget him. It was Greg."

Dee shook her head. "No, it wasn't."

"It was too."

Sissy sat up, readjusting her bikini top. "No. Greg 'oh God, please make me' Tremble was your first orgasm. Larry Crenshaw was your first lay. He, however, did not get you off. Thereby, he was quickly forgotten."

"I remember my first," Dee added for no apparent reason. "I yakked all over him and his backseat."

"And I remember my first because you heifers won't let me forget him."

"You know what really worries me?" Ronnie chewed her lip for a bit. "I worry about what he's going to do. You don't seem to grasp your true value to the power-hungry wolf."

"What are you talking about?"

"Remember all those rumors about your momma and daddy's mating?"

"Yeah. But it's all bullshit."

"But Gil is too stupid to know that."

"You think he'll try and force a mating?"

"I wouldn't put anything past him. Of course, I've never trusted or liked him."

Sissy hadn't thought about that. Forced matings were rare with most of the wolves, but Smiths were known to do them from time to time. In fact, there were tales of Smith wolves who'd died trying to force a mating on a strong female. And most wolves wouldn't try it with Sissy, but if Gil was desperate enough . . .

"I'll watch my back."

"Good. That's all I want," Ronnie said, pulling a beer out of the cooler. "That wasn't so hard now, was it?"

"You and Sissy kind of shot out of the bar last night. Everything . . . okay?"

"You mean, did we fuck like horny wildebeests last night?"

"A simple 'everything went fine' would have been sufficient, ya know."

"Yeah, but not nearly as fun, bruh."

The brothers stood next to each other, staring into the open refrigerator.

"Do you feel like cooking?" Mitch asked.

"Not really. You?"

"Nope."

"Cereal," they said together and moved to the next cabinet, pulling down all the boxes and placing them on the breakfast table.

Brendon got bowls and spoons while Mitch retrieved the milk. For thirty minutes, they ate all the cereal the Reeds had in their cupboards and finished all the milk they had in their two refrigerators.

"So you guys had a good time, I'm guessing."

"Yeah. But we have definite boundaries." And Mitch drew the little square with his fingers.

Bren blinked. "What the hell was that?"

"Her boundaries. She likes visuals."

Brendon shrugged. "Whatever. How was it for you?"

Mitch winced. "Well, you know, Sissy is a really good friend, but I've gotta be honest here"—he leaned in closer, and his brother did the same—"that woman nearly fucked me blind."

"I'm so glad I leaned in for that information."

"Sucker."

"You think you might get serious with her? Which I find disturbing and freakish all at the same time."

"I don't know. This can't be permanent, Bren. Even if I wanted it to be."

"You don't think Sissy would move to Ohio for you?"

"Even if she would, I could never ask her. The woman is a Pack animal. I'm really glad Ronnie's here because Sissy does not do well on her own."

"So you'd never take her away from her Pack."

"Would you? With Ronnie?"

Bren shook his head. "No, I wouldn't. No matter how many times I find them lurking around our apartment or waking us up in the middle of the morning to find out if there's anything good in our fridge."

"See? You get it. I've gotta abide by Sissy's boundaries no matter how hard it's going to be." And it was going to be so hard. He already knew that.

Mitch stared at the empty boxes and milk cartons littering the table. "Bruh . . . I'm still hungry."

"I'm starving."

"Fresh or cooked?"

"Wanna give fresh a try?"

Mitch stood and walked out of the kitchen and onto the porch. Several deer grazed no more than fifty feet away.

Grinning, "Bruh . . . family meal at twelve o'clock!"

"Sissy Mae Smith, as I live and breathe."

Sissy stared up at the larger woman, her face purposely blank. "Uh . . . hi . . . uh . . . Brenda!"

"Bertha," Ronnie hissed around her turkey sandwich.

"Right. Bertha. Sorry."

Bertha rested her hands on her hips. "You just saw me last Thanksgiving."

Sissy gave her a big smile and a perky, "Okay."

"And I used to hang around you every day in high school, junior high, and grade school."

"Uh-huh."

Bertha flashed a fang. "You don't know who the hell I am, do you?"

"Of course I do! You're Brenda—"

"Bertha!" Ronnie hissed again.

"Whatever."

The She-wolf snarled and marched back over to her friends.

"You are unbelievable."

Sissy had to keep her head down so they couldn't see her laughing. "I do it every time. She has got to be the dumbest canine on the planet."

"You need to leave her alone."

"But as an old friend, shouldn't I tell her about Bobby Ray's wedding?" The hate-hate relationship between Bertha and Jessie Ann Ward-Smith had been legendary. And long after Sissy had lost interest in torturing the little wild dog, Bertha simply wouldn't back off. And that was for one reason and one reason only—Bertha's thing for Bobby Ray.

"Sissy Mae . . ."

"How beautiful the bride looked?"

"Stop it."

"How happy the groom is?"

"You're never letting it go, huh?"

"You mean when she sucker punched me in eighth grade? That's ridiculous."

Before they could stop her, Sissy jumped to her feet and headed over to Bertha and her friends.

"You're going to hell," Ronnie reminded her for the millionth time.

Travis walked into his parents' house and scented the air. No one around, but the whole damn house stank of cat and sex.

Damn. That girl simply couldn't keep her legs closed. And the cat had a usefulness most of his kind didn't have. A usefulness that Travis would be damned before seeing Sissy ruin it by messing with the man's mind like she'd been doing to every male in a three-hundred-mile radius of Smithtown since the day she could walk.

He didn't hate his sister. Not like she believed he did. But Travis didn't like her. She never would acknowledge him as the strongest of her brothers, and she did that because she knew it bugged Travis. She liked bugging him. She liked causing shit. She lived for it. And if she left town and never came back, Travis wouldn't shed a tear. He had daughters and female cousins, so he didn't see much use for a sister.

He'd have to watch her closely. She could use the cat to her advantage, and Travis wouldn't let her get any advantage in this town. He couldn't afford to.

Travis left the team's playbook on his parents' kitchen table with a note telling Mitch to review it for that night's practice. When he walked back outside, Donnie was running out of the woods and motioning to him.

"You need to see this."

With a sigh of annoyance—of course, almost everything annoyed him—Travis followed after his brother. As they walked out of the woods beside the lake on his parents' territory, Travis stopped in his tracks.

"Holy shit."

"I know."

They watched as the Shaw brothers played tug of war with a crocodile over what Travis would guess was a nine-point buck. The buck was still kicking, too, but that didn't stop the brothers or the croc.

"I'm sensing the crazy gene, hoss," Donnie mumbled.

"Ya think?"

Slowly, the Smith brothers backed up into the woods. They moved silently, hoping neither the croc nor the lions noticed them. When they got to their car, they didn't say another word until they made it back to the garage.

The sobbing had been the best part. Not Bertha. She didn't cry after Sissy went on and on about the beautiful Smith–Ward wedding. As always, Bertha handled her pain with violence. But that poor little Omega she'd lit into had only been walking by. Then, that Omega's sister had gone after Bertha, which led to an enthralling fistfight. Sissy simply didn't see good ones these days. But the sobbing . . . well, that came when a male tried to break it up and got punched in the face for his trouble.

That had been the *best*.

Still, all that faded into the background as two blood-covered lions came running up. One had half a deer in its mouth; the other was trying to get it.

"I bet they were fighting with Ralph again."

Ronnie looked at her. "Why would you say that?"

"Because they wouldn't fight over half a deer. Mitch would have one half, and Bren would have the other. They'd both be happy."

"I see." Ronnie smirked. "What are you going to do when you find out you're falling for Mitch?"

"Pop you in the mouth."

With a nod, "Good to know."

Brendon had the deer, and Mitch took him down, the pair fighting over that carcass like two pitbulls over a tennis ball. The rest of the wolves sunning themselves watched in silence while Sissy and Ronnie discussed dinner plans after football practice. When the brothers went up on their hind legs and tore into each other's mane-covered necks, Ronnie asked Sissy, "Where did Dee go?"

"You know Dee. She's the ghost. Disappears whenever the mood strikes her fancy. She's good, too. Even I don't notice."

The brothers must have worn themselves out because they both crashed on either side of Sissy and Ronnie, panting, covered in blood, and appearing quite happy.

"You know except for Mitch almost getting blown away, this has been the nicest little vacation." When everyone gaped at her, Ronnie reiterated, "I said, '*except* for Mitch almost getting blown away.'"

"True. She did qualify."

Mitch rubbed his mane against Sissy's leg, and she stared at him in disgust. "You're getting blood all over me."

That's when he put his whole face into the act.

Sissy sighed. "Why do I bother?"

Football practice seemed to be going really well, except all the players kept staring at him and Brendon, and Mitch had no idea why. True, he was a fascinating specimen of male perfection, but it was starting to weird him out.

Mitch walked off the field and up to Sissy. She held out her water bottle, and he gratefully drank from it. It was a hazy, hot day, and he was simply covered in sweat. Still, he liked the way Sissy kept eyeing him.

"Your brothers keep staring at me and Bren. Think they went gay overnight?"

"I could only hope. It would make them much more interesting. But I think they saw you tussling with Ralph."

"It wasn't a tussle. He wouldn't give up that buck, and Bren and I took him down. He was ours."

"Darlin', I think you keep forgetting that you're supposed to be smarter than the croc 'cause you're only lion half the time."

"I don't know what you mean."

"Of course you don't." Sissy stood, and Mitch smiled when he noticed she'd put on another pair of shorts. Even better, though, she only wore her bikini top, and the shorts over the bikini bottoms. It was sexy as hell.

She took the empty bottle back and with her voice low, said, "Meet me in the visiting team's bathroom in three minutes."

Then she sauntered off.

Mitch cleared his throat and glanced around. The team had taken a break, heading off to get sports drinks and water from the coolers on the sidelines.

"Go behind the bleachers and around," Ronnie said, her eyes never turning away from the field. She raised her hand to wave at Brendon.

"I guess this isn't the first time you two have done this before, right?"

Ronnie looked up and winked at him. "You are so cute, Mitch Shaw."

He chuckled and walked off behind the bleachers and around the far end of the field.

Mitch walked into the ladies' bathroom and glanced under the stalls, looking for good-sized feet in flip-flops. Apparently the bathroom was the one place Sissy wouldn't or couldn't go to without something on her feet. He found himself kind of grateful for that.

"Sissy?"

"Lurking in the girls' bathroom again, huh?"

He turned around, and she closed the door, locking it.

"Just seeing where you went off to."

"Really? Sure you weren't hoping to find me with my panties around my ankles . . . all vulnerable and defenseless?" Mitch laughed. Sissy hadn't been defenseless a day in her life.

"And if I had?" He stepped toward her, smiling. "What would you have done?"

Sissy backed up against the door. "Nothing." She raised her hands, palms out. "I would have been helpless. You could take complete advantage of me."

"I could." Barely an inch separated them, and Mitch cupped her cheek, holding her in place. "And I would, too."

"I knew it," she whispered, her gaze focused on his mouth. "You have dirty bad boy written all over you."

Mitch's grip tightened, and he groaned, taking her mouth with his. Plunging his tongue inside, taking what he wanted. Sissy's hands gripped his sweatpants, struggling to push them out of her way. Mitch stepped back and quickly untied the cord holding them up. Watching him, Sissy pushed her shorts and bikini bottoms down. She'd already pulled a condom out of her shorts pocket and had it clamped between her lips until her shorts hit the floor. Then she tore the packet open, and as soon as Mitch's sweatpants were far enough down, she slid the condom on his cock. It was already so hard it hurt, and Mitch immediately reached for her.

He hiked her up, her back tight against the door, and pulled one leg around his waist. With one swift move, he pushed inside her, forcing her hard against the door. Sissy let out a yelp, but her grip tightened on his shoulder and scalp, urging him on.

Mitch gave himself several moments to simply enjoy being inside her, having her pussy tighten around his cock, squeezing the life from it.

The heel of Sissy's foot dug into his lower back, and she nipped the side of his neck. The woman had a way of telling him exactly what she wanted without saying a word. Mitch pulled his hips back and slammed forward. Again and again, he pushed into her, only to stop and grind his hips against her until Sissy moaned and gasped against his ear, her fingers digging into him. When he had her crazy, he thrust up, riding her hard until she came, burying her face against his neck and shuddering out her climax.

That's when he let go, exploding inside her, his hands gripping her rib cage so tight he feared he'd crush it.

They held on to each other, their harsh breaths easing into general panting. That's when they heard a knock at the door.

"Uh . . . Sissy?" It was Ronnie.

Sissy lifted her face, light brown eyes blinking open. "Yeah?"

"Break is over, and they're looking for Mitch."

"He'll be right out."

"Okay."

Mitch knew Ronnie had walked away even though he never heard a sound.

"You all right?" he asked when Sissy closed her eyes and rested her head against the door.

She smiled. One of her wicked smiles. "Darlin', I am just fine." She let out a satisfied sigh, and Mitch couldn't help but feel pretty good about being the one to make her so relaxed. "You better get outside, though. Before my brother whines like the big-headed baby he is."

Sissy brought her legs down and pushed Mitch back. It

took him a second to realize he hadn't wanted to step back. He'd been damn comfortable with his cock still snug inside her and his arms wrapped around her.

"I swear," she said as she headed to the stalls, "I can't wait to get you home tonight. I'm gonna fuck you raw."

"You don't make it easy to focus when you say shit like that."

"Yeah," she giggled before closing the stall door, "I know."

Sissy stepped outside, her clothes all back in place. She couldn't do anything with her shaggy hair. From what she'd heard over the years, her haircuts always made it seem like she'd just gotten laid.

Ronnie waited for her, leaning back against the brick wall, one foot raised and braced against it. "Lord, you two."

Sissy grinned. "What can I say? The boy works me."

"Yeah, I could tell."

The friends walked back to the bleachers, moving around the field since practice had already resumed. "Am I going to have to pick up the pieces of his broken heart when this is all over?"

"Doubt it."

"You say that, but I don't know . . ."

They both looked over at Mitch out in the middle of the field. He seemed to know Sissy was looking at him, and his gaze found hers. He smiled—and that's when the football slammed into the side of his head. They watched him fly off his feet and hit the ground.

Sissy winced. "Oops."

"You're distracting him. And you're gonna hear about it."

As if on cue, Travis jogged over to them. "What did you do to the cat?"

Sissy opened her mouth to speak, and Ronnie cut in before the words could come out.

"Sissy Mae."

Sissy closed her mouth.

"You promised he'd play," Travis uselessly reminded her.

"And he is playing."

"Play *well*, Sissy Mae. Ten minutes with you, and he's . . ."

They looked over to watch Mitch get blindsided by one of the team's slower players.

Sissy tossed her hair back and headed toward the bleachers. "Your point is taken."

Chapter 16

Mitch pulled out of Sissy and rose up onto his knees. He flipped her onto her stomach and yanked her back by her hips, driving into her with such force she cried out and laughed at the same time.

She gripped the headboard, pushing back as he fucked her, demanding he give her more. The woman was a demon in bed. To be blunt, she fucked like a man. She took what she wanted, and if you could keep up, great. If you couldn't, she'd leave your ass behind in a New York minute.

Fortunately for Mitch, he could easily keep up with her. He hadn't realized until this moment that he'd been looking for a lover like Sissy for years. Someone who could match him every step of the way.

After practice, they'd headed out to dinner with Ronnie and Bren. It had been surprisingly fun, he and Bren getting along better than they ever had. But every once in a while, Mitch would catch Sissy looking at him, and he knew she was thinking the same thing he was . . .

When I get your ass home . . .

They didn't even make it out of the car before they started going at each other. Once they did get out of the car and into

the house, they didn't make it past the family room—that
poor family room. It had seen much fucking over the last
couple of days. This time, Mitch slammed Sissy to the floor
and took her there. He couldn't help himself. She was such a
vicious little cock tease—he loved it.

That was four hours ago, and except for brief breaks between bouts, neither seemed ready to head off to sleep for
the night.

Mitch leaned over Sissy, their bodies slick with sweat,
and grabbed her hair. He pulled her head to the side and
kissed her neck, her shoulder. Then he pulled her head
straight back and kissed her mouth, their tongues sparring
and teasing.

He'd never met a woman who liked as rough a ride as
Sissy did. At least not one who didn't need a lot of leather
and latex involved. Mitch had never had the patience for
knots and complicated scenarios involving chains. He wasn't
averse to pulling out his handcuffs, but he was a simple
Philly boy. And what he liked was hard, sweaty, naked fucking.

Sissy did, too. But she didn't just receive. His vicious
She-wolf knew how to take. Even now, she pulled back her
right hand and gripped Mitch by the hair. She yanked hard
and demanded, "Make me come."

Mitch grinned and placing his hand flat against her back,
pushed her down. She rested her cheek against the pillow
and gripped the edge of the mattress with both hands. Sitting
up straight, Mitch pounded into her. When he knew she
wasn't expecting anything but a helping hand between her
thighs, he pulled his arm back and slapped her hard on the
ass.

"*Ow! You bas—*"

He slapped her ass again.

"*Stop doing that!*"

And again.

That's when Sissy screamed into the pillow, coming hard, her shaking body slamming back into his.

"Oh, God; oh God; oh God; oh, God." Another wave hit her, and her fangs tore into her pillow, ripping it open.

Mitch couldn't take anymore. He let go, his head thrown back as he came, the power of it sapping any strength he had left.

With a purr, he landed against Sissy's back, and she dropped to the mattress. A well-aimed elbow to his ribs forced Mitch onto his back, and Sissy turned over, curling up against his side. He slipped his arm under her shoulder and pulled her closer, his fingers stroking her neck.

He thought one of them would say something, but neither did.

Maybe for once there was nothing to say.

"Are you the hard-core Led Zeppelin fan?"

Sissy laughed as she placed the big bowl of tossed pasta on the table. "That's Daddy. He's been a fan forever, to hear him tell it."

Naked, Mitch dropped into one of the kitchen chairs. Man, she'd have a lot of cleaning to do before her parents got back.

"He's got vinyl, tapes, and CDs. The vinyls are probably worth something, too."

"He'd never sell 'em. He's too loyal to Jimmy Page." Sissy placed a bowl in front of Mitch and using tongs, loaded it up with as much pasta as she could. "I grew up listening to Zeppelin."

"Do you hate it now?"

"Surprisingly, no." Although she was grateful that Mitch had put some Eric Clapton in the CD player. "But my momma has a thing about Johnny Cash, and you couldn't make me listen to him with a gun to my head."

Mitch stared into the bowl. "What did you mix in here?"

"Why do we keep going through this? You know you love everything I make."

"Yeah, but—"

"Eat it, and stop acting like a five-year-old."

"Fine. But if I don't like it, I'm spitting it out and making dramatic gagging sounds."

Sissy filled her bowl halfway and wasn't remotely surprised when she heard Mitch groan.

"That is so good."

"Told you. I don't know why you question me."

"Am I tasting zebra?"

"What I had left."

"By the way, Brendon brought cash with him, so we're cool for money."

Sissy stared at him for a moment. "Sure he has enough to feed *you?*"

"Look, woman, I'm a growing, virile young man. I need my food."

"I still say you should be checked for a tapeworm. Or in your case, a tape-snake."

In less than fifteen minutes, Mitch had finished off his bowl of pasta and what was left in the serving bowl, and now he was eyeing what she hadn't eaten yet.

"Leave me alone."

"Come on. It'll give me extra energy for the rest of the night."

"From what I've been able to tell, the last thing you need is extra energy."

"Fine. Starve me."

Sissy shook her head and continued eating. Slowly, taking her time. And it took Mitch all of two minutes before his fingers started to tap impatiently against the Formica table.

"Are you going to be much longer?" he demanded.

Sissy could only laugh. "Don't rush me."

Mitch slumped back in his chair, his arms crossed over his chest.

"My poor, disgruntled baby."

That got her a hiss, and Sissy went back to eating her food.

"Your brother . . ." Sissy peered at him, and Mitch added, "Travis."

"What about him?"

"Have you two always been this way toward each other?"

Sissy wiped her mouth with her paper napkin. "That has to be the nicest way anyone has put my relationship with that idiot."

"I guess I can take that as a yes."

"Momma told me that when I was still in the crib, Travis walked up to her and said, 'I don't like her. She stares at me.'"

"Did you?"

"She wasn't sure she believed him at first, so she watched me for a while. My daddy would come in, and I'd giggle and wave my hands and feet. Sammy and Bobby Ray would come in, and I'd reach for them. Jackie and Donnie . . . I'd start giggling again, and Momma said it was mocking even then. But when Travis came in, I'd immediately stop whatever I was doing and just stare at him. I'd stare until he left the room. And I wouldn't fall asleep if he was in the room unless I was in either Momma's or Daddy's arms."

"Those are impressive instincts."

"Sometimes you have no choice if you want to survive."

"Is he why you left?"

"You mean to come to New York?"

"No. When you were eighteen. With Ronnie."

"Ronnie was eighteen; I'd just turned nineteen. And I left because no one in this damn town ever leaves. I mean, they go to other Smith-run towns for vacations. Smithburg. Smithville. Smith County. But they never wanted to see what else was out there. I knew when I was five I would travel. That I would see the world. Smithtown is not the beginning and end of all things, but try and tell my daddy that."

"I've never traveled"—Mitch rested his elbow on the table and his chin on his fist—"but I've always wanted to."

Sissy pushed her empty bowl away. She loved talking about traveling. "Where would you go?"

Mitch shrugged. "I don't know. Anywhere, I guess."

"Where have you been?"

"I've never even been off the East Coast."

Sissy sat back. "You're kidding?"

"Nope. And this is the farthest south I've traveled except of course, for Disney World in Florida, which I think every family is required to go to at some point. I believe it's in the Constitution."

Sissy laughed. "Well, darlin', we've gotta get you out and about."

"Where would you take me first?"

Squinting, Sissy thought about it for a moment. "I'd start you off easy. I'd take you to Ireland. They speak mostly English, and you can look up your family. And the lions there are real nice."

"Is this one of the places you're allowed in?"

"Oh, yeah. Bobby Ray helped me pay that fine years ago. I'd take you to Asia, too. The major cities, to start. Tokyo, Beijing, Hong Kong. That sort of thing."

"What about Korea?"

"Yeah." Sissy wrinkled up her nose a bit. "Maybe not right now. In another ten or so years, ya know, I could definitely . . . ask."

"Wait. Are we talking North or South Korea?"

"Well . . . both."

"That's too bad." Mitch leaned forward a bit and looked

into her empty bowl. "Guess we'll have to find something else to do since both North and South Korea are out and you're finally done eating."

Sissy slid out of her chair and backed up. "We should sleep," she giggled.

"Later." He came around the table for her and pushed her up against the refrigerator. She could feel the magnets her mother loved to collect digging into her back.

With one arm braced over her head, he used the other to slide down her neck and across her chest. His hand cupped her breast, the fingers teasing the nipple. Sissy moaned as she reached for him.

"Besides," he murmured, slowly going to his knees, "I never said I was finished eating."

Chapter 17

Jen Lim Chow, Assistant District Attorney of Philadelphia, single mother of three, Harvard Law graduate, and leopard, pulled her rental car up to the curb next to the Sheriff's Department offices and stepped out into the sweltering Tennessee heat.

Christ, what was she doing here on a damn Saturday?

Hell, she knew what she was doing here. She was trying to save her case. The biggest case of her career, and the most dangerous. One did not take down the head of a crime syndicate easily. And on first-degree murder witnessed by an undercover cop. It should have been perfect, but her major witness, the one the entire case hinged on, was now hiding in the one place he was safest from full-humans but in constant danger from a bunch of ass-sniffing canines.

She'd grown up hearing about the Smith Packs and all the Smith-run towns. She could count on one hand the number of these towns that were open to any breed. The others were mostly canine, and Smithtown was one of those. Run by one Bubba Ray Smith. Although unknown to most of the universe, he was infamous among the shifters because the wolf could hardly be called sane. Of course, there weren't a lot of Smiths one could call sane.

Walking around her car and stepping onto the clean sidewalk, Jen wondered how people could live like this. She needed a city, where things were never dull. Living here would make her go crazy. Middle of the day, and only a few people on the streets. And so friggin' quiet.

How is this normal?

Jen pushed open the front door of the office and sighed in pleasure at the lovely cold that hit her. On the drive over, she'd feared that Smithtown might not have the common amenities: air conditioning, cell phones, inside toilets . . .

"Hello?" she called out. When she didn't get an answer, she sniffed the air. But that didn't help. All she could smell was canine, canine, and more canine. To be brutally honest, she couldn't tell the damn dogs apart and usually had no desire to try. "Anyone here?"

"Can I help y'all with somethin'?"

Jen had to restrain herself from making a wild leap and digging her claws into the ceiling like a frightened house cat. She had no idea where that She-wolf had come from, but she was definitely stealthy.

"Yes. Hi." She turned to face the female with one of her patented forced smiles. "I'm from the Philadelphia District Attorney's Office."

"I see.

Keeping that pleasant smile, "And I'm trying to find Mitch Shaw."

The She-wolf stared at her with those yellow dog eyes, and Jen stared right back with her much more normal gold ones. No wonder the Smiths had to live in their own towns, between the eyes and the size of these people. Christ, this woman was easily six-one, if not more, and—Jen glanced down at the She-wolf's feet—yup! The largest feet one would ever find on a woman. Unlike the female cats, the

She-wolves' power was obvious in their body size. They could probably be starting linebackers for the Philadelphia Eagles.

"Are ya now?"

"Yes. I know he's here, but I don't know where specifically. I was hoping you or someone in your office could help me."

Slowly, the She-wolf walked toward her, and when she stood next to Jen, she sniffed her, and Jen would bet money that if she let her, she'd sniff her ass, too.

The female grunted and walked over to one of the desks. She dropped into a chair and put those giant U-boats she called feet on top of the worn wood before reaching for a cell phone. She speed-dialed someone and stared at Jen while she spoke to them.

"Hey. It's me. Someone's here to see Mitch. Yup." Then she disconnected the call, placed the phone on the desk, and continued to stare at Jen.

After three minutes or so, Jen couldn't take it any longer. "Well . . . ?"

"He'll be here if he's of a mind to be."

Jen didn't even know what that sentence meant, and she'd graduated Summa Cum Laude from Princeton.

"Can't I just go see him? I have a rental—"

"Nope."

Her need to unleash her fangs almost strangled her, but Jen held it in check—barely.

"Might as well sit," the She-wolf told her before she remotely turned on the small color TV sitting on the desk across from her. Stock-car racing . . . of course. "It might take a while for him to get here."

"Why?"

The She-wolf spared her one glance before she turned back to the television and basically shut Jen out.

Taking a deep breath, Jen turned and walked to a line of

plastic chairs against the wall. She sat down in it, crossed her legs, and waited.

Mitch didn't know they were so close to the edge of the bed until they hit the floor with Sissy on top. He was inside her, and Sissy never lost her grip even when they fell. The woman must do exercises or something because she could snap a man's cock with that amazing pussy of hers.

Her hands dug into his hair, and she kissed him while riding him hard. Her groans and growls made him crazy, and he gripped her hips in desperation, moving her harder and faster against him.

They hadn't slept. Couldn't be bothered. It wasn't every day you met your match in the bedroom. But Mitch had. He knew that now. He'd always had a feeling he and Sissy had similar sex drives, but he'd never known to what extent. Lionesses were pretty close, but once they were done fucking a man, they usually let him know by mauling him until he got dressed and left. But Sissy hadn't tired yet, and the food breaks between bouts seemed to keep them going.

Gasping, Sissy pulled away from him, her hands against his shoulders, her back bowed, her head thrown back. She ground her pussy against him, and he knew she was moments from coming. Now that she sat up, Mitch gripped her breasts, holding her nipples tight between his thumb and forefinger. He squeezed and rolled them, and Sissy gripped his wrists seconds before she came.

Before her body even finished shaking from release, Mitch rolled them both over so he was on top. He gripped her hands and held them above her head while he drove into her again and again.

"Yeah, yeah," she panted seconds before she was coming again, Mitch right there with her this time.

When he was drained completely, Mitch dropped on top

of her like a load of bricks, pretty much ignoring the grunt of discomfort that followed. It wasn't like he planned to lie there forever . . . just until his eyesight cleared and that ringing in his ears stopped.

Letting out one more satisfied sigh, Mitch rolled off Sissy and grinned when he heard her exhale.

"You have gotta stop doin' that. I'm not a couch to drop on."

"It's not my fault." And it wasn't. She did this to him. She did what no other woman had ever been able to do to him before—wear him out.

"I need food," he told her.

"We're out."

"Don't they have delivery around this burg?"

"Yeah, but—"

A voice from outside cut her off. "Sissy!"

"Shit." Slowly, Sissy rolled to her side and pushed the top half of her body up. She winced, and Mitch ran his hand down her back.

"You all right?"

"Yeah." Sissy stumbled to the window, pushed it open, and leaned out. "What?"

It took Mitch a moment, but he finally recognized Dee-Ann's voice.

"Woman in town to see Mitch. She's from the DA's office in Philadelphia."

"Did you check her out?"

"The car she's got is a rental registered to someone named Kelly Chun, but we can't find anyone by that name in the DA's—"

"I know her," Mitch cut in.

Kelly Chun was the name ADA Jen Chow traveled under when she didn't want anyone to know where she was. Mitch grinned. Chow must be really worried for her to not only leave a metropolitan city for a small town in the Deep South, but she'd also never been a fan of "canines" as she constantly called them. So coming to Smithtown was like a double whammy.

"I've gotta go see her," he told Sissy while he got to his feet.

Sissy stared at him for a moment before she looked out the window. "He'll be in town in a bit."

"Okay. I'll let 'em know. She's at the Sheriff's office."

With a nod, Sissy closed the window.

Looking him over, she said, "You may want to take a shower before you go."

"I plan to." He had Sissy all over him—and he liked it.

Mitch took her hand. "Come on."

"Come on where?"

"You're coming with me. We can get food once I check in with Jen. And you need a shower as bad as I do." From behind her, Mitch wrapped his arms around Sissy's body and kissed the top of her head. "I think you still have some of my love nectar in your hair."

"First off, stop calling it that. And second, if you *ever* do that to me again—"

"I told you it was an accident." But he still had to bite the inside of his cheek to keep from laughing.

"Accident my ass," she complained, pulling away from him and heading toward the bathroom. "There are some things that are never accidents, Mitchell Shaw, and that is definitely one of them."

In Sissy's estimation, there was only one thing worse than a rich, snobby, know-it-all heifer who thought she was better than everyone else . . .

It was a rich, snobby, know-it-all *cat* who thought she was better than everyone else.

As soon as they'd walked into the Sheriff's office, Jen Chow got to her feet like she'd been forced to hang out in a Turkish prison with the inmates.

"There you are!" she'd said. "I thought you'd never get here."

"Sorry. I got delayed."

Yeah. The delay of a quick shower that turned into a long one once Mitch shoved his head between Sissy's thighs.

Lord, the man was insatiable, and Sissy didn't mind one bit. On more than one occasion, she'd been accused of being "hard to please." And that was mostly because the male she was with wore out long before she did. By the time Sissy had turned twenty, she'd sworn off the full-human males completely since they had no hope of keeping up with her. The wolves were better, but even then, the phrase, *"Would you go to sleep already?"* had been tossed at her more than once.

Mitch had been the first who'd managed to keep up with her step for step. Or thrust for thrust. Of course, now Sissy realized that setting up those boundaries had been in her best interest. She could easily get too wound up with a guy like Mitch. A completely uncontrollable male. And lions were absolutely the worst. The males lived to be catered to, and they took shit from no one, not even other lion females. They were pleasant only when they wanted to be and downright surly for no other reason than they felt like it. They were needy and demanding and expected the world to cater to them.

Since Sissy catered to no one but herself, this attitude would definitely be a problem for her.

But, she'd been smart. She'd set up her boundaries and knew Mitch would abide by them. Mainly because he wanted exactly what she wanted. Really good sex.

Great sex.

Yet while Sissy watched Jen Chow talk to Mitch, her hand on his forearm, Sissy had that feeling again. That jealous feeling. And it annoyed her like crazy.

Chow pointed to one of the two interrogation rooms. "Let's talk. In private," she added, glancing at Sissy.

"Sure." Mitch followed behind Chow, briefly looking over his shoulder at Sissy and saying, "Be right back."

She nodded, faked a smile, and dropped into one of the desk chairs to wait.

"That New York detective . . . Mick something?"

Mitch pulled out his patience. He'd forgotten how much he needed it when dealing with Jen. "You mean Dez Mac-Dermot?"

"Yes. Her. She believes this lioness was military trained."

"Makes sense."

She dug into her briefcase. "We pulled names and did crosschecking on those not already dead or still on duty . . . and came up with these four." She placed four photos on the table. "Recognize anyone?"

Mitch shook his head. "Nope. This one's cute, though."

"Detective," she sighed. "Focus."

"I'm just saying." He grinned, and Jen studied him for a moment.

"You're looking healthier."

"I'm eating better. And exercising."

"Is that what they call it?"

"I'm on the football team."

"The foo—" Jen pushed back from the table and got up to pace. "Don't you understand my entire case hinges on you?"

"And I'm still breathing. So I don't know what you're complaining about."

"This isn't a vacation for you to spend time playing around with dogs, Detective."

Slowly, Mitch stood. "And I almost died. And if it hadn't been for that *dog* outside, I would have. So watch how you talk about these people. I'd hate for my memory to fade, Counselor."

Jen held her hands up and stepped back from him. She'd gotten so far so fast in her career by knowing when to push and when to back off.

"I'm sorry if I offended you. And I think it's a good idea if you stay here for now." She walked around the table to get her briefcase, but Mitch knew it was to put some distance between her and the unstable, dog-loving male lion she was trapped in here with. "They were on me the moment I drove past the welcome sign. I'm sure they'll do no less for any cat who drives into this town."

At the half-hour mark, Sissy realized "Be right back" might be relative, and she pushed away from the desk, wandering out of the building. It was a typical Tennessee summer day—hot and hazy. She wandered down Main Street, checking out the stores and seeing if there was anything she wanted to buy. Of course, with most of her budget going to feeding one oversized cat, she really didn't have much play room until her next paycheck. But she loved to look, and if she was feeling particularly evil, she could always charge it to her momma's account. Nothing entertained her more than those early-morning calls with her momma screaming about how she wasn't made of money.

When Sissy walked past that alley and heard a noise, she assumed it was her Uncle Eggie Dumpster diving again. But when she went around the Dumpster, she found her old Aunt Ju-ju hiding behind it.

"Aunt Ju-ju!" She crouched beside her. "Darlin', what are you doing here?"

Poor Aunt Ju-ju. She'd lost her mind a long time ago, but

Sissy had never found her roaming by herself. Someone in the family was always watching her.

Since her family's mental health had always been in question, everyone simply assumed Aunt Ju-ju had slipped her bolt as other Smiths had over the years. But Sissy had also heard the rumor that Aunt Ju-ju hadn't lost her mind until she went up against Grandma Smith, challenging her years and years before Sissy or her brothers were even born.

Perhaps that was why Sissy felt a kinship to Aunt Ju-ju even though she didn't think the woman could tell Sissy from any of her other grandnieces.

"Let's get you home, sweetheart."

She reached for her aunt, but hands stronger than she expected gripped her shoulders and eyes that rarely shifted from wolf locked on to her.

"It's Sissy I come to find. I need to see her."

"I'm right here, darlin'. I am Sissy." But she knew her aunt would never see past her madness.

"You need to tell her to watch herself. That old bitch on the hill wants her. She wants her 'cause she fears her so. I hear them calling to her."

Sissy doubted Grandma Smith or the Smith aunts feared her at all. But she didn't see a point in arguing it with her Aunt Ju-ju in a back alley.

Helping her aunt to her feet, Sissy promised her, "I'll tell her. I promise."

"That bitch hates that little girl like she hates that girl's momma. Hates 'em both equal."

There was definite truth in those words but nothing Sissy could do about it. Instead, she led her aunt out of the alley. As they stepped out onto the sidewalk, Sissy looked around for someone to watch her aunt while she went back to the sheriff's office to let them know where she'd be so they could tell Mitch.

As she looked down the street, she saw Patty Rose walk out of a small gift shop on the corner.

"Hey, Patty Rose!"

Her brother's mate froze, her entire body rigid.

She slowly turned to face Sissy, her smile bright. "Sissy Mae? Whatever are you doin' out here?"

"Just waiting on Mitch. Look, could you watch Aunt Ju-ju for a second? I want to run in and let Mitch know where I'm going before I take her home."

"Oh, I'll take her." She took hold of Aunt Ju-ju.

"Are you sure? It's no problem."

"No, no. Really, it's fine. I'd love to."

Since she seemed so eager . . . "All right then." Sissy smiled down at her aunt. At one time, she'd been tall and powerful like all Smith females. But whatever had eaten at her mind seemed to have done the same to her body. "You take care of yourself, Aunt Ju-ju." Sissy leaned down a bit and kissed her aunt on the forehead. Ju-ju usually didn't like anyone touching her, and it had been nothing but an impulsive move since her aunt was standing still for once.

Instead of pushing Sissy away like she did with most any-one else who tried to get too close, Aunt Ju-ju blinked, and her eyes went from wolf to human.

"Sweet girl," she said, patting Sissy's shoulder. "Sweet, sweet girl. No wonder they're afraid. You use that gift, Sissy, when you need to. It may be the only thing that saves your heart."

She walked off, Patty Rose following after her. When Patty tried to put her arms around Ju-ju again, the old She-wolf batted her away.

Sissy shook off the strangeness of the moment and turned right into him.

"Hey, Sissy."

Sissy let out a sigh. She'd already been distracted anyway, plus the bastard had stayed downwind. He'd crept right up on her.

"Gil." She looked up at him. She didn't have to look up as far as she did with Mitch, which suddenly made Gil seem real small. "Why are you always lurking around? Don't you have something to do? Don't you work?"

"Sure do. Own my own business now. A garage not far from here."

Folding her arms over her chest, Sissy snapped, "A garage? Like my brother's garage?"

"Don't go gettin' all upset. I'm clear across town. Not even near your brother's place."

If Smithtown was a thousand miles long, this information would soothe her. But Smithtown was small, and this was her kin they were talking about. Even if it was that asshole Travis. "You really think you can get away with this, don't you?"

"Get away with what?"

"Taking over Smithtown. Becoming Alpha Male."

"That's—"

"Don't you lie to me, Gil Warren."

Gil stepped close to her, his eyes intent on her face. "And what if that is what I want, Sissy Mae? Imagine what we could do together."

She snorted. Then she sniffed. Her eyes narrowed. "Were you just talkin' to Patty Rose?"

"Saw her in the gift shop."

"Oh. Did ya? And what were you gettin' in the gift shop? 'Cause if I remember correctly, you ain't big on giving gifts, you cheap bastard."

"I was just—" Gil's words were brutally cut off when he was shoved face-first into the brick wall next to them. The worst part wasn't that Mitch had been the one to shove him, but Sissy had the feeling Mitch hadn't really noticed Gil. Instead, he was simply moving Gil out of his way by grabbing the back of his head and slamming his face into brick.

"You ready?" Mitch asked casually.

Sissy glanced around, not exactly surprised to see they had everyone's attention. They had probably been waiting for Sissy to wipe the floor with Gil, but for once, she didn't have to.

"Yeah, I'm ready. You all done?"

"Yeah. But I could go for a sandwich . . . or two."

"You can't be hungry."

"You keep saying that like you expect my answer to change."

She grabbed his hand and headed down the street. She had no idea what happened to Gil after they walked away, and to be honest, she'd already forgotten about him.

Chapter 18

The coffee was hot and tasty, the sandwiches good and plentiful. But the company was what made Mitch smile.

Sissy had already eaten her one sandwich—*how did she survive on only one?*—and now she put her feet up in the plush leather chair and sipped her coffee from the sturdy paper cup.

"And before you ask, they still don't know who she is." Mitch bit into his sandwich. "It's a mystery."

"Thank you for that lovely view of your chicken salad."

"Sorry, baby."

She blinked, and those brown eyes locked on him. "When did you start calling me that?"

"Uh . . . this second?"

"I'm not your baby." Then she made that little square with her fingers and mouthed, "Boundaries."

"Sissy—"

The bell above the door jangled, and a familiar She-wolf walked in.

"Miss Janette." After wiping his mouth, Mitch stood and kissed her cheek. "It's so good to see you again."

"It's good to see you at all, darlin'." She motioned Mitch back into his chair before smiling at her niece. "Sissy Mae."

"Aunt Janette. What do you want?"

"What makes you think I want something?"

"Aunt Janette!"

"Sh-sh-sh," she motioned to Mitch's right side. "Mind if I look?"

Mitch shrugged, and she pulled his T-shirt away to examine his wounds. Long fingers pressed against his skin, and she nodded. "Healing up just right. Your momma did a good job." She sat down at the table, and the server placed a big mug of coffee in front of her. "Of course, those love bites make it a little hard to see."

He'd just bitten into his sandwich, but luckily hadn't swallowed yet. Otherwise, he'd be choking it all back up.

Aunt and niece grinned at each other. "I knew I saw something when I watched you two at the wedding. These eyes miss nothing. I've got the eyes of a . . . a . . . wolf, even."

Mitch ended up choking on his food anyway, but this time, for a laugh.

Sissy smiled. "We're still just friends. And that's all."

Janette looked at Mitch. "She gave you the boundaries speech, didn't she?"

"Complete with visual," Mitch laughed.

"Men need visuals," Sissy snapped. "And try chewing with your mouth closed."

"Are you going to tame our little Sissy, Mitchell?"

Sissy rubbed her face, annoyed, and Mitch answered honestly, "I'm really too lazy to try and tame anybody. If I had my way, I'd spend all day sleeping under a tree, maybe rolling out occasionally to sun my belly, and then I expect someone to bring me food. I could live like that *forever.*"

Janette threw her head back and laughed. "I do like you, Mitchell Shaw. You're funny."

He magnanimously offered her some of his potato chips, which she wisely declined.

"Have you two had dessert yet?"

"Forget it," Sissy stated with way more vehemence than seemed necessary.

"Oh, come on, Sissy Mae. He's just so dang cute." She reached over and pinched Mitch's cheek. "Wouldn't you like some pie, Mitchell Shaw?"

"No. He would *not*."

"What kind of pie?" Mitch figured Sissy didn't want to go to her aunt's house—not that he blamed her. Sometimes getting stuck with relatives was the absolute worst.

"All sorts. Sissy didn't tell you about our pie shop?"

And Mitch froze. "Pie shop? You have a pie shop?"

"The best pies you'll find this side of the Mason-Dixon, darlin'."

"How could you not tell me they had a pie shop?"

Sissy shook her head. "You will regret this, Aunt Janette."

Really, Mitch Shaw had absolutely no shame. Sissy knew this when he walked into the Lewis Sisters' Pie Shop and dropped to his knees in front of the cold case. His hands rested on the glass, and he looked at each pie like a small child would.

"I . . . I can't make up my mind," he gasped. Like Mitch needed to make up his mind. He could finish everything in that case and still be hungry less than an hour from now.

"Y'all are gonna regret this," she reiterated to her aunts, and they all laughed.

"Where should I start?" Mitch finally asked. He looked at Sissy. "Which is your favorite?"

Lord, that was a hard question. If there was one thing her

aunts could do, it was bake a pie. Even pies she'd never eat from anyone else, she'd scarf down from her aunts. Their pies had become so popular locally, they'd eventually had to open up another store in a neutral part of the region so other breeds and full-humans could go without starting those ugly fights involving everyone in town.

"Cherry."

"The cherry?"

"Trust me."

"I do," he answered simply, and she saw her aunts pass glances. She hated when they did that—it meant they were thinking up something. She hated when they started all that damn thinking. It led to trouble.

"Slice of cherry, please."

Sissy walked up beside Mitch, who'd finally gotten to his feet. "So polite."

"I'm always polite to those who deserve it."

"Mitch, darlin', you sit on down over there, and we'll bring you a slice with some milk. How that be?"

"That be perfect." He looked down at Sissy. "See what polite gets ya?"

"So, Sissy?" And her Aunt Darla dropped her elbows down on the counter in front of Sissy, her body leaning toward her niece's.

"Yes, Aunt Darla?"

"Heard you've been driving around town in Clyde."

"Mitch wanted to check him out."

"You miss it, don't you? Getting to drive as fast as you can without anyone stopping you."

Sissy's smile faded away, realizing that her aunts hadn't wanted to see her simply because they loved her. They'd trapped her! "No."

"No what?"

"Don't pretend innocence with me. I know what y'all want, and you can forget it."

Francine pushed a slice of lemon meringue across the counter to Sissy. "Now, darlin' girl—"

"Don't darlin' girl me. I'm not doing it. Forget it. And you're only asking me to do this after all these years because Momma's not here to tell you to back off."

"Because your momma has no faith in your skills. Not like *we* do."

Sissy shook her head. "Now that was just shameless."

Francine slammed her hands against the counter. "Oh, come on, Sissy Mae! Do it for us."

"No." Sissy picked up her slice of pie and the glass of milk Roberta handed her.

"Come on, Sissy. Do it for the town."

"Isn't it enough you have poor Mitch here playing against bears?"

They all looked at "poor Mitch," who seemed to be having the equivalent of an orgasm eating that slice of cherry pie.

"Mitch doesn't mind. He understands loyalty."

Sissy glared at Francine. "That was just plain mean. And I can't do it unless Ronnie—"

"She already said yes. As did Dee."

Sissy placed her food on the table and sat down. By the time her butt was in the seat, she had an empty plate with cherry residue and an empty milk glass in front of her.

"That was mine," she snarled.

Mitch grunted and kept eating.

"Well, with both Ronnie and Dee, you don't really need me."

"You know we do." Francine sat across from Sissy. "It ain't just speed we need when dealing with the Barron Pride."

Sissy nudged Mitch's arm. "Do you care that they have me going up against one of your precious Prides?"

Mitch held a forkful of pie inches from his mouth. "Do any of the Prides around here make pies like this?"

Francine grinned. "Not even close."

"Then, no, I don't care. Now don't bother me."

Darla walked up and placed three more slices of pie in front of Mitch. "This is our chocolate cream, our Boston cream, and our pecan. And anything else you want to try or a pie or two you want to take home, you just tell us."

Roberta placed a gallon of milk in front of him. "So we don't have to keep running back and forth."

Mitch looked at Sissy. "You do whatever these lovely goddesses tell you to do, and you be damn happy about it!"

Sissy rubbed her eyes, if for no other reason than to block out the smug smiles of her aunts.

Bribing heifers.

"Next time, don't agree to anything without talking to me first," Sissy snapped early the next morning, while trudging through Travis's backyard to one of the two enormous barns he had on his property. Since no Smith could own animals without the animals panicking every time one of them came around, there was only one reason there were so many barns around here. To hide shit.

Only a few of them made 'shine now, and most of them stuck with legal jobs . . . most of them. But they still kept their barns because to quote Bubba Smith, "You just never know, do ya?"

"It's not my fault. It's Shaw's. They bribed him with pie!"

"They have to be the weakest siblings," Sissy muttered. She looked at Dee. "And what's your excuse?"

She shrugged. "Momma asked."

Sissy let out a long-suffering sigh and pulled open the big doors of Travis's barn. They were still there. Three racing cars that would make any NASCAR racer drool. And clearly, her brother had been maintaining and even updating them. They positively shined, and when Sissy popped the hoods on all of them, the engines looked perfect.

"Think we should amp 'em up a bit?" Ronnie asked, her hand sliding across the roof.

"Couldn't hurt." Sissy definitely didn't mind tinkering with cars. She didn't get much of a chance now that she lived in New York, and Bobby Ray wouldn't let her anywhere near his truck. Not because he didn't trust her to fix it, but he got real panicky when she mentioned taking it for a test drive.

Sissy glanced at her watch before putting her hair in a ponytail. "We've got three days to make these babies sing. So let's get to work."

Mitch woke up when a weight dropped onto the bed next to him. He turned over and smiled at Sissy. He glanced at the clock on the bedside table. It was nearly two in the morning. He hadn't seen her all day and he'd missed her—a lot.

"Hey, ba—"

"Touch me, and I'll rip your arms off." It took him a moment to realize she hadn't changed out of her clothes or showered. And before he could find out what was wrong, she was snoring.

Frowning, Mitch glanced down at the erection that had been waiting hours for her to get home. "Don't look at me. It's not my fault. It's those evil women and their pies." Then he remembered there were pies they'd left him in the refrigerator. Well, if he couldn't fuck . . .

Chapter 19

Brendon looked at his brother while they waited for practice to start. Mitch was looking really good these days. Healthier. Stronger. Happier . . . except at this moment. He looked unusually cranky. "What's wrong with you?"

"Nothing." Mitch cracked his neck. "But let me tell you, food is not a substitute for sex. At least not good sex."

Ahhhh. Now Brendon got it.

"Yeah, I know what you mean. Ronnie was exhausted when she got home last night. She only had energy for one round."

Mitch slowly turned toward his brother, and Brendon took a step back. "But it was barely even once. I mean, by the time we were done, she was out cold, and . . . uh . . . I'm gonna stop talking now."

Travis jogged up to them, a ball in his hand. "You guys ready?"

"*Don't I look ready?*" Mitch grabbed the ball from Travis. "Let's get this fuckin' thing started."

A shocked Travis—and Brendon had never seen the man show anything but cool indifference—watched Mitch storm away.

"Everything all right?" he asked.

"Yeah. Everything is fine." Brendon shrugged. "But ya know what would be a good idea? Playing in our gear. Pads, helmet . . . all of it. Just to be . . . uh . . . safe."

They turned and watched Mitch pass the ball to one of his teammates. It hit him dead in the chest, and Brendon winced because he was positive he heard bones breaking.

Travis nodded. "Probably a good idea."

Sissy waved away the tires she didn't want. "These are good." She tapped the chosen ones. "We'll take these, and we want eight more sets for racing day."

The seller nodded and walked off. Sissy grabbed one of the tires and rolled it toward her car.

Her arms hurt. She was tired. And dammit, she was horny as a rabbit on hormones. But like most canines, once Sissy made a commitment, she stuck to it.

Besides, apparently, the lions were ahead in the betting pool among the three towns. True, it had been years since Sissy had done one of these races, but she hadn't lost her skill. Or her almost rabid desire to win.

She blamed her momma for this. All of it. This particular rivalry started back before Sissy had even been born and had been passed down from the Lewis females to their daughters. The last time Sissy raced, she'd broken her collarbone, but Ronnie had won, and the Barron Pride had yet to let it go. They could hold a grudge, and so could the Lewis sisters.

Still, Sissy knew her momma wouldn't let her daughter race if she were around. Not after she'd had to nurse a whining and unhappy Sissy back to health. More than once, Janie Mae had told anyone who would listen, "That had to be the longest three days of my life, waiting for that damn collarbone to heal."

Sissy almost hated her family for making her do the one thing she'd swore she'd never do . . . need her momma.

"Let's get these tires on," she grumbled, beginning to sound like her daddy.

Dee, who seemed totally in her element, practically skipped over to the car.

Sissy scowled at her cousin, her hands on her waist. "If you don't tone the cheer down, I'm gonna beat the shit out of you."

Dee cleared her throat and grabbed hold of the tire. "All right then."

Travis pulled his helmet off and motioned to Donnie, who limped over.

"What's the deal?" Travis asked his brother once he'd limped close enough.

"Well, to be blunt . . . he ain't gettin' any."

Travis watched Mitch take down an offensive linemen. The entire team winced when they heard poor Bart hit the ground.

Mitch was one of those players who could play any position on a team. Wherever you needed him, he'd fit and then he'd excel. And the more he watched the boy play, the more Travis realized he needed this kid. Not just for this particular game—he'd probably be wide receiver in this game—but other serious competitions they'd have over the next few years.

The problem was Sissy. She'd be the key to Mitch coming back to town when they needed him. But Sissy didn't stick with any man for long. The other side of the problem was when Sissy was putting out, she drained the boy until he was damn near useless.

A conundrum as his daddy would say.

"When's the race?"

"Wednesday. Everybody's gonna be there."

Of course everyone would be there. Nothing like a little competition between the females. The full-humans could keep their mud wrestling and wet T-shirt competitions. Travis would happily bypass all that to watch a showdown between women who'd rip the flesh from your bones when annoyed.

"All right. Let's call off practice. We'll go help Sissy."

Donnie tilted his head in surprise. "All right."

Sissy continued to bang out the dent on the front end when she saw boots standing next to her. Slowly, she looked up from her crouched position and sneered.

"What do you want?"

Travis Ray smiled, and Sissy bared a fang.

He held his hands up, palms out. "I only came to help."

"You? Help me?" Sissy stood. "Why?"

"Can't a brother simply help his—"

"Try again."

"Our loyalty is to—"

"Again."

Travis shrugged. "Five to one in the lions' favor. But if y'all win, I can clean up."

Sissy nodded. "Yeah. That sounds about right." She handed him the hammer. "Guess you better get to work then, hoss."

Mitch opened the family room door and walked in. As soon as he stepped inside, the smell of food cooking hit him right between the eyes. He dropped the football equipment the team had given him and headed straight toward the kitchen. Sissy sat on the counter, her legs banging the cabinet doors underneath, a racing magazine open on her lap.

She looked up and smiled. "Hey. Dinner should be ready in another—oh!"

Mitch picked her up and started to carry her toward the stairs. Quickly decided that was too far and dropped her on the kitchen table.

"Mitchell—"

He covered her mouth with his hand. "Not a time to talk. Just get those shorts and panties off. Now."

"Yeah, but—"

"Again with the talking?"

"Just turn the heat off on the stew."

He turned and quickly shut off the flame heating their dinner. When he turned back around, she was just getting her shorts unsnapped.

"Too. Slow." He grabbed hold of the shorts and yanked them down her legs before reaching for her panties and ripping those off completely. He had his own sweats halfway past his ass when Sissy shook her head. "What now?"

"Condoms. And don't snap at me."

He turned and reached into the far cabinet, moving a few things around and finally pulling out a big box of condoms. When he turned back, Sissy looked absolutely outraged. "Are you high? Putting those up there? What if my parents came home and we—"

"They were already there."

Sissy blinked. "What?"

"The box was already there. I'm assuming your parents had it—"

She squealed and dived off the table.

"Where the hell are you going?"

"My parents"—she pointed at the table—"they've done it on this table."

"Yeah. Probably. And now we are. Get your ass over here."

She squealed again, sounding remarkably like a girl. "I'm

not doing it on there . . . where my parents have . . . have . . . *done it.*"

"It's been cleaned."

"That's not the point!"

"You're being ridiculous. Your parents have condoms stashed all over this house. I'm sure—"

That's when she squealed and ran.

"We're going to a hotel," she yelled as she ran up the stairs. "Or . . . or live in the car! Anything but staying here!"

Mitch grabbed a condom from the box, kicked his sweatpants and sneakers and socks off, and ran up the stairs after Sissy. He found her in her room, shoving clothes into the duffel bags they'd brought with them.

"Dirty, disgusting, out-of-control old people," she raged under her breath. "If they have sex at all, it should be in their bed, under the covers, with the door closed and locked." She stood tall and spun around to face him. "What if their grandchildren had come to visit and found them doin' it on the table like a couple of . . . of . . ."

"Wolves?"

"Shut up." She threw up her hands. "We can't stay here. It's that simple."

"No," Mitch said, yanking the clothes she had clutched in her fist and tossing it across the room. "What's simple is that I have needs. Needs that need to be fulfilled. Now."

Hands on naked hips, "I ain't no whore, Mitchell Shaw. You got some needs you need taken care of, you go right on over to one of those full-human towns and get yourself a hooker."

Mitch grabbed her T-shirt and yanked her close.

"Hey!"

"Do you think that just *anyone* can help me right now? I don't want anyone, Sissy Mae. I want you. I want you now. Naked, wet, and ready. I know I could get a hooker. I could have gotten one last night. I don't want that. I want you, on that bed, legs spread wide . . . now *move!*"

Should she be worried that was the nicest, most romantic thing any male had said to her? Probably. But it was. If she were a melting kind of gal, she'd be a puddle of chocolate at his feet.

Instead, she lifted her head up high and walked over to the bed. She pulled off her T-shirt and tossed it over her shoulder. Slowly, she crept up on the side of the bed, making sure to give him her best ass wiggle. When she heard him growl, she turned, lying on her back. She spread her legs, bent her knees, and motioned to him with the crook of her finger.

Mitch pulled his T-shirt over his head and walked toward her. He knelt on the edge of the bed, placing the condom by the pillow. Watching her, Mitch slid his arms under her knees, lifting them and pulling her down the bed a bit. He lowered his head and buried his face between her thighs.

When his tongue speared her pussy, Sissy gasped, her arms reaching wildly around her. It wasn't merely his tongue either, but the way Mitch used it. He licked every fold, every crease, anything and everything he could reach . . . and Lord knew, there wasn't much he couldn't reach with that tongue.

Sissy tried to grasp something to hold her anchored to the spot. But she was spread out across the bed, the headboard and footboard too far away to reach. And Mitch didn't let up. He ate at her like a starving man, bringing her up and up only to pull back before she could come. She'd hate him if she wasn't falling—

No.

No, no, no, no. Dammit! She had to remember her own boundaries. She couldn't let the most amazing head she'd ever experienced—absolutely *ever*—get her to change her own rules. Her rules, unlike the rules of some countries she'd visited, were not made to be broken. Even by her.

Finally, Sissy reached down and buried her hands in Mitch's hair. His mouth latched onto her clit and sucked, sending her screaming into an orgasm that would blind a lesser woman.

As her body shook, Mitch pulled away. But only for a moment. Then he was back, his condom-covered cock slamming into her.

Sissy arched, cried out again. Mitch gripped her hands, pinning them by her head as he fucked her. He stared down into her face and smiled. "Christ, I missed you."

Worried she'd say something stupid, Sissy raised herself as much as she could and kissed Mitch. She could still taste herself on his mouth and tongue, and he took perverse delight in rubbing his wet face all over hers.

They laughed and fucked and came, and Sissy couldn't shake the feeling that something huge had just changed in her life.

Chapter 20

He figured they'd go to some field in neutral territory and race there. Once again, Mitch had been seriously wrong. Like the "field" in the middle of Smithtown, the "track" in the middle of the bear-run Collinstown could give Daytona a run for its money. And even more interesting was the fact that a race involving six women had drawn this kind of crowd. The stands were filled with shifter locals and any full-human mates they might have.

The usual beer and hot dogs were being sold, but they were also selling high-end paraphernalia, including T-shirts, sweatshirts, and jackets, all sporting the town names. It was kind of cute in an overly obsessive way. With a city, there were simply too many full-humans to ever get away with events like this and not have anyone notice. But here, they could simply enjoy being the out-of-control shifters they were. Mitch had to admit he loved it.

He couldn't imagine living out here full time, but there was a part of him, a part that he wasn't examining too closely, that kept seeing him and Sissy showing up from time to time. Eating pie, playing ball, freaking out because her parents still had a healthy sex life. Yeah, he was finding it easier and easier to imagine. Which reminded him that Sissy was something he could never have full time. Once he went back to Philly, it had to end.

Putting his feet up on the railing, Mitch said, "Are you and Ronnie happy?"

Brendon shrugged. "I guess. I mean, I'm happy. I think she's happy. When she isn't, she usually has no problem telling me."

Mitch grinned. "In detail."

"One time she pulled out a graph with charts." Brendon sipped his beer. "What about you and Sissy?"

"What about us?"

"Come on, bruh. I'm not blind. You two are getting way into each other."

"It can't last."

"So you keep saying, but that hasn't stopped either of you from—"

"Yeah, yeah, yeah, I know."

"Then what the hell are you doing?"

"Do I look like I know what I'm doing?"

Sissy's aunts moved into the seats behind them, and both Mitch and Bren began to stand up.

"Y'all sit right back down." Miss Francine motioned them down with a wave of her hands. "Don't mind us."

Mitch glanced back and frowned. "No Smith males?"

"Oh, darlin', they're all with Sissy and the others, getting those cars ready."

Mitch chuckled. "Really? All of them?"

Miss Francine shook her head. "I know. Poor dears."

If her uncle hadn't stepped between her and Jackie, Sissy would have decked the big baby.

Her uncle motioned Jackie away with a move of his head.

"You sure do have your daddy's temper," he said with a warm smile.

"He started it, Uncle Bud."

"I know. I know. But you need to concentrate on your immediate situation. Lord knows, you can beat that idiot up anytime you want."

"You're right."

"And guess who dragged himself out of the woods to see you?" Bud stepped aside, and Sissy's eyes widened.

"Uncle Eggie!" She jumped into the older wolf's arms. This meant a lot to her. Everyone knew there wasn't a lot that could get Eggie to shift to human, put on clothes, and be around everyone else as human except his mate and daughter.

"Hey there, little gal." His voice rumbled like ground up gravel. You felt his words more than actually heard them. "You take care of them cats for your Uncle Eggie."

"I will." She kissed his cheek, and Dee wrapped her arms around her father's shoulders from behind.

"Hey, Daddy."

"Hey, sugar bug, I want y'all to be careful out there. Remember—cats don't play nice."

Sissy cracked her knuckles and glanced over at Paula Jo Barron and her sisters. "Not a problem," she muttered.

All Mitch did was ask a simple question. "How many laps?" Which prompted Brendon to launch into his knowledge of NASCAR rules that Mitch could really give a shit about at the moment.

"And do you want to know the difference between speedways and—"

"No." Mitch looked over his shoulder at the aunts. "How many laps?"

"Usually about twenty."

Mitch and Brendon looked at each other and back at the aunts.

"Uh . . . that doesn't sound very challenging."

They all smiled, which didn't make Mitch feel any better.

The National Anthem played over the speakers, and everyone stood up except Mitch and Brendon, who didn't really think about it until Francine popped them both in the back of the head.

After they did their duty as Americans, they sat back down, and Mitch watched the cars roll onto the track.

Six. There were only six cars.

Again, looking over his shoulder, "Are there only six racing?"

"Yup," Francine said, offering him a cherry lifesaver, which he took since he was getting a little hungry.

Mitch and Brendon passed another glance. "Something's not right." Mitch now turned his upper body so he could look directly at the women behind them. "What's going on? What aren't you telling us?"

"It doesn't really matter what we're not telling you, does it? Since neither of you can do a damn thing about it now, huh?"

"*What kind of response is that?*"

"Shit."

Bren said it low, and to anyone else, they might not be alarmed, but Mitch was. He immediately turned around to look at the track and realized the cars were already tearing down the asphalt. At first, it looked like any other race, except there were only six cars on the track and three of them were different shades of gold. Then one of the lighter gold cars with the number 48 emblazoned on the side slammed into Ronnie Lee's cherry red one. Not a tap, a full slam, nearly forcing her into the wall.

"*Shit.*"

Mitch leaned forward, and just as he figured, Sissy, in the

black car, pulled up. First, she rammed 48 from behind, pulled around, and slammed into her from the side. The gold car rammed into the wall, and Mitch figured she'd stay out. But the lioness didn't. She pulled back onto the track. Even more amazing, no penalty flag for either move, nor did the cars slow down. Mitch wasn't a hard-core racing fan, but he knew some of the rules from when he'd catch NASCAR racing on his Sundays off.

Apparently, none of those rules applied here.

"It's like Roller Derby in cars."

"I'll kill her," Bren growled. "If she lives through this, I'm gonna fucking kill her."

And Mitch understood exactly how his brother felt, and he didn't like it one damn bit.

Sissy hit her brakes and barely missed getting battered by Paula Jo. Like Sissy, Paula Jo's purpose wasn't to make the last lap at the best time. That role was for her sister Lucy and Ronnie Lee. The role of Sissy, Dee, Paula Jo, and Paula Jo's middle sister, Karen Jane, was to make sure either Ronnie Lee or Lucy didn't make that last lap at all. They definitely shouldn't cross the finish line, if at all possible.

They had exactly twenty laps to either stop the other team or protect their teammate. It was a brutal game born from a minor accident that abruptly turned into what normal, law-abiding people nowadays termed "road rage." And only the females competed because the males, "just ain't crazy enough," Sissy's granddaddy had explained one day.

Sissy shifted and tore up next to Paula Jo. She was about to slam into her when Paula Jo beat her to it, forcing Sissy into a spin that nearly took her out completely. Then Paula Jo went after Ronnie Lee.

"That bitch."

And now, Sissy was pissed.

* * *

Mitch blew out a breath. "Okay. Now she's pissed."

Bren's eyes never left the track. "How do you know?"

"I know."

And as if to prove his point, Sissy tore up the middle of the track between 48 and 52. Once between them, she slammed first to the left, knocking 48 into the grass in the middle of track, and quickly swung back, knocking 52 into the wall.

"Wow."

Mitch shrugged. "Told ya."

The crowd went wild, everyone on their feet. Even the aunts behind them were screaming, "*Rip those heifers apart, Sissy!*"

Brendon leaned close, his mouth next to Mitch's ear. "One day, when it's just you and me in a soundproof room with a couple of beers, we'll discuss how frightened we are right now."

"You got it, bruh." To seal their pact, the brothers banged their fists together before looking back.

Of course, what they witnessed then only freaked them out more.

Sissy screamed. No. Not the hysterical scream like she had a couple of nights ago when she found her parents were using her entire childhood home as some sort of sex club—and that whole thing would have her shuddering in disgust for years—but one of her "*I'm ready to kill everybody!*" screams. She didn't use them often, but when she did, smart people got out of her way.

Of course, it wasn't that Paula Jo wasn't smart. She simply didn't get out of anyone's way for any reason. If they hadn't been mortal enemies, Sissy would probably like the bitch.

She saw the flag and knew they were entering the final lap. That was pretty much the only flag they ever used in these races.

Sissy pressed down on the gas and shot out past the lions to ride alongside Ronnie Lee on her left. Ronnie was ahead and could win this, but the cats were trying their best to take her out because as hard as Lucy might try, she simply couldn't handle speed the way Ronnie could.

Dee-Ann pulled up alongside on Ronnie's right. Her car had massive dents on the fender and side panels, but Sissy knew her car looked worse. Of course, she had a worse temper than Dee.

The lions had one more lap to stop Ronnie or lose. They went for broke, pulling out a move Sissy didn't remember ever seeing them do before—it must have been new.

Karen Jane pulled past Sissy and cut in front of her. Then she hit her brakes. Sissy had seconds to move, hitting her own brakes and turning her wheel; that's when Paula Jo slammed into her from behind, knocking Sissy off the track and right into the grassy field in the center.

Lucy shoved her way between Ronnie and Dee and took Dee out with a well-placed slam to her left side. Sissy's cousin spun and hit the wall.

Okay. Sissy had been mad before, but now . . .

Sissy tore across the center of the track. In a normal race, completely illegal and sometimes physically impossible, depending on the track. But there were only two rules to this game—you couldn't deliberately hit a car once the car was out, and you definitely couldn't purposely hit a driver if they were outside their car. Either infraction got you time in either the Smithtown or Barron County jails.

Sissy hit asphalt, and she sort of fishtailed when her back tires landed. But she'd gotten where she needed to be. She'd timed it so Ronnie Lee was just passing her when she tore onto the track. She cut across the track, pushing Paula Jo and

Karen Jane back. Lucy sneaked by, but Ronnie Lee would always be faster than that little girl. Sissy's big concern was her older sisters.

Gritting her teeth, she swung wild and spun, her backend colliding with Paula Jo's front. The inertia pushed Paula Jo into the back right of her sister's car. That spun Karen Jane out and right into Sissy.

The power of that shoved Sissy, and suddenly . . . Sissy Mae was airborne.

When Sissy's car flipped up and over, Mitch jumped to his feet, his heart ripping a hole in his rib cage. Then her car didn't stop. It kept going, flipping right back into the grassy field she'd illegally used to make her insane move. He lost count of how many times she went over. But when she finally landed, Ronnie Lee had made the last lap, and the checkered flag flew.

Again, the crowd went wild, and Mitch was briefly reminded of the soccer riots in Europe before he jumped over the railing and tore across the track toward Sissy's car.

He made it there before her brothers and without even thinking, ripped the crushed side door off the car, tossing it behind him. He might have hit someone, but he didn't care.

"Sissy?"

He crouched beside her, relieved to see that she at least had on all the proper gear, from a six-point harness seat belt to a helmet that matched her all-black fire-retardant racing suit and a neck brace.

Christ knew she really needed that freakin' neck brace.

"Sissy!"

Her eyes opened, and she blinked, looking around. When she finally looked at him, she asked one thing . . .

"Did we win?"

Chapter 21

They had to cut her out of the car because her seat—and her—had gotten lodged in by the crushed metal, making it impossible for her to get out on her own. Mitch helped, pulling her out completely when her uncles told him to. That's when he asked her, "How many fingers am I holding up?"

That was easy. "Eighty-five thousand!"

"Great."

Sissy stood, even though she got the feeling Mitch wanted nothing more than to stretch her out on the ground or even better, put her in an ambulance. But she kept her arm around his shoulder so he could hold her up. She glanced down at the ground and the inert form of her brother. "What happened to Travis?"

Mitch winced. "I hit him with the door after I tore it off. It was a total accident."

"Marry me," she spouted before she could stop herself.

But Mitch only grinned and said, "You say this now when you're not in your right mind. Then you'll yell at me when I take advantage of you."

Sissy started to laugh, but someone punched her in the

head from behind. If Mitch hadn't had his arm around her, she would have gone headfirst back into the car.

"You cheating heifer!"

Sissy snorted. "I didn't cheat, you blind bitch. Although I could have. But the wonder of me is that I don't need to cheat to win against your lazy cat ass!"

Paula Jo reached for Sissy, but Dee pushed past her and swung her helmet wide, bashing the right side of Paula's face. And that's when it turned ugly—because the aunts got involved.

Really, there was nothing quite like watching late middle-aged women go at it. Sissy tried to pull her aunts apart, but this involved some long held grudges. Plus, she had to deal with Paula Jo and her sisters taking on Dee and Ronnie. And it didn't help that she was still seeing at least three of everything. But anytime she stumbled, anytime she felt like she might drop, strong hands firmly held her. And Mitch never left her side.

Finally, the bears got bored, and their deputies broke it up, sending everybody back to their respective territories. Mitch tossed her over his shoulder and carried her back to her car. He dumped her in the back seat. "Hospital?"

Sissy laughed. "Not on your life. We got a party to get to, darlin'."

Mitch sighed and got into the driver's seat. "Somehow I knew you'd say that."

Ronnie Lee danced around Sissy with a bottle of Mexican beer in one hand and a cast on the other. Yeah, she'd busted her wrist with that last hit from Paula Jo's car, but that only made this win even cooler because she'd done it all with a friggin' fractured wrist!

How cool am I?

Of course, Shaw was still way pissed at her. "You should

have told me," he'd snarled. "I have a right to know when you're being an idiot."

It was sweet in a Cro-Magnon kind of way. But there was no way she would have missed this race. Besides, she loved racing with Sissy and Dee. They kicked major ass together.

Sissy had managed to keep from breaking anything, but her face had gotten bruised up pretty bad from when her car flipped. Still, she didn't seem to care as she rocked out to AC/DC with the rest of the Smith Pack at the local Smith-town bar.

But what really bothered Ronnie was Mitch. Not because Mitch had said or done anything to concern her. But because he *hadn't* said or done anything. Even now, he sat at a table with Brendon, one leg up on the table, a bottle of Bud in his hand. He said nothing but kept a vigilant eye on Sissy. And Ronnie didn't think Sissy had any clue.

She didn't see it, did she?

Mitch was or *had* already fallen in love with Sissy. A male didn't get that look on his face unless it had suddenly hit him that with one or two more rollovers, Sissy could have broken her neck. True, shifters were amazingly strong and could bounce back from illnesses and damaged organs that others couldn't, but they weren't indestructible. Of course, that's what made the race that much more fun.

But it was hitting him, wasn't it? Hitting him that one wrong move, and he could have lost Sissy forever.

And dumb bitch that she was, Sissy was completely oblivious!

"Maybe you should get Mitch home."

Sissy laughed. "Why? Will his mom worry if he's not home by curfew?"

Ronnie bared a fang, and Sissy grinned as the music went from AC/DC to Charlie Daniels, which got the whole crowd woo-hooing.

"I'm just saying he doesn't look like he's having any fun." She leaned in closer. "And I think you worried him."

"He shouldn't be worried."

"Why not?"

"Because people with boundaries don't worry about each other." Sissy shimmied her ass to the ground before shimmying back up. "His only concern should be whether I'll be having sex later tonight . . . and stop looking at me like that."

"Like what?"

Sissy raised an eyebrow, and Ronnie waved her off. "Okay. Okay." When Sissy turned around, her arms in the air, Ronnie added, "But you're an idiot."

Turning back around, Sissy honestly asked, "What'cha say?"

Ronnie shrugged. "Nothin'."

The celebration party had been great, the food spectacular, the music and beer fabulous. To be honest, it was one of the better parties Sissy had experienced in a long time, and what amazed her was that not once had she and her brothers argued.

Although as her muscles began to ache on the way home, Sissy realized she might not be doing any more races. It was time for the "young 'uns" to take over. Hell, she'd started at sixteen—why should her nieces and nephews be any different?

Besides, to her horror, she was simply getting too old for this shit.

Once they were inside the house, Mitch grabbed her hand and led her upstairs.

"Where are we going?"

"To shower. You smell like cheap booze and other cats. It's bugging me."

Sissy didn't argue and instead enjoyed Mitch taking care of her. He got into the shower with her, washed her hair, and properly put on the conditioner, which Sissy could only figure he'd learned that skill from his mother. Once they were both rinsed, Mitch dried her off and went back with her to her bedroom. He didn't say much during all this, and she didn't know why. But Sissy wasn't going to worry about it. Asking questions only led to meaningful conversations, which Sissy often tried to avoid at all costs.

She towel dried her hair and pulled on one of her old T-shirts with nothing else, figuring she wouldn't need more based on the hard-on Mitch had been sporting since they had gotten into the shower together.

He combed his hair off his face and grabbed a clean pair of sweats from the pile Sissy had tossed on a chair. "I'm going downstairs," he told her, surprising the hell out of her. "I'll talk to you later."

"You're not staying in here?"

"Nah. Not tonight."

She watched Mitch pull open her bedroom door, and on a whim, she asked, "Why?"

Sissy's entire body jumped when Mitch slammed her door so hard she had the feeling it damaged the wall.

"Did you just ask me why?" Mitch turned around, and Sissy saw real anger in his eyes. To be honest, she'd never really seen that before. She'd seen annoyance and impatience. But never real . . . rage. Not from Mitch.

"Uh . . . yeah."

"And you have the nerve to ask me that after what I just went through?"

Now Sissy was completely confused. "What did you go through?"

"What did I . . . did you . . . you can't be . . ." Wow, Mitch not finishing sentences. That couldn't be good.

Abruptly, he grabbed her by the shoulders, his fingers digging into her muscles. "Did you really think I'd enjoy watching you almost get killed today?"

"I wouldn't exactly say—"

"Shut up!"

And Sissy was so startled she did exactly what he told her to.

"First off, I had no idea what the hell you guys were up to. If I had, I would have put a stop to it."

"You would have—"

"Shut up! Second, do you have any idea what it was like to watch your car flip like that? To know you were trapped inside it and there wasn't a damn thing I could do about it?"

Since he didn't seem to really want answers to any of these questions, Sissy didn't say anything.

"And for what? For nothing. You risked your neck for absolutely nothing. So in answer to your stupid question, I'm not staying in here tonight because I'm *pissed off!*" He released her, yanked the door open, only to slam it shut again when he walked out.

Sissy had no idea how long she stood there, gawking at that closed door. It could have been minutes or hours. For one of the first times in her life, Sissy was at a loss for words.

But it was the sound of pebbles thrown at her window that snapped her out of her temporary muteness. She pushed open the window and saw Ronnie Lee and Dee standing under what she used to term her "escape tree."

Throwing on some panties and shorts, Sissy climbed out her window and into the tree right outside it. She maneuvered her way down easily, landing firmly in front of her cousin and friend.

"Let's raid your aunts' store. We need pie," Ronnie said, and Sissy nodded, recognizing the look on Ronnie's face.

Apparently, she wouldn't be getting any from Brendon either. So yeah, they both needed pie.

Brendon wasn't exactly surprised to find Mitch sitting by the lake at three in the morning, staring out over the still water. Of course, he would have much preferred if he wasn't sitting with a crocodile next to him. It was one thing to enjoy a predatory game of tug with him, but it was another to treat him like the family's pet dog.

"Hey." Bren sat down next to Mitch with Ralph on the other side. "Is he really necessary?"

"He's keeping me company." Sitting Indian style with his elbow resting on his knee and his chin resting on his raised fist, Mitch sighed. He looked like the fourteen-year-old kid Brendon had met all those years ago when his father had finally gotten around to telling him that he had another son. "Didn't I mention that before?" his father had asked, looking typically uninterested.

"Sissy went out," Mitch said on that sigh. "And I don't blame her. I lost it."

"Don't feel bad. I think I made Ronnie cry."

Mitch glanced at him. "You made my Ronnie cry?"

"Don't start. I feel bad enough without you adding to the pile-on." Bren threw his hands up. "*But that woman scared the shit out of me!*"

"Yeah, I'm sensing they don't get that. The whole time Sissy stared at me like I was speaking Gaelic."

"They play rough out here in the sticks. Or so I've been told."

"Playing rough I understand. Strapping yourself into a vehicle that could burst into flame or break into a thousand pieces and then ramming others in the same situation is way out of my comfort zone."

Brendon watched his brother pet Ralph's head. "Speaking of comfort zones . . . are you okay doing that?"

"Not really," Mitch told him, his free hand still petting Ralph. "But I'm afraid if I stop, he'll rip my leg off. I can't remember when he last ate. Did you know that crocs only eat every three days or so?"

Shaking his head, Brendon said, "Mitchell . . ."

"What?"

"You've gotta tell her, bruh."

"I don't think Sissy finds crocs that interesting."

"Not that, you idiot! That you're in love with her."

"Oh. That." Mitch sighed again. "I'd rather keep petting Ralph."

"You think she'll run?" Ronnie Lee had run when she'd found out Brendon loved her. She took off like Flo Jo.

"No. She won't run. Sissy never runs. She'll just ignore whatever I said. Ignore what we've meant to each other this last year or so, forget about these last few days. Eventually, she'll ignore me completely."

"She can't ignore you."

Mitch gave a little snort. "How ya figure?"

"Bruh . . . you're sitting here petting a *crocodile* while informing me of its eating habits. How the fuck are you going to let her get away with ignoring you?"

"You have a point. But I can't love her, bruh."

"You already do."

"I know. But I can't."

"It's times like these I want to start hitting you."

"Nothing has changed, Bren. I'm still testifying. Still going into witness protection. I can't offer her anything but running and a new name. So I can't love her. Understand?"

And Brendon hadn't realized until that moment what an unselfish little prick Mitch Shaw was. Damn him!

Mitch glanced at Ralph and back at Brendon. "I think he's snoring."

"Or those are hunger growls."

"Bastard."

Dez had rattled off the litany of things they'd done involving the Shaw case over the last two weeks. Unfortunately, her commanding officer hadn't been remotely impressed. She'd looked downright annoyed when she told Dez to get out of her sight.

Resting her elbows on her desk, Dez ran her hands through her hair. She was as frustrated as everybody else, but this woman was like a ghost. No prints, no hair, no fibers, and the armed services were less than helpful. Even among the shifters, there was still the usual political bullshit.

"Maybe she's left the country." A professional like her would have multiple passports, IDs, and contacts.

"Nah." Souza put her feet up on her desk. "She hasn't left the country. Not yet."

"And you know this how?"

"She's not leaving until she gets what she wants. And what she wants is that money. The bounty on your boy's head is substantial. If I wasn't law-abiding, I'd kill him myself for that amount of cash."

"That's lovely, Souza. Thank you."

"I'm just telling you like it is. She's gonna try again."

Dez had the overwhelming desire to mark up her desk. It was so pristine and perfect it drove her nuts. In fact, the whole office was like that. High-end and high-tech.

She ran her finger over her desk and wished she had her switchblade. "They want this trial to go forward. So I'm guessing she'll wait until he's back in Philly."

When Souza didn't say anything, Dez looked up from her desk. "What?"

"In Philly, there will be others. Full-humans who will try

to take him out and get in her way. She'll want him all to her-self—and *before* he gets a chance to testify."

Dez sat back. "You think she's found him, don't you?"

"Full-humans wouldn't have the connections, but she would." Souza raised an eyebrow. "Have you thought about going to Tennessee, Desiree?"

"Do you mean on purpose or with a gun to my head?"

After easing Ralph back into the lake, Mitch sent Bren off to make up with Ronnie. Not that their argument would last long anyway.

Mitch headed back to Sissy's house and was kind of sur-prised to find her sitting lengthwise on the top porch step with her back against one side and her feet up on the other. Christ, she was so sexy. It made him crazy.

"Hey," she said, smiling.

"Hey." He sat down on the second to last step, mimicking her pose, but he faced her and he had to bend his knees. "I'm sorry I yelled at you earlier."

"Sorry I scared the hell out of you." She laughed. "I keep forgettin' we're different 'round here. What's normal to us is considered completely insane by everyone else."

"Not completely insane. I was fine up until the time you started slamming into each other. I kept waiting for a damn flag and penalties."

"We don't do penalties."

"I know that now."

"Well . . . it does mean a lot to me that you care enough to irrationally yell at me. Like a frustrated little girl."

"And it means a lot to me to know that you're willing to risk permanent spinal injury and having to be nursed twenty-four-seven by your mother for the next twenty years simply to give a town you ran away from years ago a good show. And for no cash reward."

Sissy's eyes narrowed the tiniest bit. "Touché, Monsieur Pussy. Touché."

Mitch reached out, gripping Sissy's hand. "Wanna go upstairs and find out what other French things we can do?"

"Later." Sissy swung her legs off the railing and stood, her hand still gripping Mitch's. "Come on. Let's go to Cougar Hill and watch the sun rise."

"Cougar Hill? You named a hill after a cat?"

"Well, that's where my great great granddaddy tossed this cougar named ol' Jed off the side of the hill when he wouldn't leave Smithtown after they'd run off all the other cats. And my great great granddaddy just laughed and laughed. He thought it was so damn funny that he named the hill . . . Cougar Hill."

Mitch let Sissy lead him to this infamous hill, her hand warm and firm in his own. "Aw, Sissy, that ain't right."

Chapter 22

Smitty paced back and forth over the white sands of the exclusive tropical island beach he and Jessie Ann were honeymooning on. The whole island belonged only to them for two more weeks.

He'd never been a big scenery guy, but even Smitty had to admit the place was absolutely beautiful. They had a wonderful staff to take care of their every need, including gourmet meals, scuba diving, or simply being left alone.

It was paradise.

And for the last forty-five minutes, Smitty had been pacing the beach of this paradise, his dog, Shit-starter, right beside him until Jessie walked outside. She wore only one of his oversized T-shirts, looking disheveled and well-fucked. Smitty knew he'd never love anyone the way he loved her.

She waited until he stopped pacing before she stood behind him and wrapped her arms around his waist.

"What's wrong?"

"I don't know. But I can't shake the feeling all hell's breaking loose."

"If that's what you feel, then you're probably right. Have you called home?"

"Yup. And they all tell me everything is just fine." Smitty growled. "They're all liars."

"Have you talked to Sissy?"

"No. I was told she went back to Tennessee for a visit, but she won't answer her phone."

"So?"

"Sissy doesn't go home unless it's a major holiday, and even then, only if I go with her because I'm the only one who can stop her from trying to kill Travis in his sleep."

"If you're this worried, we should go back."

Smitty closed his eyes and gripped the small hands wrapped around his waist. Lord, he loved this woman. His mate. His wife.

"I don't want to ruin our honeymoon."

"I know. But this is much more important. What if Sissy's in grave danger . . . or . . . or . . . somethin'?"

Smitty slowly faced his bride. She peered up at him with that perfectly blank expression on that beautiful face that told him she was lying to him.

"You're bored out of your ever-lovin' mind . . . aren't you?"

It took her a good ten seconds, but suddenly, she burst out with, "*God, yes!*" She held her hands up and clarified, "Sex . . . amazing. Bored with you? Never. But in between sex . . ." She threw her hands up. "*Bored!*"

Now Jessie started pacing. "I have no Pack; I don't know what those damn kids are up to; who knows what's happening at my office; and I have no video games to distract me." To illustrate, she did this weird thing with her hands like she was holding something, and her thumbs moved back and forth. Smitty didn't get it, but he'd learned a long time ago that when it came to Jessie Ann, it was best to simply accept and move on. "And you won't even consider playing a little *Dungeons & Dragons* with me." She stopped pacing and faced him. "If I were any more bored, Bobby Ray Smith, I'd set myself on fire!"

"You could have said something."

Now that she'd gotten all that off her chest, Jessie blushed and stared at her bare feet. "I didn't want to ruin everything. This is the dream honeymoon for most people."

"People who aren't part of a Pack. We're not good on our own, darlin'."

"How do people not live with a Pack? It's beyond me." She was so earnest in that doglike way she had, all Smitty could do was smile.

"They do manage. But we don't have to." He walked up to her and wrapped his arms around her waist, pulling her in close. "How about this for an idea? We go home as soon as we can get that boat to pick us up and a flight, make sure everything is straight with our Packs, and straighten out whatever shit any of 'em started. Then you and me check into the most expensive, snobbiest, rudest hotel in New York City and fuck so hard and loud that they're eventually forced to throw us out. That way we get our dream honeymoon, but we also have our Packs within spittin' distance. How's that for a plan, Jessie Ann?"

"I can't explain it but"—Jess shook her head—"it sounds weirdly . . . wonderful."

"It does, doesn't it?"

He woke her with soft kisses and gently urged her to the shower. When she got out of the bathroom, he'd already made breakfast for her. Waffles and bacon—a shifter's breakfast of choice, it seemed.

She took the seat he held out for her and waited while he served her. He stared at her longingly all through the meal and then insisted that he would clean up and she should do nothing but rest.

At least, that's how it happened in Sissy's fantasy world where she had complete control.

The fact was Mitch fucked her awake until she screamed. Then he slapped her ass and told her he "sure would love some waffles and bacon" while he walked off to take a shower. When she followed him to the bathroom and yelled at him through the shower curtain to make his own damn waffles and bacon, he reached out and yanked her in. They didn't feel like getting condoms, so they made each other come with their hands and their mouths. When they got out of the shower, there was only one towel, and they spent five minutes fighting over it until Mitch hung her upside down by her ankles. And then he wouldn't let her up until she called him "Lord High Mitchell the Great." When he finally put her back on her feet, they had a slap fight over the whole "Lord High" thing, and Sissy got hold of the towel and took off running. She almost made it into her room, but he got to the door before she could slam it shut. Mitch insisted on drying her with the towel, but he shook her all over the place and kept the towel over her head until eventually she squealed and kicked at him.

When they finally got their clothes on, it was nearly lunch anyway, so they decided on heading into town to her brother's diner for food since he served breakfast all day long and Mitch really had his heart set on those waffles. Mitch grabbed hold of the car keys and held them over his head so Sissy couldn't get them. She, in turn, grabbed his nuts and twisted until he gave her the damn keys.

The thankfully short drive into town consisted of a lot of roaring and screams to "*slow the fuck down!*" which Sissy ignored as always. But now they were safely ensconced in a booth, and with his mouth full of food, Mitch couldn't keep from asking her, "What is wrong with you anyway?"

It was while they snarled at each other over Sissy's plate of fries that Brendon and Ronnie sat down. Ronnie's cast had been removed, and now she wore an ACE bandage. In another day, her broken wrist would be nothing but a faint memory.

When Sissy glanced at Brendon, she realized something was bothering him.

"What's wrong?" Sissy felt fangs slide across the flesh of her hand. They didn't break the skin, but the meaning was clear. Eyes wide, she glowered at Mitch. "Have you lost your goddamn mind?"

"Watch your mouth, Sissy Mae," Sammy chastised from behind the register.

"Yeah," Mitch chastised from across the table. "Watch your mouth."

"Don't make me come over there and rip out that tacky mane of yours."

"It's tawny. My *tawny* mane."

"Dez is coming down here," Brendon cut in.

Sissy and Mitch looked at Brendon and back at each other. Then they started laughing and couldn't seem to stop.

"I don't see what's so funny."

It took a moment for Sissy to get her laughter under control. "Dez. In Tennessee. *That's* funny."

"Aren't you interested in why she's coming here?"

"No. But I'm sure you can't wait to tell us."

"She's coming down here because she thinks whoever tried to kill Mitch is coming here to finish the job."

"Well, good luck to her getting into town without anyone knowing." Sissy shook her head. "It ain't gonna happen."

Brendon ignored Sissy and said to Mitch, "I think you should go into Witness Protection now. Not wait until after the trial."

Sissy's whole body went sort of cold, then hot. She hadn't thought about Mitch going into Witness Protection. For days, they'd been too busy having sex. But the thought of never seeing him again made her feel almost physically ill. But she wanted him safe, too.

"I can't," Mitch replied, finishing off the rest of the fries she no longer wanted. "I've got the game."

Brendon glared at his brother for a good long while before he snarled, "Are you fucking kidding me?"

"No, I'm not kidding. I made a promise. I'm not leaving until after the game. Besides, I think we have a good chance against those bears."

Sliding out of the booth, Brendon stood. "Can I talk to you outside?"

"Not if you're gonna yell at me."

Brendon stared, and Mitch stared back until Sissy said, "Go with him before he yanks you out of the booth."

Letting out a sigh, Mitch followed after his brother.

"You all right?" Ronnie asked, sitting back a bit when the waitress put a double chocolate shake in front of her.

"Yeah. Why?"

"Because you got this look on your face when Shaw mentioned Witness Protection."

"Yeah. Guess I forgot."

"Shaw is torn between wanting his brother safe and terrified he'll never see him again." Ronnie sipped chocolate shake through a straw. When she stopped, she said, "And you can forget it."

"Forget what?"

"Whatever you're planning to do to O'Farrell. Forget it."

"Who said I was—" Sissy stopped talking when a dab of whipped cream hit her between the eyes. "Was that really necessary?"

"It was because I know how your mind works. So let's lay this on the table, shall we? You can't call your Uncle Eustice and see if he can 'handle things' from where he is. Nor can you have his prison location moved so he'll have a crack at

O'Farrell." Damn. The woman did know her well. "And if there's one thing I've learned about Mitchell Shaw, it's that you killing a man, even to protect him, won't win you any points." She shrugged. "He's got a hard-on for scumbags. He'll do this, give up his entire life because he knows it's the right thing to do."

Sissy sighed, knowing Ronnie was right. "Times like this, I wish he could be more like my family."

Leaning back against the alley wall—he'd never seen such clean alleys—Mitch answered simply, "No."

"But—"

"I mean no, Bren."

"I'm sure Dad would—"

"I don't care what Dad would do or what Jesus would do. The answer is still no."

"Yeah, but . . . if we *handle* this . . . somehow, then—"

"Bruh, you can't even say the words. And doing it is no easier than saying the words."

Bren's shoulders dropped a bit. "I don't want to lose you."

It had been so much easier when he hated his brother and sister, believing they'd gotten all of their father's love and he'd gotten nothing but the occasional birthday card. It had been so much easier when he believed they sat around laughing about the poor cub from West Philly or simply pretending he didn't exist at all. But he knew different now. He knew he'd lucked out being able to stay with his mom and her Pride. He realized that Brendon and Marissa hadn't had anything easier growing up than he'd had. They all loved their father, but he was aloof and moody, like most of the Old School males. While his father was building an empire, the twins never had Sunday barbeques with loud, bossy women who cursed like sailors nor had nearly twenty-five relatives show up to every football game and cheer like it was the Super Bowl.

Bottom line was, Mitch didn't want to lose Bren either . . . or Marissa . . . or anyone. But he had to do what was right—he had to testify. If he didn't bring O'Farrell down now, he got the feeling no one would. And if that had happened, how many more fifteen-year-old prostitutes would get their throats slit before the old bastard died.

"Maybe something could be worked out," he lied while praying it would turn out to be true. "Maybe some kind of visitation." Mitch grinned. "But you'll have to meet me in East Booneyfuck Ohio or wherever they put me."

"You? In the Midwest? I shudder at the thought."

"I'm doing pretty good in the South. They love me here."

"Only 'cause you play ball."

"And I play it well."

"Speaking of which"—Bren glanced at his watch—"we've got practice in a couple of hours, and I need a nap."

Together, the brothers walked out of the alley and found Sissy and Ronnie Lee standing outside the restaurant. Mitch frowned when he saw Sissy's face. She looked upset, and when she saw him, she immediately tried to hide it. He didn't want her hiding anything from him.

"What's up?"

"Nothing." Ronnie Lee walked around Brendon and pulled out his wallet. "We're going shopping." She took out his credit card and put the wallet back in his pocket.

"We'll see you guys at practice." Sissy turned to walk away.

"Wait." He waited until Sissy looked at him. "Come here."

She walked over to him.

"Closer."

She smiled—a real one—and stepped closer.

"Now kiss me."

"Out here? In front of everybody?"

"Yeah. Out here. In front of everybody."

"Well, when you get all demanding and cranky, how can I resist?" She went up on her toes, her arms sliding around his neck. She kissed him slow and easy. Mitch got lost in that kiss, his arms wrapping around her waist and pulling her tight against his body. He had no idea how long they were standing there, but suddenly, Ronnie had Sissy's arm and was pulling her away.

"Lord, y'all. Get a room, why don't you?"

"Can't very well do that with you dragging me away!" Sissy looked over her shoulder at Mitch and winked.

As the two strutted down the street, laughing and pushing each other around like pups—Ronnie in tiny running shorts and a cutoff T-shirt and Sissy in her denim cutoffs and tight tank top—Mitch and Bren watched them.

And both brothers growled.

Chapter 23

With his brother off taking a nap and Sissy shopping, Mitch had two hours before practice, and that was simply too much time to sit around and think. So he went in search of food.

When he walked into the pie shop, he was surprised at how welcoming the aunts were. They kind of treated him like he was family, and he enjoyed it.

"Sit here, baby-boy." Francine pulled out a chair and patted it with her hand. He smiled and sat down at the table.

"My mom calls me that sometimes."

"I met her at the wedding, right?" When Mitch nodded, Francine smiled. "I liked her. My kind of woman. Not snooty like some of your kind can be. Now what kind of pie you want today, darlin'?"

"The lemon meringue was so good."

"Lemon meringue it is."

It was Janette who brought the pie. And not a slice either. The entire enormous thing, putting it in front of him with a pie cutter, fork, and plate. She cut the first slice for him, and Darla poured him a glass of milk from the gallon jug she'd placed on the table.

When he started eating, the four sisters sat down and watched him. It was mid-afternoon, and the place was deserted. But that wouldn't last. They got their busiest at the end of the day when people were getting desserts to go with their meals.

"So what's wrong, darlin'?" Francine asked, her elbow propped on the table, her chin resting in her palm. She watched him with warm, friendly eyes.

"Nothing. Just a lot on my mind."

"Any of that have to do with our Sissy?"

Mitch didn't see a point in lying. "Yeah. It does."

"You in love with her?"

Ducking his head, Mitch focused on his food. "Some might say."

"Is she in love with you?"

"God," Mitch muttered, reaching toward the pie to cut another slice, "I hope not."

And like that, the pie was pulled away. "What do ya mean, you hope not? You trying to tell us our Sissy isn't good enough for you?"

Mitch let out an annoyed sigh. "Of course I'm not telling you that. If I had my way, I'd give Sissy anything she wanted. Do you think I want to end my time with her? There are so many things I want to do with her, but that's just not possible."

"If you could do anything with Sissy," Janette asked, "what would it be? And keep it clean."

Mitch smiled. "Anything? I'd take her on a date. We've never been on a date."

"Mitchell, darlin', I don't understand what the problem is." Francine huffed a little. "This whole thing with you and these . . . what did you call them the other day?"

"Scumbags."

"Yes. These scumbags. That can't go on forever. They'll catch whoever tried to hurt you."

"It won't make a difference, Miss Francine. When this is all over—when I leave here—I'll be going into Witness Protection."

Francine sat up straight. "You're doing what?"

"I really thought you knew. I thought I told you." Mitch rested his elbows on the table. "Maybe I didn't. I don't know anymore. There's so much going on right now. Someone's trying to kill me, I'm in love with your niece, the game is coming up . . ."

A big slice of pie was pushed in front of him and another glass of milk.

Francine reached over and petted his cheek. "I want you to tell us everything, darlin'."

Sissy ignored Dee's laughter as she showed off her new leather jacket. "Look, heifer, fringe will never be out of style."

She yanked the jacket off, unceremoniously shoved it back into the bag, and snatched a beer out of Ronnie's hand.

Dee glanced at Sissy as she sat down next to her on the bleachers. "Rumor is," her cousin murmured beside her, "whoever tried to kill Mitch may be heading this way."

"May be. No one knows for sure. But the sheriff's department and the Elders are on alert." Sissy looked at her cousin and blinked.

"What?"

Sissy thought for a moment and then realized it couldn't hurt to ask, "You know, they say it's a lioness who did this."

"Yeah? And?"

"Dez thinks she's military."

Dee's gaze moved across the field, and she asked, "Is that right? And what makes her think that?"

"The shot this female made, nailing Mitch from where she did . . . she had to be well-trained. But other than her scent, she's left nothing. No hair, no fibers—nothing that our kind can usually find when no one else can."

Sissy knew she was touching on a sensitive subject here. She hadn't asked her cousin about what she'd done for the military because she already kind of knew from Bobby Ray. Dee's unit handled full-humans who knew of their kind and made hunting them a sport. They were usually rich, secretive, and extremely dangerous. Not only to those they hunted, but to Sissy's kind in general. And Dee hunted the hunters. She was very good at what she did, but the last time Sissy had seen her, she could tell the whole thing had been wearing on her cousin.

Really . . . there was only so long a body could do that job and keep her sanity.

Dee nodded. "I'll make some calls to old friends."

"Thanks."

Her cousin grunted as Travis called a break and sent them off the field. Mitch came right over to her, but before Sissy could stand up and drag him away to her chosen spot, he crouched in front of her, pulling off his helmet.

"Hey."

"Hey." She smiled. "Look, I found a place—"

"I was thinking we should go on a date tonight."

Sissy stopped talking abruptly, her words tumbling to a halt. "Uh . . . what?"

"A date. You and me. It'll be nice."

"Nice?" And Sissy couldn't keep the disgust out of her voice. "I don't do nice."

"Would it kill you to try?"

"Possibly."

Mitch grinned. "I'll pick you up at your parents' house. We'll go out to dinner, so dress nice."

"I don't dress nice."

"Start." He kissed her cheek and headed back to the other players and Gatorade.

"Did he just ask me on a date?"

Ronnie nodded. "Sounds like it."

"Well, what's going on?"

"Why are you asking me? I was with you until practice started."

"Dee-Ann?" But Dee had done her ghost thing and was nowhere in sight. Sissy would have to find out how she did that.

"Are you gonna go?" Ronnie asked, taking Sissy's beer and gulping down half of it.

"I guess. I mean . . . a date? Me?"

"We better leave now then. Who knows what we'll have to put together to get you dressed proper."

Mitch drank the bottled water his brother handed him.

"Where's Sissy and Ronnie going?" Bren asked, frowning.

"Home, I guess. I'm taking Sissy on a date."

It was like the world stopped. All the players gaped at him. Even Sissy's brothers. Which seemed odd since everyone seemed to know he and Sissy were fucking.

"What?"

"You're taking Sissy out on a date?"

"Yeah." Mitch shrugged at Travis's question. "So?"

"To be honest, I don't think she's ever been on a date."

"And it's not like you have to wine and dine her to get what you want," Jackie said laughingly . . . until Mitch slammed his helmet into Jackie's face. Jackie went down crying, holding his nose, too.

"Anyone else got anything to say?" Mitch asked lightly. The team shook their heads. "All right then. I say we get back to practice since I have to get ready for my date."

* * *

Sissy walked out of the shower and wrapped a towel around herself. She quickly combed her hair and stepped into the hallway.

"Okay, Ronnie, let's . . ." She stared down the length of the hall. Her aunts were at the other end, and they were waiting . . . for her.

"Wha . . . what are you guys doing here? Where's Ronnie?"

"That nice young man wants to take you out for a nice meal," Francine explained calmly. "And we wanted to make sure you didn't walk out the door looking like the local ho."

Sissy blinked. Then she tried to make a run for it.

Mitch stepped out of Ronnie's car and cracked his neck, his gaze focused on the house. It kind of amazed him how this all had come about. Sitting in the pie shop, eating and talking to Sissy's aunts, telling them things he'd never told anyone—not even Sissy. He blamed the pie. The more they fed him those delicious pies, the more he talked. But they were so sweet and understanding. It really made him feel better.

And when they had sent him off, they told him, "Make sure to ask Sissy out on a date. She deserves it." And she did, too.

Mitch reached back into the car and pulled out the bouquet of red roses. He knew it was breaking Sissy's boundaries, but she'd have to get over it. You simply didn't go to pick up a woman for a first date empty-handed. His mother would have his ass.

Taking a deep breath, Mitch walked up the porch stairs and to the front door. He raised his hand to knock, but he heard glass breaking and cursing.

"Sissy?" he said through the door.

And like that, all the noise coming from inside the house stopped.

"Sissy?" Mitch said again and reached for the doorknob.

"Hold on a minute." That sounded like one of her aunts. Darla maybe?

Leaning close, Mitch could hear whispers and what sounded like a scuffle.

Then he heard Sissy say, "No, no, no!"

Mitch stood back to kick the door in when it opened on its own and Sissy's aunts shoved her out onto the porch. Sissy spun around to get back inside, but they slammed the door in her face and locked it.

Taking another step back and looking Sissy over, Mitch said, "Sissy?" Slowly, she turned around, and he smiled. "God, it *is* you."

"Not a word, Mitchell Shaw. Not. One. Word."

"You look—"

"What? I look what?"

Mitch shrugged. "Adorable."

Sissy's eyes narrowed. "*You bastard*," she hissed before she stormed off toward the car.

"Wait."

"No!"

He caught her hand on the car door before she could yank it open. "Look, don't be mad. I've just never seen you"— Mitch dragged his gaze from her head to her feet—"in a sundress before."

A *white* sundress no less, with tiny blue polka dots, blue sandals with straps and three-inch heels, and—the killer—a matching blue headband to hold her hair back.

She looked as far from the Sissy Mae Smith he knew as humanly possible.

"You never have before, and you never will again. Now, get me out of here before I start kill—" Sissy turned back to him, but her body froze when she caught sight of the flowers in his hand. "What are those?"

"Flowers. For you."

Sissy stomped her foot and made that damn outline of a box again with her forefingers. "Boundaries," she hissed.

Imitating the box outline with his own fingers, Mitch snapped back, "Date. Now get in the friggin' car."

She snatched the flowers out of his hand and got into the passenger side of the car. Chuckling, Mitch walked around the vehicle and got into the driver's side.

Once inside, he smiled and said, "I do have to admit, you look pretty hot in that I-was-a-thirty-year-old virgin outfit."

"Shut up."

"All I wanna do is dirty you up with my love nectar."

Sissy finally smiled. "Stop calling it that!"

Sissy didn't know what was more awkward. The shoes, which were tragically a size too small? The sun dress with the tiny little ties that kept untying? The motherfucking headband?

Or this goddamn conversation?

For thirty minutes, they'd sat and tried to find something to talk about. Sissy couldn't believe it. This was Mitch. Mitch who she'd had eight-hour-long conversations with while watching really bad late-night cable, only to realize it was dawn so they'd head out to the local diner for breakfast and another two-hour conversation. *That* Mitch she suddenly had nothing to say to.

And he wasn't doing much better. He kept tapping the table with his fingers, and she briefly debated biting them off.

She'd known this would be a bad idea.

This sucks.

"What? Your shrimp cocktail?"

Shit. Sissy hadn't realized she'd said that out loud, and now she had those gold eyes watching her.

"No. This." She dropped the shrimp she'd been holding for the last ten minutes back onto its plate. "We have nothing to say to each other, and considering we are two of the chattiest people I've known, that is saying a lot."

Mitch let out a sigh. "I know. I feel awkward. I never feel awkward." He briefly frowned and added, "I make other people feel awkward."

Sissy reached across the table and patted his hand. "And you're really good at that, too."

He pushed his plate of potato skins away. "Okay. So what's the problem?"

"We are. This isn't us. I mean, I look like goddamn Gidget, and you're acting like . . . like . . ."

"Like what?"

"Like Brendon."

Mitch winced. "Ew."

"I mean, are you comfortable in that sports jacket?"

"Do I *look* comfortable? It's freakin' hundred and two degrees outside, and he made me wear this goddamn thing. He tried to make me wear a suit."

"Why?" Sissy asked dryly. "Are you planning on going to a funeral after our date?"

Finally, Mitch grinned. "Not unless it's my own."

"Take it off, Mitchell."

"Okay." He was already pulling the jacket off his big shoulders. "And you take off the dress."

Sissy's hands were reaching for the ties when she stopped and smirked at him. "Smooth."

His grin grew wider. "Can't blame a cat for trying."

"Bastard." But this time, she wasn't mad.

"Okay. Keep the dress on, but that headband . . ."

Sissy tore it off before he could finish and shook her hair out. "Better?"

"Oh, yeah."

And Sissy liked how he said that. Like the lust was getting to him.

Resting her elbows on the table, she leaned way over and tried to peek down at his pants. "You sportin' a lead pipe there, hoss?"

"At the moment, I could start my own plumbing company."

Sissy laughed, and she knew the snotty cats and bears were staring at her, but she didn't care. They'd left Smithtown and come into Taylor County. Mostly oblivious full-humans lived here, and it was considered neutral territory for the breeds. Of course, this fancy steakhouse got most of their business from the local cats, dogs, and bears. They did have a really good steak and gave very healthy portions.

"All right," Mitch said as the waiter took their half-finished appetizers away. "You've gotta tell me how your aunts got you in that dress."

"They wrestled me into it. Francine damn near broke my arm . . . what are you doin'?"

Mitch had his head back and his eyes closed. "I'm replacing your aunts—lovely as they are—with Ronnie and Dee-Ann. There." He looked at her and motioned for her to continue. "Go on. I've got the whole scenario set. It's like one of those women in prison movies from the seventies."

"There are oils involved, aren't there?"

"Baby, there are always oils involved."

The shoes eventually came off, too, tossed carelessly under the table, and Sissy's feet were tucked up under her as she offered Mitch some of her New York strip steak. Like him, she preferred her meat medium rare.

"So explain to me how we got here tonight. The aunts wouldn't tell me a damn thing."

"I wanted to go on a date with you."

"That's it?"

"That's it. Sorry that I wasn't a little more interesting."

"It's not uninteresting. But I'm not usually the first girl guys think of when they want to go to a fancy dinner."

"You are to me. I like you, Sissy. And if you draw that damn box again with your fingers, I'm breaking them."

She quickly looked down at her food, but he got the feeling she was smiling. "Fine. Be like that. I'm only trying to keep us from getting ourselves into trouble."

"It's a little late for that."

"I know."

Mitch put down his knife and fork. "Okay, let's look at some hard, cold facts. The whole boundaries thing doesn't work for two people who spend their whole lives fucking with other people's boundaries."

"Oh, my God." Sissy started laughing. "You're right."

"So let's deal with realities. I'll be going back to Philly next week. I testify, and then I'm gone. For good."

Sissy looked up at him and nodded. "I know."

"Then let's really enjoy the time we have together."

Sissy put her hand over his, and his cock became instantly hard from the innocent action. "You do understand you'll never get over me, right? Every woman you're with from now on, you'll compare to me and find them lacking."

She was joking, but he had the distinct feeling she was absolutely right. But Mitch was a take-your-enjoyment-where-you-can kind of guy. He wouldn't be Mr. Hero and cut their time together short. Instead, he would enjoy every moment, every second.

"And you'll never find a guy who'll do you the way I do. You'll be so unsatisfied in bed unless you're fantasizing about me. I hope you're ready for that."

"I guess I'll just have to suffer about that."

"And suffer you will." Mitch leaned across the table a bit. "But not yet."

Sissy smiled. "I, uh, put something in your pocket when we were coming into the restaurant."

"You did?" Mitch was usually pretty good about knowing when someone was putting something in or taking it out of his pocket. One of his favorite aunts was a notorious pickpocket, and she'd taught him a few things. But Sissy would have done her proud. Because when he grabbed the sports jacket he'd tossed onto the seat beside him and dug into the pocket, he found a black lace thong buried inside.

"When did you take these off?"

"When the aunts were arguing over the shoes."

Mitch shoved the thong back into his pocket and started to slide out of the booth. "Time to go."

"No. No, Mitchell Shaw." Sissy's smile was cruel and wicked at the same time. "You promised me a date, and a date I shall have."

"Oh, come on!"

She pointed at the part of the booth where he'd been sitting. "You just put your butt back there, mister. So we can finish our date all properlike."

With a heartfelt sigh, Mitch slid back across from her. "Can I at least sniff your thong?"

"Only when you're in the bathroom. Don't want anyone to think we're tacky now, do we?"

Sissy rested back in that lovely booth, her feet in Mitch's lap under the table. Their meal long since finished, they talked, and Mitch rubbed her feet, paying special attention to her instep.

"Okay, so what were you like when you were fourteen?"

Sissy laughed. "Fourteen? Why did you pull that number out of your ass?"

"I didn't. It's the one age you never discuss. You've discussed up to you turning thirteen when you said you woke up one day and boom, there were breasts. And when you were fifteen and started building cars. So what are you leaving out? What was Sissy Mae Smith like at fourteen?"

"I was mean, Mitch. I was really mean."

"You sound like you regret it."

"No." And she realized she wasn't lying. "I don't regret it. I regret some of the things I did, but that's not to say I wouldn't have done them again if the situation called for it."

"Words of a true Alpha."

"Yeah. I guess. But it's hard to grow up a Smith and not be a little bit . . ."

"Unstable?"

Sissy scowled. "I was going to say a little bit mean."

"Yeah, but Smitty isn't mean."

"Bobby Ray has selective memory. He may be nice when it suits him, but Lord help you if you cross that boy."

"I try not to. I need the job until I testify."

"I remember once back when we were at the mall and this bear, a big ol' buck, grabbed Jessie Ann's ass. Now we weren't hanging together, but we were at the bookstore checking out the car magazines at the same time, and Jessie Ann was in the geek section—"

"And that's the rest of the bookstore, I'm guessing."

"Cute. Anyway, she did one of her ineffectual wild slaps, but I was surprised because Bobby Ray didn't say anything. Up to this point, he was constantly protecting her. Found out he and the Reed boys waited for that bear outside the bowling alley a week later. Beat the shit out of him. He was big, too, so I think two-by-fours were used, but don't quote me on that."

"You knew then, didn't you?"

"Knew what?"

"That Smitty and Jessie Ann were—"

"Made for each other? Yeah, I knew. I was surprised he left for the Navy without her. Hell, I was surprised he hadn't gotten her pregnant by then. If nothing else, they'll have cute kids. They'll be insane hybrids with large heads, but cute." That made Mitch laugh.

"What about you?" she asked. "What were you like at fourteen?"

Mitch thought about it a minute and answered honestly. "Horny."

"You're horny now."

"I was hornier then."

"That is truly scary."

"Thank Christ I was the only male cub in the house at the time. I had my own room. I jerked off constantly."

Sissy laughed. "Thank you for that little detail."

"You asked me a question. I was trying to be as forthcoming as possible."

"Did you get in a lot of fights?"

He snorted. "I was six-two by the time I was thirteen. Only the seniors tried to fuck with me, but they stopped after they met Brendon." He grinned. "The first time he met me, I had a black eye, and he lost his mind. I told him who did it because I didn't think he really cared. He beat the fuck out of that guy. In Philly, that's a definite sign of caring."

"So how come you didn't trust him? How come you gave him such a hard time?"

"Because I was fourteen. And Marissa. Now she was mean."

"You know now, though, right? How much they love you?"

"You're not letting that go, are you?"

"Because you need to know. Look, I know Travis couldn't care less if I lived or died. Same thing with Jackie. Donnie could go either way. But it's knowing that Bobby Ray and Sammy love me and would protect me that makes up for the others. You need to know how much they love you. 'Cause let me tell you, coming down here is not one of Brendon's favorite things."

"Really?" And Mitch looked really perplexed. " 'Cause I like it here a lot."

"You do?"

"Yeah. It's nice. Quiet."

Sissy started to say something, but she was distracted when the waitress came by yet again. When she stood there and didn't move, Sissy glared up at her, making the girl step back.

"Is there something you want, darlin'?"

"Um . . ." The little full-human swallowed. "We're actually closing . . . or are closed . . . or whatever. But feel free to stay!" she spit out in a rush before running off.

Mitch looked around. "Shit. We're the only customers left."

Sissy laughed again. "Maybe it is time to go home then."

Slowly, Mitch looked at her, that gold gaze stripping her naked right there. "I think that's a very good idea," he growled.

Leaning across the table, Sissy snarled, "Then you better move that fine ass, hoss. I'm gettin' needy."

Chapter 24

They didn't even make it out of the car. One second, Mitch was shutting off the ignition, the next he had a persistent and determined Sissy Mae in his lap. With remarkable speed, she had the seat and him flat—Mitch didn't even know if seats on the Barracuda could recline back. Yet he had the distinct feeling if they couldn't, that would be the first thing Sissy and Ronnie Lee would rectify.

Even with the side windows open, they still managed to steam up the back window, and Mitch already had the top part of Sissy's dress down around her waist.

To be honest, he'd never enjoyed making out in a car so much before.

Mitch pulled Sissy's head to the side and began to kiss her neck and shoulder—that's when he saw them watching.

"Aaah!"

Sissy jumped. "What? What's—" Her eyes narrowed, and he saw her fangs slide out as she stared out the driver's side window. "What the hell are you old bitches doin'?"

"Sissy Mae," Francine explained primly, although she looked more than a little amused, "only whores sleep with a man on the first date."

"I'm really beginning to hate you."

Janette leaned in a little and looked around the car. "Nice. But Ronnie Lee will have your ass if you screw around in her car."

"Go. Away."

Darla seemed thoughtful as she stared at Sissy. "You've got titties just like your momma."

"*That is it!*" Sissy sat straight up and immediately slammed her head on the roof. "*Goddamnit!*"

"Mouth like her momma, too," Francine laughed. She motioned to her sisters. "Let's leave these lovepups to their business. We left you children dessert. Enjoy."

Sissy rubbed the back of her head and stared down at Mitch. "Would it have been that horrible to be an orphan? I mean, really?"

Mitch shrugged. "I like 'em."

"Fine. They can be your aunts then." She rested against his chest, and he pushed her hand out of the way so he could rub the back of her head.

"They only bust your balls because they like you as much as they love you. It's a compliment."

"Whatever." She settled a little more against his chest.

"Sissy?"

"Hhhmm?"

"They left us dessert."

Her head came up off his chest as if in slow motion, and those light brown eyes stared at him behind lowered brows. "And?" she asked, pretty much daring him to say the words.

"Nothing. Absolutely nothing. Dessert will be great later. *Much* later."

She sniffed, as arrogant as any lioness, and rested back against his chest.

* * *

The mood broken by her damn aunts, Sissy went in the house fully expecting to start cutting the pies or cakes they'd probably left behind. But when she turned around to ask Mitch if he wanted coffee, she found him staring at her like she was a wounded impala.

"What?" She glanced down at herself and . . . nope. Everything was in order. She'd pulled her top back up before leaving the car since she wouldn't put it past more of her relatives to be hanging around.

"Come here." She took a step, and Mitch held his hand up, halting her. "Take off the dress."

No problem there. She hated the damn thing. In Sissy's estimation, dresses had been devised to slow women down when they needed to run away. The straps on her shoulders were already untied, and she tugged down the tight bodice until her breasts were bare. She pushed the dress past her hips and to the floor.

He chuckled. "Where are the shoes, baby?"

"Uh . . . under the table at the restaurant." Sissy put her hands on her hips. "Think you can manage without the shoes?"

"I guess. But don't you think they do wonders highlighting my calves?"

It started off as a small snort, and then Sissy was doubled over on the couch laughing. Mitch had a way of doing that to her. Making her hot one second and laughing hysterically the next. When he could do both at the same time, she'd be so screwed.

When Mitch rolled her onto her back, he was already naked. He lifted her up, carrying her in his arms as he went up the stairs. He took her into her bedroom and dumped her on the bed. After she stopped laughing, she looked up at him.

"Are you ready for me, Sissy Mae?"

She snorted again. "You have to stop."

Mitch put his hands on his hips, raised an eyebrow, and said, "Ready to partake of this level of perfection?"

"I am *begging* you to stop."

He turned his head away, lifted his chin. "Of this true symbol of all that is good and right in men?"

And that's when Sissy lost it again, rolling back and forth on the bed, tears streaming down her face.

The bed dipped, and Mitch grabbed hold of Sissy's ankles, pulling her legs apart before he dragged her down to him. He wrapped her legs around his waist and dropped forward, catching himself with his hands. He hovered above her, his eyes watching her.

"Christ, I love making you laugh."

And he said it with such feeling that Sissy went warm and dripping, pushing herself up on her elbows and capturing Mitch's mouth with her own. He groaned and relaxed into her, pressing her into the bed with his weight.

With Mitch's forearms braced on either side of Sissy's head, their kiss became deeper, more intense. He slid inside her, and Sissy pulled her knees up, trying to pull him in further. Her hands reached down and gripped his ass, squeezing and digging her fingers into the taut flesh.

Something was different, and Sissy wasn't sure what. And she couldn't even focus long enough to figure it out. Mitch's thrusts were slow, deep, and powerful. Afraid she'd lose control and unleash her claws or—more importantly—her fangs, Sissy wrapped one arm around his neck, holding Mitch to her. Her free hand reached back and grabbed hold of the headboard. She felt like it was the only thing anchoring her to this world, to this moment. Damned if at times like these she wouldn't follow the man like a puppy after a tennis ball.

With him completely surrounding her, Sissy should have felt trapped. She should have been fighting to get out from under, to be right on top, taking control. She always took

control. But she loved what he was doing to her, and she
didn't want to fight it.

So she didn't. She didn't fight Mitch or herself. She simply held on to him and her headboard and let him take her
wherever he wanted to go.

Something was different. Different . . . and . . . and so damn
amazing. Mitch didn't know what to do with himself. Sissy
was warm and solid underneath him, her breath a soft pant
in his ear.

He held her face between his hands and kissed her jaw,
her cheeks, her neck. When he kissed her mouth, her grip on
him tightened, and her body began to shake beneath his.

Mitch placed his palms flat against the mattress on either
side of Sissy and raised himself over her. He took her slower
but harder, watching her face to see what each thrust did to
her. Watching to see if she was feeling anything close to
what he was feeling.

Her eyes fluttered open, and her gaze caught his. Her arms
reached up, and those long fingers speared into his hair, mas-
saging his scalp until he was purring her name. Then Sissy's
eyes clouded, her breath catching in her throat. Mitch held
off his release, instead choosing to watch Sissy's. She came
so beautifully, torso arching, head thrown back. She bit her
lip and looked away from him. But he kept fucking her until
a sob burst from her and she climaxed again. She didn't hold
anything back this time. Simply pulled him down until she
could bury her face against his neck, short, hard breaths racing against his skin.

Mitch came then. Buried deep inside her, holding her to
him.

They didn't have much time together, but the time they
were together Mitch knew he'd never forget.

Chapter 25

Paula Jo Barron, head lioness of the Barron Pride, read her newspaper and drank her beer. Some days she was so bored. Like today. It was too hot and muggy outside to do anything but sit around and sweat. And although her bar was nice and cold from the air conditioning, there wasn't much to do here. She'd already done payroll, and she wasn't in the mood to beat one of her sisters yet again at pool. And the football game in Smithtown didn't start until three o'clock tomorrow. Hell, to watch those bears kick the Smith Pack's collective ass for another year in a row, Paula Jo would risk life and limb crossing territorial lines.

But really, it was days like these where Paula Jo thought about leaving. What would it be like to leave her little town behind and find a new place? To move to a big city like Nashville or a whole other state like Texas? What would it be like to not always be here?

But as soon as the thoughts came in her head, they went right back out again. How could she leave? She didn't trust either of her sisters to run the Pride. She definitely didn't trust her crazy aunts. The current pair of males they had probably wouldn't last much longer, and Paula Jo knew

Karen Jane would only choose the replacements by following whatever her crotch told her to do and Lucy would be suckered by the first pretty face and sweet talker who came along.

Besides, if she left, what would she do for money? The Barrons were not wealthy and probably never would be. True, they weren't dirt poor either, but last month when the roof nearly caved in, they'd had to put in for a loan to fix it. It's not like they had the money simply sitting around waiting to be used.

Must be nice, she thought with only a little less bitterness than usual.

And that's when she walked in.

Definitely a lioness. It wasn't only her scent that gave her away, but also the way she moved. The way her gold eyes sized up the entire room. And even though she'd cut her hair so it was short and up around her ears, it couldn't be mistaken for anything but the gold mane of hair that it was. True, it would never be like the males' manes, but in Paula's estimation, every predator female had a little butch in her.

The problem at the moment, however, was that this was not a lioness of Paula Jo's Pride. She was an outsider, and Paula Jo ran outsiders off.

The woman's eyes caught sight of her, and instead of making a run for it, she walked over, a backpack slung over her shoulder. She wore loose khaki pants with lots of pockets and a tight white T-shirt. Paula Jo also smelled gun oil coming from her.

This female was armed.

Paula Jo glanced back at Lucy, and her little sister slipped out the back door to get the men. Other than breeding, the only use the big bastards had was for protection. Right now, their lazy asses were asleep under one of the trees out back after Karen Jane had gotten them fed.

If they would only get a day job, Paula Jo wouldn't mind

them staying, but lazy was lazy. And Paula Jo had no time or patience for it.

The woman stopped in front of her. "You run this place?" she asked. And she wasn't talking about the bar. Nor was she talking like a true Southerner. A Yankee. *Eww.*

"I do. What can I do for ya . . . before you leave?"

"How'd you like to make some money?"

Paula Jo slowly sat up straight, dropping her legs to the floor as Lucy came back into the bar, the males right behind her, yawning and rubbing their eyes. Yup, they'd been asleep again.

Lazy!

A thud on the table had Paula Jo glancing back at the female and then down at the table. She'd dropped a wad of cash on that old wood, big enough to choke a buffalo.

"This is the first half. Help me out, and there's another half."

Karen Jane, always good with numbers after her stint as a stripper, grabbed the stack and quickly flipped through it.

"At least ten thousand," she said to Paula Jo.

Lord, who do we have to kill for twenty thousand?

"What do you want?"

"All I need is for you to be a"—and the lioness grinned, showing fangs—"distraction."

"You need to go!"

Startled, Sissy looked up into Travis's face. He stood right in front of her, not even looking at the gaggle of females she had surrounding her who'd come to check out the Smithtown Team hotties, including Mitch. "Why?"

"You're distracting him, and this is our last practice before the game tomorrow. So you need to go."

"He's fumbled the ball a few times, but how was that my fault?"

"He's handling that ball as bad as his brother."

"Hey!" Ronnie piped in, insulted for her mate.

"You can't be here."

Sissy really didn't have a problem leaving, but that didn't mean she wouldn't torture her brother a little. "But where can I go? What will I do while he's here?"

"Are you trying to piss me off? Is that your goal here?"

Sissy smiled. "Maybe."

Travis scowled, but before Sissy could make him good and frothy, Patty Rose interceded. She always did. The possibility of Sissy kicking Travis's ass all over the football field was too real and too much to risk their "rise to power" as Ronnie liked to call it.

"Now y'all, cut it out. Brothers and sisters shouldn't act like this."

Sissy stared at her brother's mate. "Are you new to the neighborhood?"

Travis growled, "Sissy Mae!"

Patty Rose reached into her bag and pulled out her wallet. "Why don't you go on down to your uncle's bar and have a few drinks on me and Travis? I know a few of these ladies here"—she motioned to the females who'd been sitting behind Sissy—"would love to spend some time getting to know y'all."

"Especially if the drinks are already paid for," Ronnie muttered under her breath.

"I swear," Patty Rose went on, ignoring Ronnie like she always did, "as soon as Mitch is done here, we'll send him right over. Won't we, hon?"

"Whatever." Travis stormed back to the field.

Now that her brother was gone . . . "Patty Rose, you don't have to pay for our drinks."

"Oh, I don't mind." She placed a small wad of cash in Sissy's hand. "Y'all go on now, and I'll let Mitch know where you're off to."

Sissy shrugged. "Okay. Thanks."

With Dee, Ronnie Lee, and a handful of the young She-wolves in tow, they headed down to the bar.

Mitch pulled his helmet off and watched as Travis ran back to the field. "What's going on?"

"She'll be back. She's going to the bar with Ronnie and Dee."

"Why?"

"Because she was distracting you, and it was pissing me off."

Mitch wished he could honestly tell Travis he was wrong, but he'd not been playing his best game today. Not with the memories of last night constantly flooding his brain.

Christ, he loved her. Not a little either. Not something he'd get over one day. He loved Sissy Mae, and absolutely no one else would do for him. But he always came back to the same thing: he couldn't take her away from this. He couldn't part her from her family or her Pack. Sure, if her only brother was Travis, he'd ask her to come with him in a heart-beat. But she had Bobby Ray, and the two relied on each other the way Marissa and Bren did.

Knowing he'd have to leave her soon was breaking his heart. Thinking of her a few years from now with some wolf as a mate was making him homicidal.

"Hey, golden boy." Mitch ground his teeth together. He hated when Travis called him that. "She'll be back. So you think you can give the team a few minutes of your precious cat time?"

He started to say something, and Bren grabbed his arm, pulling Mitch back. "We've got it," he said before Mitch could start the Pride–Pack war of the century.

*   *   *

Sissy wasn't enjoying herself. And not simply because she missed Mitch, which she did. Or because it was hitting her in no uncertain terms that she'd fallen head over boots in love with the big goofball, and she had no idea how to handle that. Or how to handle it when she lost him forever into the government system.

True, all those things were bothering her, but that wasn't what was nagging at her like an uncomfortable itch.

Something wasn't right, and Sissy couldn't quite put her finger on it. There was a tension among their group of young She-wolves that had her nursing her one beer. Dee had settled for a Coke, and Ronnie Lee nothing.

The fact that Dee hadn't disappeared by now told her a lot. Dee bored easily and always simply up and left, but this time, she hadn't. She stayed. And she watched.

What was it that bothered the three friends? The girls. Why they'd followed them to the bar, Sissy had no idea, but she was ready to split. The three of them could hang at their aunts' pie shop rather than here with girls she didn't trust.

Sissy glanced at Ronnie and Dee, giving them a small tilt of her head to indicate she was more than ready to go.

Ronnie nodded and leaned forward to make some bullshit excuse about why they were leaving when one of the girls—Shayla . . . or something?—slapped her hand against the table.

"How come you're not Alpha here?" she asked with a sneer Sissy didn't much appreciate.

"Because my momma is Alpha."

"She ain't gonna live forever. You think you're coming back then?"

"No."

"I bet you're scared. Scared you're not strong enough."

Sissy shrugged. "You're right. I'm scared. Too scared to be Alpha here." She motioned to Ronnie and her cousin, and all three stood. Sissy dug into her front pocket for a couple of twenties to cover their drinks and tossed them on the table.

"Ladies," she said and stepped around the table toward the exit. But Sissy barely stepped back in time before a bottle of tequila exploded at her feet. Her bare feet.

Sissy took a deep breath, turning just her head to look at the one who had thrown the bottle. "Little girl, have you lost your mind?"

"They say you're so scary tough. I call bullshit."

"You can call anything you want, but I'm walking out of here and you're backing off."

In answer, the girl slammed another bottle of tequila to the floor, this time close to Ronnie. Too close in Sissy's estimation.

Sissy pushed her friend back and moved around the table toward the girl. The girl, like an idiot, charged forward—and right into Sissy's grip. Sissy held her by her throat and stared into her eyes.

"Take it out back, Sissy Mae," the bartender ordered her. Since this bar belonged to her uncle, she nodded and dragged the girl toward the back exit.

As one mass of She-wolves, they burst through the back door, and Sissy flung the girl to the ground. Planting her foot on the back of her neck, Sissy pressed down simply to keep her in place, not to snap anything. She didn't want to do any permanent damage to her; she just wanted the pup to learn where she fell in the big scheme of things.

But the girl scratched at the ground and desperately begged, "Get her off me. Please! Get her off me!" Surprised her bravado had left so quickly, Sissy looked over her shoulder at Ronnie and Dee. Four She-wolves were holding Ronnie back, and two males had Dee. She looked at her cousin, and Sissy knew Dee was moments from killing anyone and everyone in that alley.

What the hell was going on?

And that's when Sissy heard him.

"Hey, baby," Gil said softly, his sister and two cousins standing behind him. "I didn't think little Shayla would ever get your cute ass back here."

Ronnie started to shift, but Sissy held her hand up, halting her. Sissy was Alpha, and Ronnie had to follow her lead.

Sissy lifted her foot off the younger She-wolf's neck, kicking her out of her way.

"What is this, Gil? What do you want?"

"I'll be the first to admit I screwed up. I know I did. But I still think we make a hell of a pair."

Sissy looked back at her and Dee, and even in the situation they found themselves, all three still had to laugh.

"You know," Sissy said, still chuckling, "my momma always said you weren't too bright. And I should have listened to her."

"Your momma adores me."

"Actually"—Sissy scrunched up her nose—"she doesn't. In fact, she warned me that if you were anything like your daddy, you were cursed with the Warren small balls."

"Forget it, Sissy. You're not gonna make me angry."

"Trust me, darlin', I can make you angry. If I remember correctly, it didn't take much more than, 'No, I don't want to,' to have you taking a swing at me."

"That was a long time ago. It's over. And I'm a different man."

Sissy glanced around the group. "You call this changing? You call trying to force me into a mating changing?" She smirked. "That is what you're planning, right? A forced mating?"

"It worked for your parents."

"Lord, you are dumb. My daddy didn't force my momma

to do anything. He never had to because she wanted him. Sadly, your father can't say the same thing. But if I remember correctly, Momma left him crying and whimpering right outside of Smithville all those years ago before heading to Smithtown. You hoping to repeat that experience for yourself now?"

And Gil's anger, always a brittle thing, snapped quickly, and he took an aggressive step forward—which Sissy probably knew he'd do. Taking one step back and putting up her arms, Sissy punched Gil in the face. She did it exactly the way they'd been taught when she and Ronnie had ended up in Ireland with nothing more than a hangover and five pounds between them. Louis McCanohan had taken them in when he found them about to shift and kill some full-human scum behind his favorite pub. The sixty-year-old wolf had taught them how to fight as human so they could always take care of themselves in any situation.

Hands covering his bleeding nose, Gil glared at her. "You broke my nose."

Staying loose and on her toes, Sissy nodded. "Yeah, I did. So if we're gonna do this, son, let's do this."

Gil came at her again, fangs bared, and Sissy stepped to his left and slammed her fist into his gut. When he doubled over, she brought up her knee. She'd aimed for his jaw, trying to break it, but he moved in time and she hit his already broken nose.

Again, he dashed toward her, and Sissy danced out of his way, only to turn and double tap him twice in his right kidney. He went down on one knee, the pain probably not as bad as the embarrassment of having a female kick his ass as human.

Apparently, he didn't want to deal with it anymore either because Gil shifted and flipped around, charging Sissy. He launched himself at her, and Sissy brought up her hands, catching his front paws in them. They went down, and by the time they landed, Sissy had shifted to wolf. She scrambled away from him, her fangs bared and her body ready.

Ronnie didn't wait any longer. She shifted and tried to slip out of her captors' arms. But they shifted as well and tackled her to the ground, pinning her in place. She howled, hoping to call to Sissy's kin, but the females sat on her neck, stopping her from doing much more than snarling. Two more males had joined in an attempt to control Dee, but she was causing them a lot of damage. But not enough yet to get away and help Sissy.

Sissy didn't wait for Gil to come at her again. She went for him, her mouth open and aimed for his throat. But Gil's sister and cousins tackled her like the others had tackled Ronnie and pinned her to the ground, holding her in place for Gil.

At that point, Ronnie fought harder, knowing what they were planning and horrified beyond anything she'd known. This was more barbaric than the Smiths had ever been. A Smith male had to be able to handle his female on his own. If he couldn't, then he wasn't worthy of her.

The only man who could handle Sissy Mae Smith was back at the football field, catching passes and impressing Sissy's brothers. Mitch loved her, and eventually, Sissy would have to admit she loved him. Everybody in town knew it. The rumors were spreading, and everyone was wondering how Bubba Smith was going to take another one of his pups mating outside the Pack and the breed. Especially with a cat.

Gil must have heard the rumors and decided to make this desperate move. Or maybe one of Sissy's brothers had put him up to it. Ronnie didn't know. She just knew that she had to get to her friend. She had to get to her now.

* * *

Travis was real happy with how practice was going now that his sister had left. She distracted his star player, and to be damn honest, he couldn't have it!

He wondered if there was a way to get the boy down here every year in time for the game but leave Sissy back wherever the hell she'd be at the time. He'd have to ponder that one. A couple of days apart wouldn't kill them, could it?

He called break and jogged over to the ice chests. His mate waited for him, a sports drink in her hand. Patty Rose wasn't the prettiest thing, but she was tough, a good breeder, and an even better fuck. He definitely could have done worse.

Besides, her ambitions rivaled his own. With a female like this by his side, he'd definitely take over for his daddy once he could get the old bastard to submit.

"Thanks," he grunted. She grinned up at him, and he raised his brows. "What are you looking so smug for?"

She stepped closer. "I think I took care of our little problem."

"You mean the shed? Thought we were gonna wait to fix that."

"No." She rolled her eyes. Travis knew she thought he was dumb as dirt most days, but that was okay. Sometimes, when he was bored, he treated her like a whore. It kind of made them even.

"Then what?"

Another step closer. "Gil Warren and Sissy."

Travis shrugged, already getting bored with this conversation—and his mate. "What about them?"

"I let him have her."

"Let him have her?" He didn't understand what she meant.

She went on tiptoe and whispered in his ear, "He's forcing a mating as we speak."

Stepping back, Travis stared at his mate. "What?"

"You heard me." She smiled and glanced over at Sammy and Mitch, making sure they weren't listening. "We've been planning this for days."

His hand was around her throat, and he lifted her off her feet before she could blink. "*You did what?*"

Sissy fought to get out from under the She-bitches who held her down, but they weren't letting go, and Gil was heading right for her.

If Gil Warren thought he'd really make her his this way, he was dead wrong. A forced mating on a Smith female was just a quick way to end up with your throat cut while you were sleeping.

But for Sissy, this was about the humiliation. She'd always wear Gil's mark no matter what happened. And because of it, she'd always be considered weak. Not worthy of being Alpha Female. Travis and his mate would know this, but Gil didn't understand. He thought this forced mating was his fast ride to the top. But he was only dooming them to permanent Beta status. Maybe even Omega. And the thought of it made her sick.

No. No way! She'd never let that happen. Not while she still had blood in her veins.

With a snarl that shook the females holding her, Sissy twisted and snapped and dragged herself out from under the She-wolves. They tried to grab at her again, and she spun and snapped at them, ripping into someone's snout and making them back away from her.

With a growl, she turned around and faced Gil. She bared her fangs and motioned for him to come to her.

He took a running step, and Sissy braced her body for the oncoming fight, but a large body jumped in front of her so she stepped back and to the side.

Gil stumbled back in shock as he faced something that he feared more than a Smith female—a Smith male.

Bobby Ray bared his fangs and lowered his body as he moved around Gil. The rest of the New York Smith Pack surrounded them, easily batting away the She-wolves still holding on to Ronnie. But the Reed boys went after the males holding on to Dee since they probably didn't feel right tearing up the little girls holding down their sister.

Sissy didn't know why Bobby Ray was back from his honeymoon so soon, and she'd kick whoever the hell told him to come home, but that would be later. At the moment, she was just damn glad to see him.

Gil tried to maneuver away from Bobby, but Sissy moved to his flank, blocking him from making a run into the small stand of woods behind the bar alley.

Now that they had him trapped, the siblings looked at each other over Gil's suddenly trembling body.

They waited. One. Two. Three heartbeats—then they tore into him. Fur and blood and flesh flew across the back alley, and Gil howled in pain.

As always, Bobby Ray and Sissy moved as a synchronized pair. It was why they made such good Alphas. They didn't stop hurting Gil until Bobby Ray had him on his back with his maw wrapped around Gil's throat.

He bit down, and Gil's body went limp, paws up, eyes downcast. Gil Warren would never recover from this. He'd never be Alpha in any Smith-run town. Knowing that, Sissy threw her head back and howled, her Pack joining her.

But she stopped short when that blur of gold shot past. Sissy stumbled back as Mitch snatched Gil up in his mouth and proceeded to shake him back and forth like a rag doll. He slammed Gil's body against a wall and then tossed him to Brendon. It was then Brendon's turn to shake Gil and bang him into the wall a few times.

Gil got tossed back to Mitch, and Mitch held him by his back and stared at Sissy. She was tempted—Lord, was she tempted—to let Mitch finish Gil. But that wouldn't be today. She shook her head, and Mitch nodded.

He tossed his head, mane flipping up, and Gil flew across the alley, slamming into the wall and landing on the ground.

They all heard it, too. That sound of a spine snapping in half.

Of course, Mitch could have done worse. And in time—years, really—Gil's back would probably heal, and he'd walk again. But for now . . .

Well. It wasn't Sissy's problem.

Mitch walked up to Sissy, those gold eyes watching her. He wanted to know she was all right. Sissy nodded, and Mitch brushed his forehead against hers, rubbed his mane against her neck and snout. He'd marked her, at least temporarily, and walked off, Brendon right behind him, the rest of the team following, including Travis.

Bobby Ray stared at his sister, and Sissy, not really in the mood for this particular conversation, turned and trotted back to her parent's house and her aunts' banana cream pie—which she'd hidden from Mitch only that morning—Ronnie, Dee, and the New York Smith She-wolves right behind her.

Chapter 26

"Well, I always knew that boy had no sense." Francine placed a slice of pie down in front of Sissy. "But I never knew he was that stupid."

Sissy nodded in agreement and dug into the pie, more intent on feeding than discussing Gil Warren. Dee had headed back to her parents and told her mother everything. That led to a call to her sisters, and they'd rushed right over. By the time Sissy realized Mitch had tracked down the hidden pie and devoured it, the other aunts had shown up. With more pies in hand.

"He figured Sissy would eventually accept it." Ronnie pulled her legs up, resting her bare feet on the seat, her arms around her calves. "He had the nerve to bring up her daddy and Miss Janie."

Francine opened another cardboard box and pulled out one of her chocolate cream pies. "That was Bubba's fault. He let that rumor grow 'cause he and his damn brothers are so competitive. The way they describe it, they were Vikings descending on Smithville to take the Lewis females by force."

Sissy and Ronnie laughed at that until Francine placed

that chocolate pie in front of an empty chair and put a fork next to it. They glanced at each other, then around. When they'd first gotten home, they'd spent most of their time cleaning blood and dirt off their faces and arms while the other She-wolves were cluttering up chairs and couches or laying on the living room floor. To be honest, they hadn't bothered to check the house to see who else was there. Besides Mitch and Brendon, who would warrant a whole pie to themselves . . . ?

"Is that for me?" Jessie Ann raced down the stairs like an overeager puppy and threw herself into the chair, the pie in front of her. She looked at Francine with undisguised adoration. "I have so missed your chocolate cream pie, Miss Francine."

"Then you dig right in there, darlin'. Can't have that baby starvin' to death now, can we?"

Sissy sipped from her glass of milk before saying to Jessie, "I'm real sorry about your honeymoon, Jessie."

"Don't be," she said good-naturedly, the fork poised in front of her mouth. "I love your brother, but I was starting to crawl the walls. Besides"—she gestured to the feast in front of her—"pie."

Without another word, she took her first bite of pie. Jessie's eyes rolled back in her head, and she fell back in her chair.

For the first time in hours, Sissy smiled. The girl did have something about her. Goofy in that mixed breed way. And not surprisingly, she wore the ID bracelet Sissy had given Bobby Ray at the wedding. She knew for a fact that Jessie Ann had a diamond bracelet that had probably cost Bobby Ray a small fortune. But it was that silver-plated ID bracelet purchased years ago by a teen Bobby Ray that meant the most to her. And that made Jessie Ann cooler than most people Sissy knew—although she'd never admit that out loud.

After several more bites and rapturous responses, Jessie

asked, "Have you guys thought about opening a shop in Manhattan?"

Francine shook her head. "Not really. Think we'd sell well there?"

"I'm relatively certain the wild dogs will keep you in business until the end of time."

"That's real sweet of you, darlin'—"

"Really, Miss Francine, I'm not just being sweet. Our Pack is always looking for new investments, and you and your sisters could start a pie chain. Kind of like the Van Holtz steak house, only not as snobby." The Van Holtz Pack was the wealthiest Pack in the States and Europe, and that was due to their family-owned and -run steak houses.

"You really think so?" And Francine actually sounded intrigued rather than just humoring.

"Absolutely. Of course, your flagship store will have to be near our Pack house."

Momentarily forgetting this wasn't one of her She-wolves, Sissy automatically teased, "Good thing my brother likes women with meat on their bones 'cause your ass is gonna be gettin' wide."

As soon as the words left her mouth, she wished she could take them back.

But without missing a beat, Jessie shot back, "Cool. Now I can start wearing your jeans. I thought that was only going to be possible during the late stages of the pregnancy."

The milk Ronnie had just taken a big gulp of sprayed across the table, and Sissy almost choked on the piece of pie she'd just swallowed. As Francine clucked her tongue and cleaned up the mess, Sissy and Ronnie howled in laughter, and Jessie grinned around her pie.

It was decided while the males sat out on the porch and drank beer that Gil Warren and his tiny Pack would be pushed out of town as soon as Gil could wheel himself out. It was obvious that the reasons behind the decision varied between brothers. Smitty and Sammy Ray felt Gil had crossed a line with their baby sister, and there would be no coming back from that. He didn't belong on Smith territory, end of story. For Travis Ray, Jackie Ray, and . . . uh . . . the other Ray—Mitch could never remember the man's name— the reasoning was much more wolflike. Gil Warren had proven he was weak and a bloodline they didn't want polluting their town's gene pool. The fact that their sister had almost been forced into a mating she didn't want didn't seem to faze them at all, and Mitch easily realized why Sissy stuck with Smitty. He'd ended his honeymoon early and had traveled from New York to Tennessee to check on her. When he'd realized she was in trouble, he'd gone to her aid the same way Mitch would have if it had been either of his sisters.

Travis had gone to Sissy's aid because he didn't want Mitch too upset to play tomorrow's game.

"We'll deal with all this after the game tomorrow." Travis looked at Smitty. "You playing tomorrow?"

"Since you actually came to help our baby sister for once, yeah, I'll play."

"Good." Travis didn't say anything else—like "Congrats on your marriage" or "Sorry I missed your wedding, bruh"—and walked back into the house, his Pack of wolves following.

"Sorry about your honeymoon, Smitty."

Smitty waved off Mitch's apology. "Don't sweat it, son. Sissy did the right thing. She brought both of you some place safe."

"Yeah." Mitch smiled, thinking about Sissy. "I wasn't too happy about it at first, but I'm glad she brought me here."

"I bet you are." Then Smitty hit him. Hard.

Mitch stumbled back, trying to keep himself from blacking out.

"*My sister? My baby sister?*"

Brendon stepped between Mitch and Smitty. "Whoa!"

"It's not what you think," Mitch said, shaking his head and trying to keep the blackness at bay.

"Is that right? Then what is it?"

Mitch didn't answer right away, and Smitty snarled. "I trusted you, *boy*. And I come here and find out you're just using—"

"I love her." Mitch said it quietly, but it might have been screamed the way everything went quiet. Even the night animals stopped whatever they were doing.

Smitty folded his arms across his chest, his sudden rage disappearing as quickly as it had come. "Is that right?"

"Yeah, that's right. I love your sister."

Smitty watched Mitch for several seconds, then he pulled his fist back again. Bren tried to block him, but Mitch just sort of waited for the hit.

"You're just gonna let me hit you, aren't you?"

Mitch shrugged. "She cares about you, so I'd rather not start a caged deathmatch with you, if that's possible." He raised his hands. "You know how mighty my fists of fury are."

Smitty sized him up again, and Mitch could see him trying not to laugh. "You better keep her happy, feline, or I'm gonna let Sabina use her knives to cut your balls off." The males winced. Mostly because they all knew it wouldn't take much to talk Sabina into using her knives on anyone. Of Jessie's wild dog Pack, she was the most . . . rabid.

"I won't be here after the trial." And suddenly, he again had the attention of the entire New York Pack.

"Come again?"

He cleared his throat, and Bren stared at him like he'd lost his mind. But he didn't want Smitty thinking he'd lied to him. "I go into Witness Protection after the trial. I won't be back for Sissy. I won't be back here." And it was killing him.

But before Smitty could say anything, Travis burst back out onto the porch. "*What the hell are you talking about?*"

"I thought you guys knew this."

"What about my sister?" Smitty growled.

"What about next year's game?" Travis snarled.

Smitty looked at his brother. "Game? You're talking about your goddamn game when this is about Sissy's future?"

"Let's be realistic, Bobby Ray. It ain't like Sissy won't jump on the next steed that comes along. This boy's just a waystation."

"Hey!" the Shaw brothers said in unison.

"No offense, hoss, but you can't really think my sister has serious feelings for you, or any man."

"You got something to say to me, Travis?"

They'd been so wrapped up in their own bullshit, none of them had realized the New York Smith Pack She-wolves stood in front of the house. The men looked down at them from the porch. Jessie Ann, the cute little one in the middle, waved her hand at Smitty. She looked lost in the mass of all those much taller and bigger angry She-wolves.

"Well?" Sissy demanded, walking up the stairs with Ronnie right behind her. "Say whatever you're gonna say, Travis. To my face."

Travis glanced at Mitch and shook his head. "No. That's okay. Maybe another time."

"Don't worry. Mitch will play. And he'll play well. I'll make sure of it. So just say it."

"You don't want me to do this here, Sissy Mae."

"No," Sammy cut in. "I don't want you doing this here."

"It's all right, Sammy. Really. I'd like to hear what he has to say. Go on, Travis. Say it."

"Fine. We all know that you couldn't care less about this boy other than the fuck he can give you at the moment. When he's gone, there'll be another and another and another.

Just like always. Ain't nothin' changed. Although I was praying you'd keep this one for a few years since he does play some mean ball. But you're the same whore—"

It was the word whore that seemed to tip him over the edge, his fist slamming into Travis's face, knocking the bigger man to the ground. And as they stood around, stunned, Sammy grabbed his older brother by the T-shirt, lifted him up, and slammed his fist into Travis's face again . . . and again . . . and a few more times for good measure.

Finally, Bobby Ray and Sissy had to grab him and pull him back. Sissy had her arm around his shoulders, and she kept telling him, "It's okay. It's okay."

But good-natured Sammy apparently had his own boundaries, and Travis had just crossed them.

"I warned you what I'd do if you called her that again! *I warned you!*"

Travis sat up, his back against the porch railing. Blood covered a good portion of his face from his shattered nose down.

"You act like she hasn't been called that before," Travis snapped, trying to maintain some of his dignity.

Sammy went for him again, but Bobby Ray held him back, although Mitch had a feeling he wanted to beat the hell out of Travis himself.

Travis gave a small, taunting smile. "And Lord knows, she'll be called that again."

It was something in her eyes that Mitch caught. That split second of getting fully fed up. He reached for her, but she grabbed hold of the football helmet that one of the players had dumped by the front door. She brought it up over her head, and then as she went down on one knee, Sissy brought it back down.

The helmet connected with Travis's knee, and they all jumped and winced at the same time as they heard that bone shatter. Then that wolf howled in pure agony.

Panting, anger coming off her in waves, Sissy stood back up. "I promised Mitch would play for you tomorrow. Never said nothing about *you* getting to play. Good thing Bobby Ray is here to help out." She tossed the helmet to Donnie, who grabbed it but smartly kept his distance.

Sissy brushed her hand across Mitch's arm before she walked off, her She-wolves following behind her.

Brendon stared down at the crying, screaming wolf at his feet. "We better get him to the hospital. They're gonna have to set that." He looked at Smitty. "But we better get your wife out of the tree first."

"Out of the . . ." Smitty looked at the big tree closest to the railing. "*Jessica Ann!*"

"Don't yell at me," she snapped. "It was instinctual!" She leaned down a bit so they could see just her head, the rest of her still buried in that tree. "Angry-Sissy means I run for the hills, but I wasn't in the mood to run. Did the next best thing."

Mitch smiled. "I'm impressed a dog can climb trees."

That, of course, earned him a glare from Smitty. "Is this you helping me? I don't think this is you helping me."

Chapter 27

At three A.M., Mitch called to let Sissy know a bunch of them, including Brendon and Bobby Ray, had taken Travis to the hospital to get his leg set. The break was apparently so bad it would take more than a week to heal.

Sissy would have felt awful if Mitch hadn't sounded so proud over the phone. At one point, he even told her, "I figured I had to go with him since my girlfriend was the one who beat the crap out of him."

It had been the first time anyone had ever called her that where she hadn't automatically responded, "Who the hell are you talking about?"

Instead, she curled up on the couch, Ronnie asleep with the other She-wolves on the floor, and said, "He made me mad."

"He made me mad, too. But I'm glad you're the one who kicked his ass."

They talked for nearly an hour until Mitch told her, "It looks like we're taking him back. I'll stay with Smitty's Pack tonight. See you before the game?"

"Of course. In fact, I was thinking that . . . um . . . when

you go back to Philly, I can go with you. Just until you testify," she rushed to explain.

He was silent for a long time, until he finally asked,
"Why?"

"Because I don't want you to be alone."

"Sissy . . . that would mean a lot to me. You'll be like my
sexy bodyguard."

She laughed. "Well, somebody's gotta watch your back."

"I have to go. I'll talk to you in a few hours."

"Okay." The words she really wanted to say were right
there. Right on the tip of her tongue. But she'd never said them
to anyone who was not a blood relative or her best girlfriends.
"Um . . ."

"Sissy?"

"Uh-huh?"

"I love you."

Sissy let out a breath, her hand gripping the phone tighter.
"Me, too. I mean . . . I love you, too."

"That wasn't so hard now, was it?"

She rolled her eyes and smiled at the humor in his voice.
"Shut up."

"Talk to you later, baby."

"Yeah." She disconnected the call.

Sissy was in love, and it wasn't nearly as appalling as she
had thought it would be.

"I love you, Mitchy!"

"And I love you, Sissy!"

Then Ronnie and one of Sissy's cousins began to make
kissing noises while the rest of the She-wolves fell out
laughing.

"To the devil with all y'all!"

* * *

Mitch had only been asleep a few hours when he felt the couch he was stretched out on dip and someone slapped him in the back of the head.

Growling, he looked over his shoulder and glared. "Desiree."

"Mitchell." She grinned. "Glad to see you're breathing."

"I was sleeping."

"Yes. But I wanted to make sure you were okay."

"I'm playing ball in a few hours, so . . ." He motioned her away with a wave of his hand.

"Oh, that's nice. I come out to Hicksville to track down your little murderer, and you brush me off."

"You're not letting me sleep, are you?"

Her grin grew. "Actually, Smitty sent me up here to get you. He said I should awaken you with my dulcet tones."

Dulcet tones? The woman had a voice like sandpaper over gravel. And Smitty knew that.

"Thanks." Yawning and rubbing his eyes, he pulled himself up. "Any leads?"

Dez shrugged. "We're pretty sure she's headed this way. Your head is worth a lot right now. Maybe they'll mount it on the wall."

"Shut up."

"Or they'll stuff your entire body, and you can be put next to someone's stuffed armadillo and their tiger skin rug."

"I hate you."

She laughed. "I know. Mace hates when I wake him up like that. Although, he hates it worse when it's the dogs."

"I don't know how you got him to live with those dogs."

"Love me . . . love my dogs."

"You got a car?" Mitch abruptly asked her.

"Yup. A lovely beige rental."

"Give me a ride when I get dressed?"

"Sure," she answered simply as Brendon walked by on the way to the bathroom.

He stopped and stared at Dez and Mitch. "Dez . . . what is your deal with cats?"

They'd only gotten a few hours sleep and couldn't find *any* food left in the entire house. Damn cat. Now the Smith Pack She-wolves had finished eating their breakfast at the diner and were headed back out to the streets they'd grown up on but had left behind for the fast city life of New York.

Ronnie glanced down at Sissy's feet. "Maybe we should get those hooves of yours done at a nail salon. A little polish wouldn't hurt."

"Last I saw, I can still wear your boots. So watch the glass house you throw those boulders at."

The two friends grinned at each other but stopped abruptly as the scent hit them. Actually, it hit them all.

And like the brazen hussies they were, Paula Jo and her Pride pulled up in her topless Jeep.

"Hey, Sissy Mae."

Sissy stepped forward. "What are you doing here? Have you lost your mind?"

"I had to make a decision." She lifted her right hand, palm up. "My kind"—and lifted her left—"your kind." Paula Jo continued, shaking her head, "But in the end, it really came down to a more important decision."

Again, she lifted her right hand, palm up. "Southerner"—and then her left—"Yankee."

Sissy briefly crossed her eyes. "What are you talkin' about?"

"We've been hired to distract you. Some Yankee lion waving ten grand with a promise of twenty. We figure we can have some fun with that ten, and she can shove the other ten up her Yankee ass." Paula Jo looked Sissy straight in the eye.

"She's here for your man, Sissy Mae. And that crazy bitch isn't going to stop until she gets him."

"Hello?" Dee walked through the house and found the note on one of the living room end tables.

Went to diner for breakfast. Meet us there or at the field for the game.
—Sissy

Typical. Heifers didn't even wait for her. Of course, she did suddenly disappear on them, and she knew Sissy didn't care. That's why she made a great Alpha—Sissy didn't insist Dee spend every moment with her like most Alphas. Sissy understood her Pack and acted accordingly.

But Dee had heard about what had gone down between Sissy and Travis, and Dee hated the fact that she'd missed being there for her cousin.

And Travis deserved what he got as far as Dee was concerned. He made her glad she had no brothers or sisters of her own. Sure, you could get a Bobby Ray or Sammy, but you could just as easily get a Travis or a Jackie.

Figuring she'd already missed them at the diner, Dee decided to head on home until it got closer to game time. She went to the kitchen, and as soon as she stepped in, she caught the scent, her gaze automatically lifting at the same time as the .45 locked on her. Without thought, only years of training, Dee hooked her foot under the kitchen chair by her and kicked out, flinging the chair across the room. It slammed into the lioness, the weapon knocked from her grip.

The lioness stared at her weapon and then back at Dee. After a moment, her eyes widened as recognition dawned. "Well, well, how far we *haven't* gone."

Dee's head cocked to the side. "I thought you were dead,

Mary. They told us you were dead." And that's why Dee would never have thought of Mary as the shooter—she'd already looked into a few of her old comrades, but they were all definitely breathing and had alibis.

"As far as they're concerned . . . I am dead. God knows, we weren't making enough money at that job, considering what we had to do." She flexed her gun hand, probably trying to work out the pain the chair had caused when it hit her. "So I decided to go out on my own. Make the big money. But don't think you can get between me and my payday, little puppy. You were never *that* good."

Dee didn't have any of her guns, and the lioness's gun had skittered under the refrigerator. Quickly flicking her gaze across the clean counter, Dee saw the knife block and a hammer hanging beside a couple of screw drivers. She went for the hammer. Knives were a nightmare to fight with. Even though she could—hell, she'd been trained to, but she'd also been trained that it was an easy way to get a major artery cut.

By the time she swiped up that hammer, Mary had launched herself at Dee, a hunting knife in her hand. Dee turned her body, and Mary slammed into her side. Ramming the female's hand down on the kitchen table, Dee cracked it with the hammer.

Mary unleashed a roar and shoved, forcing Dee into the counter. With the blade gone, the lioness wrapped her hands around Dee's wrists. Dee slammed her foot down on Mary's instep and slammed her head into Mary's.

Yanking away from her, Mary shoved Dee again, this time into the kitchen table before she charged over it. Instinctively, Dee knew she had more guns outside and scrambled after her. Mary had just reached the old screen door when Dee tackled her from behind, the momentum of it forcing them through the door and out onto the porch.

* * *

"All right, so what's going down?"

Mitch glanced over at Dez and frowned. "What's going down about what?"

"You and Sissy? Man, Smitty is pissed. He called you a using bastard. Why?"

Sighing, Mitch stared back out the window. "Can't you ask Sissy these questions? I'm a guy."

"I get along better with men."

"Then get it from Smitty."

"He stormed away, and Jess went after him. Come on!" She practically bounced up and down in the seat. "Tell me! I'm a fellow detective. You *have* to tell me."

"I can't believe you're throwing that at me."

"By any means necessary."

Mitch turned and glared at her. "That is not the proper use for that quote."

"*Tell me!*"

"No. Suffer. And turn here."

"Fine. I'll ask Ronnie Lee."

"Good. Do that."

"And let me tell you, the whole no cell phone thing has been making me insane. I *knew* something was going on, and no one was telling me."

"Shouldn't you be focusing on finding my killer?"

"You ain't dead yet. So get over yourself."

Why did he like this woman? Maybe because she was strangely fascinating. Although waking up to that voice every morning . . . more power to Mace.

"The house is right up here."

She turned and drove the short bit down the dirt lane. "I hear banjos."

"Stop it. And I'm telling Sissy you said that."

"Rat."

They pulled to a stop in front of the house. Mitch looked out the front windshield. "I don't think they're here." Which really disappointed him since he'd planned to take Sissy for a quickie in her bedroom or the bathroom. Whatever worked best for them in the moment.

A noise from inside the house made it past the radio and air conditioner sounds. But something didn't sound right. He exchanged glances with Dez, and immediately, they opened their doors. Mitch was rounding the corner of the hood when some female and Dee-Ann came crashing through the screen door.

They landed, and the female, a lioness he'd guess, reached for the backpack that had been resting behind the porch rail. She yanked out a weapon, and Dez yelled, "Gun!"

Mitch had started to go up there, but when the lioness saw them, she aimed at Dez and Mitch and started firing her automatic weapon.

How the hell did everything go to shit so fast? One second, she was busting Mitch Shaw's balls, which she'd found surprisingly entertaining. And the next, some crazy blond bitch had opened fire on them.

Dez used the rental car door as a shield and waited while the blond shot the shit out of her vehicle. When it briefly stopped, Dez crouched and leaned outside the door, her .45 gripped in her hands. She got off three rounds before the bitch shot back. But then the other female, a brunette in nothing more than a T-shirt and shorts, was on her, a hunting knife in her hand.

The brunette didn't bring her arm up in a big arching move, but instead, she slashed the woman's face. The blonde roared and backhanded the brunette, sending her crashing back into the house. Then the blonde scrambled to her feet and again opened fire.

Dez ducked behind the car, and she could hear the female coming down the steps, the barrage of bullets breaking for the reload. Dez swung out again, still crouched, and again opened fire. She nailed the cat in the shoulder, but the tragedy with shifters—they didn't go down easy.

Instead, Dez had only managed to piss the bitch off. She swung her weapon at Dez. But before she could start firing, the brunette came charging off the porch and took the blonde down with one well-placed hit.

The blonde went facedown, but she used her free hand— the one attached to the shattered shoulder—to reach down and dig in another pocket of her khakis. She pulled out another blade, a smaller one, and slammed it into the brunette's hip.

Dez cleared her weapon and dug in her back pocket for another magazine.

The brunette barked in pain from the knife, and the blonde used the moment to draw herself up, knocking the brunette back. She stood and turned, the gun aimed at the brunette's head.

Dez popped the clip in, pulled back the slide, and fired. She didn't have time to aim, but she did manage to distract the blonde.

And then she heard a roar. They all did.

"Mitch! No!"

But it was too late. He'd already shifted and stood at the edge of some frightening-looking woods. He waited long enough for the blonde to see him, then ran off into those woods. And they all knew she'd follow.

She did, too. But not until she had turned back to again spray Dez's rental car with bullets.

Dez dived into the front seat, her hands over her head until the shooting stopped. Since she knew by this time, the blonde would be long gone, she stepped out of the car so she could help the brunette, who was busy picking herself up off the ground.

"You all right?"

"Yeah."

Dez held her hand out, and the brunette stared at it for a moment before grasping it and letting Dez pull her up. Blood still oozed from the wound on her hip, but Dez didn't worry about her too much. Like Sissy, she looked strong as an ox.

"Are you going to be okay? I have to go after—"

"No. You can't. They went in those woods. You can't follow."

Dez didn't know what the brunette meant by "*those*" woods." As opposed to what? Those *other* woods?

Before she could ask, cars pulled up behind them. Really nice cars that sounded like rumbling tanks.

Sissy came out of the first one. "Where is he?"

"He led the bitch into the woods," the brunette told her.

Sissy took off running, shifting in midstride. It was amazing to see. Her limbs fluidly changing from human to wolf, dark black fur bursting from her skin.

"We have to go with her."

Ronnie stood next to her now, and she grabbed Dez's arm, her clutching hand like a vise. "We can't."

"What are you talking about?" She had always thought Ronnie would follow Sissy Mae anywhere, even into hell, but she wasn't moving. None of them were.

"No one goes in those woods, Dez. No one."

Sissy was running blind, following Mitch's scent. She'd warned him not to come into these woods. And she'd warned him not to for a reason. Grandma Smith owned these woods. She owned this hill. She'd infused the ground with power. Power she'd ripped from the souls and the bones of others.

Mitch's ancestry, those Irish pagans his kin descended from, would be a bright beacon to that old woman.

Power was what that woman thrived on. It was what had

kept her alive for so long. Now, as Sissy tore up that hated hill and deeper into those woods, she had to dig down deep and find her own power. The power her Aunt Ju-ju claimed Sissy had and that Grandma Smith supposedly feared.

Because her Aunt Ju-ju was right . . . it might be the only thing that saved her heart.

Mitch tore up into the hills Sissy had warned him never to go in to. He ran as fast and as far as he could. But the lioness was faster. Even as human.

And she wouldn't shift because without thumbs, she couldn't use her gun. One on one as cat, she'd never take him.

By the time Mitch neared those ramshackle houses and that scent caught his attention, she was sliding in front of him, blocking his way.

She watched him with cold gold eyes, and he knew she was trying to figure out whether it was worth killing him now or seeing if she could get him to shift. If he stayed beast, she wouldn't have any real proof of the kill. But Mitch had no intention of helping her—and she knew it.

She shrugged. "I just need to make sure you don't show up to testify."

She raised the gun and aimed at him. He ground his paws into the dirt, preparing to leap at her. But that's when he realized he couldn't move. Not from fear, either. He simply couldn't move. At all.

And as panic was about to set in, blood splattered across his face, almost blinding him.

The lioness's arms flung out, and the weapon dropped from her hand. They stared at each other for a long moment before both their gazes looked down at her stomach—and the prongs from a pitchfork that had been shoved through it.

She opened her mouth to say something, but Mitch would

never know what as the pitchfork was forced further in and viciously twisted. The female's head fell forward and blood began to pour from her. She hung on that pitchfork until she was forced off like roadkill.

Mitch swallowed, peering up at those dog-colored eyes that now watched him. She was old. Older than seemed right. And whatever she'd been doing up here had . . . changed her. Parts of her were wolf, including fur, claws, bone structure, while other parts were human. Placing her weight on the pitchfork, she limped toward Mitch. Limped because only one leg had a foot as opposed to a paw.

He was unable to take his eyes off her, and she was less than a foot or two away when she raised that pitchfork again. He still couldn't move. And he tried. Christ, did he try.

So Mitch waited to die. Like he'd been waiting to die for nearly three years. But he wasn't resigned to dying. Not now. Not when he'd had some of his best times with one hot little She-wolf. Sissy meant everything to him, and it struck him that part of him still hoped this would all work out. That somehow they could be together forever. Two of the biggest troublemakers making a partnership that would have their relatives—and everyone else with a brain—panicking.

But he wouldn't leave these woods alive—and that realization was pissing him off.

As the farming tool began its arch down, the old female suddenly stopped.

"My, my," she said with a voice that was as fully human as the rest of her. "That's a lot of rage comin' off you, cat."

Her nose twitched, and she stepped a bit closer, took a sniff.

"You reek of Sissy Mae. You're her man?" When Mitch only stared at her, she demanded, "*Answer me, boy.*"

Mitch nodded.

"And ain't you a big buck?" The old woman snorted. It

was sort of a laugh. "Just like her momma . . . dirty little whore."

He moved, startling them both. But her paw flipped up, and his legs were locked again. He felt nailed to the spot.

"There was a time, boy, when your kind was good for one thing—something to hang on a Saturday night." She laughed at her own sick joke before hefting up her pitchfork again. "But I have other uses for you these days."

She lifted the fork. "Yeah, pieces of you will do me just right."

The fork arched down, and Mitch watched it. He wouldn't look away, wouldn't close his eyes. He'd face his death head on.

And that's when Sissy ran up and over him, her smaller wolf body jumping between him and her crazy relative.

She snarled and snapped, and the woman stumbled back.

"He's mine," the old bitch hissed. "He's on my territory, Sissy Mae. He's. Mine!"

Sissy bared fangs, her body tensing for an attack. But they weren't alone. Other wolves, four of them, all female, circled behind the old woman.

And the old woman smiled.

"It's just you, Sissy. He can't break the seal. Not like you can. And them other She-wolves . . . they'll never come up here. You're all alone. So head on back down the hill, or I'll make you watch what I do to him."

Sissy took a step back. And another. She backed up until she was next to him. That's when she brushed her head against his side, pushed her body into his, moving up until their heads were next to each other. She rubbed her snout against his mane.

Invisible chains were unleashed, and suddenly, Mitch could move, his body his own again.

The witch looked stunned. Hell, she looked terrified.

"How . . . how did you . . ."

The other She-wolves moved back, away.

Mitch took a step forward. Another. Another. Then he roared. The She-wolves ran, and the old woman glared, but the power she held was broken. Broken by Sissy. And she'd never forgive Sissy for it.

"Take him then. Hope he keeps you warm when you lose your family, your Pack for betraying your own kind."

She made her slow way back to the lioness's body. "You go on back down that hill. But don't you come back up here, Sissy Mae. You ain't never welcome again. Not here."

Grabbing the ankle of the lioness, she said, "And take your cat with you." She glowered at them over her shoulder. "And I'll be takin' mine. I have use for this one's bones."

Saying nothing else, she walked back to her hovel of a home, dragging the lioness behind her.

Mitch looked at Sissy. He trusted her to know whether they should get the female's body back or not. The cop in him wanted to try. The lion could honestly not care less.

Sissy shook her head and walked off. Mitch, after one more careful look around, followed.

Chapter 28

Ronnie saw them first, probably because she hadn't taken her eyes off the woods since she'd heard Mitch's roar.

When her friend came out, Mitch behind her, she ran to Sissy. By the time she'd put her arms around her, Sissy had shifted back. Ronnie held her and fought back tears. She'd honestly feared she'd never see Sissy again. There had been those who'd gone up the hill without invite, without permission, and they'd disappeared or they'd come back . . . wrong.

The power that old woman wielded rivaled most, and she hated everybody.

"It's okay. We're okay."

Ronnie pulled back. "She let you go?"

"She didn't have much choice."

It was a simple sentence, but it resonated through the She-wolves. They understood its true meaning. Sissy's power would never be questioned again. And only the bravest would ever challenge her for the position of Alpha.

Ronnie grinned. Proud. Sissy had come a long way from that little three-year-old who told her one day, "We'll be friends now. You're not as pretty as me."

"I'm glad you're okay, Sissy."

"Yeah. Me, too."

A naked, rushing Mitch walked past them, grabbing Sissy's hand as he did and dragging her toward the cars. "Come on. We've gotta go."

"Go? Go where?"

"The game!"

Sissy froze—they all did—and gawked at him. "You cannot be serious," Sissy barked.

Mitch faced her. "Baby, I'm the wide receiver. The team is depending on me."

Ronnie stood behind Sissy and said what they were all thinking, "Oh, my God. He's one of *them* now."

"Where the hell have you been?" Travis demanded. His entire right leg was in a cast, and his mate had put him in a wheelchair. Sissy had a hard time not giggling.

"He'll be ready in five." She and Dee rushed to get his jersey over his shoulder pads.

"He better be. The game's about to start."

"I know. I know."

Once she had him ready, Sissy handed him his helmet. Tragically, it was not the one she'd used on her brother. It would have definitely been cool for him to wear that helmet. "You ready, baby?" she purred.

"I was *born* ready, baby."

"Would you two *stop it!*" Travis snarled.

"What's the matter, Travis?" Sissy asked, her lips pouting in fake sympathy. "Your pain meds making you a little cranky?"

"Get off the field, Sissy."

"I'm going." She went up on her toes and kissed Mitch.

Behind her, Bobby Ray griped, "Stop maulin' my baby sister."

Sissy laughed and started to walk off the sidelines with

Ronnie and Dee when the team coach for the bears, Collintown's seven-foot-eight librarian, barreled forward. "They're not playing."

Travis looked at Mitch and Brendon. "There's nothing in the rules that says the cats can't play for us."

"I'm not talking about them. We told you before, Smith, we wouldn't play if her"—he pointed at Sissy—"or *her*"—he pointed at Ronnie—"were playing."

Mitch looked at her. "Uh . . . Sissy?"

Sissy rounded on the coach. "I can't believe you are still holding that against us. It's been years!"

"He was in traction for three months. A shifter! In traction!"

"*He was in my way!*"

Travis motioned Sissy toward the bleachers. "Go." He looked at the coach. "They're not playing. They're only here to watch."

"That better be true. If they're on the field at any time, you forfeit."

"So," Mitch said, clearly enjoying Sissy's high level of annoyance, "you hate the game not because it's boring or stupid as you've always said. But because the big boys won't let you play."

"Big boys? More like big babies."

Brendon watched the bears watch Sissy and Ronnie. "What exactly did you two do?"

Sissy started to answer, but Bobby Ray shook his head. "Remember what you promised as part of the lawsuit settlement?"

"Settlement?"

"Oh, forget it!" She turned on her heel and stomped to the bleachers.

As they got comfortable, Dee laughingly reminded Sissy, "Told you those bears would never let it go."

* * *

That bear hit him so hard Mitch flipped right into the end zone, the ball tight in his arms. He knew from the roar—and howls—of the crowd that he'd scored the winning touchdown.

A big hand reached out for him, and he grabbed it. Brendon hauled him to his feet and slammed his hand against his shoulders. In some cultures, it might even be considered affectionate, in others, it was just assault.

"Nice, little brother."

"I can't see straight. But that's okay."

"That bear was gunning for you."

"And where the hell were you?"

"Taking out the other bears gunning for you." Brendon grinned. "I knew I had some skill."

"As long as we keep a ball out of your hands."

"Eat—"

Brendon never got to finish his insult as Sissy ran up and threw herself at Mitch. Arms around his neck, legs around his waist, she kissed the helmet since he hadn't taken it off yet.

"You were so hot!"

With one arm under Sissy's ass, Mitch used the other to pull off his helmet. "Kiss me, baby."

She did, and all his aches and pains and exhaustion from the last few hours faded away. Her hands dug into his hair, and she pushed her body against his.

"Could you two do that later?" someone complained, but Mitch didn't know who or care.

Still, Sissy pulled back a bit and smiled at him. "I need to get you to a bed."

"Who needs a bed?"

"I'm gonna be sick." Smitty pushed past them. "And I'm tellin' Daddy!"

Before Mitch could torture Smitty a little more, he spotted Dez on her cell phone, and she was running her hands through her hair. She seemed frustrated and worried. When her gaze rose to his and then quickly looked away, Mitch knew they wanted him back to testify.

He knew Sissy understood that, too, when she whispered against his ear, "It's time, isn't it?"

"Yeah, baby."

She took a deep breath, her arms and legs tightening around him. "But we have tonight. And all day tomorrow."

"We have tonight. And tomorrow."

Resting her forehead against his, she sighed out, "*All day* tomorrow . . ."

Chapter 29

"Get up!"

Mitch tried to wake up, decided not to, and turned over.

"Get. Up!"

"What?"

"You need to move . . . *now!*"

Clothes hit him in the face. "Get dressed and get out."

"Is this how you treat all your men, Sissy?"

Ronnie appeared in the doorway. "Why is he still here?"

" 'Cause he won't move!"

Mitch sat up. "What the hell is going on?"

"Daddy."

He frowned. "Don't start calling me that, Sissy. I'm not one of those guys who finds that hot."

"Not you, you idiot. *My* daddy."

"What about him?"

"They're coming home." Ronnie picked up the clothes Sissy had thrown at him and threw them at his head. "Our parents will be home in an hour. So get your ass up."

"Brendon and you will clean Ronnie's house. We'll clean this one."

"Ladies . . . aren't you a little too old for this?"

The two She-wolves rounded on him, and he held his hands up before they could start swinging. "Fine. Fine. I'm going."

All furniture was put back in its proper place and anything damaged during the fight between the lioness and Dee fixed or hidden. Sheets were changed, nearly every available surface had been scrubbed, and any signs of feline DNA had been removed. Sissy was just flipping over the couch cushions to hide the claw tears when she heard the truck pulling up.

"They're here!" Ronnie flew down the stairs, Dee behind her. "They're here!"

"I know! I know!" Sissy pushed the cushions in and adjusted them until they looked perfect.

Car doors closed, and she could hear her daddy's low voice complaining about something and her momma's responding laugh. As their footsteps made it up onto the porch, Sissy scrambled back, her eyes searching the entire room, looking for anything that could tip her momma off.

The family room door opened, and Ronnie and Dee lined up next to her. Her momma stepped in and stopped when she saw her daughter standing there. Her eyes narrowed, and immediately, her accusing gaze swept the room.

"Move, woman. I'm exhausted." Bubba Smith stepped into the room, but he stopped when he saw his daughter. "Sissy Mae?"

"Hi, Daddy." She quickly moved over to him and threw her arms around his shoulders. "Did y'all have a good time?"

Bubba grunted. "I'd rather have stayed home."

"You can stop saying that now that we are home." Her

mother dropped her purse on the table. "Ronnie Lee, your parents are back at their house . . . where you should be."

"Uh . . . well . . ."

Janie blinked. "Good Lord . . . Dee-Ann?"

"Hi, Auntie Janie."

"Lord, girl! Come over here!" Dee went into her aunt's arms. "I'm so glad you're home."

"Me, too."

Janie pulled back. "What happened to your face? And why are you limping?" Her lips pursed. "What did Sissy drag you into now?"

"That's it. I'm leaving."

Bubba took hold of his daughter's arm before she could storm off. "Y'all stop it right now." He pulled Sissy in front of him and chucked her under the chin, his eyes warm. "So why don't you tell me what's going on, Shug?"

Mitch took the sweet tea Ronnie's mother handed him. He gave her a smile that she didn't return. She picked up her own glass and sat down on the opposite couch from him and Bren.

"So where is she?"

"Over at Sissy's."

The woman let out a long sigh. "Typical. Over there with Sissy, but not over here to see me. Or to see her daddy."

Mitch opened his mouth to defend Ronnie, but Bren lightly banged his knee against his brother's.

"You two hungry?" Bren nodded, and Miss Tala let out another sigh. "Fine. I guess that means *I* have to cook y'all somethin' since that daughter of mine ain't here to take care of her man."

Again, Mitch went to tell her she didn't have to do anything, but Bren's elbow slammed into his side.

Pushing herself up, she gazed down at the two cats. "Steak all right with you two?"

The brothers nodded.

"The boys are out back with their daddy. Guess I gotta make enough for them, too." She shook her head and walked out of the room.

"Bren—"

"Not a word, Mitch. Not a word."

Bubba walked his baby girl to the rental car. She'd told him everything . . . well, she'd told him enough. Enough to know that he could have lost her.

Enough to know she was madly in love with a damn cat. She hadn't said the words, but Bubba knew the signs. He didn't blame the cat—it just meant the feline had good taste. But he'd always hoped Sissy would find a nice wolf to settle down with. In the long run, though, all he cared about was that his baby girl was happy.

And because she was a lot like her momma, it wouldn't take just anybody to keep her happy.

"So he testifies tomorrow?"

"There's some prep or whatever, but pretty much."

"You'll be there with him?"

"Yes, sir."

"And after?"

"Daddy . . . I don't know. I love him."

"I know." Bubba kissed her forehead. "But don't forget, Sissy Mae, your Pack needs you. But you need them more."

She wrapped her arms around him and gave him one of her warm hugs. "I know, Daddy."

"I love you," he reminded her gruffly and stepped back. "Now you better get out of here. You got a long flight ahead of you."

Bubba stood on his porch and watched his baby drive away while Dee-Ann waved and headed by foot into the woods back toward Eggie's place.

"It'll be all right, darlin'." Janie slid her arm around his neck. "Don't you worry now."

Bubba brushed his head against Janie's cheek. She still had the softest skin.

"I'm going inside and taking a good look around," she said. "That daughter of yours was hiding something."

"You know," he said after kissing her cheek and watching her saunter away. "I noticed something when Sissy was telling us what had been going on around here."

"Oh?" Janie said, opening the screen door. "What?"

"I noticed that what she was telling us you seemed to already know. And you got quite a few calls from your sisters the last day or two."

His mate paused outside the door, smiled, and stepped into the house.

Chuckling, Bubba put his hands on his hips and looked out over his territory. He was so glad to be home. You could keep those boats and tours and cruises—waste of time in his estimation.

His brothers walked out of the woods, already shifted and wanting a good hunt. Smiling, Bubba pulled his clothes off and began to shift.

"Goddamnit!" he heard Janie yell from the family room. "*What the hell happened to my couch cushions?*"

She stormed back onto the porch, the couch cushion in her hand, but when she saw Bubba trotting down the stairs toward his kin, she snapped, "And I better not find out y'all are playing tug again with that damn crocodile!"

Chapter 30

"You ready?"

Mitch nodded. "Yeah, I'm ready."

They'd been back in Philly for three days, his testimony pushed off until this morning. Just as she'd promised, Sissy came with him.

He pulled at his tie again, and Sissy playfully slapped his hands away. "You're gonna end up strangling yourself."

"I hate wearing these things."

"I hate you in them. But you've got to look respectable."

He looked outside the windows of the SUV the cops had used to transport him here. It had started raining last night, and it didn't seem to show any signs of stopping soon.

"Want to just get this over with?"

"Yeah. Let's go."

He knocked on the window, and one of the police escorts opened his door. He walked around the vehicle and found Sissy already getting out before anyone could open the door for her.

She took his hand in hers, and they walked into the court-house.

* * *

Sissy knew something was up when that cranky cat ADA came up to them. "I need to talk to you and to *her*." She walked off, Sissy and Mitch following. She entered a room and waited until they were inside, then she slammed the door shut.

"Who? Who was it?"

Mitch glanced at Sissy before giving the female a helpless shrug. "I don't know what you're talking about, Jen."

She flung a file at the enormous table that took up most of the room. It flipped open, and photos sprayed out across the wood.

Mitch leaned over, moving the pictures around with the tips of his fingers. "It's O'Farrell."

"What's *left* of him," Jen snarled.

After a few moments, Mitch blinked and stood straight. "Wait. Do you think I had something to do with this?"

"Detective, everyone knows about your mother."

"My *mother*? You're blaming my mother?"

"And then there's your new girlfriend—Huckleberry Hound!"

"Watch it," Sissy sneered, "or it's time for a declawing."

"She's got an uncle in prison," the female damn near snarled.

"In Tennessee. And he don't get friendly with Yankees."

Mitch held his hand up. "Everybody stop." He looked at the ADA. "So now what?"

"What do you mean 'now what'? There's nothing now. It's over."

"Really?" Mitch glanced at Sissy and shrugged. "That's kind of a letdown."

"You know what I find truly fascinating?" Jen rested back against the table, her arms crossed over her chest. She seemed to have calmed down suddenly, even had a smile on her face, but Sissy didn't buy it for a second. The woman was pissed off. "I find the fact that the bounty on your head is already gone fascinating."

"Yeah, but with O'Farrell—"

"And it's actually rumored that you're untouchable."

Mitch looked like he wanted to loosen that tie again. "Sorry?"

"In fact, it's rumored—and, mind you, I'm just repeating what I've heard—but I have heard it rumored that if you're killed or hurt or even *touched* in any way, whoever did it will be killed in retaliation."

"Jen—"

"No. Wait. It gets better. Apparently, this is all coming from Pete O'Farrell. Not Petey. He's dead. But his son, who you would *think* would still want you dead, if simply on principle. But no, he seems to want you alive and well for years to come."

"Uh . . ."

"Oh, and people in your old neighborhood are afraid to walk past your mother's house."

"Jen, I am really—"

"No, no. Let us not speak of it." The angry cat pushed herself off the table and walked around it, picking up the file and putting the pictures back. "It is funny, though. How one can get so close to their goal, only to have it snatched from them." She shoved the file into her briefcase.

"All that work. All that effort. Gone." Both her hands on the briefcase handle, she stood in front of Mitch, looking up at him. "So tell me, Detective, are you planning to stay on the Force?"

Mitch cleared his throat. "No. I was going to resign at the end of the trial."

"Oh . . . well, isn't that lucky? Now you can go and do it today. Everything seems to be falling into place for you.

Your life is just turning *out so well.*" She spit out the last part of that sentence between her teeth before she walked out of the room.

Mitch looked down at Sissy. "Tense girl."

"Is she coming back?"

"Somehow I doubt it."

After several minutes of awkward silence, Sissy asked, "What do you want to do now?"

"Well, I . . ." Mitch shook his head. "Forget it."

"Say it."

"It'll just annoy you."

"Just say it, Mitch."

"Okay. I'm hungry."

"Mitchell."

"You asked. I'm hungry." His grin was wide and adorable. "Feed me."

Mitch stared up at his mother. "If I find out you're lying to me—ooh! Stew."

He dug into the bowl of stew Gwen put in front of him.

"I'm not lying. I didn't have anything to do with O'Farrell buying it."

Mitch let out a breath. "Okay. Good."

"See, I was gonna wait until you testified first . . . then I was going to have him killed. So you could feel like you've accomplished something. Then Uncle Joey was—"

Mitch held his hand up. "Please don't say another word."

"Yeah, but—"

"No. No more. And it will never be discussed, ever again. Right, Ma?"

"If you're gonna be that way—fine. Now would you like something to eat, baby-girl?"

Sissy blinked at his mother's abrupt change of conversation. "No thanks, Miss O'Neill."

"Roxy, baby-girl. Roxy."

"Just do what I'm telling ya, Ma. Okay?" Mitch glanced around the table and then at his sister. "Bread?"

Sissy threw up her hands. "You *ate* two hours ago."

"Why do you insist on having this discussion every time?"

"Because I keep hoping something will change . . . preferably *you*."

"I'm not changing. I like how I am. I'm perfect."

"You're delusional is what you are."

"You two"—his mother grabbed his cheeks with her left hand and Sissy's with her right, then she squeezed until their lips pursed out and it kind of hurt—"just so *fuckin'* cute!"

"*Ma!*"

Janie Mae sewed her section of the quilt while three of her sisters worked on theirs. The fourth sister, Darla, was on the phone in the main part of their pie store.

"This is gonna be beautiful when we're done, Janie Mae." Francine examined the nearly finished quilt.

They'd been working on it a couple of times a month for the last few months. Janie knew it would be for Sissy and Mitch. She knew long before Sissy or Mitch did. The two of them—thick as planks.

"I think so. I love these colors. But I'll have one of you give it to Sissy. If I give it to her, she'll automatically hate it."

Roberta shook her head. "You two are pathetic."

"I wasn't the one who got in a fistfight with Momma at Uncle Wayne's funeral."

"She started it!"

Darla walked back in, settling down in her chair and picking up the section where she'd left off. "It's all settled."

"Good. And how is Eustice?"

"He's doin' fine. Prison suits him."

"I always thought so," Francine muttered.

"They think some street dogs got into the jail somehow, so we're fine."

Janette rubbed her eyes. "How do they actually believe street dogs got into a jail?"

"Because no one wants to know the truth," Darla explained. "They'd rather believe a roving band of pit bulls is sneaking into prisons to randomly attack mobsters than that humans are shifting to wolves and tearing him apart while in the shower."

"That's just sad. Full-humans are sad."

"And how's Travis?" Roberta asked, already forgetting what they'd done to protect one six-foot-five king of the jungle.

"Oh, he's fine." Janie gave a brief wave of her hand before returning to her sewing. "Complaining like a big baby. But from what I heard, he deserved what he got. What he said to his baby sister was wrong. And Sammy handled it just right. He'll be a good Alpha. Bubba sees that now."

"I told you that boy would be Alpha of this town one day. He's smart, calm, and I like that mate of his much better."

"And you're going to tell Sissy what Travis did was wrong, right, Janie?"

Janie smirked at Francine's question. "Actually, I told her she was ungrateful, and she should have left her big brother alone."

Three of her sisters laughed, and Francine stared at her in disgust. "What is wrong with you?"

"I'm not making it easy on that girl. I will not have one of those daughters that sits around constantly talking about how great it was when she was sixteen. There is a whole wide world out there for her, and I expect her to go out there and get it. Nothing is going to hold my daughter back." She smiled with pride, thinking how far Sissy had come and how much further the brat had to go. "Not even me."

* * *

"Mitch. Wake up, darlin'."

Oh, yeah. He could definitely wake up to that voice every morning.

Smiling, his eyes still closed, he reached for her, but Sissy laughed and batted his hands away. "You need to get up."

"Why? Can't I sleep a couple more hours? It's not even light out."

"That's because it's seven o'clock at night."

Mitch forced one eye open. "Then why are you waking me when I just went to take a nap an hour ago?"

"Because you actually went to take your nap forty-eight hours ago."

Now both of Mitch's eyes were wide open. "*What?*"

"No need to yell. You needed the sleep, I'm guessing."

"Are you sure?"

Sissy grinned. "Am I sure that you slept forty-eight hours? Yeah, I'm sure. Except for you stumbling to the bathroom a few times, you've been out cold. Thankfully, it was not due to blood loss this time."

She patted his leg. "Come on. Time to get up. Your momma made you dinner."

"I am up." He motioned to the tent he was currently making with the sheets. "Time for you to get to work."

"That's charming."

"I never promised you I'd be charming." Of course, now that he thought about it, Mitch hadn't promised Sissy anything. He hadn't been able to. But now, that was pretty much over. O'Farrell was dead, and the bounty on his head miraculously gone—he would not ask about that. Some questions shouldn't be answered.

But he'd still need to be careful. Of course, he was always careful. So at this moment, absolutely nothing stood between him and Sissy making this thing forever.

When he didn't panic, try to make a run for it, or vomit, he looked at Sissy.

"Uh-oh. Why are you looking at me like that for?"

"We need to talk."

"Can this wait? Maybe later tonight?" she asked hope-fully.

"No. I want to talk now."

Sissy glanced at the door, sighed, and sat on the bed. "Okay. Talk."

"It's about us and where we want this thing to go . . ."

And that's when Sissy took her forefinger and made cir-cles with it. She was telling him to hurry up?

"If you don't want this, you just tell me, Sissy, so we can get this over with." But as soon as the words were out of his mouth, he regretted saying them. He didn't want this over with. He loved her. More than he had ever realized.

Sissy slapped her hands against her knees and stood. "I don't want this thing over with," she snarled. "But I need you to pick up the pace!"

"What the hell for?"

That's when she stalked over to him and twisted one of his nipples, which hurt like hell.

"*Ow!*"

"Downstairs, there is a living room full of people waiting for your dumb ass to come down those stairs so they can all yell 'surprise' because it's a God dang surprise party!"

"Party?"

"Yeah. Party. For you! There's food—enough even for you—cake, and to my horror . . . a karaoke machine. And to bring home how much I love your Yankee ass, I am going to be doing my rendition of The Runaways 'Cherry Bomb' with Ronnie Lee on air guitar. But I can't do a damn thing until you get that *big cat ass out of bed and into the shower and then downstairs in the next ten minutes!*"

Mitch stared at her calmly. "If you'd said that in the first place . . ."

When her eyes shifted and he saw a flash of fang, Mitch laughed and grabbed her hand, pulling her onto the bed with him. "I'm sorry. Sorry, sorry, sorry."

"You better be. And when you go downstairs, you better look surprised, mister."

"Yes'm." He kissed her nose. "I promise. Total shock and awe."

"Don't chew the scenery. Just look startled."

It had been his mother's idea, and Sissy hadn't been sure how well it would go. But so far, it had been perfect. A party for Mitch that was made up of her Pack, a good chunk of Jessie Ann's Pack, Roxy's Pride, and the Shaw twins had the place pretty well-packed from floor to rafters.

But it was nice. And fun.

Using oven mitts, Sissy pulled the large pan of mac and cheese out of the oven and placed it on the kitchen table. Wanting to give it a few moments to cool, she pulled off the mitts and turned back around.

"Oh." She took a step back. "Bobby Ray."

"Baby sister."

"Everything all right?"

"Yup."

"It's so hard to tell with you sometimes." She closed the oven door and turned off the heat. "So is there something you want?"

"Spoke to Dee-Ann today."

"And?" Sissy pushed when her brother stopped talking and stood there.

"She's thinking on it."

"Why thinking and not doing? Were you not persuasive?"

"What do you mean?"

"What do I—" She sighed. "Did you tell her we'd love for her to move here and to join our Pack? Did you tell her we'd love for her to be part of the family here? Did you tell her we'd love for her to come work for us?"

"Work for *us?* You mean work for me, don't you? Work for Mace."

"Did you tell her all that?"

Bobby Ray shrugged. "I got it across."

Sissy threw up her hands, turned away from him. "Fine. I'll make a follow-up call myself. I swear, Bobby Ray, you don't have the sense the Lord gave a rabbit."

"I've got a proposition for you," he said, wisely cutting off one of her potential tirades. Even she knew once she got going, she could really go.

"For me?" She faced him. "Do I have to give up a kidney?"

"No."

"Become a better person?"

"No."

"Achieve world peace?"

"Sissy Mae."

She laughed. "Sorry. What's your proposition?"

"We're working with that Asian wild dog—"

"Which one?"

"Jessie Ann's"—her brother snarled a little—"friend."

"Oh. Kenshin Inu. He must really care about her. He stared at her with such longing at the wedding."

Bobby Ray made an attempt to go, and Sissy grabbed his arm. "I'm kidding. I swear, I'm just kidding." Still laughing, she pulled him back.

"That's not funny."

"So what's the proposition?"

"I can't ask Mace to leave Dez and Marcus for at least three to six months. And now that Jessie Ann's pregnant—"

"You want me to go to Japan?"

"To work, Sissy. *To. Work.* Not to start shit. Not to race. Not to gamble. And definitely not to get arrested or turn all of Japan against you. Remember, I'm not stationed right around the corner like before." He stuck his hands into the front pockets of his jeans. "You interested?"

She squealed as she did on occasions like this and threw herself into her brother's arms. He caught her and hugged her.

"You'll be working directly with Kenshin and his people. All wild dogs"—he held Sissy at arm's length—"so be *nice*."

"Darlin', I was born nice. People love me. And Mitch is coming." She squealed again and hugged her brother. This time, he didn't hug her back.

"I didn't agree to that."

Sissy stepped away from him. "But you will, Bobby Ray."

Bobby Ray crossed his arms over his chest, braced his legs apart. "Or what?"

Sissy mimicked his stance. "Either Mitch goes with me . . . or get used to finding your wife hiding in trees."

"That's just mean."

"I'm a Smith. What did you expect?"

"Good point."

The siblings stared at each other for long minutes until Bobby Ray snarled, "Fine. He can go."

Sissy squealed and threw herself into her brother's arms.

"Lord, Sissy. Stop making that noise!"

Mitch sidled up behind his older sister, Marissa. He leaned down and whispered in her ear, "I heard you cried for me."

Her whole body stiffened, and she wouldn't look at him. When he'd first seen her earlier in the evening, he'd only gotten, "Glad you're not dead since Bren probably wouldn't have stopped whining about it."

To be honest, she'd asked to be tortured.

"It was . . . early. And I'm relatively certain I was still drunk."

"Or"—he moved around her until they were face to face—"you love your little bruh and were terrified you'd never be able to tell him how much."

"Arrggh!" She pushed past him. "Asshole!"

He started laughing, then Marissa was back. She grabbed his face and kissed him on the cheek—then she slapped him. Hard. It was a very Marissa kind of thing.

Without another word—or slap—she stormed off.

Brendon shook his head. "Never know when to back off, do ya?"

"No. Not even a little." Mitch held up his empty beer bottle. "Want another?"

"Yeah. Sure."

Mitch took the empty bottle from his brother and walked into the kitchen. The females were prepping more food, but he could smell Sissy's mac and cheese above it all. He started to walk over to it, ready to dive in, when he heard the knock on the back door.

Dropping the bottles in a trash can for recyclables—his mother was surprisingly "green"—he headed over to the door. But when he pulled it open, he could only stare.

"You going to invite me in?"

"Yeah. Sure." Mitch stepped back, allowing the older man in.

"Heard you had some trouble."

Mitch laughed. "You could say that."

"I'm glad to see you're okay."

"Thanks."

Brendon walked into the kitchen. "Hey, Ronnie wants a—" He stopped . . . and gaped. "Dad?"

"Brendon."

"What are you doing here?"

Alden Shaw awkwardly adjusted the pack he had attached to his back. "I got a message from your sister. It took a while to get to me, though. I was at a game park in Africa."

Mitch had to admire his father on that. He loved to run with the big cats when he could and traveled from Africa to India to Siberia constantly. Mitch didn't even know when his father was last in New York, much less Philadelphia.

"I needed to see if my family was okay." He glanced between his two sons. "You look okay."

It took a lot not to laugh, so Mitch asked, "Would you like to stay for a while?"

"If your mother doesn't mind."

"It's my party. I want you here. And she adores her son."

Alden smiled. "Well, when you put it like that." He grabbed the straps of his backpack and began to slide them off his shoulders. He turned so Brendon could help him get the pack off. And as the two took care of that, Sissy walked in the room. She winked at Mitch and motioned to the mac and cheese. He nodded vigorously, and with a laugh, Sissy went to dish some up for him.

The backpack removed, his father turned back around.

"You hungry?"

"Starving."

Mitch motioned to the table filled with food. "We've got stuff here and in the dining room, so—"

"Janie Mae?"

Sissy froze in the middle of heaping food on Mitch's plate and, spoon raised, she slowly turned. "What did you call me?"

"Sorry. When I saw you from behind, I thought you looked like—"

"My *mother?*"

Alden held his hands up, palms out, just like Mitch did a lot. "Your mother when she was nineteen . . . if that helps."

"It probably doesn't," Brendon muttered to Mitch.

That spoon still raised—although Mitch was grateful it wasn't a knife—Sissy asked, "You knew my mother?"

"It was a very long time ago, but yeah." And then he smiled. And Mitch knew that smile. He'd bet he had it a lot himself the last couple of weeks with Sissy.

Sissy's eyes briefly closed in horror. "I can't believe this."

"It was nothing really." Alden grinned again. "Just a weekend."

Damn. At least forty years or so later, and the old man could still remember it like it was yesterday. And with that look on his face—what a yesterday it was.

"You and my mother?"

Alden, trying to help, but not really, added, "It was nothing. She was just using me to make some wolf who was ignoring her jealous. Although I was more than happy to help her out."

Mitch pushed his father toward the hallway. "Dad, why don't you go see Ma?"

"Do I have to?"

Sissy let out a breath. "Everywhere I go that woman *haunts me!*"

Mitch took the spoon out of Sissy's hand, trying to ignore the thick bits of cheese, ham, and noodles stuck to it, calling his name. "You're missing the big picture here."

"I am?"

"Your mother. My father."

"You're not helping."

"And some wolf she was trying to make jealous. Imagine if that just pops up during, say, Thanksgiving dinner? Or Easter. Or a baptism. Perhaps when the local preacher is about . . . Sissy, imagine the possibilities."

"Mitchell, that is a horrible, despicable idea." Sissy grabbed Mitch by his T-shirt, jerking him close. "And I can say with all honesty, I've never wanted you more."

Sissy walked out on the back porch and sat on the stoop between Dez and Ronnie Lee.

"What's going on?" She reached over and took her godson from Ronnie's arms. He giggled and hissed.

"Dez is having a hard time dealing with her new life."

"It's a little late since she decided to breed with the cat."

"That's not it. My problem is this whole subversive underworld you people have."

"Underworld?" Sissy quietly asked Ronnie.

"Let it go."

"It's not that there are shifters. That I could deal with. But you guys have your own police, military units, government agencies. Your own stores so you can buy those giant shoes you need."

"Hey."

"Let it go," Ronnie said again.

"I mean, what else am I not aware of? What else have I not been told?"

"Desiree," Ronnie sighed, "you're not going to know everything. That is just the way life is."

"But I want to know. The only way to be prepared for the worst is to know everything."

"You wanna know everything?" Sissy tickled Marcus's ears.

"Yes! I want to know everything."

"All right then. I found out Mitch and Brendon's daddy, Alden, fucked my momma forty or so years ago. There. Now you know absolutely everything."

Ronnie put her hand to her chest, her mouth open in shock. She even wheezed a little. "No. *Way.*"

"You made your point." Dez patted Sissy's shoulder. "There *are* some things you never want to know."

"So you want me to go to Japan?"

"No."

Mitch waited, but Smitty only stared at him.

"But you're sending me anyway?"

"Yes."

"With Sissy?"

That's when Smitty's top lip raised a bit, showing some fang.

"Look, Smitty—"

"My sister," he snarled. "My *baby* sister."

"What can I say? Like me, she's . . . enthralling."

"Enthralling? You're enthralling?"

"We both are. And mesmerizing. It's our gift . . . and our curse."

"Y'all are both annoying, too."

"I've heard that before." He shrugged. "Would you prefer it was Gil?"

"That's not even funny."

"If it helps, I really do love her."

There was a bit of sneering at that before Smitty cracked his knuckles. "All right then," he finally said.

"Thanks."

"So what are you planning?"

"What do you mean?"

"Are you staying here? Gonna keep on being a cop? Or you gonna stick with us and make a hell of a lot more money?"

Mitch let out a gruff laugh that he hoped didn't sound as bitter to Smitty as it did to him. "I think I'm done being a cop. Going to Japan or not, I was hoping to stick with you and Mace. Great hours, slight chance of danger, high pay, and your sister's *hot.*"

Smitty snorted a laugh and walked off, tossing over his shoulder, "I sure hope you know what you're gettin' yourself into, hoss."

Mitch didn't, but he couldn't wait to find out.

Sissy put the last of the dishes away and helped Roxy and her sisters move the furniture back to its rightful place in the house.

"Great party, Roxy."

"Thanks, baby-girl." She cleared her throat. "And sorry about Alden."

"Don't worry about it. We'll just never discuss it again."

Roxy laughed and patted her shoulder. "Good plan, baby-girl."

With a yawn and good nights to all Mitch's relatives, Sissy headed upstairs. She opened the door to the room she shared with Mitch and stopped in the doorway.

"What are you doin'?"

"Displaying myself for your enjoyment."

He was stretched out on the king-size bed, completely naked, his hands behind his head. But it was the grin that always got her. She loved that grin.

"And what if your momma had walked in?"

"Let's not ruin the hard-on, baby."

She giggled and closed the door. "Sorry."

"Now get on over here. It's time to take a ride on the Mitchmobile."

"And I figured you'd want to talk some more," she said, practically tearing off her T-shirt and jeans and climbing on the bed.

"And fifty hours ago, that would have been true." Mitch

let out a groan when Sissy dragged her tongue along the inside of his thigh. "But I know how needy you can be."

"Me?" Sissy took her forefinger and tapped Mitch's hard cock. It swung from side to side. "That can keep time with a piano."

"Fine. I've gone a little too long without gettin' me some." He slid his hands in her hair and roughly yanked her close so her mouth was right over his. "And it's time for you to fulfill my needs."

Sissy pulled her knees up and then parted them so her thighs could straddle Mitch's chest. She gripped his biceps tight with her hands and rocked her wet pussy against him.

"Aw, darlin'. When you put it like that, how can a nice Southern gal turn you down?"

Chapter 31

It took Sissy a bit to realize Mitch was pawing at her. Not pawing at her like an actual mauling, which she probably would not have enjoyed. But as she lay across Mitch's childhood bed, naked with her feet up on the wall and her head hanging off the mattress, Mitch lay on the floor right beneath her and pawed at her hair with his hands.

"Would you like some string there instead, hoss?"

"No thanks. Your hair is stringy enough."

"If I wasn't so relaxed, I'd be a whirlwind of deadly blows." She sighed lazily. "But you're damn lucky."

Early morning sunlight streamed though the window and across the bed, and Sissy suddenly had this intense desire to be on the road. Not running like they'd been doing, but going somewhere. Traveling. Lord, she was itching for it.

"I am," Mitch murmured, his hands still playing with her hair. "Have I thanked you?"

"Of course you did."

"No. Not for saving my life. Besides, that's in your canine DNA. Like a St. Bernard."

"A whirlwind of deadly blows," she reminded him.

He laughed, wrapped his big arms around her, and pulled her off the bed.

They hadn't slept all night. Instead, they'd enjoyed Mitch's bed and each other. Laughing because they were trying so hard to be quiet. No matter where they ended up, they always had the best time together.

Once he had her on the floor with him, Mitch sat up, his back against the bed frame. He settled Sissy between his long legs and went right back to playing with her hair, running his fingers from the top of her scalp to the back of her neck. There weren't a lot of times when Sissy wanted to purr, but this was definitely one of them.

"It's been a long time since I've felt this . . . right," he continued, "and that's down to you. Thank you."

"You're very welcome." Those wonderful arms wrapped around her, and Mitch hugged her tight, his face buried against her neck. Yeah, this felt right. Perfect.

"I need to go." And Sissy felt Mitch's body go tense.

Some days . . . she was so bad.

"Go?" Mitch raised his head from Sissy's wonderfully scented neck. "Go where?"

"I'm thinking the West Coast. I need to get on the road."

She was going to leave? Just like that? After everything they'd been through together? Damn She-wolves and their traveling genes! What about what they meant to each other? More importantly, what about *him*? Who'd make him mac and cheese with that damn ham? Who'd wake him up with a stellar blow job?

"Smitty mentioned something about Japan." He figured that would make her happy, getting on the road again, but he'd planned to be there with her. All the way. Not left behind. Didn't she realize how important he was to her?

Didn't she realize how important she was to *him*?

He was all ready to give her the gift of spending the rest of her life with him, and she was going to just walk away and head out to the West Coast? So she could be around all those hot West Coast guys?

How is any of this okay?

"Yeah, but that won't be for another month. Maybe two. You know how these business deals go. Bobby Ray's not going to send us there until everything is settled."

"So when are you leaving?"

"Today. Tomorrow at the latest." She looked at him over her shoulder. "I don't stay in any one place too long. But I always come home. You should know that."

"Yeah, I guess I should." He held her tighter. He couldn't help himself. "Why West Coast? Figured you'd head off to Europe or Asia."

"Can't. You don't have your passport yet. It'll take a few weeks."

His passport. Tricky little She-wolf!

Mitch squeezed her even harder until Sissy squealed and started kicking her legs and swinging her arms.

"That was mean, Sissy Mae!"

"Sucker!" She laughed. "Don't tickle!" She batted at his hands.

"And," she went on, "I'm thinking the West Coast because you said you'd never been. I think you'll really enjoy it. It's beautiful there. If you know where to go."

He kissed her neck, her shoulder. "I can't wait." He kissed her ear. "I love you, Sissy Mae."

She grinned up at him, kissed him. "And I can't wait to show you the world, Mitchell Shaw."

Mitch hugged Sissy close to him. "And now I've got my whole life to enjoy it."

She nuzzled his chin before giving him that wicked Sissy smile. "Then, darlin', let's go have some fun."

Can't get enough Shelly Laurenston?
Try her other books in the Pride series . . .

The Mane Event

Mace Llewellyn. Brendon Shaw. Two tall, gorgeous, sexy alpha heroes who are 100% male—with a little something extra. Lion-shifters, to be exact, who can unleash every woman's animal side and still look good—make that spectacular—in a suit . . . and even better out of it . . .

NYPD cop Desiree "Dez" MacDermot knows she's changed a lot since she palled around with her childhood buddy, Mace. But it's fair to say that Mace has changed even more. It isn't just those too-sexy gold eyes, or the six-four, built-like-a-Navy SEAL body. It's something in the way he sniffs her neck and purrs, making her entire body tingle . . . Meanwhile, for Tennessean Ronnie Lee Reed, New York City is the place where any girl—even one who runs with a Pack—can redefine herself. First order of business: find a mate, settle down, and stop using men for sex. Even big, gorgeous, lion-shifter men like Brendon Shaw. But she needn't worry, because now that Brendon's set his sights on her, the predator in him is ready to pounce and never let go . . .

The Beast in Him

In *The Mane Event*, Shelly Laurenston introduced a whole new breed of heroes—sexy, shape-shifting hunks who redefine the term "Alpha male." Now, in *The Beast In Him*, one gorgeous lone wolf is about to meet his match . . .

Some things are so worth waiting for. Like the moment when Jessica Ward "accidentally" bumps into Bobby Ray Smith and shows him just how far she's come since high school. Back then, Jess's gangly limbs and bruised heart turned to jelly any time Smitty's "all the better to ravish you with" body came near her. So, some things haven't changed. Except now Jess is a success on her own terms. And she can enjoy a romp—or twenty—with a big, bad wolf and walk away. Easy.

The sexy, polished CEO who hires Smitty's security firm might be a million miles from the lovable geek he knew, but her kiss, her touch, are every bit as hot as he imagined. Jess was never the kind to ask for help, and she doesn't want it now, not even with someone targeting her Pack. But Smitty's not going to turn tail and run. Not before proving that their sheet-scorching animal lust is only the start of something even wilder . . .

The Mane Squeeze

*In Shelly Laurenston's laugh-out-loud funny, deliciously
sexy novel, a shape-shifting Grizzly and a single,
dangerous feline collide—and discover untamed,
unstoppable attraction . . .*

Growing up on the tough Philly streets, Gwen O'Neill has
learned how to fend for herself. But what is she supposed to
do with a nice, suburban Jersey boy in the form of a massive
Grizzly shifter? Especially one with a rather unhealthy fetish
for honey, moose, and . . . uh . . . well, *her*? Yet despite his
menacing ursine growl and four-inch claws, Gwen finds
Lachlan "Lock" MacRyrie cute and really sweet. He actually
watches out for her, protects her, and unlike the rest of her
out-of-control family, manages not to morbidly embarrass
her. Too bad cats don't believe in forever.

At nearly seven feet tall, Lock is used to people responding
to him in two ways: screaming and running away. Gwen—
half lioness, half tigress, all kick-ass—does neither. She's
sexy beyond belief and smart as hell, but she's a born pro-
tector. Watching out for the family and friends closest to her
but missing the fact that she's being stalked by a murderous
enemy who doesn't like hybrids . . . and absolutely hates
Gwen. Lock probably shouldn't get involved, but he will.
Why? Because this is Gwen—and no matter what the hissing, roaring, drape destroying feline says about not being
ready to settle down, Lock knows he can't simply walk away.
Not when she's come to mean absolutely *everything* to him.

Beast Behaving Badly

Some men just have more to offer. Like Bo Novikov, the hard-muscled shape-shifter hero of this wildly funny, deeply sexy new novel from Shelly Laurenston—part polar bear, part lion, pure alpha . . .

Ten years after Blayne Thorpe first encountered Bo Novikov, she still can't get the smooth-talking shifter out of her head. Now he's shadowing her in New York—all seven-plus feet of him—determined to protect her from stalkers who want to use her in shifter dogfights. Even if he has to drag her off to an isolated Maine town where the only neighbors are other bears almost as crazy as he is . . .

Let sleeping dogs lie. Bo knows it's good advice, but he can't leave Blayne be. Blame it on her sweet sexiness—or his hunch that there's more to this little wolfdog than meets the eye. Blayne has depths he hasn't yet begun to fathom—much as he'd like to. She may insist Bo's nothing but a pain in her delectable behind, but polar bears have patience in spades. Soon she'll realize how good they can be together. And when she does, animal instinct tells him it'll be worth the wait . . .